The
Raceboys

By

TJ Johnson

Copyright © 2008 by TJ Johnson

Library of Congress Control Number:
2008937331

ISBN 9780976481744

Published By
Hard Title Publishing

www.ItsFiction.com

The Raceboys

Thad Nigel Thompson, often called TNT by his fans, and T by his friends, was by far one of the best young racecar drivers on the circuit. Driving since he was four years old, he leaped through the ranks quickly. His big break came two years ago after obtaining a ride in the top racing series, and winning the championship his first year.

T had money, a beautiful house, the best racecars, and considered the top star on the track. His fans loved him, but millions of spectators hated him because he often beat their driver. He thought he was happy, but away from the track, he often felt alone.

By chance, he met Jack, and everything in his life changed. As their friendship grew, so did Thad's determination to win his second championship in just three years in the top NARC racecar series.

T and Jack fell in love almost the moment their eyes met, but keeping it a secret in the giant sport of racing was nearly impossible. T survived hundreds of wrecks, including spins, flips, and massive impacts to the wall, but could he endure losing Jack?

Their story on and off the track combines the thrill of racing, with a behind the scenes look at the racing world, and the pressure of being gay in an old boy racing league.

Information on TJ Johnson's books is available at:

www.**ItsFiction**.com

Books by TJ Johnson

The War Apart - Part I

The War Ahead - Part II

The Will

Stranded

The Raceboys

Coming soon:

A Writer's Fantasy
(About His Favorite College Basketball Star)

The Blackfeet Boys

Gay Grifters

The War Beyond - Part III

Forever Alone…Again

Web Site and Release Information:

WWW.ItsFiction.com

Dedication

This is booked is dedicated to my longtime friend Gary, one of the finest straight friends I have. He has always been there for me sharing many great laughs, always ready to help, and there for me in good times, as well as those inevitable sad times. He is a true friend, and reliable as a Timex watch. I'm so proud of him.

Gary had a beautiful blond Labrador named Bailey that he raised from a fur-balled puppy. He was one of the best dogs I have ever played with. The dog actually smiled when he saw you, and wagged his tail like a windshield wiper on high speed. He met you every day full of energy, ready to chase a ball, or take a dive in the lake. He and Huckleberry are in doggy heaven with a few of their friends, and we miss them.

ONE

Thad Nigel Thompson, or TNT as called by his fans, was by far one of the best young racecar drivers on the circuit. He had been driving since he was four years old and leaped through the ranks quickly. His big break came when he obtained a top ride two years ago winning the championship his first year, and losing by a mere six points during his second season. However, Thad became the youngest NARC driver in history to win over thirty million dollars in one season. Though appreciative of the cash, he became totally focused on winning next year's championship. Thad hated losing no matter what the sport. He was five feet nine inches, and shorter and younger than anyone else on his racing team, but he never let size bother him. He spoke his mind when he needed to, but his proud Midwestern parents taught Thad to listen before speaking. His facial skin remained smooth and required shaving only once a week or so. His kept his dark brown hair cut short and always perfectly combed. When he took his helmet off after a race, he immediately put on his carefully shaped baseball-style racing hat to cover his messed up hair. He bent his hat brim downward on the outside edges to provide more protection from the sun, and to simply look cool.

He knew his car was spinning in rapid three sixties from the collision with the number seventy-four car, but with the wind knocked out of him, he could not talk or even scream. He held on to the steering wheel and watched the view out his windshield as he continued spinning. Thad saw a glimpse of the stands, and then the track ahead of him leading to the fourth turn. He saw the pit with all the men in their colorful uniforms, and then horrifyingly he saw the line of cars he recently passed flying straight towards him after finishing the back straightaway at almost a hundred and eighty miles an hour.

He gulped and tried to suck in air and waited as he spun all the way around again while expecting the inevitable head-on collision that would kill him. Twice around and his luck held—not one single car touched him, although they whizzed by above and below as he spun like a child's toy top. His squealing spinning tires rapidly created a huge cloud of dark black smoke effectively hiding his out of control car from the rest of the swiftly approaching field of racing cars.

He heard his spotter yelling at him in his headset, but he was afraid to move even a finger to key his microphone. Suddenly, he realized his foot was still pressing the gas, so he let off and hit the brakes. As he came around the third time, he suddenly slammed hard into the wall. The sounds of the crunching metal sent chills up the backs of his crew along the pit wall. The fans in the seats on the other side of the wall leaped backwards, fearing the wall might not hold. He sighed and hoped the yellow caution flag was out, alerting the field of racecars to slow down and miss him.

He saw stars through his visor, he felt as if a steel hammer was pounding his head, and he could feel his rapid heartbeats in the temples on the side of his head. He killed the engine, but that was all he could do before he

1

passed out. The crowd stood on their feet. Camera bulbs flashed as thousands of spectators took pictures of the pitiful crumpled car. His crew chief kept calling his name on the radio, but no answer came. His spotter called him as well, but they heard no reply. The in-car camera showed him slumped over with his helmet resting on the steering wheel. The crowd and the car noise fell strangely silent.

The safety crews reached him and began speaking to him as they unbuckled the web netting in the door window next to the driver. Thad's head remained still. The EMT crewmember feared the worst. He reached in and expertly began unbuckling the five star seat belts and Hans's head restraint safety device. He unbuckled Thad's helmet, and gently slid it up and off, being careful not to move his head.

The moment the cool springtime air hit his sweat soaked hair, Thad's eyes abruptly popped open. The crewmember nearly jumped as if a corpse had suddenly moved. The man grinned, "You okay, kid?"

His eyes turned towards the man, and then he coughed, "Yeah, sure. Get me out of here, will you?"

The crewmember reached under his arm and pulled him out of the car. He stood him up, but held on to see if TNT could stand. He felt dizzy, but Thad slowly lifted his hand and waved to a sighing crowd. Applause sprung out immediately all across the arena, while his team in the pits choked back tears.

In his hometown of Marietta, Iowa, his mother leaned forward on the couch anxiously waiting for word that her only son was okay. When the good news came, she fell back on the couch feeling relieved as the tears flowed down her face. Thad Nigel Thompson escaped death once more, but more opportunities awaited him.

The top tier of the stock car racing world was called NARC, an acronym for National Association of Race Cars. This league featured the world's best drivers and hosted a long list of champions. Every driver fought hard to get to this level, and even harder to stay.

His race team owner was former driver Drew McClain. Thirty years ago, Drew won three championships before a wreck messed his legs up forever. He rode around the pits in a high-powered motorized wheelchair his mechanics tweaked for him. He could do thirty mph, and often parted the NARC racing crowds like Moses divided the sea. Thad had never seen Drew without an unlit cigar in the side of his mouth that complimented his bulldog face. Drew managed four drivers and already won two championships as an owner. His team built a lift for him so he could sit above the pits along with his crew chief for his top team. A special radio switch panel on the rack in front of him allowed him to talk and communicate with any of his teams. Though he rarely interfered with his crew chief, spotter, and driver communications, when he did, everyone knew you had just performed beautifully or badly, and his rough raspy voice could produce words of praise or venom all in the same breath. He had been tall all his life, growing quickly through three sizes of clothes in just one year as a teenager, but now his broken body settled to life in the chair.

The strength in his arms equaled any tire changer on his teams. He had been divorced twice before meeting Helen. She got him off the pain pills, alcohol, and talked him out of smoking, yet settled for a chewed cigar. She loved him and he loved her. After the accident, Drew gave up on racing, but Helen pushed him into thinking about becoming an owner. Once he made the commitment, everything about his life began to improve. He drove his teams hard and when they won, he was the first to shed a tear. He made everyone on his staff of one hundred and eighty feel like they were one of his sons or daughters. They loved him, hated him, and then loved him all the more. They would do anything for him.

Drew intended to build a dynasty, a group of race teams that were absolutely the best in the world. He built large shops with all the latest equipment, and hired a team of recruiters with key specialties. He also recruited top brand sponsors who poured millions of dollars into his teams, and he made sure he gave each of them more than their monies worth. It took two hard years of interviews and training before engine recruiter Larry Swain completed the building of the best engineering team from all over the country with doctorate degrees in engineering, physics, wind tunnels, electronics, design, and car building.

Bob Mackenzie was the team's training manager. He traveled the country searching for the right men to feel positions on the various teams. He started with young but talented crew chiefs. He wanted men he could mold into strong leaders with quick and accurate decision making skills. These men spent just as much time working with their crews as they did attending leadership training classes presented by the top leaders in the country. The speakers were salesman, psychologist, football coaches, and motivational speakers. They also took classes in Zen and Yoga to help them learn how to relax and stay in control, and how to share that calmness with his team and his driver. He insisted they excel in physical fitness programs led by the company's top trainer.

Harry Phelps was a man's man. Drew gave this recruiter only one assignment—to find the absolute best up and coming drivers, sign them to a contract, and begin their professional racecar driver training. Harry traveled the country from one dirt track to the next. He often said he has never met a stranger because in less than sixty seconds everyone he met liked him. He flirted in a friendly and funny way with every waitress he took a menu from. He left a trail of ladies wishing they could have him, but he remained faithful to his beloved wife Mary and their three daughters.

He talked with track owners by phone every day. Susie, his secretary and the real boss of his office, became his right arm as she prepared briefing reports on the results of every driver in the country. He hired a computer genius to create programs for managing all the data flowing to his office. He subscribed to every racing magazine and newspaper in the country. Susie hired two more ladies to scan the periodicals, and log every story and race results they could find. He paid finder fees to anyone and everyone tipping him about a bright newcomer. He always wanted first look even though ninety-five percent of the time his evaluations produced an unfavorable score for the rookie and a pass by Drew's company.

In Drew's corporate DMI headquarters just north of Charlotte North Carolina, Harry built a large conference theater-like room with not one but three overhead LCD DLP projectors. Each produced a high definition 102-inch diagonal screen. He used it to make presentations to Drew demonstrating the skills of the drivers he was screening. Drew always came out of the meetings completely amazed at the knowledge, data, and video Harry put together. He gave Harry a big bonus every time he found what they both considered a future champion. Harry loved the money, but he loved the treasure hunt even more.

Susie, trained as a travel agent, and easily a multi-task master, booked him on flights that often took him to four racetracks in a weekend. He jogged five miles every morning to keep his body in shape for the kind of long hour days and travel he became accustom to. Once he arrived at the track, he quickly met with the owner and the promoter winning them over with his large list of well-honed jokes, outrageous stories, and tales. He picked their brains about new young drivers racing their tracks. He met with mechanics and announcers, and quizzed each carefully while logging every fact, detail, and name carefully into his brain. He did a similar analysis on every racetrack in the country allowing him to choose carefully where he tested his top picks each year. After he walked away, he dialed a special number back to his office, and dictated everything he learned to an automatic dictation machine. In the morning, the secretaries pulled the report up on their computer screens, and input the information into their database so every word could be scanned, researched, graphed, and challenged in the future. They would email him a copy for his laptop at least once a day. Every year Drew gave Harry a new cell phone, laptop, luggage, and shoes as no one he knew talked more than most of his friends, analyzed more data on his laptop, flew more miles, and walked a dozen miles or more a day at the tracks. He also gave Harry and his wife a surprise vacation trip for her sacrifice for his company as well.

Harry first saw Thad hanging in the pits for his father's racecar on a dirt track out west. When his father pitted, young Thad leaped off a tall toolbox, ran to his driver's window, and gave his father instructions like one of NARC's highly experienced crew chiefs. He scoffed at the audacity of the child telling his father what to do, but as he moved closer, and heard what the boy was saying, he marveled at both the accuracy of his facts and the boldness of his tips. Harry delighted in the natural leadership qualities Thad displayed by ending his speech by uplifting his father with great confidence that they were going to win the race. Twenty laps later, Thad's father moved up through the field just as he son had told him to. He made his way to front of the pack, passed the leader on the last lap, and won.

Tears filled Harry's eyes when his Dad screeched his tires to a halt, climbed out of his car, and caught his son in the air as he leaped to him. They bear hugged each other before his father tossed him in the air, and caught him again with another hug. It was a shining moment he would never forget. The event made a long lasting impression on a recruiter who thought he had more than seen it all.

Harry met father and son after the crowd thinned out as they were packing the car in the trailer to head home. He congratulated father and son, but asked if his son was a driver as well. Thad responded quicker than his father, boasting he could drive anything with wheels. Harry learned the boy was driving tomorrow night on the same track. Harry told him he would be there to watch, and then took them both to a local restaurant, buying them a steak supper. At midnight, Harry left a message on Susie's voice mail to reschedule his flight home as he was staying over to watch Thad drive.

Harry spoke to the father and son before the race giving them a few tips about the race, before climbing the steps to the press box to watch the race like a spotter. Ten miles into the race, he saw Thad expertly regain control of his car after a bump in a curve by a competitor. Keeping his cool, Thad weaved his way through the field, and won the fifty lap event three seconds before second place.

Harry bought them another dinner, and told them about his boss and the teams they were building. He said he would keep an eye on Thad and made them promise to call him every week on his race results. He gave Thad a business card displaying his special private toll free number that would transfer to his cell phone day or night. He told Thad, "I want to know your race results, but also want you to tell me about what you learned in each race. If you are driving without learning—you're just going around in circles." It was a phrase Harry would tell Thad over and over until he was sure it had sunk in. At first, the instruction puzzled young Thad, but he soon understood Harry was looking for more than a fearless driver—he wanted a driver that would and could both think and learn. Harry talked with him on the phone like a father might talk to his son who was away in college, but also like they were of equal age. Thad respected Harry and his knowledge very much.

Harry's report and video presentation on Thad was the best he had ever done. Harry flew Thad and his father to Concord North Carolina to tour their DMI operations and meet his boss. Drew picked Thad when he was but

5

12 years old, telling his father to stay in touch as his son was going to drive for him, and together, they were going to win many championships. Drew sent his father twenty thousand dollars a year to help with his race expenses. At least four times a year, Drew would have his plane fly to the Midwest to pick up TNT, a.k.a. Thad or T, and his parents, and fly the group to the track for the weekend NARC race no matter where it was in the country. Unlike the NCAA, race recruiting had no rules and no age requirements. Thad got autographs from all the drivers, and delighted in going inside Drew's motorcoach checking out every bell and whistle. With his special NARC credential pass, he visited the garages, met many drivers, and watched the race from the top of the pits alongside Drew. He met television celebrities as well as sports and movie stars, and old Drew knew that when TNT went home, the experience would push him to win harder than ever before, so he could come back one day and enjoy his own motorcoach and big trophies.

On his fourteenth birthday, Thad's family and Drew watched as he drove his first stock car around the track at Lowes Motor Speedway. As instructed he drove a few laps at a slower speed to get the feel of the track, but when Drew radioed to him to pick it up, Thad's face exhibited a huge grin. He pushed the pedal down with great confidence and screamed with joy. He did fifty laps—each one a few tenths faster than the one before. Drew marveled at the ease the boy took with the car, keeping it in the fastest line he could find. Harry spotted for him and could not stop grinning. He knew from the start he had found a diamond in the rough—now everybody else knew it, too.

When Thad screeched to a halt the pit crew lifted him from the car. He took off his helmet and looked up with a grin at Drew. "How'd I do?"

Drew laughed, "You crazy rascal—you tied the track record!"

Everyone laughed but Thad. The smile fell from his face. "Dang! That's not good enough," he announced as he spun around and climbed right back in the car and fired up the engine. It only took him twenty laps to finally break the record. Drew knew he had just experienced the heart of a champion, and the soul of a competitor. He gave Harry and his wife a free trip to Cancun as his way of saying thanks for finding Thad.

Thad practiced the entire weekend, but when it came time to fly home, Drew said he was sorry, but a mistake had been made, and his flight home had been cancelled. He said Susie tried to book him on other flights, but none were available. He told him he would loan him a car to drive home.

Thad and his parents were shocked because home was a long way, but Thad quickly said, "No problem. I'll be home in two days and almost all of it legally."

Drew laughed and asked him to follow him to the garage—the showplace of their teams. You could eat off the floor it was so clean. Harry held the door to the garage for Drew who wheeled through quickly. Thad was right behind him. Drew got about ten feet into the gigantic shop and spun around. Thad looked beyond him and saw about a hundred of Drew's employees assembled like a church choir about to give a concert.

Thad looked puzzled so Drew spoke up, "Son, to say that we were impressed with your performance would be a grave understatement. My staff, team, and company wanted to do something to show you how much faith we have in you."

Drew spun to look at his employees, "Bring it out boys!" From behind the rows of employees, a team of mechanics pushed a brand new racecar over to Drew. Thad immediately saw his name on the door panel below the entry window and the paint scheme was perfect.

Drew laughed, "It's all yours. I hope it'll make you successful this summer and if so, this time next year, you'll be driving for us in the second tier league in a Mountain Dew car."

Thad was shocked as was his parents. They had never had a brand new racecar. Every car they drove was actually part of various other broken or wrecked cars. The mechanics lifted the hood and showed him the engine. He was thrilled.

"Thank you so much. I am going to win a lot of races with this bad boy."

Drew laughed, "You're welcome, but we have a problem. You need a car to drive home, but this one isn't legal on the highway."

Thad frowned. "Oh," he said solemnly.

"Maybe we can come up with something you can pull home," began Drew as he turned to face his employees, "Group B! Would you move over to this side of the room?"

As they moved Thad's eyes caught sight of a brand new racecar trailer hauler with his name in huge letters on the side."

Drew laughed again, "Will that help?"

"Yes it will!" beamed Thad.

Drew suddenly frowned, "Oh my. We can put your racecar inside, but we still haven't figured out how to pull it home." He turned to the remaining employees on the riser. "Would the rest of the group move over to the other side?"

As the employees quickly walked out of the way, Thad saw a twenty-eight foot new RV with his name once again on the side, and already hooked up to the trailer.

"There you go. You have a new racecar, a new hauler, and a new RV to pull it. Do you think you could drive that thing home?" Drew started laughing as Thad could only nod his head in shocked disbelief. Drew said, "I'll take that as a yes." The employees started applauding, and to everyone's dismay Thad did something no one else had ever dared to do—he leaned over and triumphantly gave Drew the hug of his life. Old Drew laughed harder than ever. It was a great beginning for Thad and Drew's company, and the favor would soon be returned many times over.

A few years later TNT became the first driver in history to win the top NARC championship in his rookie year. He won by 181 points – no contest, in spite of the new race for the championship playoff system. In the television interview in the winner's circle, he thanked Drew, his parents, and his team, with great sincerity, and in his order of priority. He also publicly thanked Harry—something no other recruit had ever done. His wise memory of the man who started him on his career remained an appreciative friend in spite of all the 'new' friends he daily encountered. He was a loyal company player yet a strong competitive driver on the track even against Drew's other drivers. He spoke softly to the newscasters, but yelled and screamed at his fellow drivers as he went around them like they could hear him over the high horsepower engines. His fan numbers grew quickly and they loved him, but the fans of his competitors hated him. Drew told them the louder they booed, indicated just how worried they were that he was going to beat their driver. He smiled understanding perfectly.

He did more charity and television work than any other driver on the circuit. He went to a children's hospital to see the kids in every single city they had a race. He never once missed. The kids loved him. He noted some of the other drivers just posed for a few publicity photographs in front of the hospital, but not him. Photographers had to run to keep up with him, as he moved from room to room and bed to bed, shaking hands, giving the children and nurses hugs, and kissing the little ones. He tickled tiny feet and made funny faces making a sad child in pain—smile for at least the moment. Janet Anderson, his public relation director, often had to drag him out of the hospital in a faint attempt to keep him on schedule, but she loved him for it.

When he did an interview, he took time to meet everyone on the broadcast crew, and if he went to a television station, he went up and down the halls shaking hands with every clerk and secretary as if he was running for political office. Thad did not think about why he did all these things, he just knew every hand he shook, every hug he gave, and every little kiss made him feel happier and taller than he actually was.

He was old school when it came to his fans. He stood for hours after a five-hour race in extreme heat signing autographs until the last person got theirs. He went to shopping malls, fan tents, and sometimes showed up in his golf cart in the middle of the camper zones outside the track. Drew had to keep at least four security men on him for these special events to protect him from the screaming girls, but TNT thrived on the fans, and he loved them.

His second year he took second in the final race in Homestead after his right front tire picked up a piece of scrap metal from an earlier wreck. It cut his tire—flinging him harshly into the wall. He lost the championship by six points, and found it tough to talk to anyone afterwards. He knew it was no one's fault, an accident of bad luck, but he blamed himself anyhow. It was a long winter, but he came back in February stronger and more determined than ever to win. In fact, he won the first three races of the year, and his enemy fans began murmuring he was cheating. Drew invited anyone to inspect their cars, and no one ever found a thing wrong with them. Janet produced documents to prove every car part was carefully inspected and passed every time. TNT did not care what they thought, but after a bit of bad luck, he lost the next two races before finally winning his fourth race of the new season. The win put him ahead by just twenty points, but by the Mother's Day break, he was 260 points ahead, won five races, and T felt like he and the team were just getting to the top of his game.

The last race before the break was at California Speedway—one of his favorites. TNT Television Networks was one of his many sponsors, playing on his name with a commercial about seeing TNT only on TNT Television. TNT or T, as his friends called him, thought the spot dorky, but he loved everything about filming commercials. Secretly he wanted to star in a movie one day, but not now, he had championships to win. TNT television hosted a huge dinner that evening after the afternoon race. T arrived fashionably late with Drew and bodyguards for Thad. Everyone was enjoying the huge spread of food with over two thousand people in attendance. He was whisked from one couple to the next shaking hands and signing autographs. Drew was pulled away while talking with his buddy Darrell Waltrip or DW as his friends called him. Soon the guards felt comfortable with the crowd and headed for the chow line. T did several interviews, laughed and told stories with some of the network executives by doing what he called greasing the wheel so the money would continue to roll in. His body had taken a pounding that day after being caught up in someone else's wreck. He was sore almost everywhere, but didn't complain.

He had been there two and half-hours and had not yet sat down to eat or even get a drink. He grabbed a water bottle from a passing beverage cart and downed it quickly. He finally broke away from his last group, darted down the hallway and found the bathroom, and took a much-needed pee. He noticed a young man washing his hands immediately. T could not take his eyes off him as he stared at him via the angle of the mirror. So far, the boy had not picked up that he was being watched.

He was taller than T, brown hair, and amazing blue eyes. His face looked like he had skipped puberty and acne, leaving his skin soft and smooth. His short hair was combed back with every single strand of hair carefully in place. T smiled when he saw the boy touch up a single twig knowing he did the same thing. T finished peeing, but kept staring at the boy. He guessed him to be about twenty-three years old. The boy stepped back from the mirror and carefully re-tucked in his shirt, then pulled just a little of the shirt back out to avoid having the shirt look pinched. T also did that. He pulled out too much, pushed it in again, and finally made the adjustment to his satisfaction.

He then did something that created a memory T would remember for the rest of his life. The boy adjusted his package. T nearly busted out laughing as he glanced at the boy's crotch. Quickly T zipped his fly, and turned towards the boy. The boy looked up and T smiled at him. The boy smiled back. T started washing his hands.

"How are you doing?" asked T because no other words would come to his delirious smitten mind.

"I'm fine. You?" asked the boy not recognizing Thad.

T started drying his hands and turned to face him again. "I'm exhausted and bored."

"Me, too. I came with a friend that I haven't seen in," he checked his watch, "almost three hours."

"I'm T," said T as he pushed out his hand, anxious to feel the touch of the boy's hand in his.

The boy smiled and brought his hand to T's clasping it firmly. "I'm Mel Gibson," said the boy with a straight face.

T laughed, "Mel Gibson? The Mel Gibson?"

"Most folks just call me Mel, but if you wish you can call me The-Mel-Gibson."

T knew he was being put on, and he loved it because he still had the boy's hand in his, and his heart had picked up extra beats. "Tell me the truth or I'm going to keep your hand."

The boy smiled, "You can keep my hand as long as I get to come along with it."

"That sounds fair. So what's your name?"

"Jack Langston. I'm pleased to meet you. So you are bored, too?"

"Yep, very."

Jack asked, "Have you eaten?"

"Nope, too busy having to meet and greet everyone. You want to get something to eat?" asked T hoping Jack would say yes.

"Yes, I would, but only if I can have my hand back now."

T smiled and let go slowly feeling Jack's soft fingers slide across his hand, "Let's get out of the bathroom? T led him out the door and spotted a table in the back of the room, dimly lit with nary a soul within forty yards. "How about over there?"

"Okay." They walked over. It was a booth.

T turned to him, "Listen how about doing us a favor. You go to the buffet line, get us some big steaks, with all the fixings, and come back here. I'll go get us some drinks and deserts, and meet you back here in two minutes."

"Deal," Jack smiled as he turned to head off, checking twice to see if T was putting him on. Of course, T checked on him as well, giving him a

10

smile and a wave. Five minutes later, they both returned at the same time to the table.

T had stolen a waiter's tray and filled it with beer, glasses of ice tea, soft drinks, and four bottles of water, as he had forgotten to ask Jack what he wanted to drink. Ironically, Jack had stolen a tray as well and loaded it up with food. When they arrived at the table and saw the other's tray, they both laughed

"I didn't know what to get you to drink," said T.

"I love Southern Wine, but they have no clue how to make it in California," replied Jack.

"Southern Wine. Isn't that an oxymoron or something?" asked T.

Jack laughed, "Southern wine is Southern iced tea brewed carefully, and sugar is added when the tea is hot so all the crystals turn into syrup. You add a fresh squeeze of a lemon, crushed ice, and you have the best wine in the world." Jack set the tray down on one side of the booth table. T set the drink and dessert tray on the other. "I've got bad news," said Jack.

"What? You don't have to go do you?"

"No, but there was only one steak left, but it looks to be a twenty-five pound monster. I snatched it. Sit down there and slide over," suggested Jack. T slid in to the far side of the booth expecting Jack to slide in on the other side, but he didn't. He slid in beside T. "Okay, here's a clean plate, and your utensils, my name is Jack, and I'll be your waiter," he teased.

T laughed, "I hope you're not expecting a tip."

"I heard you were a tight wad. I found salads and potatoes, and all the fixings, but sadly just the one steak."

"That's okay, you can have it," replied T politely.

"If I ate all that I would start growing fur and doing math with my right hoof pounding the dirt!"

T busted out laughing. "Shut up," teased Jack, "you're breaking my rhythm. He dragged the steak plate with the overflowing big t-bone between their plates, spread out the food so T could reach everything and smiled, "OK, time for the blessing."

T thought he was kidding, but Jack closed his eyes and bowed his head. T thought it was nice that he was religious. Jack began his prayer, "God?" he paused. "God? Are you there?" he paused again. "I hope I didn't wake You. Well, I'm pretty sure You are there, so rubadubdub and thanks for the grub. Yeah God! Amen." Jack opened his eyes and stared right into T's face as he opened his eyes. They both busted out laughing. "Let's eat."

T and Jack cut chunks out of the steak and fed it to their mouths while their hands worked on preparing their baked potatoes. After chewing and swallowing, they ate salad in harmony, another bite of steak, and then a scoop of the hot potato. Together they continued eating in rhythm until they were full.

They drank several bottles of soda, avoided the beer, and talked constantly. Jack allowed his left hand to fall off his lap and gingerly on top of T's hand. T did not jerk it away, and Jack did not apologize. They were soon holding hands—hidden beneath the table. T had never met a friend so quickly in all his life. Jack felt completely comfortable talking with T. He had yet to make the connection that T was a racecar driver.

Jack's friend was a sportswriter who contributed to a racing magazine. He sometimes invited Jack to attend a racing event with him. Jack was also a writer, but working on his first novel while doing freelance copywriting for people on the Internet. He started by writing resumes, but now wrote speeches for executives on just about any subject. He loved doing the research, and coming up with a funny opening and closing line for his clients. This paid very well and allowed him to work his own hours, and travel where he wanted as he handled all his clients through the Internet. He carried a laptop with him everywhere.

"Jack, it is late. How would you like to get out of here with me?" T bravely asked the question, and tried to prepare himself for an embarrassing negative response.

Jack looked up as if waiting for God to make his decision for him, and then said sweetly, "I'd love to."

Jack stood up, and started for the front door, and back into the large crowd of people. "Hold it Jack. I think we'd better go out the back way." He led him to the back of the hall until he found an emergency door. The sign said a buzzer would go off if they pushed the opened door. "You ready to run?" he asked. Jack smiled and nodded yes. T pushed hard on the door and the anticipated alarm went off. They took off, jumped over some bushes, and sprinted through the parking lot to T's brand new Hummer.

"This is yours?" asked Jack.

"Yep." T hit the alarm beeper on his key chain that unlocked the doors. "Get in," he ordered not waiting for a reply. He cranked the SUV quickly, and they sped out of the parking lot. For the first time in the entire season, T suddenly felt like he had escaped prison, or more importantly, he escaped himself. They drove down the freeway before taking the exit to the beach. They raced up the beach highway until they found a place to pull off. They jumped out of the car and ran to the beach. They made a pile of their clothes and then ran hand in hand into the surf. They swam and splashed one another before finally settling in each other's arms with Jack holding T from the rear with his arms around him. From time to time, they kissed and felt the other's growing penis. The warm water felt wonderful as they began talking less and making out more. Soon they were walking in the middle of the night down the beach without a stitch of clothing on. T knew if the paparazzi caught him they would have a field day with his photos, but no one knew where they were.

After they dried, they returned to the Hummer and drove to the track. T pulled up to the guard shack for the infield where the expensive driver and owner motorcoaches were parked. "Hey, Sam—you got the late shift, huh," said T, while sticking his head out the window so Sam could see his face.

"Well, hey TNT. How you doing? Come on in and I hope you sleep well. You had a hell of a race today. I'm sorry you got beat up."

"Thanks, Sam. See you tomorrow," replied T as he pushed the accelerator down slowly and pulled away.

"You got beat up today?" asked Jack worried.

"Not literally. I will show you in a minute." He parked in front of a new two million-dollar Prevost Coach, customized, and styled by Marathon Coachworks. Jack's mouth fell open. T quickly did the code for the door and pushed Jack up the steps and into the coach. He pulled the door and locked the deadbolt, not wishing to be disturbed. He began hitting a row of button. The blinds went down over all the windows, and at the same time the aisle, lights came up softly. A motorized drape began moving around the entire front window including the door. In seconds, they were hidden from the hundred of motorcoaches in the lot, and the nearby infield leftover fans in their campers.

Jack's eyes began to adjust to the dim lights and his mouth fell open. "Oh my gosh, this is gorgeous! And this is yours?"

"Yes. Sit down here, and I'll show you what happen today." T picked up a remote control about the size of wide paperback book. He hit several quick buttons and a high definition fifty-four inch wide plasma television began descending by folding downward from the ceiling. The sound system and the television came on. T hit the DISH satellite DVR button, selected the race, held down the fast forward button through driver introductions, and stopped as the announcer introduced TNT. He paused while Jack took it all in, then he raced forward at 32x until the first wreck, then the second, and finally, the last wild one that sent him spinning out of control doing several three hundred sixty degree turns before slamming into the wall.

"Oh my gosh. You're not hurt?"

"I'm just sore as hell."

"Oh my poor baby. You're in luck, because I'm exceptionally good with my hands. Turn off the television—we're getting in the shower. Let's go," ordered Jack as he pulled T down the hall. They began dropping their clothes off, moved together into the hot shower and took turns lathering each other's hair, rinsing, then washing the other's beautiful skin, then kissing, sucking, and finally drying off and heading for bed. Jack crawled on the big bed and laid back waiting for T. T locked a second door separating his bath and bedroom from the rest of the coach, just in case, and quickly slid onto the bed with Jack.

Jack rolled him over and began massaging his shoulders and working his fingers deep into the muscles. He pushed downward with his thumbs,

13

dragging slowly along T's spine all the way to his tailbone over and over again. T sighed deeply. Jack worked the muscles of his legs and when done they tried to figure out which one was bottom or top, and gave up and took turns being both. They slept arm in arm with T's soft hair floating across Jack's shoulder until his lips touched his head as if kissing him all night. They slept until way pass noon.

TWO

Thad woke up with the sun high in the sky outside, but inside his bedroom on the motorcoach remained in total darkness because the expensive dual coated electric shades kept his bedroom as dark as a cave. He turned over, pulled Jack to him, and kissed him. Jack stirred, opened his eyes, focused on T's smiling face barely seen from the glow of a digital alarm clock and kissed him back. Without a word, their hands began exploring, and soon they were making love again.

Afterwards, Thad reluctantly headed for the shower while Jack fell back to the bed exhausted. Fifteen minutes later Thad dressed while Jack took his turn in the shower. He picked up his cell phone and stared at it for a moment. He knew he had cut the power off before going to bed to avoid interruptions, but hesitantly, he turned the phone on.

He laughed as the screen indicating he missed twenty-three calls and fourteen voicemails. He unlocked the pocket door leading to the front of the coach, stepped through, and closed the door behind him. He walked to the front of the forty-six foot Prevost coach. He pushed the button for the power drapes, and they began pulling back. He hit a second button lifting the blinds. He slipped on his shoes and stepped out the door.

The glare of the sun nearly blinded him, so he reached back in and grabbed his sunglasses. He turned left and right, and realized the entire coach lot was empty. About twenty feet away sat his parked Hummer. Across the hood laid his security man and coach driver Duke Pendleton. The sixty-year-old man slept soundly with his hat pulled over his eyes. Thad slipped up, grabbed his foot, and yelled, "Boo!"

Duke jumped and then laughed when he saw the kid. "About time you got up. You missed the team flight home last night. She must be pretty to keep you in bed until after lunch. I told them to go ahead and fly home, and I would drive you to the airport and put you on a commercial flight home. Susie's already booked you a first class ticket. I guess you needed more time after that wreck yesterday." He climbed off the hood and shook the sleep from his body like an old Labrador shaking the lake water out of his fur.

Thad had to think quickly, but so far, he had fooled everyone as they thought he had slept with a girl last night. "Uh, Duke. I need a break—a break from everyone. That wreck yesterday was a wake-up call for me. I need a little vacation. Here's what we're going to do. I'll take you to the airport in the Hummer, and you use my ticket to fly back."

Duke asked, "What about the coach?" He found himself still getting use to a kid barely a third of his age giving him orders, but he liked and respected T, and would do anything for him.

"We have next weekend off so I'm driving back, but I'm going to take the whole week to do so. Tell the boss I'll be there a week from

15

tomorrow at eight o'clock sharp, so we can fly to Michigan for the next testing."

"Drew and Charley aren't going to like this."

"I know, but I had most of the week off anyhow since we don't have a race. I will call Janet so she can cancel an appearance Thursday on the Larry and Jennifer Show. I've done the show many times. With their big egos they probably won't notice I'm not there until the show is almost over."

Duke laughed, "That Jennifer girl is good looking, but my god what a mouth she has on her. I'd be getting my fifth divorce if I were married to her. Are sure you want to do this?"

"Yep, absolutely. I have never been on a trip in one of these coaches. I fly everywhere and there's so much of America to see."

"You're right and I've seen most of it, especially when I was in the military."

"You'll enjoy going home sitting in first class. They serve a lot better meals in the front of the plane. Show me how to hitch this Hummer to the coach."

"Have you ever driven a coach before?" Duke showed him how to adjust the tow bar and hook it to the front bumper brackets.

"Sure," T lied, "I used to drive a school bus."

Duke swallowed hard, "This is a lot bigger you know."

T laughed, "I'm just pulling your leg. When I began driving in the Mountain Dew league, Drew bought me my first coach. I made them let me drive it from Charlotte to Daytona. By the time I got there, I knew I could handle anything on the track and the interstate. Let's go, I'll drive."

They started for the Hummer when Thad suddenly remembered Jack. "Whoops," he said, "let me go get my wallet." He ran to the coach and leaned in. He found Jack sitting on the couch. "Hey, how are you?"

"I'm great, and you're wonderful, and smell good, too."

"Listen I only have a second," began Thad as he snatched up his wallet. "I've got to take my driver to the airport. He doesn't know about you. He actually thinks you're the girl I slept with last night." Thad laughed while Jack rolled his eyes. "Will you stay right here until I get back? I'm going to drive the coach back to Charlotte, but I want you to go with me. I won't let you say no, so just go fix yourself some breakfast, and I'll be back in twenty minutes. Please say yes," he begged.

"Okay," said Jack with a slight smile. "If you insist—yes!"

A huge grin took over Thad's face. "All right! Listen lock the door and ignore anyone that might come around, but the track looks deserted to me. See you in twenty minutes." He leaned in and gave Jack a wet kiss.

He ran from the coach, sprinted to the Hummer, and laid rubber all the way out of the track.

T kept his hat pulled down tight over his brow and to the top of his sunglasses, forgetting about the dark tinted windows of his fire engine red Hummer. He prayed no fan or media person would recognize him. During his first year in the Pepsi Cup, the team put a personalized tag on the Hummer identifying him. By the end of the year, he pulled it off and put on a University of North Carolina National Champions basketball tag. He no longer wanted attention, but rather cherished his privacy.

On the way back to the track, he left messages for Janet on her voicemail, and apologized for throwing the television appearance cancellation on her, but he knew she would handle it with great diplomacy. He guessed she would tell them he had the flu. He waved at the gatekeeper and told him he would be pulling the coach out within the hour. He slid the Hummer to a halt as he pulled within three feet of the back bumper. He sprinted around to the door, hit the remote lock button on his key chain, and pulled the door open. He ran up the steps and turned to look for Jack.

The table was set with T's fine china, including long flutes and a bucket with ice and a bottle of champagne. Jack looked up and smiled. "Hey, cutie, are you hungry?"

"I starved. You can cook?" he said as he walked up and kissed Jack on the neck.

"Yes I can, but you can't cook?"

"How'd you know," blushed T.

"Simple—these pots and pans have never been used. Pop the cork on the champagne, and I'll bring the plates."

Thad did know how to do that and quickly poured the cold golden wine, and sat down. Moments later Jack turned from the kitchen with two plates.

"Oh my goodness—I'm impressed!" began Thad as he looked at his plate of food. "There's an omelet, hash browns, toast, fresh strawberries and bananas, and grilled ham. I didn't know I had all this in the refrigerator."

"Apparently someone was trying to make sure you ate well. The cabinets and the refrigerator are full of food. There are steaks and chicken in the freezer. Dig in."

Thad smiled as he picked up his flute of champagne, "No—a toast first. To us, and boy am I glad I met you last night." They clinked glasses, drank a sip, and then began devouring the food. "Oh my goodness, this is so good. I didn't realize I was starving."

Jack winked at him, "Sex requires a lot of stamina. You'd better eat well because I'm planning on having sex with you tonight..." he paused and winked, "and several times."

"So you're going to take a vacation with me? You can get off work?"

"I'm a freelance writer. I'll check with my agent a few times to see if there is something that is crucial I need to work on, but otherwise, I'm all yours. Are we going to end up in Charlotte?"

"Actually we are going north of Charlotte to Concord North Carolina, the home of our big team operation, and not far from my house. Where is home for you?"

"I had an apartment in Atlanta when I first started writing. I hung out with gay friends and for a year or so, I went out to the gay bars. I had my heart stomped on several times, and got my feelings hurt when one of my friends slept with a boy I had fallen for. I got pretty depressed, remembered my wonderful summers in Franklin, North Carolina at a summer camp, and decided to drive towards Boone for a visit. I loved the area north of Asheville, rented a cabin on the side of a mountain, and a year later I bought a house there."

"Wow, that's cool. I don't think I have ever been to Boone. I hear it is pretty."

"It is one of the best kept secrets in the world. Great people, magnificent views, and they enjoy all four seasons. I love snow, and I love the fall when the leaves turn colors. I especially love hiking along the ridges and going horseback riding on the trails."

"I guess I need to visit there soon."

"You'd better, or I'm not going to let you fuck me again."

"Okay, okay—I will. You drive a hard bargain," laughed Thad.

They finished the meals and put the dishes in the new dishwasher drawer. They set about moving the furniture around a little and stowing everything away. "Watch this," urged Thad as he hit a button the wall, and the two bedroom slides began slowly creeping inward. They moved to the front, he pushed two more buttons, and the two front slides began moving in.

"Come on, we have to hook up the Hummer," said T as he headed out the door.

Thankfully, Jack had been with his father when he hooked up his car to their recreation vehicle before they retired to Florida. He motioned Thad to move the SUV a little closer, and gave him the stop sign. Together, they hooked up the tow bar, safety cables, and the power cable. Then they both returned to the Hummer.

Jack said, "Do you know how to put this in neutral and unlock the transmission so it will roll freely.

"Yep, I think I remember," replied Thad. He put the transmission in neutral, turned the key to the first stop and checked to make sure the steering wheel moved freely, let off the emergency brake, and then pulled a drive train knob. "That should do it."

"I think we should pull it a little ways with me in it to see if it feels right."

"Good idea. Can you unhook the power cables for the motorcoach, and I'll go fire up the engine so the air can build up the air bags and the brake system?"

Thad ran to the front while Jack unhooked the dual power cables and traced them back to where they came out ofto the coach. He opened the nearby compartment and found two power reels. He laughed as he recalled how many times his dad had struggled to coil their cables and put them in their thirty-foot camper. "This million dollar baby has power reels," he said aloud. He hit the button and the first cord automatically wound in. He hit the second button and it, too, wound in.

It took Thad a few minutes, but soon the engine revved up and the air compressors were rapidly lifting the coach to the riding position. He adjusted mirrors, the seat, and the steering wheel until he felt comfortable. He flipped on the rear monitor and saw Jack walking around the back of the Hummer. Jack bent down and watched the coach rise up on the air bags instead of the leveling legs on his father's camper. He pulled open the door.

"Everything is ready on the outside. Are you ready?" asked Jack.

"Yep, here—catch!" He tossed Jack a portable walkie-talkie. The talk button is the long one. Just press if you need me to stop, and I'll hear you in here."

"Got it, drive slowly at first."

"I will. I think I'll drive all the way around the parking lot for a test. Let's do it!"

Jack winked at him and closed the door. He ran back to the Hummer and climbed in on the passenger side. "I'm ready he called over the radio."

Thad was busy looking over all the dials and memorizing the dash so he would know what normal looked like. He shifted into drive, took the park brake off, and pressed the throttle. The big 700 horsepower diesel began moving him forward. "Yahoo!" he yelled to no one, but excited nonetheless. He drove around the lot as planned and then made his way towards the exit.

"I think all is well back here in the Hummer."

"Okay, I'll stop. Lock the doors and head this way." Thad slowed down until he came to a smooth stop. Jack jumped out, pushed the door lock button, and closed the door. He ran to the coach and came up the steps. "Lock the door and then sit down in the passenger seat. You see that black button to your right near your cup holder. Push that."

Jack did as he sat down. Quickly he lifted his feet as a motorized floor cover rolled over the step well. "That'll give you a place to put your feet," laughed Thad as he put his sunglasses on, pulled his hat down tight, lowered the left driver blind down to just above the side mirrors so he could see down, out, and back but no one could see in. He lowered the front blinds to block a little of the sun.

"Where are we going?" asked Jack.

"I don't know, uh, how about the Grand Canyon. I've never seen it from the ground—only from a plane."

"Sounds good, do you know how to get there?"

T laughed, "I think it is east of here."

"Hang on, let me get my laptop. I use a GPS software program called **Co-Pilot** to find my way around the country in rental cars." Jack undid his carrying case, removed his laptop and began turning it on. He laid a tiny GPS receiver on the dash and plugged it into the back of the laptop. He found a power outlet on the wall next to his seat and plugged in laptop charger. Seconds later the screen filled with a map and purple arrow show him where they were. He clicked on new trip, punched in Grand Canyon, found the National Park Entrance, picked it, then told the software to go, and instantly the software showed him where they were and what turns they needed to get out of town and on their way to the Grand Canyon.

"Okay, leave the track and make a right, then go about fifty yards and make a left. That road will lead us to the Interstate so we can head east."

"All right, mister co-pilot, let's do it!" exclaimed Thad as he hit the diesel horn and stepped on the accelerator. The big motorcoach lurched forward causing Jack to laugh, but also grab and buckle his seatbelt.

With just a few turns, they were on the expressway east of Los Angeles. They picked up the San Bernardino Freeway, and seven miles later turned onto Interstate 15. Neither boy relaxed until they had gone fifty miles, and left the busy California highways behind them.

"We've got about forty more miles until we reach I-40, and that'll take us near the Grand Canyon. I don't live far from I-40 because it goes right through the middle of America, and all the way to the east coast near Wilmington."

"What time will we get to the Grand Canyon? I'm doing seventy, but I don't want to go over the speed limit. If the cops stopped us, and they find out I'm in the coach, I'll be on the news in a flash. Then a phone call or two later and the media will be all over us."

"I take it you're not out of the closet," stated Jack.

"No, NARC doesn't have a single gay driver. When I was growing up you heard the word 'faggot' all the time around the drivers, but times are changing. All the rookie drivers have to attend an all day seminar on what NARC expects their drivers to say and do, and most of the afternoon session was on what not to say or do. With the cameras and microphones in your face all the time, you have to keep pretty tight-lipped even when you feel like cussing. If I'm mad I have to hold my temper until I'm deep into my hauler, and the door is closed before I can let off steam."

Jack frowned, "Uh, what's a hauler?"

T looked at him with silly smile and a wink, "Boy, you are green. Hauler is what the teams use to get two racecars to the track for each driver, along with all their tools, mechanical stuff, and supplies for pit and garage crews. There is a lounge up front where I sometimes put my uniform on, and we can have a meeting in there if needed."

"What do you think would happen if they found out about you?"

Thad sighed, "It is possible NARC might cancel my credentials and in an instant I'd be out of a job. That would cut me to the bone, but the bad part is if they didn't fire me I'd hear things said under the breath about me, or I'd see people whispering as I walked by. Someone would accidentally bump into me in the shop, or knock me off the stage. On the track, it could be worst. Let's say a guy has no chance of winning the race, and he is far out of the point's race, or in other words nothing to lose. He would be frustrated and just as I was about to complete my pass around him, he would let his car appear loose, and run me up the track and knock me into the wall. He'd apologize when the camera was on him after the race, but would walk away laughing about what he did to the faggot. In his mind, I would deserve it for being a queer. If things got really bad, someone would put me in the wall at hundred and ninety miles an hour. I'd be lucky if it didn't kill me."

"I get the picture. Okay, that settles it. I'm back in the closet because no one is going to hurt my baby," grinned Jack.

T laughed, "Thanks. I appreciate your willingness to keep our relationship on the quiet."

"Relationship? Hold on a second—I hardly even know you," teased Jack.

"You nearly sucked the end off my penis last night, and you hardly know me?" shot back Thad.

"Oh yeah—that, well, I guess I do know you a little, at least your dick."

"Before this week is over, you're going to know me more than anyone else on the planet."

"Do you think you can park this baby in a campground?"

"I think so, but we'll put you out there with the walkie-talkie to guide me in," replied T.

"There you go talking about sex again." They both laughed before Jack continued doing a bit of research with the GPS software. "There's a KOA campground that we can get to before dark. They have fifty amps service, which is what most forty-foot recreational vehicles need. However, I unplugged two fifty amp plugs when we packed up this big coach, so this baby must need hundred amps."

"I've heard Duke talk about that before. A few test tracks we went to only had fifty amps, so we'd just run about half the air-conditioning, but it's not too hot yet in middle of May. At the tracks, there are no shade trees, and boy does it get hot. Of course in the early spring and late fall, it can get pretty cold as the wind really whips through an open track. All the NARC tracks have the hundred amp service for us."

"Where are the manuals for this coach?" asked Jack.

"You're going to read them?"

"Yeah sure, or least the parts about electricity."

"They are in that cabinet up and behind your head. You have to push in on the door lock and then turn the latch to open."

Jack unlocked his seatbelt and opened the cabinet. "Good grief, this looks like a local library. There must be twenty manuals in here." He ran his finger down through the books until he found a tab for power systems. He shut the cabinet door, and sat down so he could start checking the index. He read for about twenty minutes before asking T a question. "Did you know you have a twenty kilowatt generator?"

"I knew we had one, but I don't know what a kilo-what is?"

"Kilowatt, not what. You're funny. That means we could park this baby anywhere, fire up the generator, and we'd still have hundreds amps of power."

"Cool. Do you still want to head for the campground?"

"Yeah, but if we don't like it we will free range. I'm going to crank the generator so we'll know how to do it if we need power." Jack continued reading while Thad began scanning the dash looking for the fuel gauge. It was just over three quarters full bringing a thankful sigh from his lips. It took him a while longer to find the switches for the electric mirrors adjustments, but once he did, he soon had every mirror tuned perfectly. He found a switch labeled 'NORAD' and wondered what it did. He flipped it on and nothing happen. A few minutes later, a BMW began passing and suddenly, he heard a beeping sound. He looked at the dash and realized the coach was telling him a car was alongside him. He topped a hill and reset the cruise control. About an hour later, he came upon a slow truck rig, and before he could cancel the cruise control, the coach started slowing down preventing him from running into the back of the truck. He remembered he had left the NORAD system on, and realized it must have been the radar guidance and safety system he had heard Duke talk about. T hoped it would keep him from running into or over someone.

About an hour before sundown, they pulled into the park. Jack chose the park because it listed fifty amps sites and welcomed 'big rigs', and he was sure they were in a big rig. He figured coaches did not come any bigger than this one. Thad pulled to a stop near the camp office.

Thad opened his wallet and pulled out a hundred dollar bill. "You go in and pay. Register in your name so no one we'll know I'm here."

Jack took the bill and grinned, "No problem. I don't think it'll cost that much, but I'll be right back. As he walked to the office, he caught himself doing something his dad used to do when they went on vacation—he began looking at the site numbers hunting a good spot. He found number 101 near the back away from the highway and farthest from the camp office. It was also in an area where no one else was parked.

He walked through the door and decided to fake flirting a little with the girl behind the counter so he got the lot he wanted and practically skipped back to the coach. "We're over there near the back. Pull around there and stop, and I'll unhitch the car. By the way it was only twenty-seven dollars a night."

"Gees, I had no idea it was that cheap."

"Yeah, most of them are except for the big RV resorts in the southern half of the country. They are huge and exotic, but still only about fifty a night. By the way, do you know where the gauges for freshwater, as well as the valves for the gray and black tanks are located?"

"We have colored tanks?"

"Yeah, fresh water is what we drink and shower in, and gray water is where that water ends up when it goes down the drain. When we use the toilet it goes to the black tank."

"Oh," replied Thad.

"I'll find the gauges later. This is good. Stop here." Jack sprung out the door with the Hummer keys in hand and in five minutes, he had unhitched the car and parked it. He walked to the lot with his walkie-talkie in hand. "Okay, dude, I'm ready. You've got to back in this one."

"Oh shit! You're kidding?"

Jack laughed, "You can do it—just pull past the lot, and get over on the far right. I'll tell you when to cut the steering wheel."

T did as he was told, and Jack carefully watched the right rear tire as it came near the corner of the lot, "Okay, spin the wheel as hard as you can."

They were both surprised at how easily the power steering turned the big rig. "Okay stop, pull forward about twenty feet, and cut the wheel the other way. Okay, stop, flip the wheel the other way, and roll back slow."

Jack looked left and right recalling the location of the slides, and carefully backed Thad in as far as he could go. After he shut down the generator, Jack hooked up the power and headed to the front door. "Let the air out of the air ride, and hit the leveling switch." Thad scanned the dash until he found the air control and the switch for the leveling. Once leveling was accomplished, he turned off the coach engine.

Jack came in the coach and said, "Show me where you think the water gauges are."

Thad walked down the narrow aisle and just before reaching the pocket door for the back, he opened a narrow door that looked like a broom closet. Inside were over fifty gauges and switches for operating all the power, heating and cooling systems, and lighting. Jack studied the gauges until he found what he was looking for. We are low on water and the gray tanks are almost full. The black tank looks fine. Come on, we've got work to do."

Thad put his hat on tight and followed Jack out the door. Jack found the right compartment, pulled the water hose out of a small supply door, and told Thad to hook it up and turn it on. He found the lever that allowed the water to fill the tanks, but he was looking for the usual big three-inch sewage drain hoses. Instead, he found a long one-inch black pipe that stretched like a vacuum hose. There was a nozzle on the end that fit perfect into the camp's sewer line. He began reading the labels until he found the gray valve switch. He turned it on, and heard water swoosh through the pipes for only about five seconds and stop. He searched again until he found the master valve switch and turned it on. The water made a little more noise and stopped. "Damn, there are too many switches."

"If it helps, Duke says our shit gets ground up like a kitchen sink garbage disposer, but still he didn't want any tampons in the sewer system. I guess he thought I would have a girl over, and I was supposed to warn her."

"Macerator, that's it!" exclaimed Jack as he read the label. He hit the switch, a pump suddenly came on, and the hose jumped as the water was quickly pumped out of the gray tank. "Well, that was easy."

"Easy for you. I'm hungry," complained Thad.

"Go wash up, and I'll be done in a minute. Do you want to find a restaurant or eat in?"

"I feel like pizza."

"Okay, give me a few minutes to let the pump finish, and then I'll be ready. See if you can get the slides out and close the shades and curtains. I'll ask the girl in the office where the best pizza is. Are you planning on going in?"

"We'll see if it is crowded or not."

"She suggested a place call Henrys which is just about two more blocks down on the right. I think I see it on the right. Yeah, there you go, just pull in."

"There are only a few cars out front—that's a good sign for me and hopefully, we can avoid race fans, but Duke says the best food is at the truck stops with the most trucks around it."

Jack smiled, "Do you want me to go in and check it out?"

T smiled back, "I know I'm being a pain, but if people recognize me everything becomes a zoo."

"Hold on. I'll be right back." Jack ran in and came back to the Hummer in a few seconds. "Only one couple eating dinner, and they are over seventy years old."

"Okay, let's do it." Thad brought along a ski hat from Copper Basin in Colorado and pulled it down tightly. They asked for a table in the corner with Thad sitting with his back to the restaurant. They ordered salads and a big pizza. They devoured the salads, as it had been almost seven hours since they ate breakfast. They ate half the pizza and asked for a take-out box.

"This is the first time in years I have been able to pizza in a restaurant," said T between bites.

Jack replied, "I don't know how you do it. I would go nuts."

Thad smiled, "Dad says if you love racing enough—you can put up with just about anything. I do miss going to the mall and shopping for clothes. Now I usually buy all my personal clothes online. My racecar company has a tailor that takes care of any special event clothes like a tuxedo, or appearance clothes for television."

Jack asked, "Did I mention you should eat faster?" He gave Thad a wink.

T guessed and laughed, "Because you're horny?"

"Yep, very horny. Are you?"

"Duh, well yeah. Let' get out of here." T left thirty dollars on the table, so they quickly slipped out of the restaurant, and made their way to the Hummer, and drove back to coach. They managed to put the pizza in the refrigerator before they began kissing and pulling each other's clothes off.

The next morning they got up at seven as the campground owner suggested they go the Grand Canyon early for the best views. She gave them a map, and marked the key points they should stop at. They found a McDonalds and bought breakfast on the run, and by nine, they were standing on the rim of the canyon. Jack had brought along his digital camera and began taking shots, while Thad kept saying over and over, "Oh my God. Oh my God. This is amazing."

Jack snapped his picture with the gorgeous scenery in the background. They found a small ledge about three feet down from the rim. Thad jumped down on it and then knelt down, and put his chin and hands on the edge of the upper rim. Jack backed up, knelt down, and snapped his picture. It appeared as if T was just barely hanging onto the ledge. They laughed at the picture Jack took.

They walked away from the tourists and began holding hands as they scouted about. Over the next few hours they visited most of the recommended sites, and then drove quickly back to the coach. "Let's pack up. Check out is noon."

"If you insist, but I could stay here and have sex with you for a week," protested Thad.

"You don't want to get in trouble with your owner—rumors would really start cranking. They would put you in an alcohol and drug treatment center, or in a mental hospital," teased Jack.

"I guess you're right. Let's do it."

Jack was busy studying his laptop and the GPS software. "Just keep heading east. I think we can make Santa Fe New Mexico before dark. There is a resort called Santa Fe Skies that will be a big leap up in quality as compared to last night. Is there anywhere you want to go?"

"How about we go through the Colorado Rockies?"

"Have you ever been to Colorado Springs? It is the most beautiful place in the world. From Santa Fe it is only about three hundred and fifty miles or so, but we'll be getting into the mountains."

"Sounds perfect to me," replied Thad.

Jack did the research, made a few phone calls, and soon had them booked in RV resorts in both cities. In a few hours, they were hungry again, so Jack heated up the pizza, and they stopped and ate in a rest area. By late afternoon, they were parked, and sightseeing in the Hummer. Thad turned onto a dirt road, put the Hummer in four-wheel drive, and turned up the stereo. They laughed as they bounced over the ruts in the road. They had no idea where they were going, and found themselves surprised when the road ended in a small group of cement blockhouses. It was a poor place with little grass, yards filled with junk cars, and children running about chasing each other.

"I guess we had better spin around and head back," said Thad.

Jack did not respond for a few seconds. "I feel bad for these folks. Look at that. They have a satellite dish on their roof, but broken windows all over their house."

Thad slowly turned around and soon they made it back to the highway and on to their campground. Jack grilled some chicken breasts while Thad made a salad. Jack stirred a pot of brown rice and soon they were sitting down to eat. Afterwards they watched a DVD, ate some ice cream, and went to bed. Neither boy had ever experienced awesome sex, night after night, but they never tired of the lovemaking—only tired from all the fun. Arm in arm, cuddling in tight, they slept soundly.

Jack made eggs for breakfast and then using his GPS on his laptop, they took the Hummer and drove to a ridge affording a magnificent view of the New Mexico area. Jack took more pictures while they both enjoyed the masterpiece nature created.

Jack asked, "Are you ready to get rolling?"

"Yes, I guess so. I'm looking forward to seeing Colorado. We don't have a race there, although I did go skiing in Aspen once."

"You can ski?"

Thad smiled, "You think I can only drive and have no other skills, don't you?"

Jack grinned wickedly, "I certainly do not. I just didn't know you had other skills other than driving and sex!"

Thad laughed, "You're terrible. You must put me in the category of a dumb blond."

Jack looked left and right. After finding no one within miles, he pulled Thad to him, and kissed him deeply. T reached around, felt Jack's butt, and pulled him in tighter. They allowed their tongues to explore flickering in

26

and out creating large erections below their belt buckles. Jack pulled away and just held Thad's face in his hands. "Do you know how beautiful you are?"

"Yeah, right. I'm a racecar driver—all looks and no brains, right?"

Jack kissed his eyelids gently, then his nose, and kissed an ear before whispering, "I think you are the smartest, best looking, and the most extraordinary and skillful man I have ever met. I could eat you up with a spoon." He began planting kisses down to his neck, slowly working his way to his chin, before once again thrusting his tongue deep into T's mouth.

"I've never been in love," whispered Thad. "Oh, I've had people fall in love with me—especially girls, but I've never been in love. Is this what it feels like?"

"Yes, it is, but to maintain this love we'll have to work at it. My parents celebrated fifty years of marriage last fall. Mom used to say their marriage wasn't perfect, but their love was. When I came out to them, she told me I would have to work twice as hard to find the right man, and ten times harder to keep the love growing forever. I think I know what she meant."

"I love you, Jack. I really do," whispered Thad.

Jack smiled, "And I love you, too.

They kissed deeply for a while longer before reluctantly heading back to the Hummer.

THREE

The tourist sites and the days flew by way too fast for them, but together, they did their best to savor every moment—especially the sunsets in the deserts and the mountains. Thad knew this was the happiest he had ever been in his entire life, and yet he began to fear what kind of future he and Jack might have together. Way out in the plains, Thad taught Jack how to drive the coach. At first, he drove only forty miles an hour, but in time, he felt comfortable with seventy miles an hour. The big forty-six foot coach rode like a Cadillac, but the challenges came when it was time to maneuver through a town or into their campsite. Jack would sometimes take a nap while Thad was driving, so during this quiet time T would think of all the various excuses he could make up as to why Jack became his roommate. He thought of lying and saying he and Jack were friends when he was a kid, and over the years they had lost touch with each other, but after Jack's recent divorce he called Thad's mother, got his cell phone number, and called him. He would tell people they talked for hours, as if they had remained close all these years.

He polished that story several times before trying another tale. By now, he knew almost everything about Jack including his work on a new book, and staying alive by writing speeches for executives all over the country. T's next yarn was that he had hired Jack to both write speeches for him, and to begin documenting his life for a future biographical book because he knew his fans would buy it as fast as they could print them.

A hundred miles later, he toyed with the idea of being honest and telling Drew, his boss, that he was in love with Jack, and from now on they would be going everywhere together. He scoffed at that thought, because he knew old Drew would probably have a heart attack, or run over him with his wheelchair. He could become NARC's first gay driver, setting the world and the image of a driver being a man's man, tough as nails and fearless, completely upside down. The announcement would be the headline of almost every major newspaper in the country, and on the cover of all the racing magazines. He knew every day after that he would have to watch his back, and in every accident he would always wonder if it was a fluke that caused the carnage, or redneck bigot on a mission to kill him.

The thought of the any announcement made sweat drops run down his back. He cut up the air conditioning, but he still felt hot. He also knew if his parents found out they would be heartbroken. He felt afraid they might never want to see him again, but after a while, he felt confident his mom would come around first, while his dad might take a little longer. He knew they loved him, and he hoped they loved him no-matter-what.

He had so much more he wanted to accomplish in racing. He wanted to break all the records, win more races than anyone in history, and set a new record as the winner of the most championships. He felt he already earned enough money to be happy, and unlike many racers, he held on to most of his money. He didn't buy an airplane or start his own team because other drivers moaned about how much money they spent and lost on these endeavors. Drew took care of a fleet of planes, and Susie booked him on one of the company jets for all of his trips.

He had lived in a condominium when he first came to the Charlotte area, but once the fans discovered him, he had to stay at Duke's house for a month before he found a place where he felt he could be secure. He bought a former bank executive's ranch style mansion. It was at least six thousand square feet with a pool, Jacuzzi, on a lake, and heavily treed all the way around. The entrance sported an electric gate with a high fence encompassing the fifteen acres. It amazed him that he had enough money to write a check for it on the spot, but his accountant would not let him. He listen to the guy explain for twenty minutes the tax advantages of a home mortgage, and warned he needed all the deductions he could find, so he wrote the check for twenty percent instead. He moved his stuff in a few hours later. For a year, the rooms in the house had no furniture. His folks had to stay in a hotel when they came to visit, as he had but one bed because he had no time to shop or plan until the end of race season. Janet helped him hire an interior decorator, and three hundred and fifty thousand dollars later classy furniture could be found in every room. Two weeks later, a news crew did an interview in his house, as they walked from room to room.

Jack would live with him, of that he was sure, but getting through the bumps in the road as he explained his new friend would be most difficult. As the miles trailed by, he went over dozens of stories, each time improvising new lines to the tale, and each one made him nervously chew his lip.

"Hey, wake up, sleepy head. We're forty miles from Boone, and I want to see your house!"

Jack stirred and wiped his eyes, "Don't yell so loud. You're running the mood of my dream. I dreamed I was riding east with a gorgeous racecar driver who happen to think I was cute."

T laughed heartily, "And indeed you are. Now can I see your house?"

"Of course, you can, but the coach isn't going to make it up the road. We'll have to park it and take the Hummer up the mountain. Let me think, huh, I guess we could park it at the mall."

"What day is this?" asked Thad.

"Hmm, Saturday, you said we have to be in Charlotte tomorrow night."

"Let's stay in Boone tonight, and you can show me around, but I think we'd better park the coach somewhere safe. Find a campground."

Jack booted up his computer and in a few minutes he found a campground just off Interstate 40 not far from Asheville. He made a call and obtained a reservation. "We're all set, and it is just 'skootch' off the Interstate. If we have time in the morning I could show you some of my favorite views."

29

Thad winked at him, "Skootch? Is that similar to a 'smidgen'? We'll make time to see your house, but that means we have to start having sex earlier tonight."

Jack laughed, "Let's see it is about 4:40 right now. Would five be early enough?"

With a wicked laugh, T exclaimed, "Perfect!"

They parked the coach making it into the tight spot with only inches to spare. They hooked the electrical, locked the door, and leaped into the Hummer. "Turn right and head south on Brevard Road. We have time to make it up to my favorite spot on the Blue Ridge Parkway. We're going to a place called Lambert's Leap. It's on a peak on top of the ridge and once we climb there we'll be able to turn in a slow circle, and see a spectacular three hundred and sixty degrees view of the mountains."

"Wait a minute—did you say climb?"

"Just about two hundred and fifty yards up an easy trail and it will be worth every step and more. Hustle now, but don't get a ticket. I will show you where to turn on the parkway and then we'll head south."

Ten minutes later, they reached the parkway, but as they started up the ridge, Thad wanted to pull off to see the incredible views, but Jack pushed him promising to stop on the way back. We have to get there soon, or we are going to miss the sunset."

They blew the horn as they went through each tunnel, and rolled down the windows and screamed. They both felt they were having the most exuberant and high-spirited moment of their life—made all the better because they were both in love with the other.

They were rushing around the bend and almost missed the left turn into the parking lot. "Whoa, turn left and park fast!" yelled Jack.

Thad managed to slide the Hummer to a grinding stop and parked perfectly between the lines. They popped the buckle on their seatbelts and leaped out. Thad locked the door before running as he followed Jack up the trail. He was soon puffing because Jack failed to mention the trail was a steep upward climb the whole way, but he was right—it was possible.

"Come on, old man. Are you puffing?' teased Jack.

"Yes, I am. How much farther?"

"Two bends and we're there."

"Yeah, like I believe that," shot back Thad between gulps of air.

Jack waited for him near the top. "Okay, I'm going to cover your eyes, then we'll walk about twelve more steps, and I'll remove my hands."

"I'm not falling for that. There's probably a cliff at the top, and you're going to push me off."

"Tempting," he teased, "but trust me."

T did as commanded, and Jack guided him the last steps with voice commands. "Okay, here you go. One, two, three!" Jack quickly removed his hands.

"Oh my God!" exclaimed Thad, as he slowly took in the view as Jack took his hand in his and slowly turned him in a circle. When they reached the western view Jack stopped.

"The sun is setting all the way across America, and you're watching from one of the highest peaks in North Carolina. A week ago we were on the other side of America where the sun is slowly falling."

"This is spectacular! I love it. Thad and Jack stood arm in arm watching the sun slowly slide and hide by the mountains off in the distance. Thad turned and looked at Jack, and kissed him once, twice, and three times with short sweet kisses. He ended with a long deep one. After a while, they broke the embrace, and began turning once more as daylight began leaving the deep valleys back to the east.

On the way back down to the parkway, they stopped at numerous pullovers to watch the lights begin to twinkle back in Arden and Fletcher that were suburb towns of Asheville. Jack found a place where they could see the famous Biltmore Estate, the castle like home built by George Vanderbilt over a hundred years ago.

"I'm hungry, let's get something to eat on the way to your house," protested Thad.

"Eat in or out?" asked Jack.

"I think I could be easily recognized in Asheville as there are tons of racing fans here, and lots of famous drivers, mechanics, and machine operators in this area."

"Do you like chicken Francesca?"

"What's that?"

"It's like fettuccini Alfredo with grilled chicken breast and tons of melted cheese," replied Jack.

"It sounds good to me."

Jack snapped up his phone and made a quick call to one of his favorite restaurants, Apollo Flame. After he hung up, he turned to T and grinned, "It'll be ready in ten minutes. It comes with salad, too. It is on our way back."

They picked up the food, which they thought smelled awesome, and then made a few turns, crossed some bridges and then started upwards towards Boone. After a few miles, they turned in a narrow drive and pulled to a stop at a gate. Jack got out and pressed some digits on the keypad, and a black iron gate slowly began opening.

"That's impressive," said Thad. "Your own an electric gate."

"It came with the house because some of my neighbors experienced a few break-ins. I travel a lot, so the gate keeps them from backing a van in and loading up." They pulled in the drive leading to the house. "See the killer dog signs?"

"You have a dog?"

31

"No, just the signs, but I do have an alarm system, but I'm about a mile from my nearest neighbor, and they can't see me, and I can't see them. I can walk naked to get the mail box."

"I bet that is a pretty sight," laughed Thad as he pulled to a stop in the carport.

"Come on, let's haul this food in. I can't wait any longer. I'm starving."

Jack led T to his big oak kitchen table and out the big atrium door window, so they could just see the last little bit of sunrays to the west.

Thad said, "This is some place, and very cozy."

"It is not as big as your place, but it works for me. It has two bedrooms," began Jack before throwing in, "and you can stay in the guest room."

Thad nearly spit his last bite out, "I don't think so!"

Jack laughed, "Just kidding. You can sleep with the dog."

"You don't have a dog," protested T.

"Oh yeah, I guess you'll have to sleep with me."

Thad winked at him, "I guess that'll be okay if I have to."

They ate all of their food, which nearly busted their stomachs, and went to Jack's bedroom and stripped naked. Thad thought they were going to jump into bed, but he was wrong.

Jack said with a sly silly grin, "Follow me."

He led Thad down to the basement and flipped on a single light. He walked across the room and lifted the cover off a bubbling Jacuzzi. Once Thad realized what it was he leaped in the air and crashed into the water drenching Jack.

"Whoops, sorry baby," stated T sweetly.

"To hell you are," laughed Jack as he fell into the water and into Thad's waiting arms. They soaked for about twenty minutes, but the urge for sex overwhelmed them. They headed up the steps hitting light switches along the way, toweling themselves dry, and fell into the bed hot and horny.

Jack was up early, drove to McDonalds, and brought back breakfast. Thad showered and dressed, and together they sat down at the table to eat. T was quieter than usual, and it took Jack three bites into his second bacon, egg, and cheese biscuit to notice. "Eat up while they're hot. Are you okay?"

"Yep, fine. I sort of dread going home tonight, but I'm looking forward to racing again. I guess driving fast is just in my blood."

"It's your gift or your skill, and you're amazingly good at it," replied Jack trying to cheer him up a little.

"Listen, I'm not one to hold something in very long. I like to get things off my chest, and let the chips fall where they may. I love you more than anyone in my whole life…"

Jack interrupted him, "But my breath stinks, and you want to dump me. Is that it?"

"No, no, well, yes, your breath does stink," laughed Thad, "but I don't want it to end. No one has ever come out in NARC before, and I don't know how bad the reaction is going to be."

"Well, you didn't get caught having sex in a bathroom."

"You heard about that?" interrupted T with a wicked grin. "Dang, and we were careful."

"I'm trying to be serious," began Jack again, "but that is so hard with you. I sort of figured tonight might be goodbye because I know you have to get back to your work."

"But I don't want it to be goodbye. I want you to come with me," pleaded Thad.

Jack let out a sigh, "I came all over you last night!" They laughed as Thad playfully hit Jack's shoulder. "We can come and visit each other when you're home."

"Not good enough. I want you to move in with me in Concord."

"Whoa—wouldn't that be a major problem?"

Thad sighed, "Well, I've done a lot of thinking over the past thousand miles or so. Why don't you come to work for me? You could write my speeches, and begin writing a book about my racing career. We both could make a ton of money from the book. I have plenty of offers—each assuring me we would sell a hundred thousand copies in the first week. Then you could travel with me, and we would be together."

"You're still going to stay in the closet I assume."

"Yes, for now. I want to get back on top and win the championship this year, and with you with me, I know I'll have the confidence to do so. I see how hard it is on the drivers who had to leave their wives at home."

"Oh, so now I'm your wife?" teased Jack.

Thad hit his shoulder again, "You're my bitch!" They both laughed. "You could still keep your business going as we have internet hookup wherever we go, you'd have time to work on your book while I'm testing or something, and then together we could work on my book."

"This is a bigger step for you than me, as I am used to being alone, and doing as I please. From what you've told me, someone manages your schedule, which checks with your publicist who keeps up with team responsibilities and sponsor events, and your personal manager, and then they meet with you for your final say. Is that right? When would we have time together?"

"I'll insist on being off two to three days a week for one which means the team will have to plan ahead on testing a little more. Of course, sometimes they are rained out and we are held over, but if you were with me all the time, we'd be together flying to and from anywhere and everywhere, and of course will be together every night. Will you at least try it?"

"I'm thinking," said Jack.

"Thinking about what?" asked T feeling a bit desperate and anxious for an affirmative answer.

"I'm thinking about how cute you are when you're begging for something. I am going to remember this, as it'll come in handy down the road."

"So you will come with me?"

"Yes, I'll come, well not literally, well maybe sometimes."

Thad leaned over and kissed him deeply before he could say another word.

Jack laughed, "You have cheese in your teeth—biscuit breath!"

"I'm so happy."

"What do we do if someone asks if either is gay? Or they call us a name?"

Thad dropped his head, thought a second, and then lifted his head and eyes until they met Jack's. "We'll beat the shit out of them, but I think there are people who are a bit jealous of my success, and already call me tons of names, so calling me gay or faggot is not going to faze me, but I'll have a hard time if they call you that. We'll have to act as straight as possible until we're home or alone. Are you willing to do that, and if you are, I'll spoil you with an exotic vacation right after the awards dinner at the Waldorf the first week of December?"

"Ah, now you're resorting to bribery. That's a new low, even for you. I'll do it, but not because of the vacation promise, although it does sound fun, but because I love you—plain and simple." Jack winked at him.

"Nothing is plain and simple when it comes to you—you're the most wonderful, beautiful, and loving fellow I know. I love you, too."

"I think we need a code word for love so we can say it when we feel it without getting beer bottles thrown at us."

Thad thought for a second, "How about 'vost'?"

"Vost isn't a word," replied Jack.

"Yeah, I know. Well, no I guess I didn't, but I wasn't really trying to think of a word others would understand. Here's what I was thinking, when we first met, we climbed aboard my Prevost or my coach, right? Therefore, we were sort of in pre-love. Now that we are in-love, we're no longer Prevost, just 'vost'!"

Jack laughed. "That is the dumbest thing you have ever said."

"Oh no, it is not. I've been dumber."

Jack smiled, "If you insist, but I guess it will work. So, let me try this out. "Vost you man. Race you, vost, dude! Vost you baby."

They both laughed and spent most of the day racing around the mountains as Jack tried to show him everything he could about the western

North Carolina Mountains. He promised the next time they got a few days he would take him to the Biltmore Estate in Asheville, and to see the waterfalls in Transylvania County near Brevard. The name of the county made Thad laugh heartily, as he conjured up thoughts of Dracula.

By late afternoon, they had loaded up some of Jack's clothes and stuff in the Hummer, picked up the coach, and drove back to Charlotte. They left the coach in the parking lot of Drew's headquarters under the watchful eye of the security guard. Thad drove to his house. After giving Jack the tour, they quickly unloaded his car, went to get some take-out, and then came back, ate, made love, and fell asleep.

Tomorrow would be the beginning of a new day for a new member of Thad's crew—a special member. Thad hoped Drew would understand, as well as the rest of the team and employees.

FOUR

First thing Monday morning, Thad and Jack drove to his headquarters. Thad began introducing Jack as his best friend after they cooked up a story they had gone to high school together, but had not seen each other for a long time. Thad worked his way from office to office before going upstairs to Drew's office. He knew Drew always arrived early. He stopped at the receptionist desk outside of Drew's large office.

"Susie, this is my friend Jack. Jack this is Susie—the lady that really runs this place."

She smiled, "Yeah, right. You want to see Drew?"

"Yes, unless of course he has someone with him."

"Nope, he's free, just go on in—he was looking for you," she replied cheerfully.

Thad led Jack into Drew's big office. Along one wall were the mounted wild animal heads from numerous hunting trips with his buddies to Wyoming, Canada, and Alaska. Thad always joked he was afraid to be around Drew when he had a loaded gun.

"T, you scared the living shit out of me! Where in the hell have you been?" asked Drew as he spun his wheelchair around when he realized he had a guest.

"Sorry, about that Drew. I just needed some time to get my head on straight. I left many messages for everyone. Did you get my message?"

"Yeah, I did," he began, as he set his cigar down, "that's the only reason I didn't send the FBI after you. Who is this?" Drew nodded towards Jack.

Thad smiled, "Drew, this is my best friend Jack. We were in high school together. When I felt low, I called him to talk over old times. Then I drove out to see him. We've climbed mountains and hiked through the forest, and well, he helped me to get focused again on my racing." Thad knew just what to say that would put Drew in a good mood. "After some reflection I decided I'm going to do everything I can to win you another championship!"

"That's great news," replied Drew. "It's nice to meet you son," said Drew to Jack as he shook his hand. "I'm glad you could come visit us." Then he turned back to Thad. "Listen, little man, we've got a jet waiting on you to head to Kansas for a test this morning. The boys are already there. Why don't you show Jack around a little, and then get yourself over to the airport. I'll get Janie to tell the pilots you're on the way."

Thad knew that was a polite order, but now was the time to spill his plans. He turned to Jack, "Jack, if you don't mind, I need to speak to Drew on a business matter. Would you wait out in the hall for me? It'll just take a minute, and I'll be right there."

"Sure," replied Jack and then eyeing Drew, "It was nice to meet you, sir. You have quite an operation here. Thad says you're a genius when it comes to building winners. I can see you're a hard worker," he added while gesturing to the windows overlooking the giant shop.

"Thank you, son," enjoying the flattery.

After Jack closed the door, Thad moved in front of Drew's desk, sat down, and began collecting his thoughts. "Drew, this won't take but a couple of minutes, but I wanted you to know about a small change I am going to make."

"Change? What, you don't like your new uniform? Your helmet?"

"No, everything's fine, well, not everything, you see, uh, well..."

"Spit it out boy, before you choke on it," said Drew.

"I hired Jack to work for me."

"Hired Jack—what for? What does he do?"

T would have loved to answer that question literally, but tried to get back on track, "He is a writer. He has his own business writing speeches for executives and politicians all over the country, and he is writing a novel."

"A novel, speechwriter—what do we need him for?"

"You don't, but I do. You see, he is going to write my speeches for me, and he is doing research to write a book about me. Herb has been sending book offers just about one a month, but I don't know any of the writers. I don't know if I can be honest with them. They could take anything I say and flip it around and make me look stupid. Jack is a long time friend, and I trust him with my life. I want him to write the book.

"And Drew, you're probably laughing about writing speeches for me, but I did some checking. Did you know that Larry McReynolds gets ten thousand dollars per speaking opportunity? Darrell Waltrip gets fifty thousand dollars per speech. Jeff Gordon gets over a hundred thousand. I can speak, but I don't know what in the hell to say to folks that are twice my age." T winched, "Sorry, Drew."

"No offense," replied Drew knowing he was a bit more than twice Thad's age.

"Jack can write speeches that could make me worth more than Gordon, and I'd feel good knowing I'm saying the right things to folks to inspire them to be champions in whatever job they're doing. He's great.

"But Drew, I called Jack because of this—I'm lonely. You guys are great, but there's almost no one my age around me. Sure, I can find a date, but after Herb has her sign about ten pages of legal documents reminding her he'll sue the hell out of anyone that talks about my private life, well, it sort of sours any hopes of love." He faked a laugh, "But the sex is good!

"I can't trust anyone to be my real friend because you and I both become immediately suspicious of their intentions. Some folks want to make some quick money on some gossip about me by selling a short story to a rag magazine. Some girls only like me because I'm rich. I can't tell the difference when I first meet someone. It scares me to death. I feel that everyone, and I mean everyone, is out to get me.

"Jack didn't come to me to for anything, but rather I sought him out." Thad could have shot himself in the foot for that sentence especially using the word 'come' but thankfully, Drew did not have a clue about the coming and going on in his new sex life. "I trusted him as a boy, and he trusted me before I became rich. I can give him a thousand dollars to go buy groceries and when I get back, the full change will be on the table to the penny along with the receipt. He is anal retentive about stuff like that." Dang, he thought, I wish I hadn't use the word 'anal' either.

Thad paused for his last lines, "He is going to be the key to me keeping my head on straight, and winning you another championship. Drew, I need him. Are you cool with him being aboard?"

Drew shook his head and grinned, "When your driving career is over you can always go in to sales—you're a born salesman. It's okay with me. Now do you mind getting your butt out of here, and getting on the jet? We've got work to do."

"Thanks, Drew, I'm out of here." T reached across the desk and shook Drew's hand as firmly as he could, then spun and practically ran out of the office.

He stopped at Susie's desk, "Jack is going to be working and traveling with me absolutely everywhere from now on. He's going to write a book about me, and you'd better be nice, or I'll say bad things about you in the book."

She laughed, "Don't tempt me. What can I do to help?"

"Will you tell Janet for me? He'll need a picture ID with full clearance to everything and credentials for all the tracks. Make sure he has a seat on the plane with me, and he'll stay in my coach for now. Get Janet to put together newspaper clippings, stories, and the company biography on stats, as well as my records and me. Tell her there is no hurry on this as we expect the book to take over a year to produce."

She interrupted, "Got it, motor mouth!" "Jack, since you are obviously the sweet one, please come with me, and we'll get started," she said as she stood. She led him into another office. "Just stand on the white line and smile." She went behind a photo ID camera and pressed the button on a computer, and the camera flashed taking his picture. A few seconds later, his new company identification card fell out of the machine into a tray. She picked up a new lanyard, popped the ID inside the plastic sleeve, and placed it over his head. "Listen Jack, I need a favor. Will you try to keep T out of trouble? He has so many girls swooning around him all the time. The temptation must be great. I would not want to read about some girl getting pregnant with him in my morning paper," she teased.

T said, "I'm saving myself for you—just as soon as you get rid of that husband of yours!" She laughed as the two boys hustled out of the office, and ran to the Hummer. T drove quickly to the airport.

"What did you think of Drew?" asked Thad.

"Smart, gets to the point, and I think he sizes up everyone in about eight seconds."

"That's about right. I told him about the speeches, the book, and of course, as we agreed, you're my best friend from high school. I told him I needed someone around me my age I could trust. He's fine with you being with me. We'll meet some of the team when we get to Kansas."

TNT screeched the Hummer to a smoking stop just outside the door of the waiting jet. They both leaped out of the car. T tossed his keys to the DMI employee waiting at the bottom of the stairs. "Park that for me, Jimmy, and thanks."

"Yes sir," grinned the boy as T and Jack sprinted aboard the jet.

They were in the air minutes later with T and Jack sitting in the back of the plane alone. An attendant brought them cold water bottles, bowls of fresh fruit, and a turkey sandwich with a few chocolate cookies on the side, which were T's favorite. They laughed and talked the entire ninety-minute flight, and for T the time just flew by. He was so excited to have Jack with him.

There was a SUV limo waiting for them at the Kansas airport and ten minutes later, they were at the racetrack. A golf cart took them inside and parked right beside a huge car hauler with T's picture plastered on both sides. The pit crew guys were waiting on him.

"Jack this is Sam, Bob, Henry, Mutt, Red, and Chris. Don't try to memorize their names—it's on the front and back of their uniforms so even they can remember them. Guys, this is Jack, my high school best friend. I hired him to work for me. Is everything ready?"

"Yep, just waiting on you as usual," replied Charley his crew chief with a bit of sarcasm.

"Sorry, I didn't know about the test until I arrived at DMI about an hour and forty-five minutes ago. Don't worry I'll be right out in five minutes."

T led Jack into his hauler and all the way to the rear, and closed the door to the small room with metal lockers on a left wall like a school gym. He began pulling off his clothes as fast as he could, leaving Jack wondering if they were about to have sex. T pulled on his fire resistant thermal-like underwear and his racing uniform.

He stepped into his boots and laced them rapidly. "You can watch from the pit box, but it'll get boring so do something on your laptop and pretend to take some notes, etc. If you need to go on the Internet, we have Wi-

Fi set up on the hauler. Login as Thad and the password is TNT. Okay, follow me."

Thad practically ran out of the hauler, climbed into his racecar, pushed his yellow earplugs with the tiny wires leading to his team radio in his ears, and put his helmet on. Red began helping him hook up his safety straps, buckling his harness belts, pulling each as tight as he could, and then giving the safety gear the once over. Thad put his fire protection gloves on, and Red helped him tuck his sleeves inside the band and carefully tighten the Velcro to keep them in place.

"Charley, can you hear me?" asked Thad as he pressed his radio button on the steering wheel.

"Roger, T. Gary can you hear us from the tower?"

"Roger," replied Gary, T's spotter was standing high in the grandstands so he can see the whole track. He would be in charge of helping T with his racing line, and avoiding any accidents on the track. Seven other teams were practicing and testing today as well.

"Fire it up," ordered Charley.

T threw the switch, and the engine roared to life. The pit crew began going over the car looking for anything that might be out of place. T adjusted his crotch as the seatbelt was crushing his balls. He glanced through the window netting, and smiled as he saw Jack climb up on the pit box with Charley. Jack shook Charley's hand as Charley handed him a water bottle.

"You're going to get blistered by the sun. Here—wear this?" Charley tossed him a TNT hat after shaping it for him. Jack pulled it down low to block the sun and made a note to bring his sunglasses next time. "Thanks," he yelled over the engine noise.

T pulled out and joined the other cars on the track. Gary told him the track was clear so he could pick up his speed. T worked his way through the gears, passed the pits on his first lap, and already flew by at a hundred and twenty-five miles an hour and accelerating. Jack was impressed, but by his second lap, he was at a hundred and eighty.

Charley said into his radio, "Okay T, let's go to work. I want you to test two grooves today. The rain last night washed the rubber away so we'll be on fresh track. Take it easy, pull in behind Dale, and draft him a little. I've already spoken to his crew chief. We'll do ten laps and then you take the lead, and let him draft."

After thirty minutes, T pulled into the pits with a screeching halt. The crew changed the tires, gave him T a water bottle through the window, and then T sped out again. Charley came over the radio, "Okay, T, let's find a second groove."

T came around the fourth turn looking good as he hunted his marks for a second groove. Suddenly the rear end got a bit loose."

"Whoa, boy!" yelled Gary into the radio.

"Shit!" yelled Charley. "Keep it off that wall!"

T did not yet have time to respond. He jerked the wheel to the left, then back to the right to straighten it, and roared down the front stretch. "She's a little loose in the right rear. Maybe a half pound of air,' said T in his radio.

"Bring her in, and we'll swap that tire only with the air change," ordered Charley.

Five minutes later, T came around the fourth turn again, and this time the car held to the track perfectly. Relieved, he sighed heavily.

"That's better," said Charley, "okay, pick up the speed. We've got to qualify up front this time." Charley made a note of the rear air pressure amount in his race book.

T had been right, as Jack was bored after the wiggle in the fourth turn. He popped open his laptop and in minutes he was online. He checked his email and downloaded notes for a speech he needed to write for a favorite executive of his that owned a shoe company. Every time he wrote him a speech, the guy would send him several sets of new shoes along with his check. He figured he would never have to buy shoes again for the rest of his life. He downloaded all the facts and points the speech should include. He sent an email off to his agent explaining he was doing some work for Thad, and perhaps a biography on him. Therefore, he would be traveling the race circuit for a while. His agent immediately wrote back that the break sounded like a great opportunity for him. He had no idea Jack was interested in racing, or how he got the job, but he was too busy to care with a big star's book premier press conference beginning in an hour.

Jack then clicked on T's website at www.TnTRacing.com and casually flipped through all the pages reading all the facts about T's success. He then went to Drew's site at www.DmiRacing.com and quickly realized the same web designer created both sites. He made notes on how he might improve T's site, especially the wording.

After a few hours, T pulled the car up to the hauler, shut off the engine, and climbed out. Charley came up to him, "You made good time on those last few laps. We'll try the backup car after lunch. Go chill out and relax. It'll be about an hour."

Jack followed T into the hauler where T quickly took a much-needed pee. "Are you okay?" he asked Jack.

"Yeah, sure. I checked my email, and I have a speech to write for a shoe executive."

"How do you write a speech on shoes?" asked Thad.

Jack laughed, "It's not about shoes, but the guy owns a company that makes shoes. It is a motivational speech about production success. If I do a good job, he always sends me several pairs of shoes."

"You see, I need a shoe sponsor so I can get free shoes. I get free sodas, sparkplugs, shipping services, Band-Aids, but nothing I can wear."

"Life's tough on the rich boys," teased Jack.

"Yeah it is. Let's get lunch."

They walked to the golf cart and rode over to the limo. "Bojangles, please," said T with a grin to the driver. The driver laughed as well, but did as requested.

At the drive thru window, Jack did the ordering and turned to the limo driver, "What do you want, Steve?" He made the order and they pulled around for their food.

They pulled out without anyone spotting Thad. Steve found a pretty spot to park so they could all eat. Thad hit the button for the privacy glass, and then turned on the stereo so they could talk and eat in private.

"So how did it go with the crew?"

Jack smiled between bites of chicken, "It went find. They were all nice to me."

"Excellent, we're off to a good start and more importantly, we're together." Thad leaned over and kissed him with crust crumbs on his lips.

"Ah, he tastes good, too, but if you don't mind, I have my own chicken sandwich to eat." They laughed, kissed a few more times, and got out of the car to walk a little. After sitting so long in his race car, T needed to stretch.

Twenty minutes later, they were back at the track and ready. The afternoon session took about two hours but went very well. While Thad quickly changed, Charley reminded him they had two weekends in Charlotte with the All-Star Challenge and World 600 races, and then they were on the road to Dover, Pocono, and Michigan. Thad had made the challenge by winning the Las Vegas race. He said there would be a strategy meeting at ten tomorrow at the shop.

They arrived back at T's house later that day. "So what did you think of today?" asked Thad while brushing his teeth and getting ready for bed later that night.

"I am amazed at how much money is spent on getting the little things right like testing, and all the tools and equipment you have, plus haulers, limos, and jets."

"Yep, it is a big corporation with a six hundred thousand square feet building, and since I've joined the big league we have about four hundred and fifty employees. Drew has marketing people in both the New York and Los Angeles, too. Their job is to handle the sponsors and their ad campaigns, as well as sell new sponsors. There is a lot of wining and dining to get all the money we need. Tomorrow I'll show you around the shop, and you'll meet more of my team and key players. Did you start on the speech for the shoe guy while I was going around the track all day?"

"Yes, I've written a rough draft," said Jack as they swapped places in the bathroom so Jack could tackle his teeth.

"Already, I'm impressed," replied Thad as he walked to the bedroom.

"Well, unlike most of my clients, he sends me good research notes so I have the facts and figures he wants to get across, but then I go on the Internet and search for more information. This guy is a history buff, so I look for a quote in history from someone famous that is perfect for his presentation."

"Gees, you're definitely smarter than you look," said T sarcastically.

Jack cut off the bathroom light and returned to the bedroom, "I wish I could say the same for you!"

"Ouch! That hurt," shot back T, as he suddenly yanked his boxers down, and stood there naked and posing like a model. "Now how do I look?"

Jack laughed, "Much better. You're up to genius level now." He dropped his shorts, and they both dove for the bed. After lovemaking, they slept very well in each other's arms.

The shop tour left Jack with his mouth agape most of the time. There were people building brakes, transmissions, drive shafts, while others worked on car bodies and getting ready for wind tunnel testing. He saw at least twenty-five of T's cars in various stages of preparation for a race.

"Why so many cars, do you wreck a lot?" asked Jack.

"What are you trying to say?" laughed T. "Each track has different quirks—so the cars are built to fit the track. Some cars can be used at more than one track, but it is set up slightly different to make it perfect."

They went up to Janet's office, and after introductions, she took them into a small conference room. On the table, she had laid out all the publicity materials she used to promote TNT. She had various media kits emphasizing the team in general, as well as smaller packages relating to his sponsors. She showed the folders of pictures of his racing career so far. She gave Jack a box, so he could pack all the materials to take with him as it stacked about eighteen inches high.

"Thad, you did remember we have a commercial to shoot tomorrow for RESTAR?" she asked.

"Yes, but what is RESTAR?"

"It's a synthetic oil company. We're scheduled for four hours and it is in Atlanta. We fly down at eight in the morning. Do you need a wake-up call?"

"Jack, make a note of that," began T with a sly wink, "we've got to be here by nine in the morning." He turned to start leaving.

"I said eight!" she called after him.

"I got it, I got it. I'll be here at eight thirty," he teased back as they hurried out the door.

After the strategy meeting they left in the Hummer for the day. "Have you ever been to Victory Junction Camp?" asked Thad, as he pulled out of the shop.

"No, what is that?"

"We're going there now. It is a great camp sponsored by NARC Charities For Kids who are too sick to go to a normal camp. They might have cancer or something. The Petty family started the camp in honor of their son Adam who died in a crash a few years back."

"Are you afraid of dying?" asked Jack somberly.

"Hell yeah, but there's not much I can do about it. Racing is so much fun—you do your best not to think about dying. I do everything they tell me to do, so I'm as safe as possible." He tried to think of something to change the subject, "Besides, I'm too cute to die young."

Jack smirked at him, "Yeah, you're cute alright—now only if you had a brain!"

T tried to tickle him in the ribs, but Jack fended him off.

They arrived at the camp about thirty minutes later. "Leave all your stuff in the car because you're going to need your hands free. You can put in the book I visit here and play with the kids if it'll help promote the camp, but if you think it is just promoting me then leave it out. My coming here has nothing to do with helping sponsors or obligations. I come here because I want to help."

"T!" called a little girl with a loud scream. She began running as best she could towards him. Her head was completely bald from chemo, but her smile remained huge, as Thad ran to her, picked her up, swung her around, and then smothered her in kisses.

Soon kids were coming from every building to see him. "Hey, gang, I want to introduce my best friend to you. His name is Jack. Can you say hi, Jack?"

"Hi Jack!" the kids sang out in unison.

T and Jack laughed. "Let's show Jack around. Come on," he called, as he picked up a little boy, put him on his shoulders, and began bouncing him along.

The camp director and his secretary stepped out of the office to see what the commotion was about, but as soon as he saw Thad, he smiled, "That boy is amazing with kids. Before he leaves today he will make sure he has spent time with every single one of them."

"Should I call the media?" asked his secretary.

"No, Donna, please don't. T and I have a deal—he comes as often as he can, and stays as long as he can, but he wants no credit for it. He'll also donate a hundred thousand dollars every spring, as long as we never tell anybody. Last year he got his sponsors to contribute over a million for the camp. He is one of many who keep the kids in their hearts, but no one comes to see them as much as he does.

Jack and Thad pushed the kids on swings and merry-go-rounds, played games with them and when lunch came, they sat down and ate with the kids as well. Naptime was after lunch, and a good time for them to head home.

"That was fun," said Jack. "You're great with kids."

"I should be," shot back T, "I am one!"

"Have you got everything?" asked Jack as he watched Thad put an extra pair of socks in a duffle bag.

The weekend came quickly, but T already had the itch to race. "Yep, let's do it," he replied as he led them out of the house, and they drove over to the DMI shop. He parked the Hummer on the far side. Jack's eyes lit up, "I thought we were going to the race track?"

"We are, but traffic and the crowds are so huge we'd never get there in time, particularly if they found out who was in the Hummer. We're using the company's helicopter for the short ride. Come on!" T laughed as Jack gulped, as he had never been on a chopper, and this one was brand new with the DMI logo on the side. The pilot held the door for them, as they climbed aboard. Janet was waiting for them.

"You boys ready to win a race?" she asked with lots of enthusiasm.

"You bet," replied T, as he helped Jack strap into the seat while Janet spoke into her walkie-talkie to be sure the golf cart was on the way to heliport to pick them up.

Seconds later, they took off by rapidly acending, but once high enough, the pilot began moving forward, and then abruptly banked a hard left turn to put them on the course to the track. Jack thought he might throw up, but wisely, T started showing him their house from the air, and off in the distance they could see the huge Lowes Motor Speedway. Jack relaxed and wished they had time to circle Charlotte, but minutes later they were on the ground. One of T's team members met them in an extended golf cart. They both wore their credential cards hanging around their neck, though everyone recognized TNT, but no one knew Jack.

The cart took them to the motorcoach where Duke was waiting on them. "You got me in a hell of a lot of trouble," he teased, as he gave T a hug.

"I told them to give you a raise for following my orders," shot back T, as they went up the steps. "Duke, this is Jack. He is my best friend and doing some writing for me. We're going to put your picture in my book— that'll sell a few thousand copies!"

"Yeah, right—go ahead and change. I'll stand guard duty as usual," replied Duke. He closed the front door, as they went down the hallway.

"I missed the coach," said Jack, as he turned and saw the flat screen television on with pictures of the track and of their helicopter landing. "We're on TV," he said.

"Yep, there is hardly anywhere we can go around here and not be on the tube. " Come on, help me get naked," he teased.

T did not need help, as he stripped out of his clothes, but he wanted Jack to grope and kiss him anyhow. Thad quickly changed into his racing uniform, checked his hair in the mirror, and then carefully pulled down his hat, so it would not blow off and embarrass him. He pulled open a cabinet door over the bed filled with about fifty of his racing caps, and snatched one. Quickly he shaped the visor, and squished the hat down on Jack's head and smiled. "That looks good. It'll get cool tonight, so wear this lightweight jacket," said T, as he reached into the closet and pulled out one of many such jackets with his name and number on the front and back. "Keep your credentials visible everywhere you go until my folks get to know you. Why don't you leave your laptop here until near race time? We'll be on the run for the next few hours doing promotion work and you're going with me." He leaned over and gently grabbed Jack's genitals, squeezing just a little. "I'll give you these back if you kiss me good."

Jack smiled and kissed him deeply. "Any time you need a squeeze, just come on over."

"I'm going to look forward to playing with this bag of marbles after the race. Let's do it!"

Over the next few hours, they got on and off the golf cart, as they went from one sponsor tent to another, while meeting and greeting sponsors. Janet studied all week for this, keeping her notes handy, she introduced Thad to everyone, even if he had met them before. She did not expect him to remember all the names, but often he did. He also did something many of the other drivers failed to do, but it always impressed the sponsors. When he met you, he looked you right in the eye, and never broke that look until he was ready to move on. He also listened well, as the fans often stuttered or stammered a little from being nervous about meeting a top racecar driver. He always smiled, and when he could, he made a little joke.

If a sponsor brought along his kids, Janet would slip T a hat from her big canvas bag. He would pick the small kids up, place a hat on their head, and pose for a picture. He gave all the little girls a peck on the cheek, and lightly gave the boys a firm pat on the shoulder. He always said goodbye to the sponsors while repeating their name.

The last VIP tent of the day was an important one for Drew. Inside his staff prepared a big grilled steak & lobster buffet served with all the extras including champagne, wine, and beer while a top country band played. Everyone attending was a guest of the companies Drew hoped to recruit into being sponsors for his teams. The expensive catering company placed

46

artificial turf down over the cement floor, hung fake chandeliers, and scattered waiters and bartenders everywhere. Thad whispered to Jack, "After this one we'll head back to the coach and eat. Would you mind going through the buffet and making us some to-go boxes. Try not to get me anything too greasy. Salads and pasta are usually good for me to eat prior to a race."

"Roger, will do," replied Jack with a mock salute of a two fingers and a wink.

Over the next forty-five minutes, TNT met everyone in the room as Janet introduced him to the various owners, presidents, staff, and spouses while T poured on the charm. Everyone drank plenty of alcohol except T. He kept a water bottle in one hand and took sips quite often. Jack met him behind the tent at the golf cart for the ride to the coach. It was the first time Jack had a chance to see all the other driver and owner coaches, as they breezed past the long expensive row. T told him each one ran a million or more. He saw kids playing outside, and people walking their dogs. They spotted Tony, a friendly competitor, trying to get his bulldog to pee on Gordon's tires. Everyone watched and laughed at him.

Duke sat in the front seat of T's motorcoach standing guard duty. When he spotted their golf cart, he popped the door and stepped out. They went in and immediately they were alone. "I've got to pee something awful," complained Thad, as he rushed to the bathroom.

Jack put the food out on the table, and made tall glasses of ice tea. "Thad had just washed his hands, so he placed his cold hands on Jack's warm neck. " Ouch!" exclaimed Jack, as Thad bent his head back gently and kissed him.

"Make sure I eat at a slow pace because once I ate too fast, and my stomach hurt the whole race. I can also remember before one my first races I could not keep anything down. I kept throwing up right until time for the race to start." He turned around, picked up the A/V remote, and brought the volume up on Speed Channel. They were interviewing Darrell Waltrip and asking him who was going to win tonight. DW replied with several possibilities and then said, "I'm going out on a limb because I think TNT is going to explode tonight. He's hungry for a win and beginning to hate the wall."

"All right DW!" laughed T.

After they ate, they plopped down on the couch so T could rest. Jack held his head in his lap, and gently ran his fingers through his hair until he dozed off. About thirty minutes later, Thad's cell phone began to vibrate.

Thad reluctantly stirred, popped open his cell phone, "Yeah?"

It was Janet, "Sorry, babes. Fox Sports wants to do a live interview in about fifteen minutes and just before driver introductions. Is that possible?"

"Yes ma'am, it is possible. How long is the spot?"

"Four minutes."

"I'll meet you at the cart in ten minutes."

"Thanks dear. You're the best."

Thad shut the phone and looked up at Jack while still lying in his lap, "I could have slept here all night resting my head on your warm balls."

Jack leaned down and kissed him, "You work harder than I thought."

Thad rolled up and onto his feet, "And I haven't even fired up the engine. Sometimes driving is much easier than all the hoopla before the race. The things we do to make the money. Let's do it. You might want your laptop this time. Are you going to sit on top of the pit box with the rest of team?"

"Yeah, if they'll let me," replied Jack, as he quickly put his shoes back on and grabbed his laptop.

"They will let you. It's all taken care of. Just keep your credentials in view. I'm glad you'll be up there because I like to see your smiling face when I come to the pit for the tires."

Thad was still yawning, as they made their way over to stage. A Fox Sports producer ran up to them, and told them they were set up just twenty feet away. The audio engineer put a pair of headphones on his ears. T motioned for Jack to stand off to the right of reporter. T yawned again.

"Four seconds…" whispered the producer, as he listened to the television director in his headset.

On cue the reporter said, "Thanks Bob. We're behind the stage with the dynamic TNT. He has been in the top five more than anyone else this year, but on his last outing, he wrecked hard into the wall. T, have you healed up, and ready to go tonight?"

T grinned as if he had been waiting to do this all day, "Oh yeah, it wasn't as bad as it looked, and besides, they say I have a hard head, so it comes in handy in wreck like that."

"How about tonight—are you going to win this thing?"

"Yep, maybe, I don't know. It's for a million bucks and no points so there will be drivers who normally are careful that will get a little crazy tonight."

"I heard you took a vacation after the last race."

That question caught T off guard a little, but he replied, "You know we were way out on the west coast, and I realized I had flown over America, but never actually drove across it, so I drove myself home to Concord. It was a wonderful experience, and the fellow that dug out that Grand Canyon thing is some kind of a worker. It was huge!"

Everyone around laughed as the reporter finished, "Good luck tonight."

"Thank you, Ted." T smiled into the camera.

"We'll go back up to the booth to Bob…"

T shook the reporter's hand, and gave the cameraman a high five. Driver introductions were underway, so T gave Jack a wink, "I'll see you when we are done."

Jack smiled, and then rode with Janet back to the T's pit area. Janet introduced him to all the pit crewmembers, some of which he met in Kansas. He climbed up on the box and sat with a few folks next to the Charley the crew chief.

Janet put a pair of headsets on his ears and explained he could hear the team members talk during the race. After the Star-Spangled Banner, a few jets roared over, and then the car engines fired up. They had a short heat race to put the final drivers in the big million-dollar sprint race. Thirty minutes later, the final event started. Jack recalled how loud T's car was in Kansas, but with all the cars fired up the noise shocked him. He was thankful for the earphones.

T started off in tenth place, and somehow found his car boxed in and drifted back to twentieth. After forty-one laps, there was a wreck in front of Thad's car, but somehow he managed to drive through it. Jack let out a huge sigh of relief, as did Charley the crew chief. Charley said, "That's the way to do it. Okay bring it in for four tires and gas. You've got to move your butt up quickly after the restart."

Jack heard T over the radio, "Charley make it a little tight in the right rear so I can get some grip, and I'll fly by in the second groove." T pulled off the track, and began slowing down for the pit lane, watching his tachometer carefully to make sure he did not speed and receive a penalty.

"All right, come on now. We're in the fifth stall. Drive to the sign," and then to the crew, "Okay boys, I want your best stop of the month right now!"

T screeched to a halt, and twelve point six seconds later, the tire jack dropped and out he went. Jack could not believe how fast the men were. On the restart, T got a bit of a jump and swung around the driver ahead of him going into the first turn. The crowd stood.

"Oh shit!" said Charley in the radio.

"Trust me Charley!" yelled T.

T pulled around him, and kept on going moving up to fifth place before finally pulling in line.

"Way go, T!" laughed Charley. "You just took ten years off my life. I'll need a new heart after this race."

T shot back, "Shoot, I bet you need new underwear!"

The whole crew busted out laughing, as T pulled hard inside, cut off the driver in fourth, and sailed up to third before pulling back in. "How many more laps?"

"Eighteen. You have time. Keep those tires in good shape. You can do it."

Drew wheeled over to T's pit box, and road the lift the men built for his wheelchair. After the platform stopped, he plugged his headset into a patch panel in front of him. He gave Jack a confident shaking of his fist in the air, and began yelling for Thad to move up. They all stood on their feet, as the lead cars came out of the fourth turn, and that's when T cut to the inside, just as the second car dropped to block him, T swung up high and passed him on the straight away, pulling in behind the leader. The crowd stood and cheered, and Drew gave Jack a high five.

Ten minutes went by with T trying to go outside or inside, but the lead car always blocked him. "How many laps?" he asked.

Charley replied, "Just four more—time to go, boy!"

"Charley, I'm going to drop back a little, and then pour it on in the turn up high before cutting down low. If he goes high to block, I'll be able to beat him when I cut. If he doesn't go up, I'm going to sail by him."

"Do you have enough throttle left to do that? Do have grip in the tires?" asked Charley.

"Yes, I think so, and I'd better, because I am going to do it anyhow."

Charley looked down the bench at Drew, as if asking for advice. Drew smiled, and said, "That's what I pay you the big bucks for. I don't know, but if it were me, I'd let the kid go for it," he said with a grin.

Charley laughed, "Okay, Mister TNT, time to light that fuse!"

"Yahoo!" screamed the team, as he suddenly swung very high.

The television announcer thought he blew a tire, and now heading for the wall. The first place car's spotter told his driver T's was out of it—a blown tire. They started the turn, but the driver did not believe him, and paused a second too long to think about it. T gained on him with his gas pedal down and ready for a decision.

The first place driver asked his spotter where T was. He replied telling him T was catching him. The crowd was back on their feet. Everyone yelling—even Jack!

Then the driver made a decision—he rolled high to block T, but losing some momentum, and before he could stop his maneuver T yanked the wheel to the inside and blew past him. The crew leaped to their feet, and turned to watch as T took the white flag. They all clasped their hands as if praying the car would hold together just one more lap. They knew a flat tire would slow him just enough to get beat.

T remained calm, recalling how he once lost a race in the last fifty feet to go. He knew the odds were still against him, as he left the second turn and roared down the back straight away. His crew fell silent as they watched the big television monitors. As he excited the fourth turn, they began to jump up and down in anticipation.

Charley called out to him on the radio, "Five, four, three, two, and one! You did it!" he yelled as T sailed across the finish line.

TNT let off the gas pedal and began pulling his gloves off. As he slowed down and let the cars passed him. Many waved to him. He undid his window netting, and stuck his hand out to wave to the crowd. He stopped on the backstretch, did a U-turn, and began driving the wrong way around the track, but it allowed the fans to see his smiling face.

When he reached the finish line, he did a long burnout, sending a plume of smoke into the air. Fireworks went off in the infield.

"Come on," said Charley to Jack, as he took his headphones off. "We're going to the Winners Circle." He led Jack through the pits, as they went to wait the arrival of their car and T. The officials guided Thad to a stop on the checkered black and white floor tiles. The television reporter ran up to the driver window to wait, T shut down the engine, removed his helmet, and safety gear, fingered his hair, pulled his hat down tight, pushed on his sunglasses, and on cue from the television reporter, he climbed out.

The crowd cheered as he stood on the doorsill pumping his fist in the air and shouting to his men. Fireworks streaked through the air, as confetti cannons blew bits of paper over them and fell to the ground like a heavy snowstorm. He then leaped down and Janet stood just off to the side of the reporter to cue him. The reporter began, "Thad that was an incredible pass to win the race. Tell us your strategy."

"Who has time to think of a strategy—I was just determined to win. He went high and I went low...simple." He glanced up at Janet's smiling face, "I want to thank my sponsors for their support. That's RESTAR, Cool Chips, Larry's Barbecue Sauce..."

Jack laughed, as Thad rattle off the name of every single sponsor and the reporter had to wait for him to finish before asking his next question. Soon the champagne started spraying through the air and the team drenched Thad, so he grabbed a bottle and began spraying back. Jack cleverly ran for cover behind the car. His mind became a video recorder as he took it all in, but he lifted his digital camera and took a few pictures to help refresh his memory when he wrote about today's victory.

"You stink," stated Jack, as T came into the motorcoach, closed and locked the door insuring their privacy, and came over to the workstation where Jack was busy writing.

T laughed, "Yeah, I know, but it is worth it after winning a race. Do I get a victory kiss?"

Jack smiled and looked up as T planted a big wet one on him. T said, "I am heading to the shower. The car is at inspection. They will tear it down and make sure I didn't cheat, and once we pass I will officially be the winner."

T began stripping as he walked down the hall. Once in the shower he lathered his hair and allowed the hot water to flow over his head and down his back. Suddenly, he felt a hand rubbing his back with the soap. "Want some company?" asked Jack.

"I hope you took your clothes off," laughed T, as he turned around and found his lover nude and smiling.

Jack replied, "You're beginning to smell better, but your stick shift is poking me in the balls."

T looked down and Jack was right. His erection had been instant. He began playing with Jack as they finished their shower. It had been an incredible fourteen days for them, concluding with winning the All-Star Race, the trophy, and the check for a million dollars.

The next day after winning the race left little time alone. They flew out Sunday night to New York where Thad appeared on two talk shows, did interviews for ESPN and Fox Sports, followed by more print media interviews, and finally flew home late that afternoon. They went from the private jet to T's house, threw some clothes in the Hummer, and arrived south of Boone just under two and half hours. They watched the sunset off Jack's deck as it disappeared behind a thick black cloud floating east. After eating the take-out lasagna and salad, they stripped, and went downstairs to soak in the bubbling Jacuzzi.

The rain began to fall as they were making love in Jack's bed. An hour later, they slept in each other's arms with T's face resting on Jack's chest, their legs intertwined, and their hearts almost beating as one. Thad's last thought was that winning a race had never felt as wonderful as sharing it with Jack.

FIVE

The week flew by with Drew's staff entertaining many sponsors since they were on their home turf for the second week. Lowes Motor Speedway would once again host the NARC sanctioned race, and that meant a battle with the other teams for points that determined the champion for the season. At least ten potential new sponsors were enjoying the tour of the various race shops, and on Saturday, they were escorted around the pit area before the race. Near race time, they moved to Drew's personal skybox overlooking the track. There they dined on fresh salmon, and drank cold beer and wine, while waiting for the much anticipated start of the race.

T gave Jack a kiss as he lay on the couch in the coach. "Well, I had better go pee. This is the longest race of the year—six hundred miles. I hope my bladder can hold out that long."

"I doubt you'll have time to think about it. The stadium seats, campgrounds, and pits are full, and I don't think they could let another person in, or the fire marshal would scream for a halt."

"The crowds help my adrenalin begin to boil, and it will continue to grow as the laps count up."

"Well, I want act like a wife and tell you to be safe, so I'll take a different tact, you hurry and come back in one piece, and I'll let you make love to me all night long."

T looked up into Jack's eyes. He sensed he was worried, so he smiled and planted soft kisses to his eyelids, then one to his nose, and a final one to his soft lips. "Dang, I'm getting horny already, so you'd better hope there are no delays in this race, and those pants of yours better be around your ankles when I come running in the door!"

They both laughed, and hugged tightly, before T went to make his final pee.

TNT remained in the top ten most of the race, narrowly escaped a wreck in front of him when the number seventeen car blew a right front tire and crashed into the wall. T sprinted to the grass along the front stretch, and missed the wrecked car as it slid down the track by mere inches. The crowd stood expecting another bad collision. Everyone on the pit box sighed with great relief—especially Jack. He sat down and made a note in his computer describing the event in great detail.

With a hundred and twenty laps to go, T pitted his car after the caution flag flue with a wreck behind him. All day long, the pit crew did an excellent job with tight thirteen-second pit stops. He came in the pit lane running third, but a lug nut accidentally dropped to the ground, and he roared out without it. The NARC official standing nearby immediately black-flagged him, so he had to come back in to the pits to have the final lug put on. Once accomplished, he now started in the thirty-sixth position.

"T? Charley here. I am so glad we had our bad luck now, aren't you?"

T's face wrinkled in puzzlement, but he played along, "Why would you want any bad luck, and why now?"

Charley laughed, as he turned and winked to Drew who was sitting beside Jack listening on their headsets, "If this happen on the last pit stop of the race, we would only have about fifty laps for you to overcome it. But luck was on our side, we have hundred and twenty laps for you to get to the front!"

Charley's optimism hit home with T and the rest of the crew. They began giving each other high fives, and quickly forgetting their unfortunate mistake. T smiled, "Charley, you're one smart son of a bitch, but you're right. I have to weave around thirty-five cars at a hundred and eighty miles an hour to get to the front. I also have to be sure I am not caught in any wrecks ahead of me. This is a piece of cake. Boy—are we lucky!" he added with a laugh filled with sarcasm.

"You can do it, boy. I know you can. Okay, get the grit off the tires, and get ready for the restart." Charley looked up to the roof at the top of the speedway and spoke to their spotter, "Gary, you best be on your toes. Guide T every step of the way to the front. I need your best work, and I know you can do it." He then looked at his crew, "Okay, boys—let's go win a race!"

T passed the first car coming out of the second turn, and passed two others on the backstretch, but the more cars he passed the harder it got. On lap eighty-three, the car just ahead of him became loose, spinning up the track. Gary told him to go low, and he did without hesitation. The driver regained control and caution did not go out. T kept working his way through the field, and with fifty-eight laps to go Charley saw the leader breaking from the pack for a final pit stop. The rest of the field followed him into the lanes.

Charley stood up, "Okay, men. We must give him the best pit stop of the day. I want four tires, and all the gas you can stuff in his tank. Pull off the next tear sheet off his windshield." He turned his attention to TNT, "Don't speed, but I want you to stop at the sign, take a sip of Gatorade, and be ready to go on the second drop. We're going to move you to the front so get ready!"

T screeched to a halt and the pit crew scrambled around him. Tire jack up, outside tires on, and one tank of gas in. They ran around to the other side. The tear sheet came off, T took two sips of Gatorade, the jack went up, the tires on, a second gas tank in, the jack drops, and suddenly T pops the clutch.

Gary picks him up. "You're two car lengths ahead of the leader, but don't speed on pit road. Move to the outside so the cars pitting ahead of you don't get in your way. Seventy-feet to go—keep it steady." Thad crossed the white line just ahead of the leader. "Yahoo!"

Charley screamed out as well, as he watched the slow replay of T crossing the finishing line on pit road over the television monitor, "Well done boys. Best pit time of the day. Well done." He then turned to T. "Okay, mission accomplished. Gary is going to watch the guys behind you. For the first few laps, I want you to hit your marks. We may need every second you can gain before the end of this race. I want a clean start, and remember, do not spin your wheels. You can win this race. I know you can."

They all stood for the restart, and it was a good one with T getting out two car lengths in front of forty-seven car, but two laps later, the second and the third place cars gained on him. Gary came on the radio, "Thad, they are in line twenty feet back. You have new tires, and so far today, the longer you run the better you get. Be patient, and just stay ahead of them."

T tried to stay on his marks while keeping an eye on the forty-seven car. With just twenty laps to go, the second place car went high into turn one. The crowd stood. The third place car went with him just inches off the bumper of the car ahead of him. T drifted gently upward forcing them to go a little higher than planned, and by the backstretch, they had fallen in line behind him once more. Charley let out a sigh of relief.

With ten laps to go, they began moving to the outside once more and quickly moving up to T's rear tire. Gary spoke quickly, "Don't come up T, you'll hit them and spin out. Hold your line." Charley chewed his lip while Drew lifted his hat and wiped the sweat from his brow with his forearm. Jack did not understand the tactics, but he knew anything could happen in the next few laps.

T replied, "I've got a slight vibration on the right front!"

"Damn," said Charley without keying his microphone. He dropped his head and then as he lifted it, "Son, you just keep her steady. There's nothing we can do but wait it out, and hope the tire holds. Gary, you're doing great. I want you to keep a good eye on the car right behind him."

T came back on the radio, "I see them on my right, but are they gaining on me?"

Gary spoke up, "Not yet. They would have already passed if they could. I suspect they have no throttle left."

"That's good, but they'll come down on me on turn four sending me to the grass as they cross the finish line. I'll have to do something just before they do."

"I agree," replied Charley, "but we've got eight laps to go, so let's hope and pray they begin having trouble, too."

T swallowed hard, adjusted himself in his seat, and held his line for the next few laps. He heard Gary tell him three laps to go, and the chasers remained in the same spot on his right rear corner. Over and over in his mind, TNT replayed what he knew he had to do to win the race.

"Two to go," said Charley. "Hold on son, hold on."

The crew stood just behind the wall. Drew raised his lift higher so he could see while Jack and Janet stood alongside Charley.

Gary spoke, "White flag coming. One to go, and you're doing just fine.

T whispered to himself. Third turn is the key. Get them before they crunch me.

The crowd began screaming as they all stood to watch the close finish. The television announcers could hardly talk, as their mouths were dry with anticipation and excitement.

T reached the third turn and slowly drifted just a few inches up the track as if loose. The forty-seven car reacted before his spotter or crew could say anything. He moved his steering wheel just inches upward to keep from hitting Thad, but that caused them to lose a few feet on his right rear. The driver gritted his teeth, and began turning his wheel just slightly to the inside to clip T's rear bumper while he could.

T expected the move, but they were in the worst possible spot to attempt it, as they finished turn three and prepared for turn four. He stomped the gas pedal to the floor, turned the wheel just slightly with a quick jerk. As the forty-seven car came down to hit him, the sudden movement and acceleration in the turn shocked him, and in a brief second, his bumper missed Thad's by a less than an inch. The driver did not stop his maneuver fast enough, as his rear came around the third place car crashed into his rear bumper, and together, they smashed into the wall of the fourth turn.

Gary yelled he was clear in the radio, but T had no time to reply. His right front tire blew just as he began the final straightaway to the finish line. The vibrations made his head jerk up and down. He let off the gas a bit. Fourth place was moving up after passing the wreck.

"Is he out of gas?" asked one announcer to his associates.

"I think he has blown a tire," replied another.

T gave the throttle just enough gas to keep him ahead, but he could see the fourth car moving up quickly. "Come on, come on," he said to the car, "just forty feet to go. " You can do it!" he told the car.

The vibration in the steering wheel forced him to grip it tighter than in any race in his life. He knew he would not be able to make the next turn, but he pushed that thought from his mind. The fourth car moved to his right side, but Thad could not turn the wheel to block him. The car reached his right rear tire just as he flew across the finish line. The team leaped on top of the wall, Drew and Jack screamed with excitement, but Charley clicked his radio. "Ease off the throttle, forget the brakes, and try to gear it down when you can. Move up the track a little and use the wall to stay in control."

T heard him, but the tire suddenly exploded sending tire tread and sheet metal flying into the air. The slowing cars passed him to the inside. T heard and felt the rim hit the pavement. Sparks flew in the air as he carefully moved into the wall. He felt the scraping of the metal on the wall and saw more sheet metal ripped from his car. The car came to a stop at the end of the fourth turn. He cut the engine switch off after releasing his death grip on the steering wheel.

"Thad? Thad? Are you okay?" asked Gary over the radio. T did not reply.

Charley sighed as he saw the emergency trucks heading towards Thad, "T? T? Come back!"

T sighed heavily, "I'm okay, but I'm just so weak I don't think I can get out of the car. Did we win?"

"Hell yeah!" replied an exuberant Charley. "We sure did! Don't worry—the crews will get you out of the car. Do you need a change of underwear?" All the pit crew and everyone wearing a headset turned towards him and laughed.

T got a burst of energy from Charley's clever comment, "I might. I just might. What a race. Get me out of this thing. I feel like I'm wearing it."

T got his gloves off, undid his safety harness, got his helmet off, and an emergency crewmember undid the window straps, and pulled him from the car. He walked gingerly to the waiting ambulance, while the wrecker hauled his car to the winner's circle. Ten minutes later, they released him from the infield care center, and he arrived in victory lane in a golf cart.

As the champagne began to spray, he did his bit for the waiting live television crew, ran to his crew and started high fiving everyone before making his way to the stage to receive his second trophy at Lowes Motor Speedway in a week's time. He spent the next two hours doing interviews before finally returning to his motorcoach.

Jack surprised him by having a late dinner hot and ready for him. He stripped out of his fire suit, and sat at the table in his boxers to feed his starving body. Once done, he hit the shower, dressed, and they boarded the helicopter for the short flight to the shop. By two o'clock in the morning, they were sexually and physically spent, and fast asleep in each other's arms in Thad's house.

The week flew by quickly, with Jack rapidly finishing a speech for a client, as well as a speech for Thad to deliver at the RESTAR annual dinner in Dover for their employees. The dinner was set for Friday night after qualifying on Friday afternoon for Sunday's race. They flew up that morning alone. T practiced his speech over and over. It was to be the beginning of a new era for Thad performing a motivation speech for his sponsors.

After much discussion, T realized that he had to deliver about fifty speeches a year during the thirty-six-race season. He told Jack how embarrassed he felt, as he did not know what to say to inspire folks who were a whole lot smarter and older than he. Jack made the speech patriotic, so it could be used on numerous occasions, and then emphasized teamwork as his key to success.

He also wrote various short speeches to be inserted on any occasion plugging T's favorite charities. This gave Thad a sense of pride, as he no longer felt he was just doing an obligatory appearance at the request of his big money sponsor, but actually trying to help make the world a little brighter for all.

He and Jack dressed in tuxedos purchased earlier in the week from an expensive men's store in Charlotte. Everything but their underwear was brand new. Jack set the timer on his camera, and set it on the shelf while he and T posed like two models on the front cover of a GQ magazine. They left the coach and drove the Hummer to the Dover Convention Center, parked at a side entrance, and slipped into the big meeting hall without a single photographer or autograph fan spotting them. They were escorted onto a platform where all the key corporate heads were seated. Jack found his seat at the end while the president of RESTAR introduced TNT to everyone on the platform. As soon as he returned to his seat next to Jack, the waiters began serving. At previous banquets, T rarely touched his food, as he was too nervous about what he was going to say at the end of the meal, but not this time. Jack's speech gave him great confidence, so he and Jack chatted with each other as if eating in a restaurant instead of in front of thirty-five hundred guests.

Relaxed and ready, after a two minute film on his short but highly successful racing career, and ending with last week's spectacular finish, the house lights went up and everyone stood, applauded, and cheered as T shook the president's hand. Jack sat there with great pride, as Thad delivered the twenty-minute speech with absolute perfection. Upon completion, the crowd gave him a second standing ovation. Drew turned his motorized wheelchair, and eased over to Jack while the applause continued for T.

"Son, that is the best speech any of my drivers has ever delivered. You wrote it, didn't you?" Drew shook his hand warmly, and smiled. "Since you have arrived, we have won two races, and you've turned TNT into a happy camper, and taught him how to inspire the sponsors. Thank you, thank you, and thank you."

Jack smiled. "Thank you, but a speech is just words on a paper. It takes a big heart to perform it like that. Thad worked very hard on it."

As T left the podium, he took Drew's hand, shook it firmly, and smiled.

"That was excellent—beyond excellent. It was fantastic! Thank you so much."

"It was my pleasure. We had a great time. I'll see you tomorrow," replied T, as he and Jack moved off the platform so he could shake hands with the company's employees. It took an hour, but everyone was able to meet him before they left.

58

Afterwards, they escaped out the side door and into the Hummer. "That was so much fun. I felt so proud to deliver a speech they actually liked. Jack it was so special."

"You did it with great flare—and remember, tonight you touched lives."

"Let's go get ice cream," said T.

"I'm game—where do we go?"

"Watch for a place, and we'll just pop in."

It took about a mile of watching along a strip of a road filled with all the various food chains.

"There's a Cold Stone Creamery!" exclaimed Jack.

T turned quickly, and they parked in a space just across from the entrance. T backed in a parking spot. They ran across the street and into the shop. There were only about ten people sitting at tables eating their ice cream. They each ordered banana splits with their favorite scoops of ice cream and sat down in a corner to eat. T had pulled a hat down tight over his eyes and to their astonishment, they managed to eat about two thirds of their dish before a little boy of about eight years old approached them. The child was very nervous, but bravely he spoke to T, "Sir, may I have your autograph?"

"Of course you can," said T, as he popped out a Sharpie and signed a napkin. Before he could finish some of the patrons lined up, and soon they all had signed napkins.

Jack and Thad took a last bite from their plastic bowl, quickly exited the shop, ran across the street, and crawled into the Hummer. They laughed heartily as they drove back to the track and made their way to the coach. Soon they were naked in bed and talking about the dinner, and together, they made a pact to begin making plans for other feel good appearances.

The next day Jack began researching the web as he scouted the area around Dover. He made a few calls, printed out directions, and soon they were off in the Hummer again. They picked four places to visit completely unannounced. They started with Dover Air Force Base hospital. T shook hands with every soldier and staff member there. Next, they went off the base to a children's hospital, followed by a children's home, and then ended the day at a Ronald McDonald House for sick children. Not one single media person had a hint of their journey, and it did not make the newspaper until after the race was over. T felt it was the most satisfying appearance trek he had made.

Jack suggested they create something they can give everyone that had a positive thought on it. They got with Janet when they arrived on Monday, and bounced ideas off her. She was horrified T had done the appearances on his own, but she had to admire him as well.

Jack woke before T and rolled gently over to lay his head on the pillow facing T. He had never been in love like he was with Thad. There had been times when he thought he was in love, and he could recall his best friend telling him what it was like, but in his heart he knew for the very first time he was absolutely in love with T. He studied his beautiful face, and absolutely loved his soft eyelashes. When T opened his eyes, he felt Jack staring at him. "Did you sleep well?" he asked as he planted a kiss on his lips.

"Yes, I did. I've just been awake a few minutes. You were sleeping so sweetly I just couldn't wake you. Come here," said Jack as he pulled T into his arms.

"Are you horny again?'

"Aren't you?" shot back Jack.

"Yes, I am," he kissed Jack deeply. "I am going to win the race today."

"How do you know?"

"I don't know—I just feel it."

"Well, let's eat a good breakfast, as you have a bunch of miles to drive today."

"Okay, let's get in the shower. We're going to save sex tonight after I win," replied T sounding completely confident.

"Well, I'll wait to see if you win, but if you don't I'm going to hook up with that hot rookie in the sixty-three car," teased Jack.

"You wouldn't?"

"You'd better win, huh?" laughed Jack.

Nothing fancy and exciting happen in the Dover race. The pit crew was on top of it with every stop right on target and a few tenths faster. Gary helped him through several wrecks with T keeping the car on the track and out of trouble. He took the lead with forty laps to go, and thankfully, there were no cautions for the rest of the race. He won by six car lengths. The team was overjoyed for the third time in a row. Drew felt elated as he gave Jack, Janet, and Charley big high fives, before descending to the track in his wheelchair.

TNT did numerous donuts on the track sending smoking tire plumes high into the air in celebration. He was now sixth in points and just a hundred and sixty out of first place. After he arrived in victory lane, and did the obligated interview for the television network, he turned around to see his crew and immediately received a face full of champagne spray. He laughed and charged into his crew bear hugging all of them. He leaned down and gave Drew a big wet hug as well.

"Kid, you're amazing me, and I'm not easily amazed. If you keep this up at Pocono and Michigan, we could be in first place by the time we get to Daytona. You did an excellent job out there!"

T received praised from his fans even when he was losing, but when Drew got excited and praised him, he knew he had done the best he could do.

He kept checking his watch during the press conference, and he heard Janet say they would fly out thirty minutes after the end of inspection. It was two hours after the race by the time he got back to the coach. He found Jack asleep on the couch. He leaned down and kissed him.

When his eyes opened, T pulled back a few inches and smiled, "Now we have about forty minutes until the inspection is done, and then we fly out of here thirty minutes after that. I'm jumping in the shower to get the race gunk off me. When I get out you'd better be on the bed naked, hot, and ready for the love machine!"

T spun around on his heels, and took a funny step or two towards the back of the coach. Jack laughed as he got up and brushed his teeth. He dimmed the lights in the rear, put on some music, stripped out of his clothes, and began playing with himself.

T came into the bedroom wearing only a towel. He closed the door, dropped the towel, and dove on top of Jack. "See I told you I was going to win."

"You sure did. I don't know how you knew but you did. I can't tell you how proud I was. My boyfriend has won three in a row."

"Well, don't expect me to keep it up, as winning any in a row is difficult, but four in a row would be impossible."

"Don't say impossible as long as it is possible. You have just as good a chance as anybody else, so the odds are only forty-three to one."

"Only? Yeah, right."

Jack held his face in his hands and looked him straight in the eye, "Would you shut up and hump me. I've been waiting for you all night long!"

T busted out laughing, but soon shut up as he began feeling both of their heartbeats during their lovemaking. They slept on the plane all the way back to Charlotte. Everyone assumed T was exhausted from the race, but Thad and Jack knew they were exhausted from their lovemaking and deliriously happy.

They spent Monday in Asheville with Jack guiding T through a tour of Biltmore Estate. Thad kept his sunglasses and hat on, and somehow they managed to do the whole day without being recognized. They especially liked the behind-the-scenes tour. Thad marveled at all George Vanderbilt built, but he loved the indoor swimming pool and bowling alley constructed over a hundred years ago.

Thad whispered to Jack, "I think after I win my next championship, I'm going to buy this place. We could start the year by making love in a different room every night."

"At that rate, it would take several years to finish the job," whispered Jack as they walked through the servant quarters and into what appeared to be a room housing huge boilers.

"This looks like the Titanic," said T.

"It gets cold in the mountains during the winter. It took a lot of steam to heat this huge place."

"Oh second thought, I guess I'll keep my own house, but I do wish we had gardens like they have here."

"We can build gardens on your land. You have plenty of room."

"Yeah, I guess we could. Are we about done here?" asked T.

Jack pouted, "You're bored, aren't you?"

"No, I'm not, but I am horny. It's been almost six hours since…"

"Don't even say it. I know," cut in Jack before grinning. "Come on, I know a short cut out of here, and it's my turn to be the top!"

They had been looking forward to a few days off, but after winning three straight races, TNT was the new 'it' guy. He and Jack flew to New York for appearances on the morning talk shows, and then flew all the way to the west coast to be on Jay Leno late that afternoon. They got home late Wednesday night, feeling tired and sick of airplanes.

Early the next morning, they drove up to Lake Lure in western North Carolina and deliberately avoided the elevator ride to the top of Chimney Rock, preferring to hike. By the time they reached the summit, they were both sweating in the early summer heat, but they were very happy to be away from it all. They were able to enjoy the view all by themselves for almost thirty minutes before a whole troop of cub scouts caught up with them. Jack explained that the ending for the "Last of the Mohicans" movie was filmed here, and down below in Lake Lure was the site for "Dirty Dancing".

"I think when I retire from racing, I'll become a movie star," began T. "Lord knows I have the looks for it!" He picked his nose up a bit like he was a glamour boy.

Jack laughed, "And the ego, too. I do believe you can act. Most gay people who are in the closet become the best actors of all time. They pretend to be straight all the time, faking it about women, and lying to everyone just so they can keep the big secret."

"Yeah, I know. Kind of depressing, don't you think?"

"Last year this time—were you dating anyone?" asked Jack.

"Guys, no—you're my first."

Jack smiled, "No, I mean did you date women—to keep up appearances so to speak?"

"Well, I did take dates to the awards stuff, or other special events. I hung out with Mary Jane Willis for a while. She is the daughter of Mike Willis the racecar driver and almost always at the track. She eventually gave up on me, and I hear she is getting married soon."

"What about the girls in some of your commercials?"

"They are all models, and could not care less about an athlete."

"Do you think you need to hang out with a girl at the track to keep up the game?" asked Jack.

"You think I should. I would have thought you would be jealous if I hung out with a woman." T was laughing.

"Well, we could sort of double date when we have a public appearance dinner to do."

"Double date—by that you mean you and a guy, and me and girl?" T kept a straight face.

Jack playfully hit him on the back of the head anyhow, "No, you knucklehead. Boy, the car fumes must be killing your brain cells. "I mean…"

"I know what you mean—two girls and two guys. Do you think we could find two lesbians so that everyone could be happy?"

They began walking back down the trail. "I don't know—I am just worried someone will find out we're in love with each other, and then all hell would break loose, and I would lose you."

"You're not going to lose me. I would not let that happen," began Thad, but then he paused, "I, too, worry about getting caught."

"It's going to happen. At some point, we'll make a mistake, or someone will put all the dots together, and then the headlines will read, "**Top Racer Is A Freaking Faggot!**"

Thad laughed, "You are crazy. You do know that, don't you?"

"Yeah, I know. I am crazy in love with you, and I don't want anything to spoil it. I think we should make a few plans. First, we need a plan to defuse the folks that would talk about you being gay just because you're so darn cute and single. Then we need a phase two of that plan for all the media to absorb. We can't hire a girl to be your girlfriend, but I think we should have dates for big dinners, etc. It should always be different girls so no one can really learn much about us and thus, they can't be much of a witness for an article latter on."

"I guess we could do that," mumbled Thad.

"I also think we need a plan in case the rumor mill starts. At some point, someone is going to start talking dirty about you."

"Why should they do that?"

"Because you are a star, you're a success, you're winning, and they can't stand that. They'll want to shake your confidence, and they'll do anything to beat you."

"How does this plan work?"

"I think we should allow one interview at your home. You will talk about how you built this place for a family, and you're hoping to one day get married and settle down here, and so on."

Thad busted out laughing, "You are so funny." He paused as they walked downward along the trail to the bottom of Chimney Rock. "You write it out, and tell me what to do."

Jack asked, "If someone ask if you are gay, what the hell are you going to say?"

"My mouth will say no, but my heart will say yes."

"I hope they can't hear your heart," replied Jack with a worried look.

"Why are you so concerned about this right now?"

Jack sat down on a bench, and looked left and right to be sure they were alone. "Did I tell you I worked at a summer camp during college?"

"Yeah, you mentioned it. I thought it sounded like fun. Does this camp still exist?"

"Yes, of course. It is about fifty miles from my house. During my third year, I fell for the ski instructor. He was cut like a gymnast with incredible green eyes. He had a deep tan with the whitest teeth I have ever seen. I went to sleep thinking about his body every night. We became good friends, and even though he had a girlfriend back home, by midsummer, rumors started that we were both gay. I knew I was, but I suspected he wasn't.

"Due to the tall tales being told, everything about our friendship immediately changed. We could no longer hang out together, and we made sure we were never seen alone. We remained on the opposite of everything. You know, the other ends of the camp, the other end of the dock, the other end of the picnic line, and we never took the same day off."

"The camp director called me to his office and asked me point blank if I thought Henry was gay. I told him absolutely, not and told him about Henry's girlfriend. On the next visiting day for parents and the Sunday picnic, Henry's girlfriend came to see him. He broke several rules to emphasize they were in love. They were seen kissing at the waterfront, in the dining hall, and even in the cabin. The rumor fell apart, but whenever anyone at camp wanted to get even with me because I made them go to bed, clean their bunk, or go to the end of the chow line, the rumor would start again. That was the last summer I was invited to work at the camp. I was heartbroken as I truly loved working with the kids and the camp life."

"I'm sorry, that must have been awful. So you think I could be forced from racing if they found out about us?"

Jack nodded. "I don't want to kill your racing career. You are so good at it."

"I am good, aren't I?" teased Thad. "Look, I love racing, but I know it will not last forever. Drivers are retiring earlier than ever, but I do know that I could not live without your love. I often thought I was in love—even with girls, but it must have been puppy love. Being in love with you makes me feel so alive, so human, so confident, so happy, and I won't let anything break us apart.

"However, I agree with your plans because we need to start putting as much money away as possible, so if it happens, we're set for life. When I quit racing, we can do whatever we want and live wherever we want.

"I am hungry. Let's get some lunch," suggested Thad as he stood up.

"Let's eat at the Bear's Den Inn," said Jack as he stood and began walking to their car.

"Did you say Bear's Den Inn? Do they serve 'bear' steaks?"

Jack laughed, "No, but the view off their back porch overlooking Lake Lure is gorgeous. I love their southern fried chicken with rice and gravy, green beans, cream corn, and hot peach cobbler pie."

"Shut up already. I'm starving here. How far is it?"

Jack climbed in the Hummer. "Just five minutes away. I'll drive."

"Now you're talking. Did I tell you how much I love you today?"

"No you didn't but..." Jack turned to face Thad, and ran right into T's warm wet lips as he kissed him.

"Wow, that kiss makes me horny," said Thad.

"Let's eat first—you will need the energy if you want more loving tonight."

SIX

The Pocono race started out well with T moving to the front on just the third lap picking up the five bonus points for leading a lap. He kept that position for a hundred and twenty-two laps when suddenly TNT heard a loud ping in the engine.

"Oh no," he said over the radio.

Charley came right back, "What do you mean?"

"I think we just blew something in the engine."

"Just let off a little and let's see how it does. Maybe it was just a clip or debris from the track."

"I'm losing power."

Gary called from his spotter position, "He's got smoke coming out of the back."

"Bring it in," stated Charley, his voice betraying his disappointment. He sat down with a thud. He knew they just lost the race.

T screeched the tires, and the crew immediately popped the hood. T shut off the engine. They spotted oil coming out from a seal. They closed the lid and pushed him to the garage. Twenty minutes later, they announced they had blown a cylinder and were going home. Frustrated, T changed clothes in the hauler, and walked back to the coach, too upset to even ride in the waiting golf cart. He was stopped along the way with Fox Sports wanting a comment. Politely, he stopped and gave them the bad news. Afterwards he sprinted to the coach to avoid any other stops.

Jack had been waiting for him. "What happen?"

"A valve broke or something. The engine is done for and so am I? Grab your stuff—we're going home."

"I am sorry. At least the reporters will stop asking if you're going to four-peat."

"Yeah, I guess so."

Thad did not say anything else as they rode the golf cart in silence to the heliport for the lift to the airport, and soon boarded the jet for home. They drove to Thad's house, packed an overnight bag, and drove to Jack's house. T did not feel like hiking or sightseeing. He tried not to sulk, but he hated losing. Jack smartly waited him out. They ate a quiet dinner on the back deck of Jack's house, and watched a movie on the television. It took the Jacuzzi to bring T back to life. They soaked in the hot water for about five minutes before Thad started massaging Jack's feet. Later his hands began stroking Jack's long slender legs, and soon they were making out.

By morning, Jack could hardly walk, as he never expected T to do it so long and deep after losing a race. However, the soreness also brought a smile to his face. "What would you like to do today? Do you want to hang around here and rest, or do something?"

"I need to get my mind off losing yesterday. Let's do something. What do you suggest?"

"Let's go to the DuPont State Forest and see the waterfalls."

Thad grinned, "Isn't DuPont in Delaware?"

"They had an X-ray film plant in Cedar Mountain for many years. They bought up lots of land around there mostly to protect their water rights. The plant is now closed and the state owns the waterfalls. You're going to love them and it just a short hike to each one."

"Sounds fun, let's go," replied Thad as he pulled on a shirt.

They pulled the Hummer onto the road. "Do I turn right at the bottom of the hill?"

Jack grinned, "No, go straight through, and turn right at the second light. We have to make a stop and pick up a friend of mine."

"A friend of yours?"

"Yes, you'll like him."

T gave him a puzzled look, but followed his directions anyhow. He never heard Jack mention this friend, and was almost already jealous.

"Slow down, okay, turn in that drive on the right. They went up a long drive and stopped in front of a log cabin. A big blond Labrador lifted his head from his morning nap on the front porch. The door opened and a lady came out of the door. She petted the dog, as she came down the steps to meet her guests.

Jack pulled open the door and stepped out of the Hummer.

"My lord, it is Jack! What are you doing in that car? It is so beautiful."

The dog's ears perked up, and when he recognized Jack he came running down the steps, reared up on his hind legs, planting his big front paws on Jack's shoulders, and began rapidly licking his face.

Thad climbed out the side of the car and started laughing. "I take it your dog isn't choosy about what he eats," he teased.

"Down boy," commanded Jack, and the dog quickly got down, but his tail continued wagging faster than a windshield wiper in a rainstorm. Jack knelt down and gave him a hug, and began rubbing his ears. He then stood and gave Jesse a hug.

"Hey, Jesse, how have you been?" He gave her a little kiss on the cheek.

"I have been fine. Bailey and I are just hanging out today. I'm working on some pottery out back. Who is your friend?"

"This is Thad. Thad this is Jesse, my favorite lesbian friend."

"Your only lesbian friend," she corrected. She turned to Thad, "Welcome. Would you guys like some ice tea or something?"

"Actually, I was wondering if we could borrow Bailey for the day." Jack laughed. "We're going to see the waterfalls in DuPont State Park, and I thought old Bailey might like to go."

Jesse laughed, "You know full well he would want to go. Of course, you can. He needs the exercise."

Jack grinned, "Thad, this is Bailey—the best dog in the world. Bailey, give old Thad a shake."

The dog lifted his right paw and waited for T to lean down and shake his paw. As Thad bent down to reach for the paw, Bailey suddenly gave him a big old lick right up the side of his face.

"I think he likes you," laughed Jesse.

Thad gave him a big hug and began petting him. "He is such a beautiful dog."

"Okay, you guys get going, and I'll see you later this afternoon," stated Jesse.

Jack walked to the Hummer and opened the back door, "Bailey, do you want to go for a ride?"

The dog barked with a loud deep voice, sped up his wagging tail, and leaped into the back seat with just four steps.

"I guess that was a yes," laughed Thad.

"Let's go," replied Jack as he gave Jesse another hug. She grabbed his leash off the porch chair and handed it to him.

"See you later. Have a grand day," she called as she waved goodbye.

Bailey gave the boys wet kisses on their necks as he leaned over the console to see where they were going. His tail slapped the back seat continuously, and T swore the dog was smiling at him. They took the ramp to Interstate Twenty-Six east, then took state highway one ninety-one to Brevard, from there they went south on highway two seventy-six. Just before they reached Cedar Mountain, they made a left following the signs to the entrance to the DuPont State Park. It was a rugged entrance ending in a big gravel parking lot.

"Park here," grinned Jack. As soon as T stopped, he stepped out and opened the door for Bailey. The big Labrador leaped out, and headed for the nearest tree for a much needed pee. Jack and Thad laughed as they started down the trail for the first waterfall. Bailey would run out ahead of them for a while, and then come galloping back as if to tell them something like a frontier scout ahead of a wagon train.

Jack noted how happy Thad was. He threw a stick for the big dog to retrieve it. Bailey would snatch it up, chew it a little, and rapidly run back to the boys for another throw. Bailey dropped the stick at Thad's feet, and barked to get his attention. T would give him a big pat, and then sling the stick farther down the trail. They repeated the stick and throw game over and over until Thad grew tired, but Bailey wasn't even breathing hard.

68

They reached High Falls and observed the waterfall from the covered bridge over the river. Then they hiked down the trail to the bottom. Bailey knew the route and beat them to the bottom. They walked off the trail on to a big rock at the bottom so they could look up as thousands of gallons of water cascaded over the cliff, and crashed onto the big rocks along the way down. Bailey found a big pool of water and without hesitation leaped into the cold water.

"I think that dog loves water," laughed T.

"You're right about that. He never gets tired of visiting here."

"I wish I had a dog like him," said T.

"Me, too, but with my heavy travel schedule, well, it is pretty hard to have a dog. Jesse always lets me borrow him when I need a pal to hang out with." Jack whistled for the dog. Bailey leaped out of the pool and came running. When he got near, he stopped and started shaking rapidly, sending cold-water drops flying in their direction.

"Dow, that's cold!" T took off running, but old Bailey just dashed after him.

They hiked down the river before heading up a hill. T could hear the roar of another waterfall. "It sounds gigantic."

"It's actually three waterfalls in a row called Triple Falls. We'll hike out near the middle one. You're going to love this."

Bailey got ahead of them, but then turned around to be sure they were still coming. Once satisfied, he leaped down the bank to the big rocks below. T and Jack carefully climbed down the wet rock steps, trying their best not to slip and bust their butt.

"Oh my gosh!" exclaimed T as they came out of the canopy trees covering the edge of the river and stepped on to a huge rock about thirty by fifty feet. Bailey was already playing in a safe pool away from the fast flowing stream. T looked upstream and saw the first waterfall cascading down to the second falls, which then passed in front of him and down to the final waterfall to their left. "The falls are huge!"

The roar of the water made them talk loud to each other like at the racetrack, but after a while, they took off their shirts, and lay down on the warm rocks.

"I thought you might like it—everyone one does."

T smiled, "It was the perfect place to come to. It makes all your problems seem pretty small. You're clever."

"Yes, I am, and I'm good-looking, too," shot back Jack.

T playfully patted his arm. "I can feel the sun rays on my skin and it feels great."

Suddenly, Bailey came running up the rocks towards them, and dripping pints of water with every step from his thick fluffy fur. He stopped between them and did his best shake. He delighted, as they leaped to their feet to try to escape, but he chased them in circles.

After sunning on the rocks for a while, they slowly hiked back to the car with Bailey still running in front of them never tiring of chasing a thrown stick.

Thad asked, "Where to?"

Drive the Hummer over the covered bridge. We're going to Bridal Veil Falls. They followed the road for about three miles and parked in a small parking lot. Bailey leaped out and began jogging down the trail. Thad and Jack did their best to keep up with him. Soon they were standing at the bottom of a long waterfall. It was at least a hundred and twenty yards long and about forty yards wide.

"It looks like you could slide down it," said Thad.

Jack pointed at the giant boulders at the bottom. "Only once—your body would break into a thousand pieces when it hit those big rocks at the bottom, but if want to see a waterslide, well, me and old Bailey can take you to a famous one."

They loaded up again and drove back through Brevard before turning north into Pisgah National Forest. They only had to go a few miles until they spotted Looking Glass Falls over to the right, but they only slowed down long enough for Thad to see it, and then moved north a few more miles until they turned into the parking lot for Sliding Rock. They parked their car.

"Take everything out of your pockets, take your shirt and watch off, and follow me," ordered Jack. Thad noted the silly grin on his boyfriend's face. It worried him.

Bailey wagged his tail frantically, indicating to Thad that the dog had been here before. T pulled his hat down tight just touching the top of his sunglasses. The parking lot was nearly full with several busloads of campers. T noted kids coming and going and all of them were shivering.

Jack led them around a walkway until they could see over the fence. Immediately, T caught on as he saw kid after kid sliding down the smooth waterfall, and crashing into a pool of water at the bottom. They all screamed and T busted out laughing at their expressions. Soon he overhead some wet campers talking about how cold the water is.

"Why is it cold? It is almost ninety degrees today?" asked Thad.

Jack grinned, "The water above the falls comes from deep within the mountain and hasn't seen much sunlight. They tell me the water stays about fifty-five degrees all year. Come on let's take a ride."

"Hold on! Did you say fifty-five degrees? That's cold," complained T.

"No it's not," laughed Jack. "That's freezing! Come on chicken. Bailey and I are going."

"Bailey can go down it?"

"Yep, and the kids are going to love him."

Reluctantly, T followed Jack and Bailey as they made their way to top of the falls. There was a park ranger at top that seemed to know Jack and Bailey. Jack shook hands with him, and the ranger leaned down to pet the dog. T caught up with them.

"Just follow me out and take small steps so you don't slip. When I sit down in the water, you sit down, too and push off. Don't worry about Bailey—he knows what to do."

Nervously, T followed them into the river. He immediately felt how cold it was as the chill bumps flew up his ankles. "Gees!" he exclaimed.

Jack laughed, "Come on you 'wussy'!"

Jack moved to the middle and waited for Thad to join him. Bailey barked off to his left as if saying 'hurry up fellows'.

"On three we'll sit, push, and go! One, two, three!" screamed Jack.

He sat down and immediately pushed off. T took a deep breath and pushed off. He screamed as the chill of the water sent little bumps up his back. Jack crashed into the pool of water, and immediately stood up and laughed, as he saw T crash into the water beside him. After T stood up Jack called to Bailey.

Bailey paced back and forth a time or two looking for the right spot, and then suddenly he sat down and began sliding down the waterfall. All the kids screamed and pointed at him while cameras started clicking everywhere.

"Look out!" exclaimed Jack as Bailey came sailing down towards them and crashed into the pool, sending the water flying into their faces.

Bailey went under the water and came up barking gleefully. The audience clapped as Thad, Jack, and Bailey rushed out of the water, ran up the path, sat down in the water, and did it all over again. Everyone was so busy watching the dog sail down the waterslide that no one noticed Thad or Jack.

They managed to make it down eight times until they were so cold their teeth were chattering. Quickly, they ran to the Hummer to dry off with their shirts and stand in the sun to warm up. They encouraged Bailey to shake many times to get as much water off of him as possible, but there was little use, as his fur seemed to hold the water like a sponge.

They made their way back down the mountain and feeling hungry, they stopped at a McDonalds drive-thru. Thad and Jack ordered two cheeseburgers a piece, cokes, and fries, and then Jack ordered four cheeseburgers for Bailey.

"Watch this," said Jack. Quickly he unwrapped a cheeseburger. "Bailey, catch!" He tossed the sandwich over his shoulder and then turned quickly to watch the big dog catch it in the air, chomp about twice on it, and swallowed.

"Holy cow! He sucked it out of the air like a giant vacuum," said Thad.

"Here, you try it." Jack handed him a burger, and T repeated the procedure, and then yelled catch. Pretty soon, Bailey had caught all four burgers and even a few fries.

Jack laughed, "You'd better eat your burgers quickly, or Bailey might steal one."

T stuffed the burger in this mouth and chewed quickly. Bailey kept looking back and forth at the two boys in the front seat waiting for another fry. On the drive back T just could not stop talking about what a great time he had that day. Jack just let him go on and on, knowing he was successful at getting T over the pain of the lost of the race. He had gone down sliding rock hundreds of times with campers from all over the world, but never felt as happy as sharing it with his boyfriend, and his favorite dog.

T met with Janet in the publicity department on Wednesday morning before the Michigan race. Jack came along with him.

T came into her office grinning. "Hey Janet, how are you?"

She came around from her desk, "Hey T. Hey Jack. How are you?" She gave each of the boys a hug.

"I'm good and ready to get back to racing. I've got some points to make up."

"That's the spirit. Listen, I've got about five thousand die cast cars for you to sign, and some autograph items, but before we do that, I have some requests for personal appearances I want you to look at. I put them in the three piles based on what I thought we should do, but the final decision is yours. All of them are for July and August."

"Okay, let's take a look at group number one."

T and Jack looked at the requests from all kinds of groups: colleges, service groups, and military leaders, as well as various entertainment directors for television and movies, and corporate leaders. They accepted several military requests, turned down all the entertainment requests trying to avoid unnecessary publicity, and agreed to do a corporate convention for General Motors since T drove a Chevrolet.

They went through the second group agreeing to speak at a major computer corporation's annual meeting for free, if they would donate a hundred thousand dollars of equipment to schools. Janet said she felt she sure could negotiate the deal successfully.

The last group was everyone Janet did not feel would help his career. In the past, Thad usually followed the course of her decisions, but not today. He showed each one to Jack and they chose four more. All four were children organizations. He would speak at Boys Town in Nebraska, the Texas Sheriffs Boys and Girls Ranches, and visit the Children Cancer Hospital in Saint Louis.

Janet smiled at him. "Good choices. I'm beginning to see a difference in you, Thad. I like the change."

"Janet, don't make a big deal about any of these choices. I'm doing them because I want to do them, not because they make me look good. I'd like to keep these visits private and without the media unless I need to help them raise funds."

"Got it, no problem, I will work out the details, book the calendar, and get you a copy in a few days. Are you ready to do the signings?"

"No, but let's get it over with."

She led them down the hall to a room with rows of long tables. Every square inch of those tables was covered in die cast cars, pictures of Thad, TNT hats, and more. His job was to sign them all as fast as he wanted to.

"How can I help?" asked a bewildered Jack.

"You could learn how to write my name as bad as I do," he teased, "but I guess that would be cheating. Better get some ice packs for my hand."

Janet handed him one of a dozen Sharpie pens she held in her hand. T did this about once a month. He tried to remind himself how much each of these items meant to his fans. Jack looked around the tables at the items, but eventually retreated to the couch. It took T two hours to complete the arduous task.

Jack drove them home, picking up some take-out on the way. Jack smiled at him as they got out of the car, "Let's eat and soak in the Jacuzzi."

"Sounds like a plan. My arm feels like it is going to fall off," complained Thad.

Jack laughed at him, "I guess you won't be masturbating tonight."

"No, I think you will have to help me with that."

Once inside the house and safely out of the range of cameras, they stopped and kissed. "I liked your choices today. I'll work on good speeches for each of them. Don't we need to bring the kids something when we go there?"

"Good idea. I'll call Janet tomorrow. We'll get toy companies to donate something for every kid." He sat down at the table. "Honey, I'm thirsty. Would you get me a water bottle from the refrigerator?"

Jack laughed, "Of course I will, lover-boy!"

They both laughed at how silly they sounded.

The night before the Michigan race the skies opened up and it rained all night long. The boys ate dinner by themselves in the motorcoach, watched a movie, and did their best not to talk about the upcoming race on the next day. After the movie, they ate some ice cream, checked the weather radar on the satellite system, frowned as they could see lots of green in all directions, and when they turned off the television they realized they could hear the rain on the roof. The pounding rain made it easy for them to fall asleep before eleven.

By morning, the track officials were busy thanking their lucky stars, as the sky had turned crystal blue with no sight of rain in any direction. They quickly fired up the turbine blowing machines mounted on the back of pickup trucks, and began slowly circling the track blowing the puddles of water off the track and drying the asphalt. Hundreds of other workers pushed the puddles with big squeegees to the nearest drain. The souvenir trucks began opening up their giant side doors preparing for the crowds. Trucks of food began backing in along with serving trucks to the large hospitality tents. The tables were set and by nine, T spoke at his first breakfast group for one of his sponsors. Forty minutes later, he was visiting the second group. Jack smiled, as T gave each group roughly the same speech, and then took about ten minutes of questions. He realized Thad's fans were a loyal group, but when introduced to the masses, T always received a lot of jealous boos.

They returned to the coach, so T could change into his fire and racing suit. Jack stopped him so he could count the sponsor patches, and they both laughed when he reached thirty-nine. Janet drove them over to the Speed Channel's Live Stage. T avoided the makeup girl as she tried to take a few shiny spots off his face, and when they took a commercial break, the stage manager led T to a vacant seat, put a set of headsets on his ears, and quickly disappeared.

T began talking and laughing with the host along with guests Darrell Waltrip, Jeff Hammond, and Larry McReynolds. They asked him several questions about last week's race before moving on to what he thought he would be able to do today. After the second commercial break, T was excused, and Janet drove them over to the media center where T joined several other drivers. Before long, it was time for the drivers meeting. NARC conducted a short meeting before each race while carefully explaining and reminding the drivers of key rules—especially the penalty for speeding down pit road.

Janet drove them over to the stage for driver introductions. Jack shook his hand wishing him good luck, and then Janet gave him a hug and a kiss to his cheek. They left him in line as they drove back to T's pit box. Jack chatted with the crew while T was introduced to crowds, then he boarded a pickup truck and slowly road around the track waving to his fans and laughing at the competitor fans that booed him heartily. The truck dropped him off beside his car.

T came up and shook hands with all of his crew, spoke a few minutes with Charley, and then shook hands with Drew. They all stopped talking as the Star-Spangled Banner played, and the military jets did the customary fly over. T then looked up at Jack on the pit box, gave him a thumb up sign, and climbed in the car. Charley personally checked his harness and seat belts to make sure everything was set up correctly. T took a sip from the plastic tube near his mouth and grinned at the taste of cherry Gatorade his favorite. He always became anxious at this point waiting on the guest celebrity to give the command to start the engines, but once the big motor fired up, his nerves began to relax, and his excitement and anticipation began to grow.

He was starting in tenth position, a good spot for him, but he wanted to move up quickly to lessen the chance of a big wreck taking him out of the race. He prayed the engine would hold up today and make it to the end of the race. He had a good start and quickly passed two cars before they settled into a single line. It took twenty laps before he could pass the next one. By his third pit stop, he came out of the pits in the lead and immediately thanked his crew for the twelve and half second pit stop. Jack smiled as the crew gave each other high fives.

T raced as hard as he could, but thirty-laps from the end of the race Ted Smith passed him. TNT tried to block but the other car was just a bit faster. He managed to stay on his tail and ended the race in second place. Jack wondered if T would be depressed at second, as he waited patiently for him in the coach. He packed all their stuff and laid out T's street clothes on the bed.

T opened the door and bounced up the steps closing the door behind him. "It was a good race. The motor held today, and we picked up some points. Not a bad day for a homo!"

Jack laughed at him as T stripped and jumped in the shower. "I thought you drove beautifully today. Not once was there a chance you would wreck or hit the wall. I know you like to win, but Charley said you moved up three paces to twelfth in the points."

"Yep, that's true, we have to be in the top ten before the tenth race out to make the final run for the championship."

"You'll do it. I know you can."

T leaned in and kissed him, "Yep, with your help, I'm sure I will. Let's get out of here. I want to go home."

T slept on the plane, exhausted from the long day. Jack worked on a speech on his laptop and after they landed, he drove them home after stopping to pickup late burgers and milkshakes. It had been a good trip, and T's quiet sleep told him Thad would not be brooding about taking second place.

Later in the week, they left early for California so Thad could speak at the computer company as planned. He showed how gracious he was on behalf of school children everywhere at the company's generous gift of computer equipment. He allowed the company to take all the pictures they wanted as he held up the big check representing their donation. After the audience of fifty-six hundred settled in their seats, Thad moved to the platform to begin his speech as written by Jack. He appeared completely calm and confident as he placed his hands on the podium.

He turned as he thanked the president of the company, James Hedrick, for inviting him to visit with this fine group of employees, for his hospitality, and for his gift to America's children. The crowd applauded his recognition.

T began his speech with a question, "Mister Hedrick, do you care about his company?" James nodded affirmatively. "Do you care about the people who make up this company?" T gestured with his right hand from left to right indicating the entire audience. James again nodded yes and smiled, but wondered where Thad was going with these questions.

T paused and looked around the room, "How many of you love your job?" Hands went up all around the room. "How many believe you are doing some good for the world by your creations and development of new technology?" Again, hands went up.

"No one can give their job their absolute best unless they absolutely believe what they do is important. And if they are lucky, and what they do helps their fellow man, then 'pride' begins to show." He stretched out the word pride for a stronger emphasis.

"Sometimes when I lose, and I know it is my fault, I get just a little upset." He paused and smiled as the audience chuckled. "Okay, I'll be honest—I lose my temper!" They laughed. "There are many reasons for that temper, but deep down, it is because my poor performance has embarrassed my pride. I don't like that."

"I won't pretend to know how to design and build computers, or how you create the amazing software consumers like me take for granted, but as you design you must ask yourself, is my creation going to better the world or just be a fancy selling gimmick? Gimmicks are like shooting stars—at first, they shine bright and beautiful, but all too quick their light fades as they burn up and disappear.

"You must create tools that allow the future leaders of our country to grow. Your machines should create and push forward the skills of future astronauts, pilots, ship captains, generals, scientists, doctors, policemen, and builders as well as teachers, trainers, coaches, painters, musicians, and yes, even racecar drivers.

"In my sport, like many others, there is one person that receives a lot of recognition because during the race or the game it is he that must make instantaneous, and hopefully, highly skilled and talented decisions. I must quickly go high or low, lift and push forward, pull the wheel left or right, and do all the above at over a hundred and eighty miles an hour on tracks that are banked with steep turns. The banking means I make that decision with a brain slightly tilted, and the force of gravity is pulling against it.

"Behind the scenes in our organization are thirty engineers, fifteen tire specialist, fifty car builders, twelve aero dynamic wind tunnel scientists, twenty computer programmers, six accountants, eight public relation advisors, fifteen secretaries, twelve security guards, eight hauler drivers, two coach drivers, four airline pilots, six airplane mechanics, three physical trainers, two nutritionists, and one incredible owner.

"My point is this, each of you equally have an important role in building your company and by doing so, do not forget the work you do will give the children of tomorrow the tools they need to make our world a better place for all."

He paused and then pointed to a person in the fifth row, "Your work is important." He pointed to another person farther back. "Your work is important." Then to another, "Your work is important." For twenty times, he pointed and spoke, getting louder and more enthusiastic each time he repeated the phrase.

The crowd began standing and applauding, but T soon raised his hands indicating the crowd should remaining standing but fall quiet. "You see, everyone in this room is important to the future of America and the world.

"I want you to whisper with me over and over until you believe what I'm saying. Your work is important. Your work is important. Your work is important." The crowd chanted in a whisper over and over as T quickly moved to the president and brought him to the podium shaking his hand while repeating, "Your work is important."

Without prompting, the volume began to increase until the entire group was shouting those four key words as loud as they could. Thad smiled and cheered them on. He bowed and waved as he left the stage. Jack gave him a high five as he proudly said to Thad, "Your work is important, too."

SEVEN

TNT placed in the top five in the road race at the Infineon Racetrack. He, Jack and Janet flew the next day to a huge mall in Cincinnati for a personal appearance. The crowd was huge and the police set up ropes to make it easier to control the crowd. T led his group into the center of the mall, and used the microphone on the stage to talk to the crowd. The table was set on the stage so the line filters up to the table for T to sign autographs. He sat down and started signing and smiling at everyone who came up. He had agreed to this appearance in exchange for the mall donating toys to a nearby children's hospital. After the signing, they were going to deliver the toys and T would make another appearance there.

Jack and Janet took a quick guess and came up with three thousand kids and adults in line. Janet passed out eight by ten photos of TNT so the kids would have something he could autograph.

"I think I'll go get T something to drink. I'll get you something, too," said Jack. Do you want coffee or soft drink?"

"Bottle water is good for me and thanks. We'll try to get some lunch on the way to the hospital."

Jack found his way off stage and failed to notice a man in the audience watching him. The man moved around the back of the crowd so he would be closer to Jack as he walked pass. Jack went down to the food court feeling thankful none of the crowd was after his autograph. He began to value his anonymous role. He was paying for the drinks when he heard a voice behind him.

"Jack? How are you?"

Jack turned, as he picked up the cardboard tray carrying the drinks. He saw the face of a man he hoped he would never see again. Tim English was at least fifteen years older than Jack, mostly bald, big dark eyes, and reasonably good looking though a bit chunky. He and Jack met at a club in Cincinnati one night while Jack attended a writer's conference. Tim approached him in a gay bar, and they struck up a nice conversation. Jack knew Tim was hoping for more, but he lied to Tim, and told him he had a boyfriend. Tim replied that was fine, but asked him to dinner just for the fun of it. Jack had been bored in Cincinnati for three days and reluctantly said yes.

He had a great dinner and agreed to go dancing thereafter. When Tim made his moves later in the evening, Jack reminded him of his boyfriend, and told him sex was not going to happen. Suddenly, Tim turned very ugly, and made a scene in the bar. Embarrassed at the incident, Jack ran out of there, and hoped he would never see him again.

"Oh, hi, how are you?" Jack knew his face and name, but acted like he could not recall.

"Remember me? I'm Tim English. We met in Cincinnati."

"Oh yes," Jack faked, trying to make it sound like he didn't remember him.

Tim asked, "Can I buy you a drink?"

Jack held up the carton of drinks. "I'm afraid I have all I can handle, and I must get these to my friends. It was nice to see you." Jack started moving away from the counter.

Tim followed him out of the food court. "Do you still have a boyfriend?"

"Yes, I do."

"How about having dinner with me tonight?"

Jack looked at him, "I made that mistake last time," he said coldly, but then he softened a bit, "and you're a nice man I'm sure, but I'm just not interested. There I said it, and I'm sorry if I hurt your feelings, but the truth is always the best thing to say. I hope you have a great and happy life, and I must really be going."

Jack smiled slightly, and then turned and began walking back down the hall to the signing session. He glanced back twice, but thankfully, he did not see Tim following him. The event upset him, but he delivered the drinks to Janet and Thad, and smiled when T winked at him. He moved to stand by Janet to see if he could help. Immediately his eyes caught sight of Tim standing at the end of the line. His heart stopped for a second. He knew it would not take Tim long to assume Thad was his boyfriend. He had no idea of what kind of a problem that might become. His brain raced for solutions to this dilemma, and finally decided not to move close to T for the rest of the session. He actually flirted with Janet and talked with the crowd as they waited their turn.

Ninety minutes later, Jack excused himself, as Tim approached the platform. He told Janet he had to pee and would meet them at the limo out front. Janet was too busy to argue, and T did not see him step off the stage.

Jack moved down the mall and hid behind the corner of a store so he could see the stage. Tim was indeed the last autograph seeker. Janet gave him a picture. Tim thrust the picture in front of Thad and began speaking loudly.

"I'm such a big fan of TNT! He's the man! Boy, you are one hell of a driver!"

T laughed, and thought the man might either be a little drunk or a crazy. "Whom should I sign this to?" T hoped he could get rid of the man quickly.

"If you don't mind, I'd like for you to make it out to the person I love most in the whole wide world," he said loudly.

"Great, and who might that be?" asked T with his Sharpie pen ready to write it as rapidly as possible.

Tim suddenly leaned over close to T and whispered, "To Jack, my good looking lover."

T nearly wet his pants, but he wrote what the man asked for, and then added "Best wishes, TNT." He handed the man the picture, and looked up at him.

"Oh this is so nice of you," said Tim as he winked at T. "We family boys must stick together. Thank you, thank you."

"You're welcome. I'm sorry I have to go." T stood up, snapping the pen cap closed in the process. Janet gave him an odd look, but T took her arm, and led her off the stage. He did not look back, but instead looked for Jack while leaving Tim remaining where he stood watching T walk away. Jack hurried to the limo.

"What the hell was wrong with that man?" asked Janet.

"I think he was drunk. I signed the damned picture and bailed. Let's get out of here—I'm starved," he added, trying to change the subject. "Where's Jack?"

"He had pee. He said he would meet us at the limo."

"Great, let's go."

T waved at people as they recognized him, but he never slowed down until he plopped himself into the back of the waiting limo.

T asked Jack, "Are you all right?"

Jack smiled, "Sure, but my bladder was busting. My eyes were floating."

Janet laughed, "I've arranged a private room at Roosters for lunch." She leaned up and told the driver where it was, and ten minutes later they went in the back door and made their orders. Janet excused herself while waiting for their meal.

T reached under the table and held Jack's hand. "That last guy was very strange. Guess what he had me write on my picture for him?"

"I don't know, but I'm afraid to find out."

"You know him?"

Jack related how he met Tim, and how he had been trying to get rid of him.

T asked bluntly, "Did you have sex with him?"

"Hell no!" replied Jack quickly. "I thought he was a friend. I should have known he would want more than friendship. I apologized, and told him I was not interested, and wished him the best of luck. He followed me to the food court ,and spoke to me there. I again told him I was not interested. I'm so sorry he came on stage. I hope I never see him again the rest of my life and then some."

"Me neither. He had me write 'To Jack—my good looking lover."

"Shit!"

T laughed, "I don't think I have heard you curse before, other than dang-it."

"He just makes me so nervous. When are we leaving Cincinnati?"

80

Thad patted his leg and then removed his hand as Janet came back in the room. "We leave at four after the hospital visit."

Janet set down just as the food arrived. "After lunch we go to the children hospital to help deliver the toys the mall donated, and then we'll do ten minutes with the local sportscasters. Soon we'll head to the airport and home. Thad, I know your hand has to be tired. I'm sorry." She pretended to be very sincere and they all laughed at her.

Jack and Janet pulled carts full of toys as TNT made his way into the children's ward. They handed him one toy after another as he went around to all the beds, and then moved on to the next floor. He managed to take thirty seconds with every child, signed a few arm and leg casts, and t-shirts. He loved teasing and making them smile. Six floors later, they followed the hospital administrator into the hallway. A nurse suddenly made her way to T.

"Sir, we have a child in room 609. He has AIDS. Would you consider saying hi to him as well?"

T saw the sincerity and plea in her eyes, and easily answered, "Of course I will. I want to see every single child even if they have the chicken pox."

She led them down the hall while Jack noted the administrator had turned pale and seemed upset. Jack snatched up a huge bear from the toy cart, and a Game Boy, and followed Thad into room 609. They found the boy in the room all by himself.

"Why is he here all alone?" asked T.

The nurse paused while waiting until the hall door closed leaving them alone before she answered, "This is a religious hospital, and they don't like people with AIDS. He got it through a blood transfusion. His folks rarely make it up from their home state to see him. He just loves to watch the races on television."

T smiled at her, and turned to the pale little boy in the bed. Jack could not have been more proud of Thad. He walked up to the side of the bed, and asked if he could sit on the bed. "Son, my name is…"

"You're TNT!" exclaimed the boy with a grin, and then a cough. "I watch you all the time."

"I'm glad. We've brought you some toys."

Jack stepped up to the other side of the bed, and gave the boy the big bear and the Game Boy. Janet managed to pull out a photo of T and handed it to him.

"Let me sign this picture for you. What is your name?" T asked.
"Sammy Johnson."

T quickly signed the picture, and showed it to him. "How's that?"
"Would you sign my bear, too?"
"Of course I will. Do you want me to sign your nose as well?"

81

The boy laughed and said, "No, I'd go cross-eyed trying to read it!"

"How long have you been here?"

"Six months I think. You lose what day or even what month it is, but the snow was coming down when I came up here."

"Well, how are you doing?"

"All right, I don't have much of an appetite. I know I should eat better."

"Do you get any exercise?"

"No, I just lay here until time for them to take another blood sample."

T noted the IV tube in his arm and turned to the nurse. "Ma'am, what is your name?"

"Rhonda Stevens."

"Well, Rhonda, it's a pretty day outside, if I'm careful, can I take Sammy outside in the wheelchair?"

"I don't see why not," she replied. "I think he would love it."

T turned back to the little boy, "Would you like to see my limo?"

"Hell yes, whoops, sorry, I mean, yes I would!" replied the boy grinning from ear to ear.

They all laughed as the nurse brought over the wheelchair, moved the IV drip bottle to the pole on the back of the chair, and then carefully Thad lifted Sammy out of his bed. It shocked him as to how light the boy was. The nurse put a blanket over him and then tucked it in the side to prevent it from catching in the wheels.

"Are you ready?" asked Thad.

"Let's go!"

They all followed as T pushed the boy to the elevator and down to the first floor with the administrator following in a huff. He said a few words to the nurse, but Jack did not hear what she said in reply. When they reached the lobby, the electric doors opened as Sammy took in the fresh air. Instantly, his skin just glowed, and his smile grew wider. T and Jack took turns pushing him up and down the sidewalks and over to the waiting limo. They opened the door wide so he could see in.

"I tell you what Sammy—if you'll try to get some exercise every day and start eating, the next time I'm in this area I'll take you for a ride in my limo. Is that a deal?"

"Yes sir, I will. I promise I will!"

By the time they returned to his room, the nurse had managed to secure a food tray. She slid it on the table over to Sammy's bed. T and Jack took turns feeding him until he ate everything on his plate.

"Awesome, little man. That's the way to do it. I bet you can beat this AIDS stuff if you just fight it. Do you know who Magic Johnson is?"

"The basketball player?"

"That's right. He is HIV positive, too, and he is beating the disease. You have to work hard to get healthy and eat right. I'm counting on you to do it."

T, Jack, and Janet all gave Sammy a big hug and said their goodbyes. T gave the nurse a big hug, "Thank you for letting me meet Sammy. I'll be back to check on him."

"Thank you—you probably just saved his life."

As they went down the elevator, the administrator began to apologize for wasting his time with the AIDS boy. T nearly blew is top, but tried to remain calm, "Sir, may I ask you a question?"

"Sure," replied the overconfident administrator.

"Why does this hospital exist?"

The administrator appeared confused at such as easy question, "To make sick children well."

"Wow," replied T, "I was beginning to think Sammy was in the wrong hospital, but if you're suppose to make sick children well—he's in the right place after all." T turned to face him as the doors opened, but he did not step out yet. "Sir, I want you to send all of Sammy's bills to me, and I want reports on how he is doing. You'd better make him well because that is your job. He's just a kid that's sick. That's all. I'm counting on you." T shook his hand, but kept a steady gaze to the man's eyes.

"Yes sir, I will. No problem."

Janet gave him her business card for the bills, and they all bade the hospital staff good-bye.

Janet led him across the lobby to a waiting group of sportscasters and their cameramen. Immediately the bright lights were turned on. T moved behind a podium. "Good afternoon. I have a statement, and then I will take your questions."

Jack stood there amazed at how easily T took care of business.

T continued, "I just want to thank Spencer Mall for donating toys to every single child in this hospital. They really helped make my visit with the children special. I also want to thank Nurse Rhonda Stevens and the rest of her fine staff for doing so much for all these special children. I also want to say hello to a special little boy who is very sick. He has AIDS and needs our prayers and support. The administrator here has assured me he will do all he can to help make Sammy well, and I'm counting on him to do just that." T paused while he nodded at the ashen administrator.

"I have to travel quite a bit and can't get back to Cincinnati for quite a while. I'm hoping there are some good volunteers in the area that will call the hospital and offer to help with getting these children healthy and back home. Please call them."

"Okay, boys, fire away with your questions."

The reporters had been chomping at the bit for two hours, and T took plenty of time to answer all their questions, then he went around and shook all the hands including the cameramen.

"You get an A for effort today," teased Janet as they headed to the limo.

"I love the way you handled that administrator," added Jack.

As soon as the limo door closed, T let off steam. That bigoted administrator does not want little Sammy in his hospital. I will have his job if Sammy doesn't improve quickly. Janet, please ask my secretary to keep up with his progress. I will be coming back here in ninety days. Please figure out how to work a visit in my schedule. What time is it?"

"Almost six," she replied. "You were having too much fun with Sammy for me to remind you we were running behind."

"I did have a great time with Sammy, and no problem, but let's go home."

That evening Tim sat at his table eating his dinner alone watching the newscast. The story of T's visit to the mall and the hospital came on his screen, and at the end, he spotted Jack walking alongside Thad as they left the hospital.

He dropped his fork to his plate feeling confident the boys were lovers. He just knew Thad and Jack were boyfriends, and he was going to do all he could to make Jack's life just as miserable as he had made his.

He hit the couch thinking, planning, and scheming, and then grinned when he realized he might take a ton of money away from Thad, or get a big fee from one of the trash magazines for his story. He fell asleep with a sinister smile on his lips.

Drew and his wife were eating their dinner when ESPN carried T's press conference live around the world. At first he was pleased at the huge crowd at the mall, and the giving away of the toys at the hospital, but when Thad said AIDS—it sent shivers of worry throughout his body.

An hour later, RESTAR's president called him wanting to know why his top racecar driver was hanging out with a fag kid. Drew tried to calm him down, explaining the boy needed his help, but he knew the man was not happy.

He made a call to Janet and told her to ask Thad to come see him tomorrow morning. She got the call in-flight on the way home, but Thad was sound asleep. She told him when they landed, and he nodded as if all was well so she felt relieved, but she knew from the tone of Drew's voice that he was not at all happy.

The next morning he called Janet to his office, heard her side of the previous day's events, and urged her to try to prevent this kind of thing from happening again. She promised she would because he was her boss, but she felt great pride in what T had done.

T and Jack got there about nine. They came in and sat down across from his desk.

"Boys, we've got a problem with RESTAR," began Drew as he lit up a cigar. "They have a problem with their spokesman visiting a kid with AIDS."

"Is that it?" asked T. "That's a relief—I thought it was something serious." He grinned slyly at Drew. Drew gave him a gesture as if saying, come on you know what I mean.

"Drew, what could be more important for their image? NARC is all about supporting and helping the less fortunate. We're more patriotic than any other sport in the country. Anyone that thinks that kid got AIDS from a gay person is a fool. AIDS is infecting women and children, and men all around the world most of whom aren't gay.

"The nurse asked me if I would go see the kid—what did you want me to say, no, I haven't the time? How would that look for RESTAR? I can see the headlines, racecar driver hates kids."

Drew grinned a little, "You have a point, but we need to minimize problems like this, and your press conference made it a headline."

"I know, and yes, I did it on purpose. That administrator was treating the kid badly. They have a child in a room alone and isolated from all the other children. He's a little sick kid that needs friends. They might as well have put him in a cave. I had to publicly say something so that lazy religious bigoted administrator would have to take care of him.

"Have the president of RESTAR meet me at the track this week. I'll talk to him and smooth things over."

"You sure you want to do that?" asked Drew already feeling worried.

"Yep, don't worry. I can handle him."

"Okay, kid. Listen I have been meaning to tell both of you what a great job you're doing on your speeches. That computer company wrote a fantastic letter to us." He turned his wheelchair so he could face Jack. "I know you had a lot to do with this new effort. Keep it up guys. Keep it going for us. Now get out of here I have work to do. We've got races to win." Drew gave them a big wave as they left his office. Before his office door closed, he was on the phone to RESTAR.

Thad met with his crew chief as well as his team manager on what they learned this weekend and the upcoming plans for this week's race. A few hours later T and Jack left the building.

"What do you think about Drew's comments?" asked Jack as they climbed into the Hummer and pulled out of the lot.

Thad made the turn onto the highway before replying, "I am a little worried, but I would not have done a single thing any different. The kid needed help and we could do it for him. Let's go to a movie or something. I need to get this out of my mind."

"Okay, but let's stop for an early lunch—I'm starved," replied Jack.

They ate salads for lunch and managed to get to the movie just minutes after the lights went down and sat near the back. The action adventure story managed to get their minds off the RESTAR problem. They left the theater feeling great so with the sun far to the west, they stopped at the park, and began walking around the lake.

T cleared his throat before speaking, "I wish I could hold your hand."

"I wish you could, too, but I learned something today."

"Yeah, what's that?"

Jack smiled, "I learned that whatever you do right or wrong, is front page news. We're must take great care in preventing our secret from getting out. If they hated you for talking to a kid with AIDS, what would they do if they found out your best friend was gay."

T spit in the lake, "What if they found out I was gay?" He paused before saying, "They don't allow real crucifixions in America do they?"

Jack smiled, "I doubt it, but I think tar and feathers are still possible."

Thad pondered his next thought before speaking softly, "I wish the world wasn't like that. We can't help we're gay. God made us that way."

"You think so?" asked Jack.

"He made you tall, your hair brown, your eyes blue, your smile sweet, your tummy sexy, and your ability to love amazing, so if he made all those things and more for you who else would have made you gay? I admit, I don't know why he made some of the world gay, but I believe He did. He is not a God that makes mistakes, and you and I are not mistakes either."

"The world has a lot of catching up to do, and we'll have to be careful or they'll kill us."

Thad laughed, "They'll have to catch us first. Let's go home, I'm feeling horny."

"You're always feeling horny."

"Yeah, but at home I can do something about it!"

86

EIGHT

They flew out the next morning to Daytona for one of the biggest races of the year and always near the Fourth of July. After arrival, they boarded the company yacht, a large luxury boat with a staff of twelve, and immediately set sail towards the Bahamas. The boat's accommodations were absolutely first class. Brass, glass, and gold decorated the walls, cabinets, and furnishings. They dropped their bags in a large master suite, changed into swimsuits, and ran up the steps to the top deck. There they found a pair of Yamaha personal watercrafts. Two crewmembers hoisted the crafts to the ocean. They rubbed on sunscreen, put on their sunglasses and hats, slipped over the side with each boy straddling the idling engines. Minutes later they were zooming in and around the boat as it picked up steam heading out to sea. They bounced over waves while doing their best to send water spray all over the other. Surprisingly, Jack's machine was slightly faster than Thad's, and he did not like it. Jack just laughed at him and lowered his head to cut down on the wind resistance.

The boat dropped anchor in the cove of a small, unpopulated island. The boys returned to the boat, picked up scuba gear, and soon plopped over the side into the beautiful crystal blue warm water. T had gotten his SCUBA training last season while Jack earned his patch at summer camp. They dove down to explore the reefs filled with thousands of multicolored tropical fish. Thad pointed out big tube sponges, brain coral, and a moray eel. Jack spotted a lobster in a deep crevice, and they both chased a poor small squid before he disappeared into a coral bed.

Near the end of their dive, they spotted a sea turtle, and hurriedly kicked their fins to catch up with the prehistoric looking creature. Before ascending, they pulled the regulators from their mouth, and kissed as tiny bubbles escaped their mouths and nostrils. They grinned, as they took another gulp of air from their regulators, and kissed again.

They ate dinner on the deck and watched the huge orange sun slowly descend into the water. Thad smiled, "It doesn't get much better than this. What a view?"

Jack winked at him, "I was thinking the same thing. What a view?" He pointed at T.

After dinner, they walked to the front of the boat, as the crew lifted anchor and began motoring overnight to Nassau. Pleasantly exhausted from their race across the surface, and their swim beneath it, they retired to their room. In seconds the floor was covered with their clothes, the kissing and groping began, and soon their rhythm picked up with the movement of the boat over the waves. Completely spent, they drifted off to sleep in each other's arms, feeling safe and secure, and deeply in love.

87

They devoured their breakfast of fresh fruit, orange muffins, and ham omelets with freshly squeeze orange juice while floating over a reef the locals called Shark Alley. By nine, they could see a boat steering directly from the island towards them. As it got closer, Jack realized it was a scuba boat filled with divers.

Thad laughed, "You're going to love this. Come on, we need to suit up," he said as he led him to the deck. They found their scuba gear waiting for them, and two brand new full-length wet suits.

"Are we diving with this group?" asked Jack as he began stepping into the legs of his suit.

"Yes, we're going on a shark dive," replied T without a sly smile.

Jack froze where he stood, "We're what?"

"A shark dive. I did it last year and it is a hoot. We go down with extra weight on our dive belts to a depth of forty feet, and sit on the bottom with our hands across our chest, so the sharks aren't tempted to take a bite out of us. Then a big guy comes down in a chain suit with a spear and a bucket full of fish.

"The sharks in the area are mostly reef sharks, and they are used to this performance. He'll set the weighted bucket on the bottom, spear a fish out of the bucket via a spring lid, and then wave it back and forth as the sharks dart in and out and try to take it from him. It is amazing," he added enthusiastically.

Jack began pulling his wet suit back off, "I am not going. I don't want to end up in Jaws Part Five."

Thad busted out laughing. "You're a wimp! They won't bite you—you're too skinny. They'll look for a fat old man or a pretty girl. They never go for a skinny ass."

Jack laughed and started pulling the wet suit on again. "I think I saw this on the Discovery Channel. Are you sure it is safe?"

"Would I be doing it again if it wasn't?"

"Yes, you would, because you're absolutely crazy!"

An hour later, all the divers were in a half circle with their knees in the sand, arms crossing their chests tightly, and a steady stream of bubbles escaping from their nervous bodies. The sharks began races around them before darting in and out. A big grouper hovered to Jack's right just waiting for an easy morsel missed by the shark feeding frenzy but being careful not to become the bait. Jack thought the diver in the chain suit must be absolutely nuts, as he speared a fish and began twisting it left and right as the sharks streaked through the water for it. Then again, he thought, he's the only one with a weapon.

Off to the right the video cameraman caught everything on tape. Jack would watch a while, then turn his head to the right slowly so he could see Thad's face. His eyes were wide with excitement and Jack hated to admit it, but he was having a good time, too. Thirty minutes later, the feeding was over and they all slowly made their way to the surface.

With no hat and sunglasses, it was easy for the other divers to recognize T. He sat on their boat and signed autographs for all, and gave the captain two hundred dollars before saying good-bye, as they made their way back to their boat with a copy of the video tape in a sealed plastic case.

They immediately put it in the VCR to left of the huge LCD screen in the living room of the big boat. They laughed and made jokes and teased one another as the crew brought them lunch. Soon they were steaming for Daytona Beach and back to work. It had been a short vacation, but an important one for the events that lay ahead of them.

They arrived at the track late in the afternoon by helicopter and immediately climbed aboard the waiting golf cart for the long ride to their motorcoach. They had to make their way through the pits, and noted a large group of folks on a pit tour. Janet immediately made a turn to travel around the garage to avoid being rushed by the fans. T kept his hat on tight, hoping he would not be recognized, but he knew that was nearly impossible.

Janet had to slam on her brakes as the sixty-three car suddenly backed off his trailer. The crew gave her a polite wave and a smile. They waited for the car to turn, so they could continue on their way. Out of the corner of Jack's eye, he spotted a man walking rapidly towards him. He turned his head, so he could attempt to see the man through the crowd, and immediately his heart leaped.

Jack realized the man was Tim, and he suddenly felt sick. He wondered, what is 'he' doing here? Tim kept coming towards him. Jack feared he would cause another scene so he turned back to Janet, "Let's turn around and get out of here. There's a fan coming that we don't want to see."

T turned and saw Tim, "Shit."

Janet began backing up so she could turn, but her maneuver actually made it easy for Tim to catch them.

"Howdy boys," called Tim. "You dropped this." He thrust a white envelope into Jack's hands. "Good to see you. Good luck in the race TNT. I've got to run." He turned in the opposite direction, as Janet began pulling away. Jack turned to watch him, and saw him lift his right hand giving them the bird gesture without even looking back. He knew Jack and T were watching him.

When they got to the coach and alone, Jack spoke up first, "How in the hell did he get in here?"

"A hundred bucks buys anyone a pit pass. What did he give you?"

Jack sat down on the couch, and held the envelope in front of him. He sensed it was bad news, and dreaded discovering the revealed contents. He ripped open the side, pulled out a single sheet of paper, and began reading aloud.

"Howdy boys, I hope I have your full attention. I know Jack is queer and I've seen Thad and the way he looks at you so you're a queer, too. This is wonderful for the gay population but most exciting for me. I'm guessing you don't want your little secret to get out and I'm all too happy to help you keep it that way—for a fee of course!

"My silence can be purchased for just a million dollars in cash. Chump change I'm sure to America's top racecar driver. Put it in a satchel and go to the bus station. Put it in locker twenty-nine. The combination to the lock is seven, twenty-nine, sixty-nine. The cash must be there before the start of the race. Failure to do so will result in one hundred press releases delivered to the media room during the race. I can't imagine what kind of chaos would ensue at the end of the race when you're faced with a room full of reporters asking if you are a fag. What fun that would be but of course, a million dollars will prevent this from happening. The choice is yours. The end."

"Shit!" said Thad.

They spent their free time that evening discussing the situation, and finally went to bed, and though the lights were off, they didn't fall asleep. They started hashing the problem out all over again. At first, they said nothing but angry things about Tim, but after a few minutes, Thad wanted to find him and beat the crap out of him. Jack said that would make him talk for sure. T began thinking about how he could put together a million bucks to pay him off, but they both agreed feeding Tim's greedy nature would only make him want more. In the end, they knew paying him would be something they would have to do the rest of their lives, and they did not want to do that. They lay awake in each other's arms for hours, before finally falling asleep.

Dawn came too early, and Thad had an interview to do. He dressed and they ate breakfast in silence. They were not mad at each other, but they both feared in the next forty-eight hours their world could turn upside down. They agreed Jack would remain in the motorcoach, which felt odd to Janet when she picked up T for the interview with the golf cart. T said Jack felt like he was coming down with a cold and wanted to sleep in.

Jack sat down at the computer desk with his laptop and stared at the screen for a long time. He needed to work on a speech for a client, as well as come up with idea for T's speech at an army base the following week. He also wanted to create a series of one-liner comments for Thad's appearance on a late night talk show on Tuesday night. He looked at the screen for almost twenty minutes without writing a single word. Jack had never experienced writers block, and perhaps he thought that wasn't the real problem in this case. Over and over in his mind, he played out his brief friendship with Tim, and wondered what he possibly could have done to make him betray the trust every gay man gives when he meets a new friend.

He remembered reading a gay article suggesting all closeted gay men should be for out of the closet for the greater good of all gays, because once the world sees the caliber and the quantity of so many homosexuals, there could in fact be more acceptance of gays. The flipside of this argument is every individual is entitled to his privacy and a choice of when, and if he wants to come out. The poll at the end of the article showed gay men split right down the middle on the issue.

Jack remained in the closet during his high school years after seeing a boy he knew beaten up by a group of athletes. He hated himself for having kept his homosexuality a secret, because he never fell in love, or enjoyed dating the boy of his dreams. He went from one coast to the other for his college education, and far away from anyone he grew up with. He chose a huge school with gay organizations, and his Internet searches revealed a dozen gay nightclubs in the city surrounding the school.

After arriving on campus, he began his out of the closet experience as he told anyone who asked if he was gay—yes! He flirted carefully with boys he felt attracted to, but it wasn't until his second year he began his first real love affair. It lasted three months before suddenly his boyfriend fell out of love with him, and in love with their neighbor's adult son. He quickly pushed the depressing thought from his mind.

His father used to tell him when faced with a difficult decision to take a piece of paper and draw a line down the center creating two columns. The left column for why he should do something, and the right side column for why he should not. Jack smiled as he opened a spreadsheet wondering what his dad might think of his electronic piece of paper. He type in Pro in the first column, and Con in the second column. He began listing his reasons under the Pro column as to why he should remain in the relationship with Thad. The listings came quickly: attraction, great sex, humor, love, confidence, great sex, laughter, love of the outdoors, great sex, funny, loving, amazing, partner, talented, skilful, great sex, etc.

His Con column began with: closeted, superstar, recognized everywhere, sponsor opinions, works in a redneck bigoted sport, and then paused, and wrote: subject to blackmail attempts.

He stopped typing as the last listing made him instantly forget about all the other reasons. He sighed and dropped his head. He shook his head in disbelief. He had sworn he would never go back in the closet, but easily did so with Thad because he loved him so much. Of all the six men he had seriously dated since college, he knew only T truly loved him. Just the sight of him made him smile, and when Thad kissed him, he completely melted in his arms. Jack knew T adored him, and the feeling and confidence that gave him lifted his spirit making his soul come alive.

He started another list. If he stayed with Thad, Tim would label him a homosexual. Instantly the entire motorsports professionals would call him a queer, a faggot, and he would become the butt of numerous jokes, and jeers. It would drop Thad from being the king of the road to a scorned driver who threw away his career. His sponsors would drop him, Drew would fire him, and no one on any other team would hire him. Instantly his career would be over.

How to stop Tim? His first idea was a simple one—just shoot him! However, he was not a violent person, so perhaps he could 'accidentally' run over him with the motorcoach. He knew Thad could pay Tim off, but if Tim wanted to ruin him, he would not stop with just one million. He could call the police, the FBI, or maybe the CIA, but all of them would feel betrayed when their favorite sports star came out of the closet, and became in their minds a turncoat faggot.

He soften, and wondered if he could talk Tim out of blackmailing Thad, but he shook his head again knowing he had told Tim numerous times he was not interested in him, and so far, he had failed to listen to a single word he said. Tim would not stop.

Frustrated, and feeling defeated, Jack closed the spreadsheet without saving it, and opened his word processing software. He began typing a letter to Thad.

Dear Thad,

I love you so much that I can't possibly allow this blackmail to happen. We can't pay him off, and there's no way he is going to stop until he ruins me, which means he destroys you. I can think of no other way to prevent this than for me to go away. If I were not here, no one would take his blackmail threat seriously. Janet could get you a hot date and everyone would think Tim is just trying to bilk you for the money, which is true. The FBI could arrest him, destroying his credibility, and maybe lock him away for a very long time, but they would mean the story would go public.

However, if I was around, suspicions would grow, and before long, someone angry because you beat them, would accuse you of being a queer, and the whole mess would start all over again. It would be a repeat of what happened to me at summer camp.

I dreamed we would have this amazing life together. I feel ten feet tall when you hug me, and even taller when you make love to me. I have never felt that way before, and may never again, but I love you so much that I cannot let this man bring you down.

Thank you for allowing me into your life and for loving me. I have never felt so wonderful in my entire life. I will think of you often, and I pray you will drive safe, but win. I wish all the happiness possible, and I will miss you, but we must go our separate ways. It is no longer possible for us to be together. It must end now.

I'm going away and I'm not going to Boone. It will not be possible for you to find me, so please don't try. I love you. I love you. I love you.

Jack

He read it over three times, made a few corrections, as was his habit when he wrote anything, and then sent it to the wireless printer. He signed it, folded it in half, wrote Thad's name on it, and then laid it on the bed. He stopped for a moment, wishing he could tear it up, but he knew he could not.

He quickly packed his clothes, closed up his laptop, and made his way out of the coach. Duke was wiping down the front of the coach after removing the bugs he hit on the way into the racetrack the night before.

"Hey, kid. How you doing?"

Jack smiled, "Hi, Duke. You sure take good care of this motorcoach. It is a beauty."

"I'm glad you two guys didn't wreck it in the desert."

"Thad drove it very carefully because he said you would kill him if he got a scratch on it."

Duke laughed heartily, "He's right." Duke noted the luggage but said nothing.

"See you later. I've got a meeting to get to."

He turned and began making his way out of the motorcoach lot, through the tunnel to the outside world, and began walking away from the track. It took him an hour to catch a cab, but finally he did. It was hot in July in Florida making his face red. As he wiped the sweat from his brow, he knew exactly where he wanted to go—somewhere cooler.

"Airport," he told the driver.

The interview lasted longer than Thad wanted it to, but they experienced a power failure, and had to wait for the cameras to warm up again. Janet began driving him back when she got a cell call from Drew. He asked her to drive T over to the media center. T felt frustrated, as he wanted to get back to Jack, but told Janet it was okay. Drew met him at the entrance and together they walked inside.

"I have someone I want you to meet," said Drew.

They walked over to a table with a man sitting with his back to him.

"Thad," began Drew, "this is Kyle Rickman the famed RBC news anchor."

The man turned and stood. T immediately realized he was taller than he appeared on television at six feet four inches. His hair was completely white, his face tan from years of golf and sport fishing, and his radiant blue eyes focused directly on T's face.

93

"I am most pleased to meet you, sir," began T as he stuck out his hand.

"And I you," began the man as he shook his hand firmly and smiled with perfect teeth. "I have followed your career for several years, and I must say I have never met a driver with so much talent. You are an inspiration to all of us racing fans."

Thad smiled, "It was probably easier for me to follow your career as my parents are big fans, so I grew up watching you on the network news every night for most of my life."

Kyle grinned slyly, "I think you just aged me by twenty years."

"Oh, I am sorry I didn't mean…"

Kyle laughed, "I'm just kidding. Please sit down because I want to ask a favor of you. I have been after my news producer for several years to do a prime time special on today's generation of racers. He has finally agreed. It'll be a two-hour special, and I want you to be our single guest. We'll look at your life, your career, your victories, and show America how a racecar star is born. It'll be fantastic and seen worldwide by millions of people. We'll show your home, your family and friends, and you can introduce America to the lucky girl you're dating. It will be an Emmy winning show."

Thad gulped as his brain rushed at the horror of having his real private life revealed. He stumbled for words, "Well that is very flattering. I appreciate the offer. I will talk it over with my team and get back to you. It was a great pleasure to meet you," he began as stood up and shook his hand again, "and I hope you're going to stay and watch the race tomorrow, as I'm going to win it for Drew." He gave Drew a slap on his back, then turned, and quickly made his way out the door.

Janet drove him to his motorcoach after he told he had to pee badly. He waved at Duke who was finishing up the cleaning job and bounded into the coach locking the door behind him.

"Jack?" He went to the refrigerator, opened a bottle of juice, and began taking a long swig from the bottle. He began walking to the back of his coach expecting to find Jack asleep on the bed, but the moment he saw the note on the bed with his name on it in Jack's handwriting, he knew something was wrong.

He set the bottle down on the nightstand, and sat down on the bed. Slowly he picked up the note and began reading. His heart rate picked up and his eyes watered. He read it again as a feeling of great sadness began to take over. He folded the note and put it in his nightstand drawer, and lay back on the bed. Seconds later, slow tears dripped down his cheeks. He had not cried in years, but he could not help it. He loved Jack with all his heart, and he saw this calamity as completely his fault. His world had pushed Jack away because almost everyone in his sport would hate Jack if they knew he was gay just as they would bring out the tar and feathers if they knew the great TNT was gay, too.

After the tears stopped, he propped up the pillows, and flipped on the satellite television. He skipped through channels mindlessly while thinking through the situation. He wanted to run out of the coach, leap into the Hummer, and start searching for Jack, but in his heart he knew when Jack made his mind up, there was little he could do to change it. He also knew Jack would do exactly as he said, and go to a place where he could not find him, and he did not have a clue where that was.

He rolled out of the bed, picked up his drink, and moved to the dining booth. He took out a piece of paper and began making a list of things he needed to do to take a strong offense to Tim's threats. He ate some lunch while he refined his list, picked up his cell phone, searched through his phone directory, and made a call.

"Hello, is Traci there?" he asked.

"Just a minute."

T waited recalling the last time he saw Traci just last February when he was in town for the two weeks of Daytona and the opening of the racing season. He had taken her to the movies, and a few quiet dinners, and she watched from the pit during the races.

"Hello?"

"Hey, Traci, it is Thad. How are you?"

"Hey, boy, where have you been? It has been a long time since I heard from you," she said.

"I'm sorry. This season and the chase, well, it has been incredible. I don't have time to hardly eat or think. I've just got to get back in the top ten because I am going to win the championship this year."

"You're forgiven, but I missed you."

He thought she was being sweet. "Listen, I know this last minute, but I've got an appearance to make this evening at the RESTAR hospitality tent, but after that, I was wondering if you would go out to dinner?" He hoped she said yes, and graciously she did. He told her he would pick her up at six and bade her good-bye. He hung up feeling like a dog for using her friendship to bail him out of a jam.

He then dialed Duke on his cell phone even though he was just outside. "Duke, hey bud, I may need a little extra help at the RESTAR event tonight. Janet and I ran into this crazed fan, and he said some ugly things. Do you remember Traci? Well she is coming with me, and I'm afraid that man could scare her off. I need for you to keep him out of my zone. Let me describe him to you." T described Tim perfectly.

He hung up, called Janet, and asked her to come visit him in the coach. They chatted for a while before he told her what he was thinking. "**The Entertainment Tonight Show** has been after me for an interview for quite a while. I'm in the mood to do it tonight. Are they here?"

She grinned as she had been trying to schedule this for a long time, "Yes, they are. I got a call from their producer this morning."

"Tell them I'll talk to them right after the RESTAR event and before I go out for dinner. I can give them five minutes."

"No problem, I'll set it up," she replied.

"What do you think of that **PEOPLE Magazine** reporter that has been hounding us?"

Janet smiled again, "Zeke is funny, and I think he would be very fair."

"Okay, tell him to be here at nine tomorrow morning and yes, they can bring a photographer. We'll do the story right in the coach—a behind the scenes story. It'll be fun."

Janet rapidly made notes, and before their meeting was over, he had agreed to do five interviews though still thinking about the TV special with Kyle. She could not imagine what had changed but she was thrilled, and she knew Drew would love it.

After she left, Thad sat there shaking his head. The only way he could force Jack from his mind was to keep talking. While he talked to Duke and Janet, for those brief minutes, he had felt better. However, once Janet closed the door to the coach, the silence inside seared his soul. He wanted to curl up on the couch with Jack, and above all, he wanted to strip naked and make love to him.

He paced back and forth several times and settled on a plan. He changed into jogging clothes, and left the coach to begin jogging around the track like he used to. He knew what would happen, and he no longer cared. A hundred yards down the track the photographers started chasing him. They took his picture, and when he got near the first turn, the fans camping in the infield began screaming at him. He stopped and began signing autographs and posing for pictures. He picked a pretty girl just over eighteen years old, signed her hat, and gave her a quick kiss. Every one of the photographers caught the picture. He said goodbye and returned to jogging. At the other end of the track, he did the same.

After showering, he ate a sandwich, and came out of the motorcoach. "Duke, let's ride over to Daytona USA. I feel like hanging out with our fans."

Duke drove the golf cart, and together they entered the museum. The ticket booth clerk made a phone call, and they soon met the manager who escorted them in. He signed hundreds of autographs, made jokes with the fans, and smiled for every picture and once again found a girl to kiss.

As he was signing, he noted a man in a Yankee baseball gap standing off to the side. T leaned into Duke and whispered. Duke nodded and drifted towards the man so he can see his face. Once he had the man's face in his memory, he walked up to him. T tried not to watch, but he stole glances in their direction when he could.

"Sir, you don't know me, but I thought I would tell you something about me. I served honorably in the Navy Seals, and earn several medals in the first Gulf War. I know how to break a man's neck with a simple, but powerful quick snap. I also know how to gut a man with a single stroke of a knife. I attended a school where I learned how to torture a man as painfully as possible, forcing him to tell me what I wanted to know.

"Thad is my friend. You are not my friend. If I see you again, well, I might have a battle flashback, and mistake you for the enemy. Did I tell you I never left an enemy soldier alive?"

Duke smiled at him. Tim said nothing. He quickly turned and left the building. Duke rejoined T, and after a few minutes, they left the building. Thad went immediately back to his coach, went to his bed and fell down to take a nap. He smelled Jack's pillow and slowly pulled it to his face and inhaled the scent he found on the pillow. He felt confidant he could defuse Tim's threaten attack, and hoped once he got things back to normal perhaps Jack would return.

He awoke to find he only had about twenty-five minutes to shower and change into his racing suit. He took extra time to make sure every hair was in place and that his face looked good. He even trimmed his eyebrows and made sure he had no nose or ear hairs poking out. He laughed at himself, but he knew over the next few days his picture would be taken about ten thousand times.

He left the coach and cranked up the Hummer. He picked Traci up and immediately made it back to the track and over to the huge RESTAR hospitality tent. When they climbed out of the Hummer, the photographers took his picture as he helped Traci from the SUV. He held her hand as he led her through the crowd to the side of the tent.

"My goodness," began Traci, "the crowds just attack you. I don't see how you handle it so well."

"It is all part of the job, but don't panic it'll be over soon, and then we'll get some dinner somewhere a little more private. You can answer any question the reporters ask, but just remember they'll try to get you to say something you might regret tomorrow when everything you said, or implied, will be in print all over the world."

"That's ominous," she replied.

"Why don't you come on stage with me? I get lonely out there by myself."

"Are you sure?"

They both turned as they heard the stage announcer rattle off a list of T's accomplishments. A RESTAR assistant guided them to the back of the steps leading to the stage. "And now ladies and gentlemen, please welcome TNT!"

The crowd of five thousand stood and cheered as he led Traci up the steps and held her hand as they crossed the stage. T took the microphone and went right to work. "Good evening folks. I'm so glad you're here, and I hope you're ready for a good race tomorrow. I have a secret to tell you, but you must promise not to tell anyone outside of this room. Can I trust you to do that?" The crowd yelled yes.

T looked down at the news reporters and spotted amongst the group of fifty the video cameras for Entertainment Tonight. "I'm not sure I can trust this group of reporters. Do you think they can keep a secret?" The crowd yelled no.

T laughed, "Okay, I'll tell you anyhow. Tomorrow, I am going to win the Daytona 500!" The crowd immediately stood and cheered. He then went on to tell how things were going this season. He answered questions from the audience, and twenty minutes later, they left the stage with their ears ringing from the cheers and applause. They left the tent and rode to the motorcoach. The news crew was all set up and waiting for him.

Outside they met the reporter from Entertainment Tonight and turned to go inside.

Traci leaned into him and whispered, "Should I wait over by the Hummer?"

"No, I want you here. You make this a whole lot more fun for me. I'll keep it as short as I can."

Janet introduced the producer, light stands were turned on, and a few minutes later, he began the interview. He talked about his favorite charities, the kids at the hospitals, and Victory Junction Camp. He talked about hoping to settle down one day, but admitted with his high pressure schedule that it was very tough to even think about settling down for a while. He said he only wanted to marry once, and that marriage last a life time, and he would hold out until he had the time and opportunity to marry the person he loved most in the world."

They asked him what he looked for in permanent partner. "I need someone that enjoys the same things I do. I love to hike to waterfalls in the mountains, I love horseback riding, I want to see more of America like the Grand Canyon, and high country in Colorado."

As soon as they were done, he gave the crew a tour of the motorcoach, and then waited for them to remove all their camera gear and light stuff. He then changed clothes, led Traci back to the Hummer, and left the track. "Okay, Miss Traci, I'm all yours. Thanks for coming with me. I'm so glad you're here." He reached over and squeezed her hand.

"I don't see how you remain so calm. I was a nervous wreck."

"You get used to it. I'm starving. Are you hungry? I hope so. I made reservations at Dinos. Is that okay?"

She smiled, "It is very okay. I've always wanted to go there, but you have to know the right people to get in. They say the food is fantastic."

"I must know the right people," he grinned and winked at her, as Janet really knew the right people, but it was he that leaked to the press he was eating dinner there. They pulled up to large restaurant. T received a card for his Hummer from the parking attendant. They turned to enter the restaurant, and saw about eight photographers ready to snap their picture. T did not hustle in the door, but stopped and allowed perfect pictures for all with Traci as his side.

After dinner, there were more pictures. As they drove away, T yawned, "I've got to get to bed as I have five hundred miles to drive tomorrow. How about coming with me to watch the race?"

"I'd love to," she replied.

"I'll pick you up about 9:30 if that is okay? Please dress comfortably with good walking shoes, as everywhere we go is a bit of an asphalt hike. It'll be a long day, but we'll get some dinner afterwards if that is okay with you."

"Of course it is," she said as he helped her out of the Hummer in front of her condominium. He walked her to the door and gave her a quick kiss.

He drove back to motorcoach, waved at a few driver friends, shut and locked the door. He stripped down to his boxers, and walked back to the kitchen. He fixed himself a bowl of ice cream, and immediately thought about Jack. He started to put his cell phone on the charger when suddenly he realized he had Jack's cell phone number in his directory. He scrolled to it and thought for a moment about whether he should call or not. Finally, he took a breath, highlighted the number, and hit the talk button. It began ringing.

Across the country, Jack was almost asleep in the cabin. His day had been a long one, leaving him exhausted from the journey, and the gut wrenching choice he had made earlier. He missed Thad especially as he lay in the bed in alone. He looked over when the phone rang, and out of habit, he almost picked it up and answered it. He slowly picked up the phone and read the Caller ID. He recognized the number immediately and sighed. He so wanted to open his phone and answer T's call, but he knew if he did, he would give in and come back to him. He slowly set the phone down and let it go to voicemail.

Thad listened to all four rings before voicemail kicked in. He listened to Jack's wonderful warm and friendly voice instructing him to leave a message. Hearing the sound of his lover, made his eyes moisten, but he fought to hold back tears. The beep came too soon. "Jack? This is Thad. I respect what you did, but I don't much like it, but you were probably right—at least for a while. I am going to take this as a challenge. I have gone right to work to defuse Tim's threat. Duke had a heart-to-heart talk with him yesterday, and I have made sure I'm seen with a pretty girl on my arm. I think this will all blow over in a few weeks. I hope you'll come back to me. Please call me. I don't think I can bear not hearing from you. I love you. Call me." T hung up feeling somewhat hopeful and yet depressed. He went to bed after setting the alarm. He closed his eyes hoping to dream of Jack.

Jack turned over without listening to the voicemail. He would do that tomorrow, but for now, he desperately needed to fall asleep. It took awhile, but emotionally spent, he drifted off and the dreams of T began.

NINE

His morning flew by. Thad picked up Traci on time and returned to the motorcoach just as the crew from **People Magazine** arrived for his interview and their photographs, which they did in the coach with Traci to give the story and the pictures an 'at home' feel. Thad wanted the biggest stories possible, so he made an appearance at the Media Center with Traci at his side, attended the driver's meeting, and before long, he heard the command to start his engine. As they did the warm up laps, he began quietly talking to himself. "I've got to win this race. The biggest tool I can use to destroy Tim's attack is to win. No one would believe a faggot could win the Daytona race. I have to win."

As the pace car left the track, he saw the green flag drop, and he took off. It took him twenty-five laps to pass enough cars to get to the front, but he did. His fans stood and cheered and everyone one else booed, but he did not care as he was grinning from ear to ear.

There were several big wrecks behind him but so far, he had been able to stay out front and dominate the race. He reached a hundred and sixty-one laps when suddenly he felt his right front tire hit something on the track, and flung it hard into the bottom of the car.

"Charley?" called T over his radio. "I think I just hit a bolt or something hard with the right front.

"Is it still handling well?" asked Charley as he clicked on his microphone button.

There was a long pause before T came back on his radio. "The right front is going down. I'm coming in. Get ready."

Charley issued orders to the pit crew and thirty seconds later T screeched to a halt on a green flag pit stop. He took a sip from his Gatorade straw, as he felt the right side go up and the tires changed. Six seconds later the left side went up. The gasman squeezed in two cans of gas, the jack dropped and he popped the clutch and tore out of the pit.

"Watch your pit speed?" warned Charley.

"I've got it. What place am I coming back out in?" \

Charley check with his associates and replied, "Thirty-first."

T grinned and said sarcastically, "Is that all? I thought I would be forty-third. It is a good thing we had this problem early, huh?"

Charley laughed at him. "I'm glad I could help change your outlook on a race problem. Now that everything is just rosy, get off your butt and put the pedal down, and let's get back to the front!"

T laughed, "I'll pass them two at a time!'

"Quite a few cars are out of the race due to crashes and engine troubles. Let's start making our way up, but don't get caught up in any wrecks in the process."

"I'm switching to invisible. Oh, and by the way, I'm going to win this race!" T laughed as he worked his way up to speed.

Charley looked at Drew and Janet and mouthed, "Invisible? What the hell is he talking about?"

T passed his first car on the third turn, and with the race winding down, he kept on passing cars. He was in tenth place when a caution came out with just forty laps to go. "I need a great pit stop guys. Now is the time for under the thirteen seconds!"

T slid into his pit, and the crew ran around his car, changed four tires, added gas, pulled a tear sheet of the glass, and dropped him at twelve point seven seconds. He crossed the pit line in fifth place. "Way to go guys. We picked up five stops. We're going to win this race!"

T focused on the cars and drivers ahead of them and memorized the list in this head. He began to recall the driver habits of each of them. When the green flag dropped, he had the best start of his career and passed number four. The crew jumped into the air. With the thirty-two laps to go, he passed number three on the outside. Two to go, he thought.

Charley came on the radio, "Having fun?"

T laughed, "Hell yeah. I hope you have the champagne ready. We're going to win this race!"

Gary, his spotter broke in on the radio, "T? Getting around the fourteen car is going to be tough. He is drafting close off the leader. Can you take him on the outside?"

T pushed his microphone button, "Yeah, I think so, but I may have to lean on him to break up the draft."

Charley broke in on the radio chatter, "Charge his rear, and shake him up. Let him know you have the fastest car. Once he starts blocking, he'll lose his draft advantage. Then pass him quick. If you wait too long, the seventy-two car could get too far out front."

"I got it. No problem. Out." T did not want to talk anymore because that required thinking. He wanted to concentrate on getting around the fourteen car.

At eighteen laps to go, T reached the rear bumper of the number fourteen several times. He then moved high and grinned when the fourteen came up to block him. He cut low and the block came with him. He went high and low several times and on lap eleven he faked high, got his nose on the inside in turn one, and passed him by turned two. The crowd rose to their feet.

Charley screamed out over the radio. "Excellent. That's the way to do it, and just one more to pass to make the win."

T had no time to revel in his maneuver. He remained two car lengths back from the first place seventy-two car. The laps began to tick off as he finally reached his rear bumper. He knew their spotter would tell him about his handling of the fourteen car.

He began drafting for lap eight and seven to go, but in turn one, he moved to the outside. Seventy-two moved up to block him while expecting him to drop down low. T started low, and instantly pulled back into his high line. The seventy-two car started low and realized the fake a second late. T moved a third up alongside the seventy-two car. He put his gas pedal down and was even with him on the high side when they came out of turn two.

"I hope these tires hold their grip," said T to himself. They remained neck and neck on the backstretch. On the turns, T crowded the seventy-four making him stay low. He passed him on turn four and moved in front on the backstretch.

"Yahoo!" yelled Charley over the radio. "All right son. Just keep it steady and don't blow that engine. We have six to go."

Gary began calling off the laps and the position of the very unhappy seventy-two car, but without clean air, the former leader began to fade. T crossed the finish line, and slammed his gloved fist into the steering wheel. He had wanted this win more than any in his life. Minutes later, Drew came on the radio to congratulate him, and told him he had just moved into ninth place in the championship race.

T spun the car around, dropped his window net, and stuck his bare fist out of the window and began waving to the crowd. Janet ushered Traci to the winner's circle, while they waited for T to do his burn out and bring his car into Victory Lane. The television crew stood by as did sixty other reporters. The groups from **The Entertainment Tonight Show** and **People** magazine were also there. On cue, T emerged from the car with his hat and sunglasses on. He motioned for Traci to come to him. He gave her a hug as the cameras snapped their quick kiss, and then began the required television interview with the winner. Soon the champagne was flying through the air, as the crew and T soaked each other with the spray from the bottles. Janet and Traci made a dash behind a wall to avoid the melee of jubilant crewmembers.

The reporters from all over the country began making their way to the media center. As they pulled out a chair from the white clothed tables, they found a single page of page facing down. They chatted with the other reporters knowing the top three place drivers would be entering shortly.

NARC's media director tested the microphones as they waited. He saw a few of the men reading the piece of paper, but had no time to ask what it was all about. The reporters read it with most giving it a smirk, wadding it up, and tossing it to the table.

The side door pushed opened and the drivers for the fourteen and seventy-two driver came in and sat down at the head table. A moment later, TNT entered the room with a big smile on his face. He had Traci at his side, and showed her a place to stand and wait for him. He moved to the center of the platform. The reporters stood and gave him a standing ovation— something they rarely did.

The press conference began as an assistant in NARC's media department picked up one of the sheets of paper, read it, and nearly gasped for air. He carefully made his way to his boss and showed it to him. The man's face went white, but they soon felt this had to be a hoax, and hoped none of the reporters brought this up.

T answered almost twenty questions before the media director finally called a halt to the session, so T stood and thanked everyone. He, Traci, Janet, and Drew made their way out of the meeting. The media assistant handed Janet the sheet of paper as she walked out the door. She walked off to the side and read it, and then immediately folded it and put it in her pocket.

They drove over to the fan gate where fans could stand along one side of a chain linked fence and the drivers on the other side. Through a small slit, they could pass things to him for an autograph. TNT signed as many hats and shirts as he could before time to board the golf cart once again and head over to their motorcoach.

Drew went off to meet with some sponsors. Janet asked T if she could speak to him alone for a minute. T looked at her pleading silent eyes and said sure. He asked Traci to wait at the golf cart, and he assured he would be right back.

Janet led him into the coach and sat down in the dining booth. T got a Gatorade from the refrigerator and sat down across from her. "What's up?"

Janet handed him the folded note. "I was handed this in the media room by a media assistant. I saw a few reporters fiddling with a copy during the press conference, and I am shocked that no one asked you about this. Who wrote this?"

T did not answer her, as he took his time reading the note. A knot formed in his stomach, and he suddenly could feel his pulse along the side of his head. "Do you remember the crazy male fan that ran up to us while we were waiting in the golf cart?"

"He wrote this?"

"He has been stalking me. Yesterday, he was the guy that caught up with us in the golf cart. As I was signing autographs at Daytona USA, when Duke spotted him following me again and well, Duke had a 'word-of-prayer' with him. I guess he decided to get even with me."

"Gees, I would have expected a crazed female fan wanting to have a baby with you than this creep," she replied.

"This isn't signed, and it would take an investigation to discover if the guy did write this," stated T. "What should we do?"

"Nothing, as an investigation would fuel the fire, and suing him would bring on even more publicity. We ignore this crap, and chalk it up to the price of fame."

Relieved, Thad smiled, "I guess you're right." He hoped this would be the end of her questions. He was wrong.

"Just one more thing, how did he get Jack's name? Everyone on the planet knows you, but how would he know Jack's name."

"I don't know," he lied. "I haven't a clue. Are you going to tell Drew about this? I hate to upset him."

Janet did not reply right off. Drew was her boss, but Thad was her job. She usually did what was best for her job. "No, I guess not—unless something else happens. Where is Jack?"

T lied again, "He couldn't concentrate on writing his book while traveling and keeping up with me. He's a good friend, but I've got a championship to win, and have little time for anyone."

"I better go. I'll send Traci in. I'll see you on the plane." Janet stood and left the coach. T fell deep in thought, but quickly smiled when he saw Traci.

"Sorry about that—just a bit of business to handle. Are you hungry?" asked T, as he pulled a platter of fresh fruit from the refrigerator, set it on the table, snatched two plates from the cabinet, and two forks from the drawer, and sat down at the booth. He stuffed two pieces of pineapple in his mouth.

She sat down opposite him, "I had a hot dog during the race—but this looks good," she added as she winked at him.

"That's not fair," he laughed, "I got nothing but Gatorade and gas fumes during the race, and I am famished!"

Later Duke gave Traci a ride home, while T hurriedly changed clothes, and rode the golf cart to the helicopter. After boarding the jet for the ride home, T remained silent and pretended to sleep. Drew looked back at him, and thought he would be bouncing off the walls after wining, but realized the race and the win must have taken a lot out of him.

Janet also noted his silence, and began rethinking their conversation about the note. She had run the page through the shredder on the plane, and wondered where Jack was. She did not feel T had told her the whole truth, but knew better than to challenge him. She liked Jack, and loved the changes he made in the way T worked with his fans, children, and his speeches. She would miss him, too.

On a larger NARC plane sat a hundred and twenty journalists in route back to Charlotte from Daytona. Steve Appleton had folded the piece of paper he found in his chair in the media room and stuffed it into his jacket. He glanced to his left and the photographer sitting next to him was sound asleep with his head leaning against the window. He pulled the note out and read it again. The note gave no clues as to who had written it, though he wished it had, as he would have followed up by interviewing the writer.

He folded the note and returned it to his pocket. He pulled out his reporter notebook and began making a list of questions about TNT. Had he seen him with a woman on his arm or holding hands? Yes. Was the same woman at each track? No. Did any of the television interviews reveal a girlfriend? No. Was a woman living with him? Not sure—no one knew anything about his home life. Has there been any gossip about his sex preference among the other reporters and drivers? No.

He looked back over his notes and realized he had no credible evidence that T could be gay, but still, the thought of scooping a story with his name on it printed in every newspaper in the country could be the leap to network news that he desired. He wanted the move to the Charlotte paper, and pretended he liked the NARC assignment, but in truth, he hated everything about racing. He thought the drivers were spoiled rich bastards who flaunted their money in their giant motorhomes and fancy jets. He barely made fifty thousand a year, while every driver in the top series made more than double what he did.

He had covered pro football, basketball, and baseball, and in two to four hours, you were done and gone, but not in NARC. It took a weekend to cover the sport, and all day on race day, and sometimes late into the night. The thirty-six-weekend race schedule had worn him down, and he blamed the breakup with his long time girlfriend as collateral damage from the grueling schedule.

One nice thing about flying on the NARC media jet he liked was their Internet connections for every seat. He pulled out his laptop, plugged in the Ethernet connection, and two minutes later, he was online. He went to DMI's website and searched every page about TNT. He read the publicity materials, and looked at every single picture. He then went to NARC.com and did the same thing. Not satisfied, he did a Google search for TNT and discovered there were over five thousand hits. He scanned through the keys, read everything about his younger years, and studied every photo, and not once did he find T hanging onto some babe. He failed to find any comments about his plans to marry. After a hundred pages, he rubbed his eyes feeling weary from the long day.

However, he knew he still had nothing more than a hunch. He went to his newspaper website, and typed in a secret web link, punched in his name and privacy code, and instantly he had the entire archives of the hundred and twenty year old newspaper library at his discretion. He began searching again for everything on TNT. He saw photos around town of T going to dinner or lunch with various celebrities, or DMI friends. The only woman he saw on a semi-regular basis was Janet Anderson his publicist. He had met Janet, and made a mental note to try to have lunch with her this week.

As he scanned forward to pictures for this season, he noted people in the background. He eliminated anybody on his crew, hoping to find a civilian hanging out with T. Earlier this season he found no one in the same picture, but after Mothers Day he began to see a guy with brown hair and a bit taller than Thad in the background. He began rolling forward, and although this guy was never photographed standing beside T, he was in many of the pictures. He emailed one of the photos to himself.

The stewardess said they would be landing in a few minutes, so he closed his laptop and notebook and prepared for landing. He spent the time mulling over his thoughts and decided he had little evidence of anything, but it did peak his curiosity, and tomorrow he would get on the trail like an old hound dog—refusing to quit until the trail ran cold.

Thad got to DMI before dawn the next morning, and almost fell asleep in the makeup chair. Shirley did her best to get him clean-shaven, hair done, and television makeup applied. He walked into the small studio Drew built just last year to make it easier for the networks and flag stations around the country to interview his drivers. A producer led him to a stool where the lighting director quickly adjusted the big white lights eliminating any shadows or hot spots on Thad's face.

T cleared his throat and asked, "How many?"

The producer looked at his clipboard, "Twelve live spots and ten taped for later broadcast. We're also doing a spot for RESTAR's new sweepstake spots."

"I want to do a free spot for Cincinnati Children Hospital."

The producer wrote it down. "Whom do I send it to?"

"I'll have Janet get you the address. Thanks."

The producer helped T with his tiny headset inserted into his ear, and hid the wire around to the back of his neck. He then clipped a small lapel microphone to his shirt. "Six minutes."

The director in the booth asked T to test his microphone. "One, two, three and I already have to pee!" The crew laughed as T grinned. The camera brought his face into focus and zoomed in to a headshot. He then walked over to a second camera and made a half screen shot with T in the left side of the screen. He did this so the networks could add the anchor or footage of yesterday's race.

The first spot was with ABC's Good Morning America. It was a five-minute spot. He did the same for the other networks, and then started working on the big flag stations in Chicago, Atlanta, and Los Angeles. He took a short break, and then did spots for ESPN and Fox Sports, cut the promo for RESTAR, did several local channel promos encouraging folks to watch NARC and his RESTAR car. Finally, about ten o'clcok, he cut several spots for the hospital publicity department.

"Time for breakfast," he announced, as he pulled the microphone and headset off, and made his to the door. He walked to his Hummer, drove home, heated an egg and sausage biscuit in the microwave, and downed it with three bites and a glass of milk. He brushed his teeth and fell in the bed.

Janet had sat in the booth during the tapings, but once completed she went upstairs to her office. She answered about a dozen emails and sorted through requests for appearances. When her phone rang, she was surprised the caller was Steve Appleton, as he had hardly responded to any of her publicity emails, nor asked for an interview. She sensed correctly Steve was not just interested in the DMI drivers.

"Hey, Janet, great race yesterday. Congratulations," he began with enthusiasm.

"Steve I am so glad to hear from you. I thought we were on your blacklist or something."

"Not true, just a rookie race reporter trying to figure out how to keep up with a hundred drivers in the three series. I am so swamped I can't even remember the name of my dog. Come to think of it—I don't even know if I own a dog!" He was really pouring it on thick.

Janet laughed, "Funny, and you have obviously had too much caffeine already today. What can I do for you?"

"I was wondering if you would meet me for lunch and no, I am not asking you out on a date. I'm working on a piece about T called "Winner away from the track" for next Sunday sports section, and I have a few questions. How about we meet at noon at Applebee's, the one near you and Concord Mall?"

She looked at her book and smiled, "I can do it. I'll see you then."

"Great and thank you, and I will see you there."

After Janet hung up, she buzzed her secretary and asked her to put together the latest headshots of T for her, along with the usual press kit stuff. Her next call was from a producer with **Entertainment Tonight**. He reported the footage at the track with TNT was excellent, and the story would air in three parts starting tonight. She asked for a copy of the interviews, and he promised he would send them.

An hour later, an editor with **People Magazine** called to report they were going to press Tuesday night for a Wednesday release with TNT on the cover, and the story inside with six selected pictures. She asked for the name and address on the lady accompanying T at Daytona. Janet gladly gave it. After she hung up, she immediately called Traci to warn her, and encouraged Traci to keep her comments simple. She added when asked personal things to feel free to say 'no comment' or simply no. She knew the folks at **People** would call Traci shortly, and she was glad she beat them to it.

The morning flew by but she arrived at the restaurant on time. She spotted Steve at table and made her way to him.

"Thank you for coming," he said as he politely stood while she seated herself.

"My pleasure and you're up early today after the flight home from the track last night."

"I slept on the plane," he lied.

"I wish I had. There's so much more to do when Thad wins. The media always swarms the winner for a few days until the next race. He did live interviews all morning from our satellite studio. By now, the adrenalin has run out, and Thad is sound asleep."

They ordered lunch and then Steve began his plan of attempting to fish for the truth. "I received a very strange handout in my seat in the media room after the race. I looked around the room and realized everyone received the same page, but already many reporters were wadding it up and throwing it away."

"May I see it?" she hoped he would think this was her first reading of the blackmail attempt.

"Of course," he said as he produced it from his writing pad.

She scanned it again. "This is preposterous, a figment of some loony, or someone attempting to blackmail TNT."

"Who wrote it?"

She handed it back to him, "I wish I knew so our lawyers could sue him immediately. If you find out, will you let me know?"

"If you'll give me the scoop on your plans if I do."

She smiled, "Deal."

She continued by asking, "Why does this garbage interest you?"

"I agree it sounds like blackmail, but was Thad approached by the author asking for money."

"No he was not."

"Then why would someone try to dish dirt on T like this?"

"I don't have a clue."

"Well, before I dismiss it, I decided to do a little research. I searched all our media files from the beginning of Thad's career to yesterday. I could not find a single picture of him with a woman until the night before the race, and at the race yesterday. Who is the girl by the way?"

Janet sighed and gave him the info on Traci.

"I also read every word printed on him, and I could not find any reference of a girlfriend. Are Traci and T dating?"

"No and yes," she replied. He has a very difficult schedule during race season making a relationship nearly impossible. He does see her from time to time, and has for about two years."

"Isn't that sort of a copout? Out of the forty-three racers, seventy-five percent are married, and half of them have children. What's his problem? Is he a closeted homosexual?" He watched her carefully for her reaction to his blunt question.

Inside Janet was about to explode, but she sensed he wanted an angry reaction. She did the opposite, and laughed loudly. Other patrons turned from their meals to see what she was laughing at. She attempted to talk several times, but would abruptly burst into laughing again. "I'm sorry. That is hysterical. I'm with T many hours of almost every day. We travel together and hangout at the track. T embarrasses me with his attraction to women. He spots a pretty girl and immediately says something. Thankfully, I am happily in love with someone else, so I am never tempted, but this man really treats a woman with great respect. He buys flowers, and never forgets a special day. This not a copout, as you put it. Thad's only in his early twenties and way too young to get married."

Thankfully, the waitress brought their meal, and they began talking about everything but TNT. After the meal, Steve brought an envelope from the chair beside him onto the table, and began pulling out a series of eight by ten photos. "While searching through the articles and photos of Thad, I noted that all of last year, and most of this year, he never once hung out with a best friend or even a drinking buddy. However, over the past few weeks, our photographers snapped numerous pictures of Thad, and I began to note this guy. He handed her a picture that showed Thad sitting with Janet in the golf cart, and Jack sitting in the back seat. Before she could answer, he handed a series of ten photos to her: T and Jack on the pit box waiting for qualifying, T and Jack at a hospitality dinner, a television interview, talking to Drew, and laughing with the pit crew.

Janet then told him what she knew. "His name is Jack, a school friend of Thad's from his early years. He is a writer and came to visit for a while to help write several motivational speeches for Thad to deliver, and to do some ground work on an early biography of Thad. Jack is completing a book of his own at the same time, and he thought he could finish it while hanging out with T around the track. Wrong! He could not keep up with Thad's schedule, and had to retreat to finish his book."

"No last name?"

"Yes of course he has a last name, however, I promised to keep his name out of everything. He does not wish publicity, and he will not do an interview about his friend Thad. End of story." She began standing. "Thank you for lunch," she began as she handed him a press kit, "here's the latest promo material on Thad. If you have any other questions, please give me a call. If you don't mind, send me an early copy of your story."

"Of course," he replied standing as well. "Thank you so much for meeting me."

"My pleasure." She shook his hand and smiled, and then turned and left.

Steve sat back down, pulled out his credit card to pay for the lunch, and put the pictures back in the envelope. He had expected her to deny T was a homosexual, but it surprised him she did not try to deny the man in the photo. Instead she answered quickly, gave him part of his name, explained perfectly why he was with Thad, and why he was no longer there. It almost sounded too perfect, but he had no reason to distrust her answers. His boss, the editor of the newspaper, had a saying he said excessively for Steve's ears,

"You use bait to catch a fish, but you use air to catch what is not there for the catching." However, he knew he would have to find more to go on before telling his boss about a possible story on Thad.

He drove to his office and began to think of how he could find this guy named Jack. He flipped through the bio until he found Thad's hometown. He then went on the Internet and searched for a list of schools Thad would have attended. He searched for the phone numbers and began calling. Twelve calls later, he found Thad's high school. After a few more calls, he found his middle school, and eventually his elementary school. He asked the school secretaries if they recalled who Thad's best friend was. He obtained names like Bob, Sam, and Ted but no Jack. He then asked if they recalled a Jack as his best friend. Not one could recall a Jack. He hung up puzzled. It wasn't a big town—someone had to know Jack.

He then made a big decision and loaded up the photos, his notes, his list of schools, and drove to the airport to fly to Thad's hometown to begin searching for Jack. He wasn't completely confident there was more to the story, but sensed something was wrong about Janet's explanation.

TEN

Thad woke late in the afternoon still feeling exhausted from last weekend's race, the spin moves he made with the media to promote a heterosexual image, and when alone in his house—the loss of Jack. He hoped it would only take a few more weeks before Jack could return. He showered and deliberately did not shave hoping to create a stronger macho image. After heating up a frozen dinner, he sat down on his long empty sofa with a pad and pen, and began making plans on how he could promote his image. He looked at his Palm Pilot, and scrolled through addresses and phone numbers until he found what he was looking for. Her name was Becky, and she lived near Chicago the site for next week's race.

Although he felt guilty for doing so, he turned on his cell phone and dialed her number. He told himself it was okay to continue with heterosexual friendships, but in his heart, he knew the girls were hoping he would fall in love with him. They talked for a while before he asked her if she would like to join him at the track for the weekend. She immediately answered affirmatively. T gave her the details and said he would pick her up late Friday afternoon. He sighed heavily after hanging up feeling tremendously guilty.

He checked his voicemail hoping Jack had called him. He made notes on the calls he wished to call back, as he rapidly deleted the current messages, but when he reached the end of the list, he sighed, as there was nothing from Jack. He frowned, and reluctantly began returning the calls.

Janet had made three calls to him, each one sounding more urgent so he dialed her first. "Hey, sorry I missed your calls. After working in the satellite studio all morning I came home, turned the phone off, and crashed."

"I sure you were beat from the big weekend in Daytona. We've may have a problem." She told him about the lunch meeting with Steve Appleton, including the photos he had with Jack and Thad together."

"What's the problem? Jack is just one of my friends."

Janet paused, "I think he believes there is more to the friendship. He wanted to know who Jack was, and I knew he would not stop until he found out. So I explained Jack was one of your school friends, wrote some speeches for you, but had to leave because he could not concentrate on writing his book."

"All that is true, so what is the problem?"

Janet switched hands on the phone and pushed a strand of hair back from her worried brow. "I sensed Steve was going to continue investigating Jack because he also had a copy of the memo from the media room in Florida accusing you of being gay and in a relationship with Jack. The fact that Jack recently left probably peaked his never ending reporter curiosity."

Thad rolled his head back, and then left and right trying to relieve the stress in his neck. "What should we do?"

"I think we should continue promoting all your good works, and to continue to treat the accusation as an attempt to blackmail you. You're on **Entertainment Tonight** for next three nights. We were lucky that Traci was with you while they were filming. Tomorrow I'll receive a copy of the feature story of you in **People Magazine**."

"That's good, but I think we should keep up the exposure. What other offers have you had for interviews."

Janet ran through a long list and Thad agreed to five more interviews—two in Charlotte and three in Chicago at the racetrack.

"Janet, am I flying up Friday to Chicago?"

She checked the schedule. "Yes, we leave at nine Friday morning."

"I think I want to go up on the private jet instead of with Drew and the gang. I want to fly to Greenville South Carolina. I heard about a children's home called Boys Home of the South, and it is near a former Air Force Base called Donaldson. She if you can arrange for a visit about ten. Then we'll fly to Memphis and visit that children's hospital named after Danny Thomas. By three we will stop in Cincinnati so I can check on my little friend Sammy Johnson.

"Are you writing all this down? Good, now call that sporting goods company called Ted's and tell them if they'll donate ten thousand dollars worth of equipment for the Boys Home, I'll put a patch with their name on my uniform for the Chicago race and call out their name with the rest of the sponsors."

Janet laughed, "You're shrewd, but a great idea."

He smiled, "I am not done. Have my accountant cut a check for fifty thousand to the hospital in Memphis, and have the graphic department make a four-foot long replica check to give them. I also need for you to call **Toys 'R Us** in Cincinnati and get them to donate a ton of toys for the Children Hospital. Tell them I'll do a commercial spot for them in exchange.

"Make sure we have tons of media there so I can promote each of the children facilities. I want to get maximum exposure out of this side trip. Find out what I can do to help kid groups in Chicago."

"My team and I will get right on this, and bring you up to date on Thursday."

Thad smiled, "Thanks and don't worry about Steve what's-his-name. He is an unknown reporter barking up the wrong tree, and after he hits a dead end, that'll be the end of his story."

"I hope you're right, but I think he is a tough one."

Thad laid the phone down feeling like there would always be people in the world who would do anything to bring him down. However, for the first time in his life, he had felt real love from Jack, and he knew beyond any doubt he was in love, too. He had never been in love, as most of his life racing had been his only focus. He noticed good-looking guys, but never spoke with them fearing he would be found out. He convinced himself he must act the part of a heterosexual he-man if that is what it took to win championships and make a career as a racecar driver. He thought maybe he could find a partner after his racing career was over, but that could be twenty years. After falling in love with Jack, he now felt two decades too long to wait for love.

Somehow, he thought, he must find a way for Jack to return while remaining a top driver. He did not know if that was possible because he knew if they were found out, everyone but Jack would be against him.

He picked up the DISH satellite remote control and flipped through the guide until he found the airing of **Entertainment Tonight**. He clicked to the channel and began waiting for the show to air. He picked up the cell phone and called his mom.

"Hey, Mom, guess who?"

"Hey, honey," she replied. "It is so good to hear from you. Congratulations on winning the race yesterday. The Daytona race is a big one to win."

"Yes it is and it felt great yesterday, but I'm exhausted today so I'm just hanging out at home. I just took a long nap. How is everything at home? Is dad okay?"

"We're good, and very proud of our son."

"That's great. I thought I would tell you for the next three nights I'm featured on **Entertainment Tonight,** and I'm in **People Magazine** that comes out Wednesday. Let me know what you think of the stories. I think the interviews went very well."

"I'll be sure to watch, and I have a subscription to **People** so the mailman will deliver it to me."

"Mom, there are several news organizations that are writing stories on me, and they may even look you up. They'll try to get you to say something personal about me so they can sell more papers with their sensational headlines. You're certainly free to do what you want, but I'd appreciate it if you wouldn't talk to them."

"Okay, honey. I would be too nervous to talk to them anyhow."

They talked on for a few more minutes before he said goodbye. He turned up the audio as the magazine show came on. He watched all the promos and thought Traci looked awesome. Every shot of him had her at his side. Mission accomplished, he thought. He liked the fast paced promos for continuing the story tomorrow, and it ended with him climbing out of the car in victory lane.

Afterwards he drove the Hummer to a local restaurant to pick up his take-out order. He hurried in and out with his hat pulled down tightly over his sunglasses. He returned home and sat at the kitchen table and ate, but feeling lonely.

Steve had flown into Des Moines Iowa and rented a car. He drove about eighty-five miles to the town of Marietta. It was late afternoon so he checked into a Holiday Inn Hotel, changed clothes, and went to the exercise room to work out. He followed it up with time in the sauna and a soak in the Jacuzzi. He got out of the water when a group of ten-year-old boys jumped into the small pool.

He ate while reading the local paper, especially the stories on Thad's victory at Daytona. He made some notes in his reporter pad, purchased a map, looked up the addresses of the schools, and marked each one on his map.

He arrived at the high school by eight-thirty the next morning. He met with the school's secretary, a guidance counselor, and even Thad's senior high school homeroom teacher doing a little redecorating in her room. He asked a series of questions before finally bringing up Thad's friend Jack. None of the school staff recalled Jack as a friend of Thad's. He then went to the school library where a nice librarian obtained the annuals for Thad's freshman through senior years for him. He chose a good close-up shot of Thad and Jack outside a hospitality tent and laid it on the table beside the books to refresh his memory. He began thumbing through every picture in the books and it took about ninety minutes. Disappointed, he thanked the librarian for her help and made his way to the middle school.

There he followed the same procedure, and felt a bit amazed the small town of Marietta had a middle school that also had annuals, but the results were the same—no Jack. At the elementary school, he had to settle for class pictures, and interviews the principal, secretary, and even the janitor, but no one knew of a Jack in school at about the same time as Thad. They all had great stories to tell about Thad's school year. He made notes in case his hunch played out so he could write a total story on the secret life of successful racecar champion Thad Nigel Thompson.

He found the house where Thad grew up and knocked at the door, but no one answered. He knocked again and there was still no answer. Thad's mother watched the reporter as he crossed their front lawn and knocked on the neighbor's door. He spoke with Mrs. Madison a few minutes, crossed the street, and went to every door on their block. She remained hidden at the corner of the drapes, and felt great relief when he finally got in his little blue rental sedan and drove away. She had followed Thad's advice by avoiding him.

On the flight home, Steve made notes and questions about his visit. So far, he had found no one that knew Jack. As was his custom, he played his own devil's advocate by punching holes in his potential story. Maybe Thad met Jack at a summer camp, a sport league, or in another town while visiting a relative. Maybe he was a cousin, or someone who moved into the town for a few months, and then moved away, and the locals just simply did not remember him. Maybe Thad had said school friend as a simpler explanation as to how they met. He wondered if Thad had been in trouble, and met Jack at a counseling session for reckless driving, drinking while driving, or even drugs.

By the end of the flight he had little to report to his boss about his theory, so he decided not to tell him about the note he received in Daytona, but rather told him he was doing an in depth story on who he felt was going to be this year's champion. His boss liked the idea and left him alone while signing off on his travel expense report.

Thad turned the television off, stripped off his street clothes, and fell naked in the bed longing for Jack as he began playing with penis. He thought back over his conversation with Janet and recalled her saying Jack was a school friend from Thad's past. "Damn," he said aloud.

He realized he should never have said school friend and wished he could take it back. He thought a good reporter would most likely find that fact to false. He no longer felt confident, and at night he often lay awake, either thinking about the pending disaster if they found out he was gay, or thinking about Jack and wondering what he was doing.

About four in the morning, he recalled the name of Bailey, the Labrador belonging to Jack's friend. It took him a while longer to remember the lady's name. It was Jesse. He then fell asleep.

By nine the next morning he was half way to Boone. He drove to Jack's house hoping to find him there, but after climbing over the gate, his knock at the door went unanswered. He saw no recent tire tracks in the driveway. He went to the mailbox, and found nothing but junk mail there. He climbed in the car, closed his eyes, and tried to remember the route they took to Jesse's house. He began to drive and after a few wrong turns he found her house. He stepped out of the Hummer and immediately Bailey came running to him, and leaped up as if attempting to give him a hug. Thad dropped to one knee, gave the dog a hug, rubbed his ears, and laughed at how rapidly his tail was flying back and forth.

"I think he remembers you," said Jesse as she came out on the porch.

Thad stood and walked over to her, "Do you remember me?"

"Yes, of course, you're Jack's boyfriend."

Hearing the truth made him smile. He decided not to respond affirmatively. "Jesse, may I speak with you?"

She sensed something was wrong the moment he arrived alone and without Jack. "Come on in. Would you like some lemonade?"

"Yes, that would be fine. Thank you."

Thad and Bailey followed her into the house. He sat down on her sofa as she brought the glass to him. He took several gulps while collecting his thoughts.

"Jesse, I know you don't know me very well, but I really need someone to talk to. There is no one in my world that can help me."

116

"You're in love with Jack aren't you?"

Her boldness stunned him, but he nodded affirmatively. "I would have to deny that if you told the reporters..."

She cut him off, "I hate reporters, and your secret is safe with me. Jack is a long time friend. We both volunteered for a fund-raiser in conjunction with the first Gay Pride parade in Asheville. That was four years ago. When my partner died of AIDS a year later, Jack is the friend I counted on most. He helped me through the final days, took care of all the funeral arrangements, and lived with me until I could get back on my feet.

"Did he tell you four months after the funeral he bought Bailey for me?"

"No, he didn't," replied Thad. "No wonder he cares about Bailey so much."

She smiled, "See, he never takes credit for doing good deeds. He came home one day with this small six-week-old little ball of fur. I had never owned a pet in my life, but when he placed Bailey in my arms, well, I was instantly smitten. Jack knew he would soon have to get back to traveling with his work, so he wanted me to have something I could love, and he knew when this puppy grew he would protect me.

"Bailey became my guardian angel. He listens to me when I'm sad, and practically laughs with me when I'm happy. Bailey and Jack got me back on my feet again, and helped me to stop feeling sorry for myself. I'm working again and became a trainer for Hospice—you know the folks that can come to your home when a love one is dying. It is a great group that allows people to die with dignity and in the comfort of their home surrounded by their loved ones."

She paused and reached over and squeezed Thad's hand. "Honey, we could sit here for hours talking about me, but I think you need to do the talking."

Tears swelled in his eyes, and Thad's pent up feelings finally let loose, "Jesse, I love Jack with my heart, and I know he loves me, too."

"So what's the problem—other than it is illegal for gay folks to get married."

Thad smiled, "In my racing world, the word 'gay' is a four letter word. Remember my sport started as a redneck league, but has become a conglomerate of business and technical folks from all over the country. It is a huge business requiring the support of big sponsors. Those sponsors worry constantly about their image. Therefore, the image of the gladiator encircling the track at hundred and ninety miles an hour creates a gigantic hero that no one could possibly live up to. People of all generations want your autograph, and they want to touch you. My boss expects me to act in a certain way, so the sponsors remain happy which keeps the checks coming in.

"There's a huge camaraderie between the men in his crew, the shop, and his boss. They would not accept a homosexual gas or tire man, and they certainly would not accept me as a driver."

She sighed, "But you're the best there is at your sport." She laughed at herself, "I'm sorry, Jack didn't tell you I was a huge Dale Earnhardt Junior fan until you came along. I've read every story about you. You had my heart long before me and Bailey met you. So, let me see if I understand, Jack does not like living in the closet, but apparently, he was doing so for you. He doesn't flaunt being gay like the queens in the Gay Pride parade, but rather prefers to a quiet but honest life. If asked if he was gay, he would say yes and say it proudly.

"You, on the other hand, feel trapped because you love the sport of racing almost as much as you love Jack." She squeezed his hand again.

T looked into her eyes and knew every word she spoke to be true. Thad said, "In Cincinnati, a former rebuffed acquaintance of Jack's showed up at an autograph signing. He approached Jack first, and then surmised Jack and I were lovers. He had me sign his photo of me to Jack. It was humiliating but I did it, and then we got the hell out of there.

"I thought that would be the end of it, but this man showed up in Daytona, and demanded money for his silence. Jack and I did not pay him. We discussed this situation over and over looking for a solution. Before we came up with a plan, Jack disappeared. He left me a note saying he never wanted me to lose my career over him, and that he would go away, write speeches for his clients, and work on his book."

"Have you heard from him?"

"No, not a word, and he doesn't answer my calls to his cell phone. I have no idea where he is, and I desperately need to talk to him, and to hold him."

"I know, love is such a wonderful thing, but sometimes, it can be very hard. So what are you going to do?"

"After I dried my tears, I set about a plan to appear as macho as possible. I did interviews with a pretty girl at my side. You should watch Entertainment Tonight and pick up this week's People magazine. I have lined up tours of hospitals and orphanages, and arranged for another girl to be with me in Chicago on Friday. I will not pay this man a dime because I know that will not bring Jack back. I don't know if I'm doing the right thing. I don't know what to do?

"There's a reporter out of Charlotte that is on my trail. He believes a memo handed out by the blackmailer in Daytona, and he is seeking Jack out. I checked this morning's newspaper before I left and there was nothing in it, so he hasn't found Jack either."

"If you came out, the blackmail would stop, and so would the hounding by the reporter, but what do you think would happen to you at the track?"

His brow wrinkled and she could see the lines of worry on his face. "Well, my sponsors would probably drop me, and then my owner could drop me as well. There is a clause in my contract allowing my boss to cancel if I am arrested, or caught driving drunk in a street car, do drugs, or become involved in a sex scandal. I guess this comes under sex scandal.

"At the track, my pit crew could begin making mistakes, people would call me names, I would probably get punched from time to time, and on the track they could accidentally crash into me. I would go from hero to zero in a flash."

"Honey, there isn't a good answer on what you should do, because only you can decide what is best for you. Jack loves you enough to step away, so you would not be hurt. He loves you enough to let you go."

"But I don't want to be let go. I want to be with him. I want to feel his soft kisses on my face, and to hear his heartbeat in my ear as I lay on his chest. I want to feel his arms around me, and I want to make love to him all night long."

"Oh dear," she smiled, "you are going to give me hot flashes, and I am lesbian for Pete's sake!" Jesse pretended to fan her blushing face.

He smiled as he sighed loudly. "If you hear from him, will you tell him I love him, and that I want him to come home?"

"Yes, I will, but so far I haven't heard from him, but I do think he will call. He always checks in on me from time to time."

"Good," Thad dried his eyes with his hands. "I don't know what I'm going to do but for now, I'm just taking it a day at a time."

"That's all any of us can do—just put one foot in front of the other and try to keep going. It is how I got over my partner's death, but then again, Bailey dragged me forward. He gained a hundred pounds in his first four months. What a dog!"

They both laughed as Bailey jumped up at the sound of his name and started wagging his huge friendly tail. T got down on the floor and played with Bailey for a while, and then gave Jesse a hug and left. He left a card with his private cell phone number on it on the coffee table, and he hoped she would soon call with news about Jack.

Steve spent the rest of the week continuing to research every article on TNT. He studied every photograph they had on file, and began interviewing the photographers who covered NARC. They produced more unpublished photos, and found several shots of Thad and Jack laughing as they waited for an event to start. He felt they were certainly good friends, but he could not find a single photo of the boys holding hands, or displaying any physical affection.

Disappointed, he knew he was going to either drop the story, or begin using his bag of tricks. His instinct told him to keep going so he went to

119

his editor with an idea. He showed him a picture of Thad and Jack standing shoulder to shoulder in the pit watching qualifying. "I want to publish this picture because this guy is Thad's long time best friend, and I must find him."

The editor sat back in his big leather desk chair after studying the photo, and removed his glasses. "Why do you need to talk to him?"

Steve immediately knew he was going to have to tell his editor his hunch, or his story would come to halt right then. "Two reasons: One, I can't find a single childhood friend that will talk about the real Thad."

"The 'real' Thad," replied the editor stressing the word real.

"Yes, and that brings me to reason number two: I think Thad is a homosexual."

"Oh my," replied the editor, "how did you come to that conclusion?"

Steve produced the note he received in Daytona. "This was passed out in the media room in Daytona. No one took it seriously because Thad had just won the race. He's a superstar. They probably thought it was a joke."

"And you didn't?"

"I admit I first thought so, but then I wondered if there had been a failed attempt at blackmail. Can you imagine if Thad was gay, how much money he would pay to keep it quiet?"

"That's a big if, but he might have decided not to pay a dime, hence, the release of this vague note," replied the editor. "Have you found anyone else that would say he is gay?"

"Not yet? However, somehow things don't quite add up. I was told this guy's name is Jack, but his publicist would not release his last name. I was told he was a school friend from his childhood, but I have been to all his schools, and not one person knew who the man in the picture was. They also could not recall a friend of Thad's called Jack. I even went through all the annuals searching for his picture in hopes of finding his name was not really Jack at all."

The editor asked, "What did you find?"

"Ah, the question is what didn't I find. Quite simply, this Jack does not exist anywhere in Thad's past. I think Janet Anderson lied to me, or she was lied to by Thad."

"Okay, so a few things don't add up, so where's the story?"

"There has never been an out of the closet person in NARC—not even a pit crew member, but most certainly not a sensational driver who could win another championship this year. It's just like the most of the other major pro sports—no one has come out of the closet while they were still playing. However, in NARC, no one has come out even after they retired. If Thad is gay, this will be the biggest sports story of the year."

"But wait a minute, we're not a tabloid newspaper," warned the editor.

"You're right, we're not. I don't want to print a story until I have the facts, and know for sure Thad is gay. That is why I'm here. I need your help."

120

"How so?"

"I must find this guy they call Jack. He is the key. I think he may be Thad's secret lover. I want to publish his picture after trimming Thad out of the picture with a simply caption—do you know this man? If so, email me at Steve@CharlotteTimes.com. If I'm lucky, someone will know him, correct me on his name, and tell me how I can find him."

"You'll be very lucky, but I'm game. We haven't hurt anything by trying."

"We'll put it in the Sunday edition."

"I would like to cover the Chicago race this weekend."

"Okay, I'll get Martha to make the arrangements. Keep me posted. I hope this hunch is found untrue, but if it is true, I want to be the first newspaper to print the exact truth and nothing less."

"Yes sir," replied Steve as he stood and left.

Thad arrived early at the airport on Friday morning to begin his long day with three promotional stops before arriving in Chicago for the race. The first flight was a short one to Greenville South Carolina. Janet carried her notebook outlining all the details she and her staff had arranged in just three days. They touched down to find a large freight truck with a painted sign displaying Ted's Sporting Goods on the side. As Thad stepped out of his Lear jet, Ted Livingston met him.

"Good morning," said the tall former pro baseball player with thinning hair, and a warm friendly smile. Thad thought he like looked more like a former basketball player because of his height.

Thad shook his hand firmly, "Ted, I can't thank you enough for your willingness to help these kids."

"My pleasure and I think it is going to be a great day for all of us."

"Why don't we take some pictures of us in front of your big truck?" Thad knew Ted's staff would be eager to take all the promo shots they could. They moved over and stood in front of the truck as the photographers from most of the local and national medial took their shots. Thad did a quick interview with the local sportscaster for channel four. Fifteen minutes later, they left for the drive to Belton and the Boys Home.

Thad arrived in a limousine with the big truck trailing behind him. A member of Janet's staff had arrived earlier, and arranged the kids in rows so that when Thad stepped out of the limo they could get a photograph with the kids greeting him. The administrator stood by on the sidelines, and let the photographers get their shots. Thad shook his hand and thanked him for allowing him to visit. Of course, the administrator was equally thankful.

Soon the doors of the big truck opened and the men began unloading all the sporting equipment. The children carried in basketballs, baseballs, footballs, and the men carried in the bigger pieces. The administrator gave

Thad and Ted a tour of their campus. Thad picked up younger boys and posed for pictures. T learned that Ted was quite a ham as well, so he started handing him children, and Janet's team got a great shot with each man holding two children each with their new TNT racing hats on.

In Memphis, the press throng grew to three times the size of Greenville. Thad took his time as he went to see every single child, and left multiple toys from Toy 'R Us in their hands. An executive for the company had flown in so Thad graciously agreed to drive over to a local store on his way back to airport to pose for promos there as well. The store was thrilled and the children smiled gleefully. Janet checked the second stop off as a big success as well.

Tim sat on his couch flipping through the television channels trying to find something to watch. He called in faking sick, but actually depressed. He had started counting his blackmail money, and felt cheated when he came home from Daytona with not a single dollar of Thad's money in his pocket. He was shocked when not a single member of the news media believed him. He had been afraid to put his name to the announcement because he thought the police might arrest him for blackmail.

After stopping on the CNN channel, he nearly dropped the remote when he suddenly saw Thad's picture on his screen. The story showed him visiting the hospital in Memphis, and then cut to a live shot with their reporter on the scene. "Thad, I understand this had been a busy day for you with stops in Greenville and Memphis, so where are you stopping next?"

Thad smiled and announced, "I'm on my way to Cincinnati to visit the children's hospital, and my little friend Sammy. By late afternoon, I'll be in Chicago to practice and prepare for qualifying for this weekend's race."

Tim leaped from the couch and ran to his room to dress. He left the house without locking the door, and drove quickly to the Cincinnati Children's Hospital. He parked his car and walked to the lobby where he found a group of reporters already gathering for Thad's arrival. He leaned against the wall behind the group and waited.

ELEVEN

Thad and Janet arrived in Cincinnati feeling euphoric and pleased as to how well the day was going. Janet's assistant checked her watch and began passing out media kits to all of the reporters waiting for Thad's arrival. T personally carried the four-foot long check out of the Lear jet by himself. A group of photographers had been waiting at the airport so he quickly posed with the check, and immediately felt guilty for doing so.

After they managed to get the long cardboard check in the limo T leaned over to Janet and said, "I wish I hadn't done that. I'm giving the money to the hospital because the kids need it. I should not have made it look so self-serving."

Janet smiled, "Get over it. When folks see you promoting this hospital with your own money, they are going to start sending in checks left and right to help this place. Try to find a way to encourage the locals to volunteer their help here, too. These kids need people with friendly faces."

T smiled, "You are so right. Okay, I'm over it, and I will ask for volunteers. Did I ever tell you just how clever you are?"

"Yeah, right," she replied with a laugh.

They pulled up to the hospital, and suddenly felt like they had arrived at a movie premier. With all the media reporting Thad was coming back to Cincinnati, the fans began swarming on the grounds of the hospital. The hospital rented a roll of red carpet, and T soon opened the door of the limo and stepped out the carpet. He stood there a few minutes allowing everyone to take his picture before pulling the big check out of the car. He made his way inside, and quickly moved to the elevator. He found the previously unsmiling administrator inside and now smiling from ear to ear.

"We're so glad to have you back," said the man politely.

Thad shook his hand and grinned, "It's great to be back. Let's do the check thing after I see how well you are taking care of my little friends. How is Sammy doing?"

"I am pleased to report he has gained ten pounds since you were last here, and he is doing his physical therapy. His doctor says he is doing very well."

"Thank you for taking care of him." T paused and then asked, "Can Sammy eat pizza?"

The administrator was taken back and swallowed hard before replying, "Yes, I guess he can from time to time."

"What pizza place do you recommend near the hospital?"

The administrator quickly tried to think, and then recalled his daughter liked Pettie's. "Pettie's Pizza," he replied.

Thad removed a hundred dollar bill from his pocket. "Sir, if you could do me a favor. While I am visiting the kids, would you pick up four large supreme pizzas and soft drinks, and deliver them to Sammy's room for me. Sammy, Janet and I are going to eat lunch with him?"

The door opened so Janet and Thad stepped out of the elevator leaving the administrator remaining inside feeling stunned at the request. They turned the corner and started laughing. Janet managed to speak first, "You are hysterical. I wish we had pictures of his face. He did not know what to do."

"It felt good to boss him around a little. Okay, let's get to work."

Rhonda Stevens met them in the hallway outside the children's floor. Thad smiled and gave her a big hug, "How's my favorite nurse doing?"

"Great, and our buddy Sammy is doing so much better. Shall we go see him first?"

Thad grinned slyly, "That is tempting, but no I want to see him last. I have a surprise for him. Let's go see all the kids and afterwards, your administrator is delivering lunch to Sammy's room. Would you like to join us for some fresh pizza?"

An astonished smile appeared on her face, "My administrator is buying lunch?"

"No, I paid for it, but he is picking it up. Do you think he expects a tip?" asked Thad sarcastically. "Come on let's go. I'm ready!" replied Thad. "I'm anxious to see the kids." He went from room to room, interrupted therapy sessions with many apologies to all, met new kids, and spent about ninety minutes going from one to bed to the next. He signed autographs, tickled toes, gave out kisses to the girls, and hugs for all the boys. He could not have been more enthusiastic. He left everyone feeling happier and confident.

He asked, "Is that the last room?" he asked as they reached the end of the hall.

"Yes, are you ready for Sammy?" Rhonda led them down the next hall and into Sammy's room.

Sammy's eyes brighten as he gave Thad a huge smile. Thad went to him and gave him a big hug, "Howdy, pal? How are you? Are you feeling better?"

"Yes, I am. I can't believe you came back to see me?"

"I told you I would. I hear you have been eating and gained a few pounds."

"I have. I have gained ten pounds," said the boy proudly.

Thad gave him a high five, "That's the way to do it."

They talked for a while, and then the door to his room suddenly opened. The administrator walked in with four boxes of pizza and plastic grocery bag of soft drinks. He set them down the table. Thad immediately walked to him, "Sammy, this is the administrator, and he was nice enough to pick up lunch for us. Do you like pizza?"

"Yeah, sure," replied the boy gleefully.

"Good," replied Thad as he turned to administrator and shook his hand, "Sir, thank you very much. You have been most helpful today. Would you mind doing me just one more favor?"

Warily the administrator responded with a soft tone, "It would be my pleasure."

Thad grinned, "Would you go downstairs and get the media ready? Tell them I'll be down soon, and I'll present you this check." Thad pointed at the big check leaning against the wall.

The administrator smiled at the sight of the check, "Yeah, sure. I'd be happy to." The administrator left.

They all waited for the door to close before speaking, "How in the world did you get him to pick up the pizza, and then easily send him downstairs?" asked Rhonda.

"He's all about money, so I just politely reminded him of that by pointing at the check."

They all laughed as Rhonda and Janet scooped out a plate of pizza for Sammy and Thad. The four of them ate until no one could eat another slice. Thad spent about an hour with Sammy and made him promise to keep working on getting well. Sadly, he forced himself to say goodbye, and asked Rhonda to share the remaining pizzas with her patients and staff.

T tried to see himself in the stainless steel reflection in the elevator, "Did I get the pizza off my face?"

Janet gave him a quick check as they rode the elevator down to the lobby. "Yep, you'll do. This visit was so much fun. Are you ready for the presentation?"

"Yes, I am. I'll try to promote the hospital as best I can, and then we're off to Chicago and get ready to race."

The door opened and the lobby was packed. The security guards put up red ropes to give him a path to walk to a small platform with a podium and pile of media microphones all poised around it. The administrator waited on the back of the stage. Thad and Janet made their way there. Thad leaped on the stage and began speaking immediately.

"Ladies and gentlemen, I am so happy to be back in the great city of Cincinnati, and to visit one of my favorite hospitals. I am pleased to see the children doing so well, especially my little buddy Sammy. He has gained ten pounds and looking great. I want to thank the administrator, and all the staff for the special work they do for the kids. I am pleased to bring along a little check..." Janet handed him the four-foot check, "for fifty thousand dollars to help these kids get well. I want to encourage all my sponsors, and all the racings fans around American to please send in their checks to help."

The administrator walked forward and Thad presented him the check and posed for pictures. Once the check ceremony completed, Thad turned back to the microphone. "I would like to ask the great folks in Cincinnati to volunteer to help these kids with your time. They need to see more smiling faces. I am counting on you to help. I'm so glad the media is here to help us promote this great institution, I have a few minutes before I have to fly to Chicago to prepare for this weekend's race, but time for some questions."

Thad began answering questions from the reporters as Janet looked over the group. She recognized various faces, but when her eye caught sight of Tim, she nearly choked. Instantly she knew who he was and wondered why he was here. She turned back to T and began hoping he would wrap up the question period so they could get out of there. He did about ten questions before he saw Janet pointing at her watch, indicating he should wrap it up.

He gave her a slight puzzled look, but did as requested, "Well, that's it folks. Thank you so much for coming. Let's go racing!" There was immediate applause from the hospital staff and visitors, and even some of the reporters.

Just as T stepped off the stage and turned to the door, Tim leaped on the far end of the stage, moved quickly to podium, and began yelling, "I know a big secret about Thad. Do you want to know what it is?" Everyone stopped moving and talking, and turned back to the stage. Thad and Janet were almost to the door. Tim pointed at him, "Thad is a homosexual, and in love with Jack Langston!"

The room fell silent. No one knew what to do. The administrator smiled slyly. The head of hospital security acted first ordering two of his men to remove Tim from the podium and the hospital.

Tim struggled to free himself from their grip, "Did you hear me? He is gay and trying hard to keep it a secret. America's top racecar driver is a homo, a fag, a queer and doing his best to hide it."

The reporters all turned to look at Thad. Janet's face turned red. Thad slowly smiled, "I hope they have room for this guy on the top floor. He obviously needs some help, if you know what I mean. See you at the races." He took Janet's arm, smiled at the crowd, and walked out the door to the limo.

"Wait! Wait!" exclaimed Tim as the guards began pushing him off the stage. By the time they had him out the door the limo was gone. The guards let Tim go, and told him to get off the property.

As Tim began walking to his car, Steve Appleton walked up. "May I ask you a few questions?"

Tim was angry at being escorted out of the building so he turned around quickly as if ready to hit Steve, but immediately smiled and let loose his fist. "Sure, but I think I had better get out of here."

"Let's go to the park across the street and sit down and talk. I would like to interview you."

"Sure, let's go."

Steve opened his courier case and lifted out the eight by ten photos of Thad and Jack. "Do you know the guy standing next to Thad?"

Tim looked through several of the photos and grinned, "Yes, I do. That's how I found out about Thad. Jack and I met a while back, and well, he rather had a thing for me, but I told him no as he was too young for me. Poor thing couldn't stand the rejection, and he called me forever. I had not seen him for about a year, but a few weeks ago, he turns up in the mall here in Cincinnati. Thad was doing an autograph thing. I realized they were a couple, and confronted Thad by having him sign an autograph picture to Jack. He did it, but they left immediately afterwards."

"But how do you know they are a couple?" asked Steve.

"I flew down for the Daytona race, and got a pit pass. I spotted them together several times," replied Tim with great confidence.

"Did you see them show any affection? Were they holding hands? Did they kiss?"

"No, I only got to see them for a few minutes."

"So you have never seen them do anything sexually together? I don't see how you can surmise Thad is gay. You said Jack came on to you—did the two of you have sex together? Did you and Jack share any gay moments?"

"No, we did not."

"And you did not see Jack and Thad having a gay moment either—so where's the connection?"

Tim thought for a minute and then answered matter-of-factly, "Have you ever heard of gaydar?"

Steve laughed, "Yes, I know what that is. You're saying you can tell whether a man is gay or not from a distance. Is that all the evidence you have? That's not enough to accuse somebody. His lawyers will probably sue your ass. Have you thought of that?"

"Let them try and my lawyers will dig up the dirt on them. I'll make millions," bragged Tim, though he had no lawyers at all.

Steve thought for a second and then pulled the slip of paper he received in the media center at Daytona. "Did you type and hand this out?"

Tim looked at it and smiled, "So what if I did?"

"I am trying figure out why you are so bent on bringing Thad down. He obviously is not in love with you, nor shown any interest in you, so what is the point of putting out this memo, and then jumping up on the stage at the press conference and making your brief speech? What do you gain from all this?"

Tim fidgeted with the collar on his shirt a few moments, "I just thought it would end Jack's idea of having me."

Steve frowned and rolled his eyes at this guy's ego, "Okay, let's say you want to stop Jack from chasing you, why bring Thad into it? Doesn't he have a right to his own privacy? If Jack were an item with Thad, why would Jack still be after you? You're much older than Jack, and I'm sorry, but Thad is a way better looking."

127

"You don't get it, do you? The way to hurt Jack is to hurt Thad's wallet and fame."

Steve heard the whole statement, but the part that stuck in his mind, the part about Thad's wallet, brought him to his next question. "Was this memo in Daytona an attempt to blackmail Thad? Were you trying to get money from him? Is that what you're doing?"

Tim answered quickly, "Oh please. My mom is rich. Why do I need his money?"

At that very moment, Steve knew Tim was lying. He changed his tact, "Okay, so I'm going to write this big story, but before my editor will let me print it I have to have all the facts. Let's start with the easy stuff. What is your full name? What is your age? Where were you born? What is your address? What is your telephone number? Do you have a criminal record?" Steve kept asking the questions because he knew he wasn't going to get answer from any of them.

"I don't have to tell you anything!" Tim stood to leave, and then turned around, and smiled slyly, "If you don't print this story I'll find someone who will, and it'll be your lost."

"Maybe, but I only want to print the truth, and if you're not willing to confirm who you are, and your motive, then you're not a source I can use."

Tim turned and left. Steve put his photos and papers back in the courier case while thinking. He had assumptions, but no evidence. He had pictures, but nothing seedy. He would have to keep digging as he suspected there was a story here, but not the way Tim was telling it.

Unfortunately for Thad, the television stations showed a clip of Tim getting up on the stage at the end of Thad's presentation. They said they could not confirm the man's accusations, but kept the audio up so the television audience could hear what he said. By the time Thad's plane landed in Chicago there were a dozen reporters from various television networks with a major sports network going live as he came out of the plane.

"Thad? Thad? What is your response to the man's accusations in Cincinnati?" yelled the reporters.

T frowned, "I think the man's elevator doesn't go to the top floor, if you know what I mean." Thad and Janet kept moving to the waiting Hummer.

"But sir, he called you a homosexual. Are you denying you are gay?"

"I'm not going to get in a spitting contest with you. The man needs help. Let's don't beat him up about it. I'm sure with proper counseling he will be fine. My job is to race and win, and that is exactly why I'm here in Chicago." He turned and slid into the car and pulled the door closed.

"But are you gay?" The Hummer pulled away as the reporter finished his question.

Thad rubbed above his nose with his thumb and index finger, "I'm getting a headache. This Tim guy is driving me nuts. Is it illegal to have him kidnapped, and shipped to Greenland or something?"

"Yes, it is. I thought you answered well, but you did not say you were not gay. I think they will ask you again and again until you answer negatively."

"I didn't see it that way. The man is trying to bring me down and for what reason? Did I do anything to harm him? No, of course not, but he is a sick bastard..." he paused and sighed before adding, "that needs help."

"Drew is going to hear about this one, but not from me. All the sports networks were there, and he is a fanatical ESPN and Speed channel fan. I'm surprised my phone isn't already..." her phone started ringing just as she finished her sentence. "ringing." They both looked at it. She saw the Caller ID and hit the talk button, "Drew, how are you?" She rolled her eyes at Thad.

"Are you in Chicago yet?"

"Yes, sir, we just touched down, and on our way to the motorcoach. We did three cities today and all were a huge success."

"I just saw the clip on that nut at the hospital. I don't want you to go back to Cincinnati. We can't afford that kind of publicity."

"I understand. The man is most likely deranged, and probably assumed because Thad's little friend Sammy has AIDS that Thad must be gay. It is really sad, but we're putting it behind us and moving forward for this weekend's plans. When are you flying up?"

"Tonight in time for the Pepsi dinner so I can keep these sponsors happy. I'll see you in the morning."

"Right boss, so fly safe. Bye." She looked up at Thad. "He doesn't want us to go back to Cincinnati again. I guess he is right—we can't afford another incident with Tim."

"But that's not fair to Sammy. I promised I would be back." He paused and looked out the window as they drove away from the airport. "I'll just have to fly in unannounced and in secret—maybe even at night. I won't disappoint that little boy."

"Okay, but let's keep that just between you and me, okay?" She reached over and patted his knee. "Let's hope that bastard doesn't show up at the track."

Thad chewed his lip and replied, "If he does, it would be very tempting for me to accidentally run over him." He smiled to let her know he was kidding.

She smiled back and squeezed his hand. "Hang in there. We've got a race to win, you know, so try to cheer up!"

Thad rushed into his motorcoach and locked the door. He turned the stereo on, tuned in his favorite XM Satellite Radio channel, cranked it up, stripped, and walked to the shower. Twenty minutes later, he came out of the coach and drove to Becky's house. She had received his email the day before inviting her to the Pepsi dinner. She appeared at the door in a beautiful blue informal dinner dress. Thad smiled as he held the door for and gave her a little cheek kiss.

"My goodness you are gorgeous," he said.

She laughed, "Modern science still works. Grab my dress bag and suitcase, and let's go. I'm starved."

"Yes ma'am," replied Thad. Unlike many girls he dated, Becky was a lady who took charge from the get go. She had taken second in the Miss America Beauty Pageant three years ago, and served as a hostess for both Miss Illinois and Miss America Pageant organizations. She received her training from a twenty year veteran hostess who taught her that when she was traveling with Miss America she was to always take charge, and don't take no for answer. She handled her personal life in much the same way.

Thad trudged behind her pulling the suitcase while she waited for him to open the car door for her. He laughed as he helped her in the Hummer and loaded the luggage in the back.

"I like your new Hummer. It suits you. How's the stereo?"

T punched the power button, and adjusted the volume. He knew she hated rock music so he dazzled her with XM's channel 71 and smooth jazz. The music of Dave Koz filled the car.

"Now that sounds awesome. Good pick. Where are we eating dinner?"

T stepped on the gas after glancing at the clock. He had twenty minutes to get to the dinner at a huge Marriott not far from the track. "The Marriott, for the Pepsi dinner," he replied, "where I have to give a short speech, but former pro football player Roger Stauback is the featured speaker. If the food isn't good, just fake it, and we'll get something as soon as we can get out of there."

"I met Roger as the Miss Texas Pageant a few years ago. He was a judge and a true gentleman." She reached over and gave T's hand a squeeze. "I'm glad you invited me. It is the first weekend I have been at home in a long time. I'm looking forward to the race."

"Let's hope I win. I've got to keep moving up in the points."

"You'll get it. You're a winner—on and off the track."

They arrived at the dinner via a back entrance and almost immediately spotted Drew. T walked towards him holding hands with Becky. He introduced her to him and old Drew's face just beamed at the couple. He made a few jokes and then a blunt remark. "Thad, why don't we just get this marriage thing over and done with? I just shook hands with Eddie Jones, NARC's chaplain, and I'm sure if I ask, he'll marry the two of you right now! You'll never find a prettier lady, and I am a good judge of beautiful women."

130

Thad wished he would stop, but he didn't. Drew leaned towards Becky, "He needs a woman that knows how to take charge, and I'm told you are excellent at making decisions."

Becky smiled and winked at him, "Not me, I'm actually very shy person."

Thad and Drew both laughed as Drew responded, "Honey, you're anything but shy, and I like you. Thad, please introduce her to my wife. She's gone to the powder room, but we'll see you on stage. Thad, do you have your speech ready."

"Yeah, it is one that Jack wrote for me." Though proud of Jack's work, he wished he had left his name out of his response. He quickly added, "Janet and I had a great day with our promotions. Our sponsors should be pleased with all the exposure they received."

"Very well, I'll look forward to hearing you. Well, let's go eat. I'm starved," added Drew as he led them towards the stage in his motorized wheelchair.

As soon as Thad and Becky walked onto the stage, the audience of just over five thousand stood and cheered. Thad waved at the crowd as the Master of Ceremonies introduced him and former Miss Illinois Becky Yost. They both stood as the spotlight found them and waved at the crowd.

Becky whispered to him, "Gees, I guess I should have worn my diamond crown."

Thad shot back, "Yeah, and I should have worn my helmet because next to you I feel pretty ugly!"

They were still laughing by the time they sat down. The dinner was surprisingly very good with their conversation mostly spent on catching up with what had been happening in their lives since their last date. After dessert, the speeches began, and T was second on the bill. He talked about the importance of taking care of the less fortunate, and told stories about the children he had recently met in the hospital. He thanked Pepsi for their sponsorship and support of his team, and he ended by saying he was going to win tomorrow's race and the championship. The crowd cheered and applauded as he left the podium to return to his seat. Drew gave him a high five as he went pass and sat down with Becky.

"You are absolutely charming. What a ham you are!" she whispered.

"Thanks. We have about thirty more minutes—are you okay?"

"Yes, of course. I'll be fine."

They listened intently to Stauback's speech on motivating employees. Thad made some mental notes on points he wanted to remember, but especially loved the part where Roger said you can never make a mistake when you have another's best interest at heart. While the crowd stood to applaud Roger, Thad felt he could have led Becky through the curtain for a quick exit, but he wanted to meet Roger, so they waited a little longer for the program to end.

As they left the banquet hall, they ran in to a group of reporters. Holding Becky's hand, T stopped so they could take their pictures. Several asked for a comment on Sunday's race. T obliged, and just as he was about to say thank you and head for the parking lot, he heard a voice from the back ask him a question, "Thad, do you have a comment on the man accusing you of being a homosexual in Cincinnati?"

The hair stood up on Thad's neck, and he could feel Becky's hand tense up. He sighed before responding, "I hesitate to respond because I feel this man has a sickness, and because my personal life is my business. I have never answered personal questions before, and I'm not changing that practice. Good day gentlemen."

As they drove away, Thad began to apologize to Becky for the encounter. "Oh honey," she began, "I've been called every name in the book including a dyke all because I told a security guard who had not done his job that he was a lazy louse. The more famous and successful you become, the harder they try to bring you down. That's the price you pay for being a racecar champion, and it has nothing to do with your driving ability." She paused and reached over and squeezed his hand, "Although I was tempted to take Drew's advice and marry you in front of the Pepsi crowd." She laughed, as did Thad.

"Yeah, me, too, but I'm not ready to settle down. I feel like I am a man on a mission. I want to see more of the world, and experience all the adventure I can before I settle down and have kids."

"Then you should do exactly as you want to do, and to hell with anyone that gets in the way. That's a tip I use quite often. Don't let anyone push you into anything you don't want to do. When you meet the person you just can't live without, I hope they'll enjoy seeing the world with you."

The next day Becky watched him practice and qualify, but then he took her shopping where she returned with a few items to help decorate his coach. He wondered what Jack would think of her interior design touches. They decided to grill out and avoid the media, enjoying lemon peppered grill chicken, a Greek salad, and red skinned potatoes, and a bottle of wine.

Becky wanted sex, so Thad cut the lights off and let her take charge. He wasn't sure he would be able to obtain an erection without closing his eyes and thinking of Jack's body, but once achieved, he rolled a condom on his tool just seconds before she mounted him. Afterwards, she remained at his side while she slept, but it took T over an hour to drift off. His mind replayed the trip on Friday, and the question of his sexuality creeping up in almost every encounter with the press. NARC's media friends enjoyed the openness of interviewing their drivers, just seconds after a win or a wreck, so that it would be difficult to attempt to avoid them. He felt very frustrated Tim once again spoiled his attempts to appear to be anything but a homosexual.

132

Steve and his newspaper's photographer secretly followed Thad everywhere he went on Saturday and Sunday. He hoped to get a shot of Thad and Jack, or Thad and any other male, but always at his side was Becky. He also watched for Tim but apparently, he had not made the trip up to Chicago.

Becky waited in the golf cart with Janet, one of her new best friends, during driver introductions. The crowd of two hundred thousand usually booed him, but this time Thad heard some drunks yelling 'faggot' at him, as he came across the stage and boarded the pickup truck for the customary ride and wave around the track. From time to time, he heard the word again from someone in the crowd. He never acted like he heard their jeers as he continued smiling and waving at the folks wearing his team's colors.

Becky gave him a kiss as he climbed in the car. Her warm smile displayed a little worry, as if knowing he could die today in a bad wreck, and hugged him tightly. "I'll be saying prayers for your safety today."

He smiled back and replied, "Don't forget to pray I'll win, too."

Thad had no less than four narrow escapes in avoiding wrecks ahead of him—one of which sent him on a wild ride across the grass onto pit road, and then back out on the track without losing position. He kept his focus and pushed forward, and with a hundred miles to go he managed to move up to third place.

Charley came on the radio, "We've got just one more pit stop so how's the car?"

TNT came back on the radio, "Keep it the same. It's a little tight, but I'm afraid to mess with it. I can win this thing."

"Your lap times are a half a second faster than the leader. Just stay in control, stay on your line, and keep moving up. Unless we get a caution, we'll pit with forty-eight laps to go."

"Ten-four," he replied.

Becky had been watching from the quiet and comfort of the motorcoach. She had twisted a dishtowel into a tight knot, as she gritted her teeth while watching Thad miraculously drive through some impossible wrecks. The last one had him driving blindly through a thick cloud of smoke. She hadn't realized his spotter had told him what to do and said another quick prayer.

Fifty laps later, T came on the radio, "Caution flag stop. Come on boys. I need your fastest time of the day on this one. I want to come out just one spot better."

He followed the leader down to pit road while watching his speed carefully. He knew one mistake could cost him the race. Drew looked down at his pit as TNT screeched to a halt. The pit crew leaped over the wall and began a flurry of well-practiced activity around his car. T closed his eyes for a second hoping to relax a little, as he sipped on his clear tube of Gatorade. When the left side popped up, he opened his eyes, put his left foot on the clutch, and shifted into first with his right. Five seconds later the jack dropped, he popped the clutch and spun out of the pit box with a twelve point seven pit stop.

"Watch your right!" screamed the spotter into the radio.

T got a quick glance to his right and pulled with a jerk to the left just scrapping into car number sixty-one. He carefully maintained his speed and came out of the pit number one. "Yahoo!" he yelled as he crossed the white line. Way to go guys! Best pit stop of the day. Tell me you put some gas in this thing."

Charley laughed, as he watched the pit boys give each other high fives, "Oh we put a gallon or two in."

They all laughed heartily, as Drew complimented the crew over his radio, and then spoke to Thad. "Son, a win here could move us back into the top ten, and maybe even seventh or eighth, so be patient and make the engine last."

"You got it boss. I'm going to win this race!" Thad was jubilant as he followed the pace car around the track.

A few minutes later, just as he was mentally going through everything he had to do, and prepare for the restart, an unknown voice suddenly came over his radio. "You're a freaking faggot Thad, a fudge packer, and as queer as a three dollar bill. I'm going to put your ass in the wall!" The radio clicked.

Drew reacted first, "Who said that?" He looked all around the pit and felt their eyes watching him. It wasn't one of them, and it wasn't the voice of anyone they recognized. Someone was on the team channel.

Thad remained absolutely still behind the wheel, as the pace car began to speed up. "Shake it off," he said to himself. "Ignore them. Show them. Beat them."

Charley quickly came on the radio, "Thad, when your car is better than anyone else, they're going to try just about anything to rattle your cage. Don't pay any attention to that crap. We have a race to win. Are you ready to do it?"

"Yes sir, I am!" exclaimed T.

The pace car pulled off to the pits, and he led the field carefully to the green flag. Anyone of the top five places could win the race, and he knew they were all waiting for him to make a mistake. He jumped out about four car lengths in front of second, and then held to his line. Forty-one passed second place car with twenty-two laps to go and moving up quickly.

Gary, his spotter, came on the radio. "T forty-one is moving up. He may have the car, and you'll have to hold him off. You just stay on your line, and I'll keep my eye on him. I'll tell you when to start worrying about who is behind you. For now just drive the wheels off that thing."

"Roger," replied a solemn but determined T.

At ten laps, Gary came back out on the radio, "Okay Thad, he's just two car lengths back. Stay on your line, and don't begin blocking until you have to."

Charley broke in next, "T how much engine do you have left? Can you give us a little more speed?"

"No, it's on the floor most of the time. I'll have to hold him off."

Forty-one moved almost to Thad's bumper with just four laps to go. T began watching his mirror as much as he was the track ahead. With three laps left, T felt a slight tap by the forty-one.

Drew broke in on the radio, "He is just trying to distract you. Hang in there."

Forty-one tapped him again and then cut low. T immediately cut him off. He swung back high and T blocked him again.

"Get out of the freaking way you faggot!" said the same voice as before over T's radio.

"Damn! Who said that?" asked Drew.

Charley came back on, "Ignore it Thad. Drive your ass off. There's just one lap to go. You can do it!"

T reached over and turned his radio off just as he saw the forty-one car break high again. T easily pulled the wheel just enough to block and prepared for another attempt. They rounded the second turn with no less than a foot between their bumpers.

"Two turns left," whispered T as he checked his mirrors carefully.

Forty-one hit him hard going into the third turn. The car shook and wiggled as he struggled to hold his line, but managed to somehow stay in front of the forty-one.

Boom! He felt another hit going into the final turn. T held the steering wheel as tight as he could. Forty-one tried to cut to the inside and got a fender to T's left. T eased down on him, but the forty-one did not get out of the gas with two hundred yards to go. Forty-one reacted by turning upwards giving T a bump at an angle pushing T up the track enough for him to get a little more ground on the inside.

T fought hard, and slammed the accelerator pedal down to the floor once more. Forty-one gained a little, and T could no longer see him in his rear mirror, but easily could see him in his left side mirror. Not good, thought Thad. He could see the finish line and felt the forty-one might be able to beat him to it. He pulled downward rubbing fenders with the forty-one and holding him to his position. The forty-one tried to go lower to get away from him, but T just came on down.

With fifty yards to go and no more options, the forty-one yanked the wheel hard to the right and hit Thad's car. His car lifted from the track, he caught air, and spun sideways in front of the forty-one.

135

"Oh no!" exclaimed Charley.

"Oh shit!" said Gary from the rooftops along with the other spotters.

Thad's car was in front of the forty-one car, and rolling sideways over and over with just forty yards to go. Desperate to win, the forty-one continued t-boning Thad's car as it rolled over. He hit the roof thinking he would bounce him out of the way, but instead his bumper caught in the roof supports, and he could not break free. The crowd stood and watched in horror as the forty-one car pushed T over the finish line on his side with the driver side down on the pavement.

Just as he crossed the finish line, the forty-one car slammed on his brakes in attempt to break free from Thad's car. As he came loose, the momentum on Thad's car caused him to begin flipping and rolling down the track like an airless football. The third place car had not anticipated the forty-one slamming on brakes and slammed into his rear. This sent the forty-one in a burst of speed down the track. The forty-one tried to jerk his steering wheel to the left to avoid Thad's car, but the steering shaft locked on the last impact, and he slammed into the trunk of Thad's car spinning him around harshly, and directly into the third place car, and together they all slammed into the wall of the first turn.

Becky eyes went wide. She could not believe what she had just seen. Neither could his pit crew, his spotter, Charley, or Drew. Janet knew she had never seen a worst wreck. Everyone in the pit area stood still. The television cameras zoomed in looking for any sign of life in the car. One of T's inside cameras had smashed and broke in the crash. The emergency vehicles arrived, and began swarming around the twisted mess of metal. The television and radio commentators continued speaking about the race while their eyes remained on Thad's car.

Cautiously, Charley clicked his microphone button, "Thad? Can you hear me? Are you okay?" He sighed and repeated, "Thad? Can you hear me? Are you okay?"

There was no reply. He didn't know the radio was in the off position.

TWELVE

All two hundred and fifty thousand fans stood in silence waiting to see any sign of life in T's car. The pits crews stood on the pit wall attempting to get a view of the scene just pass the finish line and slightly into the turn. The television announcers soon had little to say. They feared Thad was dead, and immediately went to a commercial break. Drew pushed the button that lowered his wheelchair to the ground. Becky rushed out of the coach and began running to the pit where Janet met her and hugged her tightly.

Charley pushed the red microphone button once more, "Thad? Can you hear me buddy?"

There was still no reply.

The emergency crews could not get through the maze of bent twisted metal. They sprayed their fire extinguishers all around the car hoping to prevent a fire.

"Get the saw!" one of the men yelled to his partner.

A tall man with white hair ran to his truck, opened a side compartment on his emergency vehicle and pulled out a gas powered circular saw with diamond teeth. He ran to Thad's car, set the saw down, and pulled the starter cord. It roared to life. Everyone along the pits knew the use of the saw was not a good sign—meaning the driver cannot crawl out of his car on his own.

The television networks began showing their slow motion replays of the finish of the race. Drew and Charley watched their monitors, hoping to see any sign of life in Thad's car. They stared at the only working in car camera, but all they could see was his lifeless arm. When the network television picture came back live, they saw the tall man sawing through the roof. Janet turned Becky away from the monitor. "Hang in there, honey. He'll be all right," she said as she rubbed her shoulder.

Ten minutes later, the crews peeled back a section of the roof. One of the crew reached in and began unbuckling all the straps and cords keeping Thad in his seat. He remained unconscious. Carefully he unbuckled his helmet and slid it off. He pulled his glove off, and put his bare fingers against Thad's neck to feel for a pulse.

"He's alive!" said the crewmember.

He put his glove back on and pulled the seat belts out of the way. He reached inward as far as he could, but realized Thad's right foot was pinned. "Give me a knife!" he yelled.

His partner set the saw down, and quickly pulled his hunting knife from his waist belt and passed it into his partner.

"His right foot is pinned. I'm going to remove his shoe and see if I can pull his foot free." He began cutting away at the shoe until the cords were loose. He held the knife in his teeth, as he gently pulled T's foot out of his boot. He handed the knife out. "Okay, I think we're ready."

He worked himself back out of the car, and then he and his partner reached inside, and slowly began pulling Thad out of the car. "Support his neck."

"I've got him, you hold his head," said the taller one.

"Okay, a little more and we're free."

Someone rolled a stretcher up, and they gently laid him down on it. The EMT technicians began swarming over the limp body. They put a support collar around his neck, and a strap over his forehead holding his head still to the stretcher. They checked for broken bones, and listen to his heart and lungs. One of the EMT's looked up at the emergency crew as they stood by awaiting a decision. They hoped he was still alive.

The EMT smiled and gave them a quick thumbs-up. The cameraman on the scene captured it, and in a second, the entire track saw the thumb on the monitors as well as the entire nation. Drew sighed heavily. Charley pulled off his headset and wiped tears from his eyes. Becky lost it and sobbed heavily.

They began rolling the stretcher to the ambulance and moved away from the hot wrecked cars as a welcomed cool breeze rambled across the track. Thad's face remained wet with sweat and the breeze felt cool against his skin. Just as they lifted the stretcher to set him inside the truck, he opened his eyes. One of the EMT men almost dropped the stretcher as the sudden eye pop scared him.

"That's a good sign," said the other. "Come on, get him in."

Thad could not focus, but he could see the blue sky. He remembered the end of the race, but did not recall being flipped and eventually t-boned across the finish line. The door closed and the truck headed to the infield care center.

"Come with me," urged Janet as she began grabbing Becky's hand and dragging her to the emergency hospital in the center of the track. Drew began ridding his wheelchair in and around the pit area and working his way there as fast as he could. Charley left a few men in charge of packing up the pit equipment, and the rest of the men followed him as he ran to medical center as well.

NARC informed the television announcers that Thad was alive, and he won the race. However, the usual Victory Lane Celebration had been cancelled. Soon the networks pulled away from the race coverage and went back to regularly schedule programs.

Reporters surrounded the medical care center awaiting any news. The driver of the forty-one came out of the care center just as they were wheeling in Thad. He gave the still body a stare before pushing his way through the reporters. The rest of the drivers and crews began their tear down while the officials began moving the remaining intact top five cars to inspection. There was little they could do with Thad's car as a flat bed wrecker winched it on to the bed, and hauled it away.

Becky and Janet had seen Thad rolled into the hospital, but they could not see his face. Thad had fallen back into unconsciousness in the ambulance. The crowds tighten around them. Reporters began asking Drew and Charley all kinds of questions, but Charley followed Drew's lead and made no comment.

Inside the medical care center, the doctors and nurses began cutting away his uniform until he lay there naked. They got an IV shunt in his wrist and quickly began hydrating him. A doctor easily noted the swelling around his ribs, his arms, and his legs. Gently, he felt his neck area and decided to immediately do some x-rays. A big mechanical arm swung over his body and began taking the pictures. In a few minutes, they could see he had four cracked ribs, but amazingly nothing broken. His neck looked good as well. They were all relieved.

"His blood pressure is good, heart good, breathing good, and nothing broken," said the doctor as the nurse made notes. "Ammonia stick," he ordered. "The nurse pulled a drawer out of the cabinet behind her, found the capsule, and placed it in the doctor's hand. He broke the capsule in half and immediately placed it under Thad's nose.

Thad's nose wrinkled, then he flinched, and opened his eyes. The doctor removed it. "Thad, can you hear me?" asked the doctor.

Thad swallowed hard and whispered, "Yes."

The doctors and nurses smiled.

"It hurts to breath," said Thad.

"I should imagine so. You're okay, but you have a few cracked ribs that I'm sure hurt, plus a bunch of other bruises. I bet you have a headache as well."

"Yeah, you're right. But I'm okay?"

The doctor leaned over so Thad could see his face and eyes. "Son, you're banged up, your brain got shook around a little, but you're going to be okay. I'm putting some pain medicine in your IV, and it will make you sleepy, so just let go and relax. We're going to transport you to the downtown hospital, so I can get a MRI done. Just relax."

"Wait!" blurted Thad. "Before you knock me out, tell me something."

"Sure kid, what?" The doctor motioned for the nurse to hold still for a second, as she was about to inject the painkiller.

Thad swallowed and then flinched at the pain. He took in a breath slowly and replied, "Did...I...win?"

The doctor and his staff smiled, "Yes, you did. Way to go. Now just lay still and relax." He nodded to the nurse who injected the knock out drug into his IV.

The doctor walked out of the emergency room, and out the front door. He waved his hands urging everyone to quiet down. "Thad is alive. He has several cracked ribs, many bruises, and one hell of a headache. I'm taking him in for an MRI, and we'll know more by nightfall."

"Any chance he could die?" yelled a reporter.

"None. He only asked if he had won. I told him yes!" The doctor turned around before anyone could ask other questions. NARC's media director took over.

Becky and Janet hugged each other. Even old Drew and Charley hugged. Drew called to Janet. "We can take my helicopter to the hospital. You and Becky follow me."

Drew yelled at folks to get out of his way with the girls following him. Charley ran to his crew and gave them the news. He also picked up the trophy. Duke began packing up the motorcoach. He brought all of Becky's stuff to the front of the coach, and waited for his orders. He sat in the front seat and watched the crowds disperse, as well as the long line of car haulers as they snaked their way out of the track and began driving home. It had been an exciting, and thrilling victory, but scary. He said a quick prayer for T's recovery, and expressed thankfulness for saving him.

By nine, the doctor related the results of the MRI to Drew, Janet, and Becky. He had already told Thad who was awake. "He'll be fine, but I'm planning on keeping him overnight as his brain got shook around pretty harshly. He's a tough kid. He'll be very sore, and those ribs are going to hurt for a few weeks, but he'll be all right."

Drew sighed and asked, "How soon can he race again?"

"We'll see how he is doing tomorrow. Every time he wakes up he asks if he won the race, and I keep telling him yes."

"Thank you for your help," replied Drew, "whatever he needs just get it for him. I'm going to the business office to arrange to pay his bill. Just make him well. Thank you."

As the doctor left Drew turned to Janet, "Are you all right?"

"Yeah, now I am."

"Good, do you think you can stay with him? I have some work to do. I'll call you from time to time. I will fly home tonight, and you and Thad can fly home tomorrow. I will have a doctor standing by when you land. Thad's pilot is waiting at the airport. I'll tell him to check into a hotel, and call you with the number to his room."

"Okay, no problem."

He turned to Becky, "Honey, this is just a sad part of racing. Thad loves to race, and he knows a wreck is always a possibility. I guarantee you he is far happier he won, and in fifth place in points. He'll be fine. Do you want me to give you a lift home? We can swing by the coach and pick up your stuff. Duke has packed the coach up and standing by for my instructions."

140

Becky turned to Janet, "Are you going to be okay by yourself?"

Janet nodded, "I'll be fine. I've been through this before. It was your first time, and I know how dramatic a day like this is. I'll call you after I talk to him in the morning."

"Okay," she replied, then she thought a second, "I'm going with Drew to get my stuff, and then go home. I'll change clothes and drive my car back here to be with you."

Janet smiled, "Thanks. I'll save you a spot on this wonderful couch."

They both smiled, as the waiting room furniture was just about as uncomfortable as possible. Becky followed Drew out of the emergency room where his driver was waiting for him. They rode back almost silently and Becky could tell Drew was deep in thought so she politely remained silent.

At the track, Becky excited the car as Drew asked Duke to take her home in the Hummer, and then begin his drive with the motorcoach to Charlotte. Becky waved goodbye to Drew.

Drew had his driver take him to the NARC office hauler. He rolled up the ramp, and asked to speak to Bob Isby. Bob had been the leagues race director for fifteen years and well respected by all. Drew was waved on in and met with Bob in his private office.

Bob asked, "How's your boy?"

"Sore, beat up, bruised, a few cracked ribs, but otherwise just fine. They're keeping him overnight, but the MRI was good. No neck or spine injuries—thanks to your safety technology group. I think every safety device on that car was used to the max and it saved his life."

"We'll be studying this wreck for quite a while. I'm so glad he is okay."

"Bob, did you hear that anonymous voice over Thad's radio near the end of the race?"

"I heard about it. I have my radio specialist assembling a tape for me. It should be ready in a few minutes. I take it someone was trying to rattle his cage."

"You can certainly say that. They said some nasty stuff to Thad. It is a wonder he could concentrate. How did they do that?"

"No one can legally broadcast on our channels, but illegally anything is possible. It had to be someone that knew how to do it, and how to do it secretly. I don't know if we can find out who it is unless someone can recognize the voice."

"Let me know if you can. I'll sue the bastard all the way to hell and then some."

Bob sighed, "I'll let you know. Are you flying home?"

"Yeah, I guess so."

"I'll call you tomorrow."

Drew shook his hand, "Thanks, Bob. We'll go to our backup channels next week."

"Have a safe flight."

THIRTEEN

Jack woke up a bit later than usual, took a hot shower, and slowly shaved. Almost everything he did reminded him of Thad so he started singing just to get him off his mind. He dressed, ate a bowl of cereal, brushed his teeth, and walked to his rental SUV and drove to town. The drive through the mountains to the town of Frisco Colorado never ceased to stimulate his wonder of the great outdoors. There were mountain peaks with snow on them even though it was early July and the middle of summer. The Dillon Reservoir Lake seemed to be made of crystal as it sparkled in the morning sun. He cut off the air conditioning allowing the scent from the mountain trees to invade the car as he hit the buttons to make all the windows go down including the rear one.

He rounded one of the many hundreds of hairpin turns in the road that led him to and from Frisco. He had stayed in the log cabin with its magnificent views a few years ago to work on a story, but it was the first time he had used it to get over a man. With thoughts of Thad creeping back into his brain, he turned on the radio, found a country station, turned the volume up, and tried to sing along even though he really didn't know the words.

The town of 2800 residents grew to 10,000 in ski season, but during the summer, it was just quiet and beautiful. He found a grocery store and parked his car. He pushed the cart through the aisles while filling his cart with lots of fresh vegetables and a variety of fruit. He bought a few chicken breasts, and even a steak, his favorite Amos peanut butter cookies, and smiled when he realized it was two for four dollars, so he picked up his second favorite a box of oatmeal and pecan cookies. He snatched up a few bananas, a gallon of milk and half gallon of orange juice, a loaf of bread, sandwich meat, and finally Breyers Light Carmel Crunch ice cream—another favorite of his. He knew most of his cart was full of comfort food, but with no around to hug him it was the best he could do.

"Looks like you're going to stick around for a while," stated the lady at checkout counter. She had a pencil over her left ear and a cigarette over her right. Her hair had been hurriedly pulled back and tied with well-worn elastic thingies, as Jack called them, and she looked exhausted. Jack guessed she spent at least eight hours a day behind that cash register. He had no idea how anyone could do that.

He smiled at her, "Yep, I've got to change out the city air in my blood system, and it has been so long I am afraid it might take a while. No need to starve while breathing."

"You'd think at 9000 feet above sea level I would have great lungs, too, but all I do is cough," she complained while stifling a cough."

Jack politely stated the obvious. "Smoking will kill you at any altitude. If you smoked in the middle of the forest with no one around for miles, you'll still get lung cancer." He paused and winked at her as he added, "But what I do know is that maybe you'll prove them all wrong."

She laughed, "As she tossed a thumb at her partner in the next line, "Mabel, I told you this boy was smarter than he looked."

Mabel replied without even turning around, "Yep, and he has a cute ass, too."

Jack's face blushed a little pink and he laughed, "Well, you two fine ladies surely must be on the welcoming committee. Have a great day."

"You come back to see me, uh, I mean us real soon. There's always a bargain at Fred's Market—especially if Fred is out of town!" The girls laughed as Jack pushed out the door and put his stuff in the car. He spotted a few newspaper racks, went over, and bought a USA Today newspaper. He drove mindlessly around town just to recall what stores were where, and though there was a new Blockbuster, the rest of the town appeared to be about the same as before. He turned on the highway and made his way home.

It had been a few hours since he had put the groceries away. He spent the rest of the morning working on his book, trying to make sense of a new chapter he had been working on for more than a week. He finally sighed and got up to fix himself a sandwich. He used a thick coat of Miracle Whip on both slices of bread. Then he peeled a banana and sliced it for his sandwich. He closed the bread together and took a bite while he fixed himself a big glass of cold water. He laid a bag of grapes on the table and sat down to read a bit while finishing his sandwich.

He had read most of the front page until the column of sectional headlines caught his eye. "Thad in Nasty Crash" was in bold print. The fine print said turn to Sports Section page one. He flipped passed the business and lifestyle sections and dropped his sandwich as eyes focused on the picture of Thad's car all crumpled and twisted. A second picture showed the power saw being use to cut their way into the car. Finally, a third picture showed T lifted from the car unconscious. He shuttered at the sight, but quickly devoured the article afraid to find out that the man he loved most had died.

As he read the comments from the doctor and heard that T's first words were, "Did he win the race," Jack began to cry repeated sighs of relief. He knew Thad had to be okay.

The log cabin was cheap during the summer, but one of the amenities installed for the more expensive snow season rates was a cable modem with cable television. He rarely had the television on during the day, but quickly he picked up the remote and turned it on. He flipped through the channels until he found the Speed channel. They were replaying the race, and he could see T's car in tenth place and appeared to be doing fine. He clicked the up channel until he stopped at ESPN's news channel. They were showing a NFL training camp story, so he hit the recall button and watched more of the race. After a minute, he hit the button again and went back to ESPN. He did this about eight times until ESPN began showing footage of the car wreck, the removal of Thad from the steel cage that held him, and then a shot of the hospital. The reporter ended by saying the doctor reported T was doing very well, but kept overnight just to be sure. He said it would take some time to heal the four cracked ribs, but he expected Thad to be ready to drive in two weeks.

Jack thought this to be good news, but hit recall once more anyhow. This time he saw the accident happen in real time with T's car flipping over and over before being spun around and t-boned into the wall. He left it on the channel listening to every word from the announcers until satisfied the ESPN reporters were telling the truth. He then cut the television off, and sat there with his half eaten sandwich lying on the paper towel on the table.

He thought to himself what if Thad had died, how Jack would have overcome the guilt wondering if the wreck was somehow his fault. He looked at his cell phone and speculated if he should call Thad, but he knew reaching him in the hospital would be impossible, as the fans and the media probably swamped the place. He thought about calling Janet, but then she would ask where he was, why he had left, and he didn't want to lie to her.

After a few minutes, he picked up the lifestyle section and began eating his sandwich. He made a mental note to watch ESPN's Sport Center show tonight for any news of T's condition. He spent the rest of the day writing and editing with little progress. Late in the afternoon, he took a hike along the shore of the beautiful lake. He knew it froze over in the winter, but he could not fathom how the big lake would look as an ice chunk. The manager of the development told him the temperatures remained around zero in the first quarter of the year. Jack could not imagine anyone wanting to live here during the winter, but he sure loved it during the summer. I guess people are attracted to Fresco for different reasons and different seasons, he thought.

He sat in front of the television that evening eating a salad and slurping some spaghetti he had made. He knew it was rude to make a noise while sucking the noodles in, but he loved doing it when he was alone. It was one of the many fine habits he picked up in college along with sucking Jell-O off the spoon he held just in front of his mouth. Doing these stupid things always made the lonely boy smile.

He wished he could have borrowed Jessie's dog, but he knew Bailey belonged with her, and he was so glad he kept her happy. He laughed when he had a thought he might rent a dog for the rest of the summer. After all, there were signs along the road for renting just about everything in Fresco: houses, cabins, apartments, townhouses, cars, skis, sleds, snow suits, snow boots, snow bibs, and more. After about forty minutes, ESPN played a video of T getting out of the hospital, and then replaying the crash scene. At the end, they cut back for a wave from T before the limo took him to the airport.

Jack cut the television off, realizing by now that Thad was probably home. He looked at his cell phone again. "To call or not to call...that is the question!" he said aloud to no one, and then laughed at his pitiful

Shakespearian voice that made it sound more like Darth Vader in Star Wars. He quickly left the phone and its temptation on the table, and walked to his bedroom, stripped naked, grabbed a towel, and went downstairs and climbed in the Jacuzzi—another summer perk most likely paid for by the rich winter guests.

After he relaxed a while, he allowed a lower water jet to shoot some bubbles under his butt and up between his legs. He stiffened somewhat then played with it while thinking of T. In his mind, he knew leaving Thad was the right thing to do, but his mind wasn't the problem. It was his heart, and his heart felt broken. No matter what he did, he could not push his thoughts of Thad's love away. He had thought he had been in love several times before, but gay relationships for him had always been difficult. There is an extra layer of trust that must be accomplished between two lovers in the gay world, or so he thought. When he was young and wanted gay sex he couldn't find anyone that was gay to have sex with, but by the time he hit twenty-one, and began learning and traveling, he knew he could find gay sex in any town in the world—maybe even in Frisco.

But finding someone that loves you more than anyone else, and give up looking for all that gay sex—now that is a person you want to keep. He thought about the men he dated, and if he put his sex life down on a spreadsheet with the pros and cons compared, he would have a long list of cons and only one pro—Thad.

He knew the only way their relationship would work was if Thad came out of the closet to everyone, and then and only then, could their love really grow. He realized his thoughts were selfish, and he did feel bad for it, but to be in the closet all day long just about drove him crazy. How do you store away those thoughts you have about your lover all day long? How do you save up the times you wanted to lean into him, hug him, kiss him on the nose, pinch his butt, or sing to him? How do you put those hundreds of daily desires on hold on a hard drive to recall when alas you were alone? He laughed again at his analogies realizing no one could make a relationship fit into a certain cookie cutter molds.

He knew a person could not stop their heart by themselves, and then start it again several hours later because they would be dead. How could he or Thad put their hearts on hold waiting for those precious few private moments before they fell asleep? What remote button do you hit for restarting a moment of affection, a wink, a smile, a squeeze of the hand, or a tweak of the nose? Or a pull of the ear, a caress of their thigh, a pat of the back of the head, a clinch of intertwined fingers, the depression of a new dimple, a giggle, a laugh, and finally a kiss?

It is not humanly possible, he thought, to ever really put love on hold because like the heart muscle, love is a living thing and if stopped—even for a brief while, it will surely die.

Before he closed his eyes to sleep that night, he knew that it was Thad who would have to decide what was right for him. He knew Thad would never have stopped him from writing because he knew Jack loved to do it and it was his career. Therefore, he could not expect Thad to stop racing for him. Jack knew he wanted to love and be loved, and yet still continue his work, and he just hoped that somehow Thad would figure out a way he could love and be loved and continue to win championships.

Thad made Janet go home after swearing he would be fine, and he would call her if he needed her. The doctor had given him some pain pills because he knew the ribs were going to be very sore. Janet had brought dinner over for him, so he sat at the table and ate while watching ESPN's Sport Center, but when the video of the wreck hit the screen he grabbed the remote and punched the movie guide button, and began thumbing through the movies until he found one he liked and went back to eating.

He sat in the recliner for a while and fielded a call from his mom, and then Drew and even Duke, but soon everything in the big house became still and quiet. He managed to get out of his clothes and climb in the Jacuzzi. The warm water felt good, but he stayed in too long while doing a lot of thinking. When he went to climb out, he got dizzy and quickly sat down on the step to keep from falling down on the hard floor. Once he cooled off a little, he made it to the kitchen, took out a fresh bottle of water from the refrigerator, and went back to the recliner. Once his skin returned to room temperature, he pulled a light blanket over his naked body and fell asleep.

Somewhere in the middle of the night, Thad dreamed Jack was by his side and kissing him. He pulled the pillow to his chest tighter as if holding Jack. He saw his warm radiant smile that always brought a grin to T's face. He kissed Jack's neck and teased Jack by rubbing his soft hair beneath Jack's nose. As expected, Jack suddenly sneezed loudly. Thad laughed and pulled him into a tighter embrace.

When T awoke the next morning, he could hardly move. The soreness had set in, leaving him painfully stiff. He tried to stretch, but finally gave up, and willfully pulled himself up and out of the recliner. "Ugh, ow," he exclaimed, and then a word that summed it all up, "Shit!" He thought about getting in the shower, but decided to return to the Jacuzzi after dropping his blanket to the kitchen floor, removing two water bottles from the refrigerator, and slowing making his way to the tub.

It took almost an hour before he felt good enough to get out. He downed the last of his water, and made it to the shower. He decided to forego shaving or shampooing, as he didn't think he could handle the pain of lifting his arms over his head. After drying off, a headache made even his eyes hurt. Somehow, he put some clothes on. He made it back to the kitchen after dressing and took another pain pill. He popped a frozen sausage, egg, and cheese biscuit in the microwave. He ate it slowly with a large glass of orange juice. He had just made it to the recliner when the phone rang.

"Hello, T? It is Janet. How are you?"

"I think Duke backed over me with the motorcoach," grumbled Thad.

"Does that mean you don't want to go jogging around the lake today," she teased.

"No ma'am. I think I'll stay in the recliner."

"Good boy," she replied. "Our doctor is on the way over there. He's bringing a Velcro shoulder harness that will give those ribs some stability so they don't move around while healing. It's a bitch to put on, but you'll thank him for it afterwards—if you don't pull his ears off when he tightens it!"

Thad rolled his eyes, "Boy, I can't wait. More torture." Then he changed the subject, "What's the schedule like today?"

"Nothing. We have this weekend off. Do you remember or did your brains turn to pudding?"

"Oh, yeah, I forgot."

"I've already moved everything to the end of next week to give you as much healing time as possible. Do we need to line up a back up driver for Indianapolis?" She knew the answer, but wanted to hear him say it.

"Hell no, I'll be fine. I just don't know how they are going to get me in the car. Can they cut a hole in the roof and lower me in that way?"

"Waltrip has a roof escape hatch in his car because he is so tall, maybe we'd better put a sun roof in for you."

Thad laughed, "That'll be the day. Why don't you enjoy some time off while you can? Mom is coming to stay with me to cook, clean, and nurse her baby back to health. Thank you for all those many things you do for me. I hope you have a good vacation."

"You're sure you'll be okay."

"Yes, I'll be fine. Mom will put about three quarts of chicken soup in me, and I'll be fine."

Janet thought a second, "How will chicken soup help your ribs?"

"Heading to the bathroom twenty-five times a day helps you stretch!" he replied with a grin.

"Okay, well, I'll have my cell, so call me when you need me."

"Yes, ma'am and thanks again. Bye now."

Thad had lied about his mom coming, but he knew it was the only way to get Janet to go with her boyfriend to their planned trip to Calgary. She was flying out that afternoon. He fell asleep on the recliner only to be awakened a few minutes later by the doorbell. He grumbled as he made his way to the door realizing Janet must have given the doctor the gate code.

Without looking out the door, he opened it and said, "Come on in, Doc. Thanks for coming."

148

Thad sat on the kitchen table while the doctor examined him. He then looked at the pain pills and approved of the prescription. "They only gave you three days worth. If you need more call me, but I hope you don't. We don't need for you to get dependent on these things."

"Don't worry; I hate pills almost as much as I hate shots."

The doctor looked at him slyly, "Oh, thanks for reminding me. I do have a shot for you."

"Me and my big mouth," replied a suddenly somber Thad.

After the shot, the doctor had T hold one arm out a time while holding the ribs on the same side with his other hands. He slid what looked like a ski life jacket over that arm then over his shoulder and back. He then put the other arm out and carefully put the jacket sleeve over it. The maneuver hurt a lot.

The doctor walked around to face T and pulled the vest together adjusting the Velcro straps while gradually making the vest tighter. Once completed Thad suddenly felt better.

"How's that feel? See if you can stand up and walk a bit."

Thad slid cautiously off the table and walked across the kitchen. "This is much better. The support helps a bunch."

The doctor smiled, "Well, it will help the ribs heal, but to be honest, the shot I gave you had some pain medicine in it so you wouldn't kill me when I put the vest on. It'll wear off in a few hours. This would be a good time for you to walk around the house a little to keep the soreness out, and then take a good nap. Sleeping will be uncomfortable, so I'd leave the vest on. It is made of nylon fabric so if you shower, just wear it in the water, and towel off as best you can. And believe me you don't want to put it on without the shot—at least not for a few days."

"Thanks, doc, how long before the ribs are healed?"

"About six weeks," came the quick reply.

"Six weeks! I've got to race next week."

"Oh, you can race, but it is going to hurt a lot. The following week it will also hurt, but not quite as bad and so on. I don't recommend you race at all for six weeks, but you're not going to listen to me anyhow. I hope they can get your race suit over the vest because I'm sure you will not enjoy driving without it. Here's my card. Call me if you need me."

Thad walked him to the door and made it to the recliner. He picked up the house phone from the end table and hit speed dial five. "Hello, is this Apollo's."

"Yes, sir, it is. How can I help you?" asked Carol.

"Carol I need a large Supreme pizza with extra cheese. Is Bobby working today?"

"Yes, he is. Is this Thad?"

"Yes it is—alive and almost well. Bobby knows the code to the electric gate. Do you mind if he delivers it?"

"No, that'll be fine."

"Good let me give you my credit card number and give Bobby a twenty dollar tip on the card for me."

"Got it, will do," replied Carol. "Give us about twenty minutes, okay?"

"Thank you."

After devouring several slices of pizza, T went back to the recliner with his cell phone in hand. He flipped through the directory until he found Jessie's number and hit the call button. It rang a few times until she picked up. "Hello?"

"Hi, Jessie. It is Thad. How are you?"

"How am I? I'm fine, but then again I wasn't flipped over like a pancake at the Waffle House in my car, and then bulldozed in to the wall, and smashed by the following car. So how are you doing?"

"Well, I'm a little sore…" T flinched at a sudden pain in his left side, "okay, I'm a lot sore! But I'm alive and I won the race."

"Honey, you sure love to win. I'd give up first place not to go through that."

"I'm tough," replied Thad with a grin.

"Yeah right," said Jessie sarcastically, "and how many places do you hurt."

"Oh just a few…hundred places." They both laughed. Thad asked, "How's Bailey doing? I sure wish I could borrow him for a few days. I've got ten days off and can hardly move."

"Well, I'm sure he would like to visit you no matter what kind of shape you're in."

Thad smiled at the thought although he doubted he could even throw a ball for old Bailey right now. He paused while she spoke next.

"He hasn't called yet."

T sighed, "I am sorry to bother you. I just had to know. If he does, tell him I love him, and I need him so bad."

"The ribs killing you?" she asked.

"My heart is broken, but yes, the ribs do hurt as well. Gosh, Jessie. I don't know what to do, but I need to talk to him. Thanks for your help. Is it okay if I call back in a few days?"

"Sure honey. I feel so bad for you."

"I will be fine. Give Bailey a hug for me and tell him to take good care of you. Thanks. Bye."

Jack went to bed around the usual time of eleven, read a little in a book he had started before he met Thad, but never had time to read with T around. Loving and being with him was far more fun than reading about it in a book, he thought. He cut the light out forty minutes later, and closed his eyes. Then he turned the other direction. After a few minutes, he pulled the extra pillow to his chest to cuddle it. For the next ninety minutes, he tossed and turned, fidgeted with the blanket, readjusted the pillow, and just could not fall asleep.

With the closing of his eyes, he saw on his eyelids television monitors playing a collage of video clips of Jack and Thad together. He would open and close his eyes and the video would continue. He tried to think of something else but the video would pop up in his head every time.

He even did what most horny guys do when they can't sleep, or any other excuse. After ejaculation he cleaned himself up, made a trip to the toilet, dove back in bed, cuddled up with the pillow, and his brain still kept bringing up the video.

Eventually he did fall asleep, but about half past four, he thought he was awake, but only in his dreams. He was flying through the air like a helicopter over the race track, and then he came in closer, as if he was going to crash right on the asphalt. He wanted to scream but no words would come. Suddenly, he spotted T's car racing out of the fourth turn. Somehow, his flying body moved over the car as if protecting Thad like a hummingbird over her chicks.

Jack glanced up ahead to see where T was going, but instead of a finish line, he saw a giant brick wall, and T's car was heading directly for it. He again tried to yell to T to put on the brakes, but it appeared Thad just applied the gas pedal a bit more as they began accelerating. Jack screamed as T's car slammed into the brick wall and Jack flew harmlessly over it.

He suddenly woke up with a start. He was face was hot, his heart pounding, and his palms sweaty. He got out of bed, wet a washcloth, and wiped the sweat from his body. His brain knew it was a dream, but he feared it might have been some kind of premonition and this scared him. Was Thad going to die? Was all this somehow his fault?

He fell back in the bed and remained wide-awake until time to get some breakfast.

Jack made it down the mountain to the gas station, picked up a newspaper, and came back to the cabin to look for any stories on Thad's recovery, but he didn't find anything. He flipped on the television and watched ESPN's SportsCenter for a half hour, but again there were no racing stories. He had forgotten they had a week off and thus, no news for them to report.

He walked to the couch, picked up his cell phone, and called Jessie.

Jessie looked at the Caller ID and quickly clicked the green phone button, "About time you called! I was worried about you, and obviously you weren't at all worried about me and Bailey." She was just teasing him, but there was a bit of truth to her greeting.

"I'm sorry. I've been rather bummed out. How are you and Bailey?"

Jessie smiled, "Don't worry, we're fine. I'm just giving you a hard time. The question is—how are you?"

"I've been better. I don't physically hurt, but I'm not sleeping so well. I left Thad…"

She interrupted him, "Yeah I know. He came here hoping to see you, and he called yesterday. He is begging me to call him if I hear from you."

"How's he doing? Is he okay, from the wreck I mean?"

Jessie sighed, "He cracked four ribs, and they hurt like hell. I think he is there all by himself. However, honey, his heart is broken. I have never seen a man so in love with another, and so hurt and crushed by your leaving. Why in the hell did you do that to him? I thought you guys were made for each other. Bailey loves him. What more could you ask for in the way of approval?"

Jack's eyes watered and he swallowed hard, "I love Thad so much, but that's the reason I had to let him go. You know I'm out of the closet, although I don't go around with a pink triangle on my head, but in Thad's world, you have to stay in the closet with the door nailed shut. The only time we had to be ourselves was when we were alone in bed together.

"Do you remember that guy Tim from Ohio that I told you about?"

Jessie reached over and scratched Bailey's ears. "Yeah, I do. He was the jerk that wouldn't leave you alone?"

"Good choice of words. He spotted Thad and I in a mall and made a scene. We thought it was over, but then he showed up in the Daytona, and tried to blackmail Thad for a million dollars."

"Holy gees," exclaimed Jessie. "I hope you knocked his block off!"

"I wish, but again we're in the closet in the race world, and we just tried to ignore him. He then put out a flyer to all the media members. T bluffed his way around it, but it really upset him. It made me realize that if he remains in the closet, this kind of the thing could just keep coming up, and if the press believes any of it, they would just hound us wherever we go. What kind of life would that be? We'd feel like poor Miss Diana and all that paparazzi crap.

"I want to be free to walk down the street with him, go shopping, see a movie, have dinner out, and hold hands. I'm not looking to have sex on the sidewalk—just affection."

Jessie laughed, "I don't think sex on the sidewalk would be much fun anyhow. You'd probably get sand or bits of glass on your ass! And that could hurt!"

Jack smiled, "You know what I mean. I want to be in love all day, not just a few hours before bed."

"Okay, spill the beans. What was sex with a superstar like?"

Jack laughed, "I only have to say one word—heaven!" They both laughed, as he continued, "I have never felt so loved in all my life. He only had to look at me with those eyes, and I immediately felt like I was the king of the world!"

"You sound like it, but I'm sorry you couldn't find a way to make it work. Are you going to call him?"

Jack closed his eyes, "I don't know. If I did, I think we might get together for a few days of bliss, and then on the next race weekend, I'd be pushed back into the closet. I don't think I could handle that."

Jessie took a breath and said, "Honey, did you ask Thad what he wanted to do? Did you tell him how you felt, and how being put back in the closet hurts you?"

Jack open his eyes as a slow tear slid down his cheek, "I can't ask him to come out for me. Everyone has to come out in their own time and place."

"Jack that sounded like the standard answer we all say. I asked—did you tell him how you felt, and did you ask what he wanted to do?"

"No," he whispered his voice cracking.

"Then you've run away before the bank's been robbed. I listened to Thad, and I saw through his eyes that he deeply and wholeheartedly loves you. How can he come out if you're not there to cheer him on, to help him decide, to support him, and help make the pain go away. You've left him on the end of a diving board with no water in the pool!"

Jack laughed, "You're sure have a funny way of putting things."

Jessie laughed as well. "Jack, darling, Bailey and I give Thad two thumbs and four paws up. That's the best rating ever!"

Jack chuckled. "I know. He's the best."

"Okay, what's done is done. You've given him time to think on his own. That may have been good for him, but why don't you give him a chance to talk to you, and see how he feels about the mess. You might be surprised at his answer."

Jack asked, "What if he says he wants me, but we have to stay in the closet?"

Jessie thought a second, "Ask him for how long. Maybe he needs to do it in the off season, and not right before the big chase to the championship."

"Oh, so you're a racing fan now. Did he make it into the top ten for the chase?"

"Yes, he did. They tried to wreck the shit out of him, but he still won the race." She paused before adding, "If he would go through that for a silly old trophy—I wonder what he would do for you."

Jack sobbed, as tears continued streaming down his face. "You really think I should call him."

153

Jessie smiled, "Honey, if you don't, then I have to call and tell him you called, but tell him you don't want to talk to him. It'll break his heart. You have nothing to lose by talking it out, but you sure have a lot to gain if you do. Love conquerors all. I'm sure it is going to be hard, but the journey together will make your love stronger. You know I learned the hard way that life is too short, and the person you love most could die. I thank God for every precious moment I had with her. You've already missed some wonderful time with Thad by leaving. Don't miss any more."

"Okay," he said finally. "Don't call him. I will, and I'll tell him you said hi."

"Thank you. It will be fine. Just talk to him. Use your old spreadsheet thing to show him the reasons for staying in the closet and reasons for coming out. He may be a racecar driver, but he isn't stupid. He'll figure it out—just give him time and your love."

"I know, but I've got my work to do…"

She cut him off, "Yeah, and I bet you haven't been able to write one word since you left him. Am I right?"

Jack smiled, "Yes ma'am. You're right."

"So you see, you do love him more than even your own work. Call him."

"Okay, well, I had better go charge up my phone before I call him. Thank you Jessie, you're my best friend. Give Bailey a hug for me. I love you."

"I love you, too. Stay in touch and let me know how you're doing."

"Okay, bye."

FOURTEEN

Thad screened his calls and spent the day either watching a movie on television or soaking in the hot water. His arms and legs were feeling somewhat better, but his shoulders, back and ribs still ached like he had the flu. He checked for a temperature but had none. He dressed and decided to walk around outside for a while. He had a hard time tying his shoes, but he managed to do so. He carefully made his way down the steps, walked around the pool, and took the path to the lake. Although the sun was hot, it felt good to breathe some fresh air. He walked all the way to far south of his fifteen acres, and then walked back to the house where he immediately gulped down another cold bottle of water.

He warmed up a slice of the pizza after taking the big box out of the refrigerator. He had just taken the last bite when the phone rang. He grabbed a water bottle and headed to the recliner before taking the call. Just as he set down, he looked over at the Caller ID. His heart leaped with joy.

He asked rapidly, "Jack? Is this you? Are you okay?"

Jack smiled, "It is I. The question is, how are you and what did you break?"

"Uh, four cracked ribs, and they hurt like hell when I move, but I have to move to work out the stiffness in the rest of my body." He paused and added, "I've missed you, and I love you very much."

"I've missed you, and I love you, too."

"I think I know why you ran away—you wanted to protect me, but I can tell you I feel miserable without you here."

"Life and love is just not very easy is it? I love you with all my heart, but I can't love you for just part of a day—when we're alone."

Thad sighed heavily, "I know. It hurts me, too."

"It wouldn't be fair of me to ask you to come out of the closet for me, because everyone has to decide if and when they want to. I feel lucky that I came out sooner, but no one really cared in my case. I was thankful my family sort of guessed it, and didn't make a big deal about it. I know mom's church wouldn't approve, but there are people there she doesn't approve of either. She just keeps saying a prayer for them."

"If this was a perfect world, I could come out, love you with all my heart and show it all the time, and still race for the championship," stated T.

"But the world is not perfect, and I'm sure you would take some ribbing from the racing community," began Jack before Thad broke in.

"More than likely they would tar and feather me!"

Jack smiled, "I think you would look cute in feathers, but I'm allergic to feathers, so don't let them do that to you, or I couldn't sleep with you."

"Where are you? Can I come see you?"

"I should come see you—you're the wounded soldier."

Thad replied quickly, "No, the paparazzi are already trailing me. I keep the gate closed, and so far only allowed the doctor and the pizza boy in. If you'll allow me to come to you, we could spend some quiet time together talking things out. Will you let me do that?"

Jack replied without hesitation, "I'm in Fresco."

"Fresno California?" asked Thad.

"No Fres-co in Colorado, stated Jack.

"And they said you weren't a poet. You made a rhyme. Do they have an airport there?"

Jack replied, "I flew in a commercial airliner to Denver, rented a car, and drove west to get here. It is in the winter skiing communities like Keystone, etc. However, I did pass an airport when I went to town yesterday. I saw a Lear Jet like one of Drew's there."

"That's good news. I could fly into there. How do I find you?"

"I will pick you up. What time?"

"I dunno. Later today. I'll call the crew to get the plane ready. It's probably a two-hour flight. What is the weather like—is it cold?"

Jack laughed, "It's hot during the day, and cool at night. We're at 9000 feet above sea level and on a lake. It's a very small town. I think we'll be safe."

"I'll call you before we take off to tell you when to meet me. Please don't tell anyone I'm coming—except Jessie, of course. Thank her for telling you to call me."

Jack grinned, as he knew Thad was smarter than he looked, "No problem, I'll get dinner ready. Fly safe. I love you."

"I love you, too."

T hung up and immediately speed dialed his pilot Al Trevors. "Al, I need a big favor. I need for you to fly me somewhere, and I want you keep it a huge secret. The newspapers are hounding me as well as the boss. I need to go away, get some rest so I can heal, and be ready for next week's race. Can you do that?"

"I have to file a real flight plan. That's the law, but the rest I can keep under my hat."

"Are those flight plans public information?"

"Well, yes they are, so that if any air controller has a need to check on a plane he can pull it up on his computer."

"If you file a plan and in flight, are you allowed to change your mind?"

"Yes, I am and that happens, but I always call in and let them where I'm going," replied Al.

"Where do you call?"

"Usually wherever I am at the moment I need to make a change."

"So not here in Concord?"

"That's right—it could be anywhere."

"Okay plan a flight for Denver with a little extra fuel—if you catch my drift."

"What time do you want to leave?"

"Is a half hour possible?"

"Yes sir, Katie's out of town visiting her mother. May I tell her how long I will be gone?"

"You'll be back tonight and we'll schedule a return for me next week. Are you sure that will be okay with your plans. You'll have a full week or more off once you get rid of me."

"Yes sir and thank you. I'll see you shortly."

Thad hung up jubilantly. He went to his computer and emailed Janet that he was going to the beach to rest in seclusion, and he would call her next week upon his return.

He then made his way down the hall, began throwing some clothes in his sports bag, and caught sight of his face in the mirror. He looked a little rough. He had taken a shower that morning, but quickly decided to shave. Afterwards, he put on some aftershave, stuffed a jacket in the bag, locked the doors, and set the alarm. It hurt getting in his SUV, but he was thankful for the vest, and hit the button to close the garage and second button to open the electric gate.

He drove out as he watched the gate close behind him in the mirror. Just before he reached the private airport in Concord he swung in to a Wendy's, went through drive-thru, and bought three single hamburgers all the way except no onions, large fry, and two more hamburgers and fries.

He slowed down as he pulled up to hanger, and looked all around for other folks from DMI or other race teams. The place looked deserted as everyone was on vacation. He felt lucky Al was still there.

It hurt to get out of the car, but he carried the food to the plane. "Hey, Al, I bought you some lunch, but would you mind doing me a favor? There's a sports bag in the back seat. It hurts like hell for me to carry it with these cracked ribs. Would you get it for me and lock the car. Here are the keys."

Al caught the tossed keys, "No problem. Go ahead, get on board, and we will be in the air in about ten minutes."

Thad put Al's lunch on the co-pilot seat where he sometimes sat while watching Al fly, but not today. His ribs were killing him. He went to the back of the plane, pulled the side table up from the locked position on the recliner next to his seat, and set his food down. He went back to the galley and fixed himself and Al large soft drinks. Al came aboard the jet, stowed Thad's bag, and locked the door.

"Thanks. You didn't have to buy me lunch," said Al as he made his way to the cockpit.

"Well, I was starved and I didn't think you could drive this bird through the drive-thru at Wendy's," replied Thad with a grin. Al laughed. Thad continued, "I hate to leave you alone, but I'm going to take a pain pill, eat my lunch and fall asleep in the recliner. Wake me when we get there, and thanks again for your help. How long until we're close to Denver?"

"Two hours and five minutes."

Thad smiled, "Don't file it yet, but you're actually taking me to Fresco, Colorado—just west of Keystone. There is an airport for jets there."

"I know it. I've taken folks skiing there. The last time I landed there, it was minus two degrees. I think it'll be warmer this time. It is 82 in Denver and the skies are clear. No problem. I'll make it happen."

"Thanks, I just don't want the press to know where I am and hound me. I need some down time."

Thad sat down and immediately called Jack to tell him he would be there in about two hours and fifteen minutes after allowing a little more time to go west of Denver. He then took the pill, ate his lunch, and fell asleep.

Jack sat on the hood of his rental car and watched the horizon to the east. He had already been fooled once when a jet flew in, but as it slowed on the runway, he realized it was a private jet for Virgin Airlines, and the guests aboard drove off in a big black limo. He had no idea who they were and didn't care.

Twelve minutes later and on time was T's white Lear Jet. Jack held his breath until he saw the letters "DMI" on the tail. He instantly knew it was the right plane. Al recognized Jack, pulled the plane to a stop near his car, and shut down the engines.

Thad awoke went the tires hit the tarmac, stowed away his leftover food, and tried to wipe the sleep away from his eyes. He undid the seatbelt, waited for Al to open the door, and put down the steps. He followed Al out the door, and smiled when he saw Jack waving at him.

Jack walked over and shook Al's hand, "Hey, Al. How was the flight?"

"It was a good one and Thad slept the whole way. He took a pain pill. Here's his bag, as it hurts him to carry it. I hope he can rest here in this beautiful mountain paradise."

"I have a doctor standing by should he need it—but I think he'll be fine. My mom will cook dinner for us—nothing like a home cooked meal to make you feel better."

"Yep, you're right." Al turned to watch after Thad as he slowly made his way down the steps.

"Hey, Jack. Thank you for letting me hideout at your place and recover. These ribs hurt like a son of a bitch."

Jack laughed, "I thought you racecar drivers were tough." Al laughed. Thad smirked.

"I am tough—behind the wheel, but walking is another thing entirely," shot back Thad, as he turned to Al. "Hey, big guy, thank you for helping me. I will call you Thursday night for a time to pick me up on Friday, so we can go directly to Indianapolis. I left a tip on your seat because with your wife away I'm sure you're going to starve, so go out and enjoy a good meal on me. Thanks again."

"Sir, you don't need to do that—you already bought me lunch."

Thad laughed, "Wendy's is a tie-you-over food. Please eat a real meal, okay."

Al laughed, and climbed back aboard to begin his flight home. Jack stowed T's bag in the back seat and helped him into the car. T was sweating by the time he shut the door.

"You don't look so good," said Jack as he started the rental car.

"I'll be fine. I hope this car has air conditioning. I'm hot."

Jack turned it up and gave T a little tour of the town that took about five minutes, and then made his a way along the lake before turning up towards the log cabin he rented.

"It's a beautiful place. It reminds me of Sundance."

"Yes, it is and if I want to, I don't have to see another human all day," bragged Jack.

"Stop that. You're making me horny." They both laughed.

Thad held Jack's hand all the way to the cabin, but they didn't kiss until they got out of the car, then in the cabin, then again after they stripped, and a long wet kiss in the Jacuzzi.

"You looked like a sissy in that life preserver," teased Jack as he playfully splashed him in the chest.

"I don't care. Tease me all you want. I am not taking it off. It hurts like hell to put it on. I'll probably wear it until it rots and falls off. I keep it tight which keeps the ribs from moving. Let's just hope they heal fast."

"We'll feed you lots of milk," stated Jack as he put his hand into Thad's crotch.

"Milk? I was hot for something a bit more…sexy."

Jack grinned, "Milk has vitamin D which helps build bones. Maybe it will help your ribs."

Thad took Jack's hand and pulled him close so they could kiss long and hard. They drank lots of bottled water and stayed in the tub almost an hour. They went to the bed after drying off and made out some more. Jack wasn't sure T could have sex, but Thad sure wanted to try.

With T on his back, Jack gently spread his bruised legs, found a little k-y to lube his tool, scooted up close to T's genitals and carefully slid inside.

Jack ended up doing all the work while making sure he did not put any weight on T's chest although they did manage to kiss. They fell asleep side-by-side.

T woke an hour later to breathe in the wonderful smell of baking lasagna. "He carefully rolled out of bed. Is that wonderful smell your 'mother's' cooking?" He walked over to Jack and kissed him.

Jack was finishing a salad he had made. "My mother?"

"I heard you tell Al your mother was going to cook for us."

"That was lie. I learned how to tell those from you. I thought it would ease any thoughts Al may have had about us."

"Oh, I see. I was looking forward to eating your mother's cooking. I didn't think she would poison me, but your cooking, well, I guess I will have to take my chances."

Jack laughed, "Yep, you are. I hid the car keys and you can't walk far in your condition for help."

"Walk far? Do you mean because of the broken ribs or because you fucked the tar out of me!"

They both laughed as T made his way to the table. Jack let him start on the salad while he brought over a hot loaf of sliced buttered French bread, and then carefully using oven mitts he set down a huge casserole dish of lasagna.

"Oh my—this smells great," stated T as he dug into his salad and ate a piece of the steaming bread.

Jack served him a large helping of the Italian dish, "Now it is very hot so let it cool a little or you'll burn your tongue, and then I can't kiss you."

T laughed, "Yes mother dear, I promise."

After dinner, they walked down to the lake to enjoy the reflection of the setting sun across the crystal waters. "This is a beautiful place," stated Thad as he walked gingerly down the path looking carefully for a root or loose stone to trip him up. He knew if he fell it would hurt something awful.

Jack walked just a step behind watching him for the same reason. "Yes, it is. In the winter this lake freezes to the point where you can drive a truck across it."

"Brrr, it must get cold up here. I've never been snow skiing. Most of January is tied up with testing new cars before the February Daytona race. December is the only full month we have off and along with the last week of November. Racing is tough on families with thirty-seven weekends tied up so they try to make up for it by being home for the three big ones: Thanksgiving, Christmas, and New Years."

"How thoughtful," said Jack sarcastically with a slight smile.

T smiled, "I have been thinking about how heterosexual families make life a success and with the exception of a few, the wife travels to the race for the weekends and in most cases the kids come, too. They all live in the big motorcoaches, set up huge grills alongside, and cook and grill most of their meals along with racing friends or the crew. I only know of a few divorces with Gordon's being the most publicized so the togetherness must be the key to marriage surviving."

"It must be tough on the family watching their partner go through mile after mile always wondering if they would crash and die today."

Thad sighed, "Boy, you're gruesome today. Listen, after Earnhardt died, new safety measures were designed, engineered, installed, and now the car is safer than ever and no one has seriously been hurt."

"Except for a few ribs, right?"

T smiled, "Smart ass." He reached back and took Jack's hand in his. He decided to change the subject. "So what have you been doing out here?"

"Just thinking."

"That must have hurt," laughed T.

Jack squeezed his hand, and turned T just enough to kiss him. The kiss lasted a minute or so as their tongues explored and members stiffen. As they broke the embrace, they kissed each other lightly just once more. "I never get enough of that."

"Me neither." T spotted a bench under the shade of a tree with the entire lake in front of them. "Let's sit a spell."

"You sound like an old cow poke."

T grinned, "I feel like an old cow that got poked!" They both laughed. Jack sat down and put his right arm around T's back for comfort while being careful not to put any weight on him. T reached across with his left hand and gently squeezed Jack's crotch.

After a wink and a smile, T took a deep breath and began, "I was right about why you left, wasn't I? You were afraid your staying would hurt me, force me to come out, and then the whole world would know."

Jack quickly replied, "That's not true. I couldn't stand your bad breath any longer."

T balled up his fist, and lightly popped Jack's thigh. "Shut up for a minute. This is hard enough. I appreciate your concern for protecting me but..."

Jack interrupted him, "That's not the only reason. I couldn't handle been dragged back into the closet with you. I'm not a flaming queen, but it is a long day when I can't touch you, lean into you, pat your knee, give your butt a pinch, or kiss you. I can't be myself and..."

T jumped in, "And I can't be myself either. I know. Maybe I should retire."

Jack laughed, "You're only in your third year, and you have a chance to break another record by being the youngest driver to win two championships in just three years."

"I know that. Drew reminds me all the time, but while you were gone, I realized you can't hug a trophy when you go to bed at night. The darn

161

things will let you kiss them, but they never kiss back," added T trying to be funny.

Jack said quickly, "Yeah and you can't fuck them either!"

The boys howled at the thought before T tried to continue, "I want you in my life for the rest of my life."

Jack jumped in, "And you said I was the poet."

T laughed and continued, "Most racers retire about forty years old if they're good. Times have changed. I already have thirty-two million dollars in the bank. My accountant, Sam Young, has put about eighty percent of that in secure investments and then borrowing against that to buy land. We buy and sell land every year for housing and business developments. His goal is for the money we have put in the bank to continue growing the rest of my life. I could quit and live just fine as far as money goes."

"Yeah, but what would you do for living. I can write the rest of my life. What would you do to keep from becoming bored? You can only do the nasty so many times a day."

T sighed, "Hell if I know. I had thought about building a race team."

"But if a gay man can't make it as a driver what makes you think he can make it as an owner?"

T frowned, "I don't know."

Jack jumped in, "Okay that's one thing you could do, but let say you stay in the closet, continue racing, and eventually retire. They'll invite you back for interviews, or maybe start a race, or give you award, and you don't have a wife with you, but they found out you're living with a good looking man, the rumors will still hurt."

"Which good looking man are you talking about?"

"Me stupid," replied Jack as he caught himself from sending a playful elbow into T's sore ribs. "Hear me out for a second. The world is changing, not fast enough, but changing. There are more gay people on television, in movies, and selling their songs than ever before. There are gay lawyers, accountants, bankers, insurance salesman, teachers, dancers, and about any other job, you can think of. I know there are gay men right now in racing—they're just keeping it a secret just like you.

"So let's say the world's most popular driver came out of the closet. Here's what I think you should do. First, you avoid the rumor mill entirely. You have Janet arrange the biggest press conference ever. You make sure every television and sports network is there along with every writer for newspapers and magazines. You promise something really big, and you do it on the morning of race day, so it will be too late for Drew, the officials, your sponsors, or even your crew to do anything about it.

"You also do as many interviews as you can before race time, explaining there are gay people in every job and role in the world. You feel it is your obligation to be truthful while doing all you can to help mankind by continuing your support of hospitals, medical research, children homes, and anything you can do to make their world a better place to live in.

"Then you challenge your sponsors to do the right thing, and continue their support of you because you're a good driver, and you need their support for your charities. Call each sponsor by name and challenge them to match the fifty thousand you are going to donate that day to twenty charities. They'll look foolish if they don't, and besides, you just gave their company a huge free commercial.

"Then you praise DMI and Drew. Tell them how you respect him and his leadership, and that you've always known him to be a fair and honest man. Tell them you look up to him like a father, and that you're more determined than ever to win him a second championship. Let him know how he can count on you, because you'll never let him down, and you know you can count on him, too.

"Praise your crew and engine builders in the same manner. Tell them you'll fight as hard as you can, and will never give up on wining.

"Praise the fans while acknowledging there are some fans that love other drivers so much they boo you, and that you understand that, but ask them to unite with you in supporting these charities as well as many others. Ask them to get involved in making this world a safer and healthier place for their children to grow up in.

"Before you go to this press conference, in the private of your motorcoach, I will personally call you every gay vulgar name I can think of including queer boy, faggot, and fudge packer!"

Thad started laughing, "Fudge packer? Why in the hell would you call me all those names?"

"It's simple—if you can handle your boyfriend calling you those names, then anyone else that says them will be only as irritating as a gnat flying around your lunch. Their words would mean nothing. Like the children's rhyme says, "Stick and stones may break my bones, but words will never hurt me!"

T grinned, "You're weird, and obviously had too much time on your hands. What would I do next?"

"Simple, you expect them to boo as usual when your name is introduced, but when you put that helmet on, you turn all that noise off, and concentrate on doing just one thing."

"What's that?"

"You win, you idiot! They may not respect you as a gay man, as that may take a while, but it would be hard not to respect the guy that wins the race, and goes on to win the championship. After all, this queer has already won one title in your first year, and took second the following year. There aren't many straight drivers that can do better than that."

"It isn't that easy to win," replied T. "What happens after the race?"

"It's the same as before the race. You don't get in a hurry, and you do every interview you can to show the world that you are a champion, and a great guy that just happens to be gay. You spend the next day talking to your sponsors and arranging charity events. You deliver checks and toys everywhere. After a month of doing this you'll be exhausted, but no one will ever be able to put you down."

"That sounds like a lot of work. How do I know I can handle all this?"

"Because I'll be right there with you. Janet and I will work together to book you as much as possible, and I'll write speeches that'll bring a tear to the eye of the biggest bigot in town. It will be tough in the beginning, but in the end, you'll win."

"And one more thing, this is the perfect time to do this. If you came out in the winter before the season or early in the season, DMI and the sponsors may have had time to replace you, but not now. You're close to winning a championship, and the owner and sponsors aren't going to pass up on a chance to enjoy that exposure."

T looked him in the eye, "Have you got this written down somewhere?"

"Yeah, it's on my laptop."

"Good, you've given me a lot to think about, and I may need to read it to absorb it. I am glad you care enough to try and help me."

"Thad, it would be impossible for me to love someone as much as I love you without trying to find a way to help. Come on let's head up the trail to the house. The wind cools quickly this time of the year now that the sun is almost down. How about let's get some dessert to go with your dinner?"

Thad was known for a sweet tooth and smiled, "What have you got?"

Jack laughed, "Me—stupid!"

FIFTEEN

Exhausted from the travel, the nervous apprehension and excitement, the good food, and the sex, the two boys slept soundly for the first time since Jack left Thad at the racetrack. Jack made sure he didn't roll into T's damaged ribs by putting his back to him, and letting T snuggle close to him. Observers would have thought they looked like deformed spoons, but they were spooning. They woke late, and had no clue what time it was, or what time zone they were in. It had been twenty-four hours since Thad had taken his last pain pill, but the soreness returned to his ribs, so reluctantly he rolled out of bed, made it to the bathroom for a much needed pee, and then called back to Jack.

"Do you have any Aleve, Tylenol, or Ibuprofen?"

"Turn around and look in my shaving kit. There is some Tylenol there. Just take two."

"Yes mother dear, and thanks. I need a shower. Do you want to help?"

Jack came into the bathroom in the nude. "I'm game. Let me get the water going for us."

Jack made fun of T's rib vest. "I have never seen a grown-up wear a lifejacket in the shower. Gees—it's only about a half inch deep in here. Come to think of it, I've never seen a child wear one into a tub!"

"I'm glad you didn't, or you'd be a pervert or a weird uncle. I can't shampoo my head."

"Turn around, and I'll do it for you."

Thad gladly obeyed, as Jack tenderly washed his hair, took the sprayer to rinse him, added conditioner, and rinsed again. They he took the liquid soap and washcloth, and carefully washed the rest of him especially his private parts.

Thad smiled, "Hold on, we need to scrub underneath the vest. I'm going to undo the front so it is loose, and then maybe you can do my chest and back."

"Are you sure?"

T smiled, "No, I'm not. I haven't done this since the doctor put it on. Let's try it slowly."

Jack helped him loosen the Velcro straps. Once undone Thad took a breath, and slowly he peeled it back. He let out his breath, and took another one.

Jack whispered, "How is it?"

"I can certainly tell a difference, and I think if I walked or rolled over I'd probably pass out, but it is better than it was the day after the wreck, so I'm making progress. Go ahead and put some soap on me, and I promise not to cry."

Jack laughed, "That's good. I wouldn't want to be accused of making a grown man cry in the shower with his lifejacket on!"

T took a mouthful of the shower water, and spit it at Jack in response.

After they dressed, with Jack taking charge of dressing T, they decided to get some breakfast. "Are you hungry?"

"Starved," replied Thad quickly.

"I haven't bought breakfast stuff, but I have a suggestion. There's a place called Granny's about four miles from here, and they absolutely produce the best waffles and omelets in town. Why don't we go there?"

" Are you sure? I don't want to be recognized."

Jack smiled, "This town is used to celebrities who come here to ski, so I don't think they really care who you are. We could put your sunglasses on and my hat, and as stiff as you walk they'll think you're the son of Frankenstein!"

"You're funny, but why wear your hat?"

"Because it is not a racing hat, and it says Keystone on it—one of the more popular ski spots out here. You'll look like a local, or ski bum who probably took a bad fall and broke four ribs."

Thad smirked as Jack put the sunglasses on T's face, and the stupid hat on his head and pulled it down tight. "I think the blood has stopped reaching my brain," complained T.

Without a moment's hesitation, Jack reached over and squeezed T's penis through his walking shorts. "It feels fine to me!"

They both laughed and made their way to the car.

T enjoyed the scenery as they drove into town. They were late for the regular breakfast crowd, and still too early for the lunch crowd, so they pretty much had the place to themselves. Jack bought a paper, and together, they found a booth and sat down. Jack quickly went to the sports section and scanned it finding nothing about Thad in the columns and certainly nothing about him leaving town. He then jumped to the lifestyle section and scanned it looking at the celebrity news, and again he found nothing on T. Satisfied, he folded the paper, and told Thad they were in the clear.

When the waitress appeared Jack took charge, "Mable, we'll both have super large glasses of very cold milk, two ham and cheese omelets, bacon and sausage on the side, grits for him and hash browns for me, and then a side plate of four of your small waffles. Also we'd like a big bottle of maple syrup, and if you have them—a bowl of sliced strawberries."

After she left T chuckled, "She didn't write any of that down. Do you think we'll get all that food?"

"Yep and I bet she brings us toast and jam, or biscuits. I come in about every three days, and she has never messed up my order. Eat this big brunch, and we'll eat a very light late lunch to even things out. You're going to like the food. How do you feel?"

"The Tylenol has kicked in, and I smell better, so overall I feel great. Thanks for the help."

Jack winked at him, "I decided to order so that no one here would hear your voice. I hope you don't mind."

"Absolutely not, I love being pampered. Can we take another shower when we get home?"

Jack laughed, "Of course we can, but I was thinking about driving you up to that mountain over there." He pointed out the window.

"It's a huge mountain. Are the roads smooth, or are we traveling by donkey?"

"Funny, it is a newly paved highway, so I think you'll do just fine. Did the doctor tell you to move around to loosen up the soreness?"

"Yes, hence the need for the lifejacket. The safety equipment in the racecar saved my life, and the head device kept me from breaking my neck, but the roll bars kept me from being squished like a sardine in a can. Thanks to the technology, I was lucky. My arms and legs are sore as is my neck, but it is better every day."

"That wreck looked awful on television. I about had a heart attack."

"How'd you hear about it? Did someone call you?"

"No, I saw it in the paper, and then started watching Speed Channel and ESPN. I didn't feel better until they captured a sound bite from you leaving the hospital. Once I heard your voice, and saw you walk to the car, I finally relaxed a bit. You scared the shit out of me."

"It wasn't my idea to get wrecked, but I did win."

Mable brought a large platter of food to the table. After she left Jack added, "Let just hope you don't have to win the championship by going through that every week."

Thad looked at all the food and grinned. "You talk—me eat!" in a Tarzan-like voice.

Jack laughed, "Not a chance. I'm eating, too!"

Thad started with a bit of everything. Sausage, omelet, bacon, waffle, and even the biscuits she brought to the table. He drowned a waffle in syrup, and gulped the milk. It took them thirty minutes to clean their plates and Mable smiled as she cleaned the table. Thad gave her a twenty, and together, the boys left the restaurant and began the journey up the mountain. They took Highway 9 with Jack driving slow enough that the curves in the mountain road did not hurt Thad. They cut through the town of Breckenridge and began climbing. It took about a half hour with Jack pulling off at various lookout points, so they could enjoy the view. Thad reached over and held Jack's hand enjoying their time together.

At the top, they got out of the car and walked over to a bench. There were a few tourists, but mostly the area was deserted. They sat there enjoying the view and after a while, the tourists left.

Thad suddenly let out a yell, "Oo-wee!" They both laughed at the echo.

"I thought you had hurt something," said Jack.

They talked about the view, and how wonderful it was in Colorado, but Jack reminded him that in a few months it would be cold as hell where he was sitting. They spotted a big winged bird, but neither knew if it was an eagle, hawk, or just a buzzard. Jack had been careful to let Thad talk about whatever he wanted to, but in time, T brought up the discussion of the previous night.

"I've been thinking about your plan, you know, me coming out of the closet in the biggest racing sport in the world, and laying my head down on the chopping block for all to take a whack at…"

Jack broke in, "But your ass would be so cute while you're bent over. I might be tempted to show the bastards what a fudge-packer is." They both laughed.

"I can't tell you how frighten I am. I am risking giving up everything I've worked for. All those go-karts, midget cars, and dirt cars I drove to get to the top series. For several years, I ate nothing but baloney sandwiches three times a day. I couldn't afford a big breakfast like we ate this morning." He paused as he gazed off to the east as far as he could see. The day was perfect with clear skies, a slight breeze, and bright sunshine. It wasn't hot at this elevation, so they were comfortable just sitting there thinking and talking. Jack reached over and patted T's thigh before taking his hand in his.

T continued, "They are going to call me lots of names, and may even punch me from time to time. I'll never know if they wrecked me because they wanted to win, or wanted to kick my ass. We might have to increase security to protect me from the drivers and crews as well as the fans."

"We can do that, because I do not want you to get hurt, but neither do I want you to give up the sport you love so much. I love watching you compete, and I am proud of what you accomplished, but I am humbled by all you can do with your huge stardom by helping kids and maybe now, even help find the cure for AIDS."

T winked at him and returned to his gaze, "I am worried about all those kids and younger drivers who look up to me. I hate to disappoint them."

"I bet they are the first ones to support you. Why would they turn down your help? You are going to do more for them after you come out than you could possibly have done before. Plus, you're going to add a whole new group of fans that will really admire you."

T looked at him with a puzzled expression. "Who is that?"

Jack smiled, "I'm glad you asked. All over the planet, there are millions of gay people afraid to come out of the closet, too. They will see that

168

if you were brave enough to do it on live television in front of the entire planet, and then perhaps they can be brave and tell their parents, friends, and schoolteachers. Times are changing. I knew I was gay when I was about fifteen, but kept thinking I would grow out of it, but kids are coming out even sooner now—some as young as nine or ten. You're twenty-three and already an old gay man compared to them."

T laughed, "Gee thanks."

"Here's a fact—teen suicide is three times higher in young gay teens that straight teens. We can do something about that by funding gay youth support groups all over the country. Our goal should be to create a gay support group in every school in the country. We are not trying to talk someone into being gay—only creating support if they are gay."

"Gees, you sure think a lot. I prefer masturbation!"

Jack punched his thigh, "Okay, so while I was thinking you were massaging your brain. I can't wait for your ribs to heal so you can massage that rascal inside me."

"It'll be my pleasure to help you," added T in a faked English butler style of accent. They both laughed.

Jack stood up, "Come on, let's go. Have you ever seen a herd of buffalo?"

"I don't think I have ever seen one live buffalo," replied Thad as he got to his feet and began walking back to the car.

"Do you see that valley down to the west? In the valley is a man who owns a big ranch with five thousand buffalo. He grows them and provides this area of the country with awesome buffalo steaks."

T smirked, "What does it taste like?"

Jack smiled as he turned the ignition, "Like the best steak you have ever had."

Jack drove back towards town by going around the curves and bends of the road, as it made its way down and around the mountain. Thad's ears popped after they dropped about a thousand feet. Jack found the ranch after spotting the sign for the Double Bar Buffalo Ranch, and made a left turn. The road was a little smaller, but still in good shape. He slowed down anyhow to protect T from any pain to his ribs.

After they went a few miles, they crossed a bridge made of two inch steel pipes. Jack explained the pipes scared the herd and the horses so they will not cross the bridge. A half-mile later they broke out of the heavy forest and into a wide-open range. At first Thad though he was looking at a huge pile of turds that covered several acres, but then he realized the 'turds' were moving. A mile later, he realized he was looking at a huge herd of buffalo, slowly grazing their way across the fenced pasture.

"My goodness they are huge," stated T.

169

"The bison weigh about two thousand pounds, but imagine in the centuries before the white man came to America, the bison came from Asia most likely across Alaska and settled into the plains. They were huge, weighing close to five thousand pounds, but with all this room to run around in, they managed to trim their bodies down to battle weight. When the first settlers crossed the Mississippi heading westward, there were ten million buffalo. For centuries, they roamed the plains free and happy. Our white men guns nearly killed them all. Thankfully, laws were passed before they became extinct, and ranchers discovered a market for buffalo steak and burgers. Slowly, the demand has grown, and now they ship the beef all over the country—even to New York City."

Thad asked, "How'd you know all this?"

"I read newspapers and articles, and once curious, I 'googled' various sites. It was really pretty easy. I can learn just about anything on the web, including the best positions for men to enjoy sex."

Thad laughed, "Looking at the size of the dicks on those big male buffalos is making me horny."

Jack grinned, "I'm not surprised. It is bigger than my arm!"

The boys laughed, as they drove slowly around the pasture, and then made their way back to Breckenridge. "I need to make a quick stop." Jack pulled into the parking of a medium size building with the faded word 'saloon' on the front. Thad noticed there were hitching posts for horses along the side of the place.

"What the heck is this?"

Jack smiled, as he closed the door. "Just sit tight, and I'll show you."

He walked in through the saloon's swinging doors, and off to the far right he saw the long bar leading to the back. There he saw a huge refrigerated display filled with extremely large steaks. Looking through the windows, he picked out two buffalo steaks. The lady wrapped them in butcher paper, and stuck them in a bag. He also bought two large baked potatoes and salads with fixing, and paid for everything before returning to the car.

He opened the door and reached in with the bag, "Here hold this."

Thad took the bag and let it rest on the seat next to him. "What is in there? It's heavy."

Jack backed out of the parking lot, and started driving towards the cabin. "It's part of a dead buffalo!"

"A what?" exclaimed a shocked Thad!

Jack hit the steering wheel as he laughed, "Its buffalo steaks, potatoes, and salad for our dinner tonight."

Thad looked into the bag. "Good grief, they are huge."

"All the steaks in the saloon are huge. That's a cool place. You go in, pick out your steak from the butcher, and they put it on a platter. You then go to the back where there is a huge grill that about twenty people can stand around. You plop your steak on the grill, add some seasoning, and while it is

170

cooking you head off to the salad bar. The waitress will bring you some ice tea and a huge baked potato. After about eight minutes you go turn your steak over, and before long, your salads are done, your potatoes are melting in butter, and you're forking your steak off the grill."

"That sounds like fun."

Jack lost his smile, "I know, but in the spirit of keeping your visit under the radar, I thought we should eat in the cabin, and besides, when I eat that much steak—I really get horny!"

"Home it is," replied Thad quickly. "I can't wait to eat your steak, uh, I mean your buffalo steak!"

They both laughed, as they crossed the intersection and turned back on highway 9.

On Tuesday morning, Thad awoke before Jack with the ribs feeling better, but his butt wonderfully sore. Carefully, he crept out of bed, and closed the bedroom door before going to the bathroom. He pulled on a pair of boxer undershorts, and walked to the deck on the backside of the cabin overlooking the lake. He saw a fish jump out of the water below, and a big bird circling high overhead. The air was not yet hot, but warming quickly. His bronze skin glistened in the morning sun. He ran loose fingers through his hair knowing he must look a wreck. He felt the stubble on his chin, and then rested his armed against the life vest that continued to support his ribs. He felt he was healing very well, and even took the vest off for a while yesterday, but he knew come Sunday, he would need it again to get through the race.

He surprised himself by being anxious to drive after just one weekend off from the horrifying, multi-spin, multi-flip disaster he survived in the Chicago race. Driving for him was as easy as riding a bike for a ten year old, but driving over 180 mph just absolutely thrilled him. It was a speed rush, second only to watching Jack's eyes just about pop out when his jism exploded deep inside Thad.

After their initial talks on the mountain last week, he said little about his decision to Jack. He did not want to be talked in to doing something, because if he allowed that, and things went wrong, he did not want to blame Jack for it. The decision had to be his, and his alone. He knew how Jack made big decisions with the spreadsheet listing the reasons to do or not do something, but for him, he could handle the process with his own brain.

He counted off on his fingers of his left hand the reasons to stay in the closet, and slowly began making a list of reasons to come-out with the fingers of his right hand. One list was far longer, but was it the right decision for him. He knew Al would return for him in just three days, so one way or the other, the time had come for him to make a choice.

He didn't like to think about losing Jack if he decided to stay in the closet, and yes, he wondered if he could survive without Jack. For a brief moment, he wondered if there was another gay man that was willing to stay in the closet, but as soon as the thought occurred, he pushed it from his brain, and admonished himself for even bringing it up. How could he respect someone—anyone who was not willing to be brave, stand on their own two feet, and tell the world how proud they were to be an honest gay man.

Thad knew he liked the feeling of being a sports hero, though he felt guilty for doing so. He often felt that racecar drivers were like gladiators, and the racetracks modern day coliseums. Sure, people wanted to see their favorite driver win, but they yearned for a good old fashion wreck, or even a fistfight to stir them up. Rarely did anyone in a bar say what an incredible move he did to pass the twelve car on lap sixty-three, but rather they talked about the big wreck he walked away from, while failing to remember he lost the race. At least after the Chicago wreck, they could remember the bent up car, and that he won, he thought.

He recalled Jack talking about the kids in need of a hero—a brave person they could look up to. He also thought he could use his media power and cash to help sick kids, and that he would continue to do, but what about the kids who were not sick—just sick of the way the world thought of them. He knew gay kids needed education and counseling, too or they could pick up a virus like AIDS or Hepatitis, or in fits of depression take on drugs for relief. He heard that roughly ten percent of the population is gay. To put that on his level, he thought about twenty thousand gay people sitting at a racetrack that held two hundred thousand. "That's a lot," he whispered to no one.

He glanced across the lake once more, realizing he was going to miss visiting Frisco, so he made a mental note to come back during the warm season when the air was clean and pure, the traffic small, and the locals friendly. And next time, he said to himself, I'll be the top and Jack will be bottom!" He laughed, and walked back into the bedroom.

"Jack? Jack? Get your ass up. We've got things to do," yelled Thad.

Jack rolled over and opened his eyes, then quickly shielded them from the bright morning sun. "I thought we did about all you could handle last night. My dick and my lips are still sore, and don't make a joke about what your evil mind is picturing!"

"Get up! We're going to Granny's for a big breakfast, and then back to take on an enormous project."

"What's that—we going to paint this place?" asked Jack as he stood up in the nude.

T rolled his eyes before horny thoughts began leaping about his brain. He resisted, "No, we've got to plan our attack. Janet will be back in the office today from her vacation, so I have just three days left to plan. You're looking at the first out of the closet gay racer in the world."

Jack looked at Thad's pitiful blue boxers and lifejacket, and found it hard to imagine him a champion of any sport. "I think we'd better get you dressed, so folks won't see you in those old boxers with your lifejacket on, and try to hand you a dollar to get you by."

Thad and Jack cackled as they headed for the shower, dressed, and out the door they went with great excitement and anticipation.

Jack hooked up his laptop to his portable printer and to his Wi-Fi card, so they could print out their lists, and prepare to send notes to Janet. Thad planned to call her on his cell phone soon, and swear her to secrecy. He would not tell her his real motive, but lead in a direction he needed for her to go. He began by asking her not to tell Drew about any of these plans. Second, he emailed her a list of all the media he wanted to be present at a nine o'clock news conference on Sunday, the day of the race in Indianapolis.

"But what do I tell them is the reason?" She protested. "I have to tell them something."

He gave her a half-truth, "Tell them I am going to announce the biggest charity fund-raising drive ever, and that I'm personally going to give away fifty thousand dollar checks to twenty charities. I'm working on the list right now, and shortly I'm going to email you the list of benefactors. I need for you to make sure there is a representative from each of these institutions there to receive the check. They can each bring along six kids to be my guest at the racetrack.

"Arrange a hospitality tent with credentials for each group and lunch, and I will make an appearance in front of them, and make sure we have a race cap and t-shirt for every kid there. Are you getting all this down? Get them seats in the stands, and yes, I'll pay for everything."

Janet had her headset on, and was typing as fast as she could. "Yes, I believe I have the details down. Do you realize how much that is you're giving away?"

"One million dollars," replied Thad slowly, "one spectacular million dollars! Cool, huh?"

"I know you can afford it—I just never heard of a driver giving away a million dollars of his own money in one day before."

"They don't call me TNT for nothing. I also want you to make sure all my sponsors are there. I'm hoping they match my checks." He paused to allow her to catch up. "Now if word leaks out, the shock value will be lost. There are only three people that know about this plan: Sam my accountant and us. I will get everything ready on the financial end. Find someone in graphics you can trust, and get those big checks made for us, but I want you to lie, and tell them I'm going to hand one of these out at each of the next races."

Janet broke in quickly, "There are only twelve races left."

He smiled at Jack, "Whoops, okay, we'll hand out two each week until we run out, or I might get even more generous."

Janet kept typing while asking, "Why are you doing this?"

173

"Why not? Sam has made me ten times that in the last two years. It is the least I can do. Just think of it as my way of tithing. I don't want you to tell Drew until thirty minutes before the press conference. It is going to be a fun weekend, and by the way—thank you for doing this, and yes, I'm also going to win the race!"

She laughed, "I think your head may still be like Jell-O after last week's wreck, but I love you for doing this. You're going to help so many people."

"I hope so. I'll check back in with you Thursday."

"Where are you?"

Thad rolled his eyes, "I'm in heaven, of course!"

She laughed, "You must be."

T smiled, "I'll meet you at the track in Indianapolis on Friday morning in time for practice."

Okay, I'm going to work. Have a safe flight."

"Thanks again, and I love you."

Thad hung up. Janet hit the off button for the call. Thad had never said he loved her before. She realized that he really did appreciate the work she did for him.

She spun around to her computer where she kept big databases of all the sponsors and their contact numbers. It took three hours, but she called every one of them, and spent the afternoon composing a press release for all the media. She rewrote it ten times until she was sure it would rub the curiosity of every journalist around. The next morning, Janet and her assistants spent the morning booking flights for the kids and charity receivers for all twenty institutions. Since the Cincinnati hospital was on T's list, she thought she would surprise Thad by asking the hospital if they thought Sammy could fly over. A tear fell from her eye when they said he was doing so much better, but they would see how he feels by the weekend. She hoped he could come because Thad would be thrilled to see him. She also swore everyone to secrecy.

Thad looked over at Jack as he was busily typing away on his laptop while listening to the phone conversation. Without looking up, Jack said, "You realize if you chicken out on coming-out of the closet, you'll still have to give those kids their million bucks!"

Thad laughed, "I know, but if I survive coming out, I think I'm going to do the same on the anniversary date next year, and the next."

"Now you're talking. The gay dollar is a mighty thing as the politicians are learning."

"What are you working on?"

Jack stopped, and looked up, "I'm doing two things at once. I'm writing your coming-out speech, although you can say whatever you want. I just thought a few phrases might help you through it."

"No, you go ahead and write the whole thing. I scared shitless," replied T.

"Don't go getting me excited. I have a lot of work to do."

"What was the other thing you're working on?"

"We go to the track on Friday right? Do you think I should remain hidden on your motorcoach for the weekend?" Jack didn't wait for him to answer, "I think I should. It might let the cat out of the bag, so to speak, and fire up the rumor mill. I prefer to surprise the bastards on our own terms." Thad laughed at him as Jack continued, "So, I was online researching charities you should visit on Friday and Saturday. One of them is called The Arc. It is an organization that supports children and adults suffering from disabilities. This group makes sure they are treated right and get the support they need."

"That sounds good."

"Also there is a dyslexia foundation, and a bicycle group that provides bikes for kids. In addition, there is also a program called "Kars4Kids." They want people to give them their car instead of trading it in, and then they will sell them for cash."

"Cool, I'll donate one of my cars to them, and autograph it. They could do a raffle or auction, and make a ton of money."

"Which car?"

Without hesitation T smiled and exclaimed, "The yellow corvette!"

"You love that car, but it is perfect. It will raise a lot of money."

"I'll ask Duke to see if his brother can drive it out for us."

Jack smiled, "I was thinking you could appear on all the local network affiliates live. When the race comes to town, the local sportscasters are run over by the national media. We'll visit them after visiting Indianapolis Veterans Hospital. For a few minutes, they'll have you all by themselves, and they'll love you for it. You'll have a busy day or two, which will keep you from worrying about Sunday morning." He turned his laptop towards Thad. "Here, email Janet and ask her to send you the practice and qualifying schedule, and the time of the drivers meeting. Timing is going to be so important."

Thad sat down and typed out the email. She sent it back a few minutes later. He then called Al, and told him what time to pick him up Friday morning. He asked Al to be sure he was flying alone as sometimes he would bring other drivers along with him, and to remember to keep his pickup area a secret.

By dark, they were exhausted from all the brainwork required for the day, and answering Janet's numerous emails without giving away what the real plan was. Jack ordered pizza, made a huge salad, and together they enjoyed a bottle of wine instead of the usual beer Thad would have opened. He didn't think he would like it, but he was tipsy by the second glass, so they soaked the soreness and the buzz away in the Jacuzzi.

175

On Wednesday morning, T took off the lifejacket, and together, they took a long shower. He went most of the day without it, but put it back on late in the afternoon, as the ribs began aching again. That night they waited until the last minute before hustling into the local theater in the dark to watch one of the summer blockbusters.

Thursday went just as fast except that Jack could tell Thad was becoming nervous. He not only had to give the best speech of his life—but he had to live with the consequences forever. T read Jack's speech over and over, and thanks to his ability to memorize most anything, he soon had it down pat. Jack made a few last minute alterations, but neither boy slept well their final night in Fresco.

They arrived at the airport at ten to watch Al land. Jack already left the rental car at the agency, and he set down the rest of his stuff alongside Thad's duffle bag. He often teased Thad that with all his millions he should buy a good set of luggage. T just gave him a 'what's the big deal' look, and Jack laughed.

Al didn't ask any questions, but shook hands with Jack. Thad told him Jack was working on a big speech he had to give on Sunday. Soon they were in the air and off on their journey. Jack hoped everything went as planned, but on the flight he began making a list of things that might not go as well as planned, and creating alternate plans, comebacks for bigoted remarks, and more worrying. Ironically, once the plane was in the air, Thad seemed at peace and fell asleep.

SIXTEEN

"Are you sure you have your credentials?" asked Thad as they were landing in Indianapolis.

Jack opened a button on the front of his shirt, and pulled out the credential lanyard including the photo the league officials took. They kept a copy on file for matching if required. "I have them."

Thad took out his money and wallet. "Here take these. There's about a thousand dollars in there in case you need something, or my charge cards if you need to buy something."

Jack put them in the zip pouch of his laptop case. "Stop worrying. I'll be fine."

Thad smiled, leaned over, and kissed him. "They'll be a helicopter waiting to take me to the track as soon as I land. Practice starts in fifty minutes. My crew chief, Charley Gast, is probably about ready to have a coronary by now. You're okay with taking a cab to the track?"

"Right. I'll get there during the height of practice so that everyone will be busy. I'll wear my hat down low and make my way to the motorcoach. What about Duke?"

"Do you know the code to the door lock?"

Jack smiled again, "Yep got it. It is your birthday backwards. Boy, you are dyslexic."

Thad laughed, "I thought I was creating greater security. Duke will pick me up with the golf car at the heliport. I will tell him I have a guest staying over this weekend, so he'll stay out of the coach. Keep the door locked, so that when I get there I'll have to unlock it like no one is home. They'll be plenty of food aboard, so please make yourself at home as before. Make or order some dinner as I'll be starved." He looked at his watch, "Just under three days to go, or about seventy-one hours and counting."

"You'll be so glad when it is over, but it is not too late to back out." Jack squeezed his hand.

"Nope, once I set my mind to something I am a doer, and I'll get it done."

Al put on the seat belt light and soon they were on the ground. Thad walked gently down the steps, while Jack waited patiently inside in case there were any photographers there to get a picture of Thad arriving for the race weekend. Thad climbed aboard the golf cart that took him to his helicopter.

After a few minutes, Jack peeked out the window and found the tarmac empty. He said goodbye to Al, who was going through his flight logs, walked to the private terminal, and out to the street and hailed a cab. Thad told him which gate for the cab driver to drop him at, so he wouldn't have to walk too far. He was shocked at how big the track was, as he had only seen parts of the race on television. He pulled out his credentials, and stood in line to go through the security gate. The guard half looked at his laptop case, and his bags including T's duffle bag, as a person with his level of security could just have walked through, and they would not have stopped him. He pulled his hat down low, spotted the motorcoach lot, and began walking.

It was a twenty-minute walk, but the noise was deafening, indicating that practice was in full swing.

"Where in the hell have you been?" asked Charley, as he came into the hauler, and found T almost naked except for his boxers and rib vest. "From the looks of your tan I'd say the beach and sun were very kind to you."

Thad didn't correct him. "Thanks. He sat down and pulled his thermal socks on, then he stepped into his uniform and looked up at Charley. "Would you mind helping me get one arm at a time in the sleeves?"

"You got to wear that vest?" asked Charley as he pulled a sleeve out, reached in, and pulled T's arm through.

"Yes, unless, you want me to cry like a baby on the track from the pain," grinned T.

Charley realized he was serious, "I guess four cracked ribs would hurt like a mother. Gentle now, and will get that last arm in. Are you going to be able to get in the car?" He guided his arm through the sleeve.

"Hell yes, but just slow and easy." He zipped up, and thankfully discovered enough room for the vest. "Tell the crew not to slap me on the back, even if I win qualifying."

"Roger that. I'll kill the first one that does. Come on, the car is on the track and ready. I think we have built a winner for you."

Charley led him out the door carrying his helmet for him. "That's good," replied T, "'cause I'm going to win this race."

"That's what I want to hear," replied Charlie, as he stepped on the pedal of the golf cart.

Jack stopped, and saw T's car warming up before picking up speed. He marveled that T could drive a car that fast with the rib damage he experienced. Except for a few kids and babysitters, the motorcoach lot was empty. He found T's coach, punched in the code, stepped in, and locked the door, but realized Duke had left the window blinds up. He sat his bag down, and walked over to the console trying to remember how to close the blinds. It took him a while to find the right switch, and when he flipped it, the blinds electrically went down all the way around the coach. He sighed with relief except now he had to find a light switch or two.

He put all the bags in the master bedroom, hung up their clothes to get some of the wrinkles out, and hooked up his laptop, so it could start downloading their emails. He went to the kitchen and found the refrigerator full of fresh food including a spiral sliced ham, loaded baked potato salad— one of T's favorites, a tub of coleslaw, a big bowl of chopped fresh cantaloupe and watermelon, sliced French bread, and a huge apple pie with chopped pecans, with melted chocolate and caramel dripped all over it. He lifted the pie and was shocked to find that it weighed at least twelve pounds. "Good lord, one bite of this pie would put a pound on you," he said to himself.

He fixed himself something to drink, found the remote for the satellite television, retrieved his laptop, and sat in the recliner to watch practice, and check their mail. The mail was still downloading, so he opened his spreadsheet for today's schedule. Thad would appear at five television stations today, and this afternoon he was going to the Veterans hospital. When the emails stopped, he realized almost all of them were asking for a new confirmation that everything was on schedule. He answered them all, and watched as qualifying time trials began. Thad had drawn fourth from the last, and Jack was thankful T was in the last ten to go out, as Jack felt this would help Thad.

Jack picked up the phone, and called the sports directors for each of the stations to assure them Thad would be there, and asked if they were promoting the hell out of this opportunity. Before hanging up, he would ask the person to transfer him to the news director. He would then tell each one of them that T would be appearing at the Veteran's hospital today at three. He got the email addresses, and emailed them a Press Release for the event.

Janet watched from the pit box, as T pulled his car to a stop, and remained inside while they prepared his car for qualifying. She turned to Charley, "Why doesn't he get out?"

"It would hurt like a…oh never mind. He is just thinking hard," he added.

She climbed off the stand, and walked over to T's car. "Hey sailor, give a girl a ride?"

T looked to his left, and flipped up his visor, "Hey. How was the vacation?"

"It was awesome, thank you very much. And how was yours?" She knelt down beside his door, so he would not have to strain to look up at her.

"Well, the ribs have been a pain, but it did force me to rest. How are you coming with your special project?"

She looked around to see if anyone was listening, "We're good. I'll make a lot of reminder calls tomorrow and Sunday morning, but I think it'll work. At this late notice, I had a bitch of a time getting a bus to meet the kids at the airport, but I did."

"Thanks, I owe you one. This is a good thing we're doing. I hope you feel that way."

She smiled, "I hear you don't want to get out of the car. Are the ribs killing you?"

"Oh it is not the ribs, it is the stereo in this car. It is just awesome," he teased.

She laughed, "Yeah right. They could at least give you an XM Satellite Radio in there."

"You'd think, but right now I'd settle for a swinging door. Would you hand me a squeeze bottle of Gatorade. They're in the blue cooler."

She retrieved it, and handed it to him, "No problem. You want me to clean the windshield and rotate the tires for you. I give Green Stamps for full service."

T laughed, "You're a trip. Oh, wait a minute, let me see your left hand." She blushed, as she showed it to him. "He finally popped the question. That's why you're such a smart ass today. Congratulations. I'll give you a kiss when I get out of this car."

"I will be counting on it. You be careful out there. I'll be on the box if you need me."

"Yes ma'am. Thanks."

T sat alone for the next twenty minutes, as he watched all the cars ahead of him go through time trials. Their times were good, and T was worried.

Jack stopped making calls when he saw T pull out for his warm-up lap, "Come on buddy, you can do this," he muttered to himself. "Step on it and get that pole!"

His first lap time put him in third, but he never let up on the accelerator. He kept the pedal down on the floor, and drove a perfect line, putting his car easily in first place with only three more drivers to go. He pulled into the pit, made a left turn, and drove to his garage. The crew guys were excited, and pounding the car with their hands. T took his gloves off and then his steering wheel. He began to slowly unbuckle the seat belts, and harness and headgear straps. He wanted to take his helmet off, but felt it would pull too hard on his ribs.

Charley came up to his window, "That a boy! That was just awesome! Let me help you get out of that car." Charley guided him up and out without pulling his rib cage too hard.

"Get this helmet off me," he begged.

Charley unclipped it, and pulled it off. "You're hurting, I assume."

"Just sore," replied T with a sigh. T was sweating, so Charley undid the top of his suit for him, and then got him another Gator Aid bottle.

"I am sure you are."

T asked, "How many cars to go?"

Charley turned around until he could see the leader board. "Just one so we're either on the pole or on the outside lane. Either one will be fine. Way to drive."

"It is an awesome car. A little tight in turn three, but my goodness it had the horsepower."

"I like the sound of that."

All of sudden the crew started yelling and cheering. T asked, "Did we win the pole?"

Charley turned around after seeing the official time on the leader board. When he saw their car number, he grinned. "Yep, you're on the pole."

"Charley, do you remember what I said about the crew and my ribs?"

Charley suddenly turned pale, "Yeah, right. No sweat." He quickly pulled his headset up, and told the crew the situation.

Janet drove up, "How about a ride to Victory Lane for the pole trophy?"

T walked slowly over, gave her a kiss on the cheek, and congratulated her on the ring. "I'm so happy for you. When's the wedding?"

"Drew said I had to wait until the off season, and that I could have three days off." She laughed.

"I think he meant three weeks," laughed T as he sat down in the cart.

"I may need your help with Drew," she winked at him.

He laughed, "You got it. We'll send him hunting in Alaska!"

Jack knew the pole award would take about twenty minutes, so he tried to quickly finish his calls and emails, and started pulling the food out for their lunch. He made a pitcher of sweet tea, T's favorite meal drink, found a lemon, sliced it up, and set it on the table. He glanced up to see the beer sponsor present him with the pole award plaque that T held close to his chest, and never once lifted it above his head. He did a few interviews, and then Jan dropped him off at the coach. She started to come in, but he told her he needed to go lay down, so she waved goodbye and promised to check on him later. He felt guilty for lying to her.

After she drove off, he quickly punched in the code and came up the steps pulling the door behind him and locking it. He turned around to see a smiling Jack, and a table set for lunch.

"Dang! You'd make a great housewife," laughed T. "How did it go coming to the track and getting in?"

"No problem. No one saw me, but of course, I had the right credentials to make it possible. Way to go on the pole." Jack leaned over and kissed him. "Gees, you're hot. Let's get you out of that suit."

"You're hopeless. How can you think of having sex at a time like this," grinned Thad.

"I just want to see you naked...again!"

In the bedroom, Jack carefully peeled T out of the upper part of the suit, took off his boots and socks, got the rest of the outer suit off his feet, tugged to get the fire suit off which was the hardest, noted his boxers were

181

soaked with sweat, and yanked them down, and then carefully took the vest off. "How are the ribs?"

"They are almost done, got any barbecue sauce?" shot back T. Jack rolled his eyes at him. T continued, "They hurt a bit."

"Do you want a shower, or do want me to wipe you down with a hot wash cloth?"

"Boy, are you nice. I might keep you, if you don't mind sucking me every now and then." They both laughed. "Just wipe me down, and I'll take a shower after our nap, so I smell better for the visits and interviews."

With the tenderness only a person in love could do, Jack cleaned him up, got new shorts on him, and together they set down to eat. T was famished, and after all the walking Jack had done after arriving at the track, he was starving as well. They talked about the plans for the afternoon while they ate. After Jack put the food away, they ate a slice of the pie.

"I'm stuffed, but boy was it good. You put all that together?" asked T as he squeezed Jack's hand.

"To be honest, it was all in the refrigerator, and there's plenty more if you get hungry again."

"Okay but let's stop and pick up some fresh corn. From the helicopter, I saw acre after acre of tall green corn stalks. It made my mouth water. We can microwave it, and eat it with the ham. Come on, let's take a nap." T got up and drank the rest of his tea. By the time, Jack cleaned up the kitchen and reached the bed, Thad was already asleep. Jack dimmed the lights, found a light blanket, and pulled it over them, and together they slept for almost two hours.

Jack help T dress by putting a big oxford dress shirt over his vest leaving the tails of the shirt hanging out and loose. T watched for wandering eyes, and finally gave Jack the 'coast is clear' sign, so he ran to the backseat of the Hummer and once off the track, they stopped, and T got in the passenger seat and Jack drove. He had the GPS set up to guide them to the Veterans Hospital. The director was waiting for them when they walked in the lobby. T brought a pocket full of Sharpie pens for autographs, and was ready to go to work. Several news media folks were there along with their cameramen. He allowed all the pictures they wanted, while the director guided him up and down every one of the six floors until he had seen every patient. Video and still shots were taken from time to time. Jack smiled at how wonderful T was with everyone he met, and he thought their plan was off to a great start. Thad spent extra time with those recently wounded in battle. He signed everything from casts for broken arms and legs, to prosthetic limbs. It was a moving experience for them, and by the time they left it was four o'clock.

"What's next?" asked T as he downed the rest of a water bottle. "

"Channel seven and the sport director is Steve Lyman," replied Jack, as he punched in the street for the GPS to get them there. Jack gave him his laptop. After pulling up a picture of Steve from their station's website, T memorized his face.

"Pull into that convenience store. You got any money on you, as I don't have a dime. I need water. Go buy a dozen bottles of water."

Jack left the air conditioning on high, and quickly made the purchase. It was a fifteen-minute drive, and after that short amount of time T emerged from the SUV all smiles and friendly, and acting like he never felt better. Jack marveled at his stamina. T saw Steve come out the door, and immediately said, "Hey, Steve. I just love this beautiful part of the world. You're very lucky to live in Indianapolis." Jack grinned and rolled his eyes.

Since these station visits had been kept secret from Janet none of the national news media knew anything about it, and only later that night when the locals presented their news stories did a few clips show up on the network media.

"Are you hungry?" asked Jack as he drove away from the last station.

"I'm exhausted. I don't think I have ever smiled so much in a single day. Now I know how a beauty queen feels in a Christmas parade." He rubbed his jaw. "Yep, I'm starved."

"Should I get some take-out?"

"Yeah, there's a Texas Roadhouse not far from the track. You feel up to a steak?"

"Yeah, sounds great. Get salads and potatoes." Jack began driving while T used his cell phone to order and gave the waitress Jack's name."

"Take the next exit and turn right," urged T. When they pulled into the parking lot of a big grocery store, T pulled the visor straight down. "Do you have cash?"

"I have your cash," replied Jack as he opened the door leaving the air conditioning running. "I'll get the fresh yellow corn and be right back."

A few minutes later, they pulled into the steakhouse parking lot. Once again, Jack said, "I'll be right back."

"Don't forget to tip the girl. She sounded nice."

"What if I see a cute guy in there? Can I give him a tip, too?" teased Jack.

"You'd better hurry your ass back with food, as I'm already getting hungry and horny!" They both laughed, as Jack slammed the door and T locked it. He did not want to meet any fans or anyone in the racing community.

He had just about fallen asleep by the time they got back to the motorcoach. Jack pulled up to the front of the motorcoach. They both looked, and didn't see anyone paying them much attention. Jack got out and retrieved the bags of food from the backseat, while T went around and opened the coach door, and ran right into Duke.

"Hey, Duke," said T loudly trying to warn Jack, but he was too late. Jack had stepped around the corner of the coach before he heard him.

"I wondered where you were. Hey, Jack. How are you?" asked Duke.

Jack had both hands full, but replied, "I'm good"

T was thinking fast and added, "I asked Jack to help me with the speech I have to give Sunday morning. We stopped for take-out, so we could work through dinner."

"Do you need anything?" asked Duke. "I'm heading to dinner at the hotel. My feet are killing me. I will never get used to walking so much on cement and asphalt."

"We're fine. I'll see you tomorrow."

Once inside, T locked the door, as Jack took the food to the kitchen counter. "What do you think? Will he tell the others?" asked Jack.

"I don't think so, but if he does, we'll stick to the same story. You're here helping me on the speech, but let's try to keep you hidden for just one more day."

The starving boys ate every bite of the dinner, and split a piece of the apple pie after Jack warmed it up in the microwave. T added a scoop of ice cream on the top. Afterwards they turned off the lights, and went straight to bed.

While T finished his late breakfast, Jack was checking his emails and the itinerary for the afternoon. T had practice at eleven, and then they ate a late lunch, followed by a short nap. Jack drove them to the Indianapolis Dyslexia Institute after the power nap, and about ten miles out of town he would visit a children's home. Suddenly, he recalled an old movie he had seen on television while fixing dinner. He went online, did a Google search, and found the Boys and Girls Town in Omaha. It was famous and huge. He scrolled down through their website until he found their phone number. Four calls later, he was speaking to Henry Wilkins, the director. On Thad's behalf, Jack explained that T had recently heard about their fine institution, and wondered if he could visit them on Monday afternoon after the race. Of course, the director said yes, so they set up a time. Jack then asked him if he needed anything. The director could have rattled on a long list of things, but he tested the waters by saying they could use school supplies for the fall term. Jack asked him how many kids and wrote the information into his notes on his laptop.

Jacked smiled, "I'll take care of that, but how about something bigger?" Jack loved asking the directors that question. He could almost feel their heart jump over the phone.

The director hesitated, but finally said the air and heating system had gone out in library, and it was just too hot to use in the summer and sometimes too cold in the winter.

"How much for a new one?"

"Three hundred thousand," replied the quick hopeful director.

"I'll see what we can do. What brand do you want?"

"Rheem."

"Very good. Let me do some research, and we'll see you about two Monday afternoon."

Jack quickly did a web search for Rheem, found a contact list, wrote down the president's name, and then used Anywho.com to find his home listing. He dialed the number, "Bob Miller? Bob, how are you? Very good and yes, I'm fine, too. This conversation is going to sound a little odd, but I work for Thad Nigel Thompson, or as the kids call him TNT. He is making a stop on Monday in Omaha to meet the fine kids at the Boys and Girls Town in Omaha Nebraska. We've just learned they need a new heat and air conditioning system for their library. It is about 20,000 square feet, and the director says it will cost about $300,000."

"That sounds about right," replied the confused director.

"Well, if T paid cash, and did a promotional spot for your company would you provide the unit and installation for less? He'd really like to help these kids, but he can't do it without your personal help."

The President smiled knowing that he paid over $400,000 for a celebrity to do his commercials last year, and now he could get the hottest racecar driver in the world for less than $300,000. "Jack, I tell you what I'll do. If T will do four commercial spots for us, I'll do everything for free."

Jack about wet his pants, and wished he hadn't drank so much orange juice while talking. "That would be fantastic. One more thing, do you think you could meet us on Monday in Omaha at the campus about two for the presentation? It is okay to bring along your camera and video crews. We want you to publicize this event, so that other companies will want to help Thad make this world of ours a little bit better for all—especially the kids."

"No problem."

Jack added, "If you have any questions, just call me at this number. In addition, could you get someone to make a big check or something to present, so it'll show up good for the cameras? I've invited the local media and all the network news crews to attend."

The company President smiled, "You bet I can. I'll see you on Monday."

Jack hung up adding Omaha to their travel list, and made a call to Al so he could make flight plans. Then he looked up the number for Office Depot in Omaha, and called asking for the manager who was thankfully working on Saturday. He explained the kids needed school supplies, and asked him whom he should call to get his company involved. Four phone calls later he was talking to the head of that company while sitting on his cart at his favorite golf course. By the time they hung up Jack arranged for a truckload of supplies to be there, and he had to ask T to ask the driver of the number 99 car Tim Jones to be there as Office Depot sponsored that car.

Jack looked up to see practice ending, cleared the table, and started the microwave on the corn he had cleaned that morning. T showed him how to put the ears in the Pyrex dish adding salt, pepper and lots of butter, and just a few teaspoons of water, and covering it loosely with plastic wrap. He pulled out the leftovers, and made another picture of tea. T came in the door and locked it.

"How'd it go?"

T smiled, "Good, but there is a little shimmy on the right side. Charley and the boys will work on it tonight. Just between you and me that car will fly. I have never driven faster. I made sure to drive fast, and then let off the gas before the lap finished so my friendly competitors couldn't see how fast I was going."

"Aren't you clever? Come on let's get you out of that suit. You look hot." They walked to the bedroom where Jack unzipped the suit.

"I feel like a hot penis in a condom," complained T.

"You wish," shot back Jack as he began wiping him down. They both laughed, sat down, and T ate a whole ear of the hot buttered corn before stopping for tea, and more food.

"I booked us at the Boys and Girls Home in Omaha Monday afternoon. I've already told Al, but you need to tell Duke to stay over one more night in the hotel so we can stay onboard the coach until Monday."

T gulped another mouthful down, "No problem."

"And you need to ask Tim Jones if he can meet us there at two."

"Sure, but why?" T took a much-needed swig of the cold iced tea.

"Because I found out the kids needed school supplies, so I got Office Deport to donate them, and they sponsor his car, yada yada. Oh they also needed a new heat and air system for the library."

T stopped eating, "How much is that going to cost me?"

"Nothing, I got Rheem to donate it for free if you'll do a few commercial spots for them. Is that okay?"

T laughed, "Hell yes it is. Way to go."

Jack felt proud of T's support.

T asked, "Did you say Rheem? I wish you wouldn't talk about sex while I'm eating!"

They both laughed as they finished eating and slept well during their nap. That afternoon they visited the Dyslexia Institution with T telling the reporters he had Dyslexia, and knew these folks needed plenty of help. He urged the community to support them. They were on the list for tomorrow's presentation as was their next stop. The boys both had fun at the Children's

186

Home playing with a group of kids, visiting rooms, and just hanging out. Jack made a note to send the kids TNT racing hats and t-shirts. By six, they were exhausted from the fun and the heat.

"Should we do take-out on the way back to the track?" Jack was driving, and T was leaning against the window almost asleep.

"I usually do pasta and salad the night before a race. Let me think a second. Oh yeah, there is a place here that makes the best Fettuccini Alfredo with grilled chicken and Caesar salads. What is the name of it? Uh, Robertos! That's it. Go to exit 67 and hang a left." T got on the phone, and made the order.

Janet had been so busy Friday night hosting a dinner for one of Drew's sponsors for another car that she missed the nightly news in the local area. She was giving tours of the hauler and the pits on Saturday, and didn't sit down to rest and read the newspaper in her hotel room until late Saturday afternoon. She turned the TV on, and ate Chinese take-out with chopsticks—a skill she was proud of. She soon saw pictures of T at the Veterans home and television stations. She read the stories and wondered why she didn't know about this. She began flipping from one local station to the next until she hit upon a video story showing T meeting the sports staff followed by a quick interview. This puzzled her. She sat down her dinner and called T's cell phone.

T was waiting for Jack to return with their dinner when his phone rang. He looked at the Caller ID. "Hey Janet, how's the bride to be?"

"I'm good, although Drew is wearing me out with the new sponsor stuff for his the number 44 team. Hey, I just read about you in the newspaper about your appearance at the Veterans hospital. Why didn't I know about it? I should have had the press releases out, and gone with you in case something came up."

"Sorry, it was no big deal. A friend just asked me if I would, and I had nothing to do and said yes. I was so proud to be an American when I met the soldiers and the great staff there. It went great."

"And on the news I saw you at the local television stations."

"That's my fault, too. I was leaving the hospital, took a wrong turn, and couldn't figure out where in the hell I was in Indianapolis, and you know men won't ask for directions. I tried to get back to the track for an hour when suddenly, I saw the big TV antenna and the satellite dishes. I went in, introduced myself, and got directions, and while there, I just went around chatting with everyone. One thing led to another."

Not satisfied, she press on, "What about the other stations? How'd you end up at those?"

T rolled his eyes, "Well, I remembered that we must at all times be fair to the media. If we do an interview for one, we must work in another, so I just made my way from one to the next." He saw Jack coming, "Hey, I've got to go in and eat. I'll talk at your later. Bye."

She said bye and put the phone down trying to recall if T had ever done this before. She went back to her cashew chicken stir-fry dinner while leaning back and resting her exhausted feet. She fell asleep with the television still on.

With dinner done and the kitchen cleaned, the boys settled down to watch a movie, but all they could think about was the big press conference in the morning.

T looked up to at Jack's face with a sad, soulful look, "Don't you think you should be on the stage with me so I can't chicken out?"

Jack laughed, "You can chicken out right now if you want to. It has to be your decision, and I'm here to help either way."

"Spoken like a true diplomat, and a big chicken. Was it this hard for you to come out?" Thad reached over and intertwined his fingers in Jack's left hand.

"Well, I came out right after college. My school was several states from my folks, and in my freshman year I accepted the fact I was gay when a cute guy asked me out."

"How'd he know you were gay?"

"I don't know because I didn't even know. He was funny and great to talk to, so I went out with him. It was several dates later before we had sex. I wanted to tell my parents, but I didn't think my dad would take it very well, and I was afraid he would cut off my college support. I came out to the family once I had a full time job, an apartment, and my own car. I was wrong about my dad—he said he had known for a long time, and he loved me anyhow. Mom was the problem!"

"She didn't like the fact that you were gay?" asked Thad.

"No, she was fine with that. She didn't like the idea there wouldn't be a wedding to help with, or grandkids to help raise!"

They both laughed before giving up on the movie and went to bed. Jack had wrongly assumed T might be moody and not want sex the night before the race and his big press conference. He was definitely but pleasantly wrong.

SEVENTEEN

T read the speech several times a day for the past few days and successfully memorized it. He put a copy in the side pocket of his uniform in case he forgot something. Jack helped brush his hair, but laughed when T crammed a race hat over his work. They kissed several times, and Jack asked him one more time if he was sure he wanted to do it because Jack had become nervous as well. Suddenly, there was a knock on the coach door. Jack drifted back to the bedroom while T went to see who it was. He glanced up at the security monitor and realized it was Harry Phelps head of driver development, the man that watched T drive since he was a little boy, and got him the contract with Drew. He owed Harry a lot. He opened the door.

"Hey, Harry. I'm so glad you could come today. I'm going to win this race!"

Harry smiled, "I bet you are. Listen, have you got a minute, I need to talk to you."

"Uh," stumbled T, "what's up?"

"Can I come in?" asked Harry as he began moving toward to the door.

T knew he was in a jam so he said loud enough for Jack to hear him and the entire west wing of the stands, "Sure Harry. Come on in. I've got a press conference in a few minutes."

"It won't take a second." Harry sat on the couch and got immediately to the point. "I was in Daytona when that note was passed around about you being queer. I laughed it off at first, but as I traveled out west to see a few wannabe racecar drivers, I got to thinking. I had recalled a few years ago, right before you signed with Drew, that I had seen you looking at another young driver."

T grew nervous, "Hey, what are you talking about? I don't remember that."

"Yeah, you do. His name was Alan Martin. I saw you guys a few other times hanging out, shooting pool, and I could tell you were sweet on him."

T became very nervous, with no idea where his friend was going with this discussion, so he tried to end it, "Harry, I've got to go. I have that press conference."

Harry stopped him cold. "I know you're gay." He paused for a second, "And I think this is what this press conference stuff is all about." He paused again. T could feel his heartbeat in his neck. "Thad, you don't know this, but I had a beautiful daughter. Her name was Susie, and she was a heck of a tomboy. I bet she would have made a fine racecar driver or a mechanic. She was also a looker and the boys were after her, but she fell for another girl in nearby town. They were caught before she could tell her mom and I that she was gay. She held on for a year, but the rumors in town got to her. She drove my car right off the overpass and crashed it down on Interstate 85 at rush hour. She was hit three times and died instantly. I know she meant to do this because she left us a note saying how sorry she was that she had let us down and disappointed us.

"She was my only child. How could she ever have done anything to let us down? We loved her..." he caught himself as the emotion built up, "and still love her. She didn't need to kill herself. If I had known she couldn't handle it, I would have moved us to another state. It was my fault she died— not hers. That's why I came to see you before this press conference. If you're about to do what I think you're going to do, there are going to be days when stupid people will make your life hell. I don't care what they do or say, life is still worth living. Once you're out of the closet, as the kids call it, you're free from the secret, but you still need to be careful. My wife and I love you, and if you need a place to hold up or you just need to talk, you call me. I'm proud of you, what you have become, your driver abilities, and what you're about to do. There isn't another driver on the track as brave as you are." Harry stood to go, but Thad stopped him.

"Harry, wait a second." He turned to face the rear of the coach and called, "Jack, please come here."

Sheepishly, Jack came up to Thad's side. "Harry, I'd like for you to meet Jack. Jack this man is the reason I drive a racecar. He taught me about racing in the big leagues, and he taught me how to be a man. I can't lie to him. Harry, you're right. I am gay and so is Jack. We love each other very much. Don't you worry—I am not about to kill myself. In fact, I'm going win this race and the championship. You just sit back and watch. But I need two favors: Could you keep this under your hat for just a little while longer?"

"Sure son. No problem. Jack, I'm so happy to meet you." They shook hands with warm smiles.

T smiled as he hugged Harry, "And Harry, Jack is going to take my golf cart and drive over to the media room. Would you go with him and stand in the middle in the back so I can see the both of you when this happens?"

Harry hugged him tight and then gave Jack a hug, "You bet. You ready to go Jack?"

"Give me one second," replied Jack as Harry wisely went out the door.

T and Jack kissed long and hard, and hugged for a long time. Thad called Janet and asked her if she would come pick him up. Jack and Harry drove off before she got there.

Janet drove up and T bounded out the motorcoach door trying to pump himself up. "Hey Miss Bride to be—is everything ready to go?"

He sat down on the golf cart seat as she stepped on the pedal. "Of course, I'm always ready. The kids are so cute. I have them in three rows on the platform with recipients on the front row. I'll be down front giving them their cue, and handing you another big check to give away. Wow, I still can't believe you're giving away a million dollars in just fifteen minutes!"

"They need that and more. Thank you for all your help. I may not say it often enough, but I really appreciate all you do, and I am so grateful for your help and loyalty." He paused and swallowed hard, fighting to hold back the emotion building inside him. He asked, "Did you get Drew here?"

She laughed, "Yeah, but he is as curious as a cat. He helped me get all the sponsors there, too. Speed Channel got wind of this press conference, and they're going to run it live on their Race Day Show."

T gulped and took another swig of his squeeze bottle of Gator Aid. When he got to the media building and the auditorium, he saw the Greyhound bus the kids arrived on, and he knew he couldn't let them down. He saw Harry and Jack step thru the center doors, and he wouldn't let them down either. "Janet, see if everything is ready, and I'll walk right down the center aisle."

"You're the man and just like Elvis!" she teased as she walked into the room and came right back out and gave him a thumbs up. As he reached the doors, she yelled, "Ladies and gentlemen, and kids of all ages, please welcome championship driver Thad Thompson!"

T entered the room by winking at Jack and Harry. He shook some hands as he went down the aisle, and when he got to the stage, a young kid caught his eye. It was Sammy. T stopped shaking hands and immediately went to him, picked him up, and hugged and swung him around. He held his little body in his arms in spite of the T's sore ribs, and told everybody to please be seated as he walked to the platform.

"Before we got started, I want to introduce you to the sweetest, bravest boy on the face of the earth. This is my friend Sammy. Life has been tough on Sammy, but Sammy says he has been tough on AIDS, and the disease doesn't have a chance of winning." He looked at Sammy as the camera bulbs flashed taking their picture, "Sammy, I dedicate today's race to you, and by the way," he turned to look the cameras straight in the lens, "I am going to win it, too! And that's a promise," he added as the auditorium and the kids clapped. He returned Sammy to his feet and smiled at the kids, and then turned and smiled at the front row seats full of sponsors and their leaders. He saw Drew and winked at him.

He took a breath, looked at the back of the auditorium, and found Jack smiling at him. "Ladies and gentlemen, I have several important announcements to make today, and I'll try to do them as fast as I can because we have a race to win. Thank you so much for coming. I see before me my boss, team owner, and friend Drew McClain. I would not be here without you. I love you."

He turned to the front row on his left. "As I call out my sponsor names would the representatives from each company please stand, and hold your applause until I get them through them all." He began rattling off the

191

names just like he did during an interview or after a race win. No other sport shamelessly plugged their sponsors like championship racing drivers.

He turned around and waved to the kids and the adult leaders with them. "Behind me are representatives and the kids from twenty of my favorite charities. I bought them tickets for today's race, and Janet has found hats and t-shirts with TNT on the front of them for everyone. Thank you for coming." The audience again gave them a hand.

"These charities and many others all over the country need help. No other sport in the world has loyal fans like we do. We need to challenge our fans, our sponsors, and our team owners, and encourage each into giving their time and their money to help. I have heard speeches about how we should do this or that, or the government should do this or that, but I believe in putting my money where..." he paused for effect "where my heart is! Today I'm going to hand out a big check to each of these groups here today. With Janet's help we'll get started."

Janet handed him the first big check. The representative came forward, shook T's hand and the kids all stood with them as they held the fifty thousand dollar check up for the pictures. He continued until he had given away all the checks. Janet sat back down and T looked up to see Jack's smile once more.

"I don't know if you folks had your calculators with you or not, but that was one million dollars, and it will go to great use, but that is not enough. I'm going to ask my sponsors and my team owner Drew, to figure out how they can help these groups as well. I'm willing to do whatever I can to help my sponsors increase their sales so they can afford to help others. If you need me, I'll be there, but I'm counting on you to be there for me, and help these charities!"

The crowd applauded including many in the normally nonchalant press corp. Not yet ready to totally jump into the frying pan, he deviated from their planned speech just a bit. T said, "I'd like Harry Phelps to step forward. He's in the back of the room. Give the group a wave, Harry," he urged as he smiled. "I'd like for Drew McClain to spin around in his wheelchair." He smiled as he did so. "Drew, don't get excited because I don't have a check for you today." The folks laughed. "I just wanted the world to know that Harry and Drew are essential to my early driver development and bringing me to the big leagues. I owe them for that, and their loyalty and friendship. I just wanted you to know, and I love you." He paused and then smiled, "You can turn back around Drew. That's enough praise for now. I don't want you to get the big head!" The crowd chuckled as Drew blushed.

T looked up, smiled at the group, and winked at Jack. "I've known all my life that I could drive anything from a bicycle to a scooter, to golf carts and cars. I've known about other things in my life, but never gave them much thought as racing always came first. I am sorry to admit that most of my young adult life I only cared about winning, and forgot about the plight of others not as fortunate as I have been. With your help, I hope to fix that from now on.

However, there is another group that is not on this stage today that I want to talk to you about. Let me begin by saying I've seen the magazines and heard the race announcers call racers heroes. I thought it was cool, but I didn't really think of myself as a hero. I think heroes are like firemen, policemen, or soldiers. The special group I want to talk about has very few heroes to look up to. After doing a lot of research, I learned there were many in this group across the country, only they don't get the press that I do.

"This youth group I'm talking about is gay." He paused for a second to let the word sink in and the room fell instantly quiet. "These kids figured out who they really are, but are forced to keep it a secret from family and friends, as well as strangers that would beat and kill them. Often no one in their circle is willing to stand up for them. Sometimes when they confess to a guidance counselor, they are scorned. If they go to their pastor or priest, many times, they are kicked out of the church and the parents notified. Many are pushed out on the streets to live on their own—told never to return home again.

"Some are abused because they are hungry and need food, and so they give the only thing they have—their youthful bodies. These are lonely kids in need of someone to step in and be their hero. I'm going to do that today. I'm going to help them, I hope my sponsors and team, and all of you will help them today.

"There's a lot of ignorance in the world. In some countries, if a youth is found out to be gay, they don't just kill them, they deliberately torture these children for several days. Kids in America are spit on, kicked, beaten, and neglected all because they are what God made them.

"I don't plan to preach to you today, but no one chooses to be gay. They can no more change who they are than a person can change the color of their hair or skin. When we get to heaven, maybe God will tell us why he made some people gay, but until then, we have to trust Him to know better than we.

"The suicide rate for these young gay people is three times higher than it is for your teenagers. How lonely it must be for them when they have no one to talk to, no one to share the anxieties with, and many times no place to live.

"No other group in America has been the victim of more hate crime attacks than gay people. People hate them for just being who they are—how stupid.

"In spite of what some church leaders preach, I believe people are born gay. They say gays try to recruit more gays. How dumb is that? You have to be born that way. You can't catch it, and you can't give it away. It just is. You can't recruit any easier than you can teach an elephant to fly, or a whale to walk around a circus ring or drive a car.

"God gave me the talent to drive a racecar and thank goodness, or I'd be making burgers at McDonalds. We don't know why and it is not our job to know why, but I believe God makes some people different. Maybe He has a sense of humor: some tall or short, some fat or thin, some light or dark in color, some with thick or thin hair, and some with no hair at all like Drew. We don't get to decide on which trait we are born with—we should just be thankful for what we are given. I think that is the way gay people are.

"There are many talented gay people in our civilization. I won't name them all as that would takes hours, but here are a few names: Alexander the Great, Aristotle, Julius Caesar, Leonardo da Vinci, Michelangelo, Walt Whitman, Tennessee Williams, Oscar Wilde, Billy Jean King, Rock Hudson, Nathan Lane, Melissa Etheridge, K.D. Lane. In addition, who hasn't laughed with Ellen Degeneres and sung along with an Elton John song.

"There have always been gay people, and there always will be. Mel White wrote to Jerry Fallwell to try to get him to stop persecuting gay people. He wrote, "The Scriptures have been misused to defend bloody crusades and inquisitions; to support slavery, apartheid, and segregation; to sanction the physical and emotional abuse of women and children; to persecute Jews and other non-Christian people of faith; to support the holocaust of Hitler's Third Reich; to oppose medical science; to condemn inter-racial marriage; to execute women as witches; to excuse the violent racism of the Ku Klux Klan; to mobilize militias, white supremacy and neo-Nazi movements; and to condone intolerance and discrimination against sexual minorities."

Thad added, "A favorite quote of mine is, "Some minds are like concrete, thoroughly mixed up and permanently set."

"We can change the world a little at a time with the power of our sport. We can avoid being like the concrete by stopping the bigots. We can change people's minds over time. It just takes one hero at a time to step up to the plate. We have nothing to lose but everything to gain.

"I would rather be rejected by people for what I am, than be accepted by people for what I am not." The time had come, he sighed heavily and looked straight at Jack with a twinkle in his eye, "Before I give my final announcement of the morning, I want to thank you all for coming and to beg you not to forget these charities really need our help."

Thad felt up until that point the press remained silent to what they felt was another temporary cause a celebrity decided to endorse. They didn't give it much thought and much of T's speech went in one ear and out the other.

"My final announcement is simple, though it took years for me to get ready and prepared to make it. I'm going to win today's race and this season's championship—not as a straight man, but as a gay man. For I, Thad Nigel

Thompson, is and always will be…gay. I am the first racer out of the closet, so to speak, and I'll be the first to the finish line. Thank you."

The audience remained eerily silent and shell shocked until the news crews started making a dash for the door to file their story. There was some polite applause, but mostly the room became a sea of chaos. Several reporters made their way to the front and wanted to ask questions, but Thad politely replied, "After the race boys—after the race."

He winked at Janet, stepped down and gave Sammy a hug, and walked straight up the aisle, gave Harry a big hug, and walked out the door and over to his golf cart where Jack was waiting. Quickly they drove to the motorcoach and went inside.

In the media center, Steve Appleton sat in his chair completely stunned. He had been so close to breaking this story, but couldn't make a factual case, and the biggest story of the season fell through his fingers. Every reporter now had the story, and all the digging he did remained useless.

"I give it about three minutes until everyone in and on the racetrack hears about it," stated T.

"It went great. I'm so proud of you. You didn't get a single egg thrown at you."

They turned on the television to watch the pre-race shows. It wasn't long until the story of the million-dollar give away came along, followed by T announcing he was gay. The announcers were still in shock, and rambled on before going to a commercial break.

"Well, there's no way for me to go back in the closet now," stated T as he kissed Jack.

"You're right." Jack smiled after kissing T again, "Now the hard part."

"That was the hard part. That was the hardest thing I've ever done," replied T as he went to refrigerator. "I need something sweet. Let's eat a piece of that pie. That'll get my adrenaline pumped up for this race."

Jack laughed, "The hardest part will be showing them a weak, limp, silly old gay boy like you can whip their redneck butts and win this race!"

Thad stuck a spoonful of the pie in Jack's mouth, "Ooo, I love it when you talk dirty to me!"

During driver introductions Thad expected the boos to be louder than usual when he was introduced on stage at the finish line and indeed they were, but he did notice there were people standing and clapping for him this time that were not wearing any of his team's colors. While taking the ride in the back of a pickup around the track, he waved at the fans while a network reporter and his cameraman asked him about his car for today's race. He knew where the busload of kids were sitting, as well as Sammy, so he waved frantically to them. When he returned back to his pit, his crew gave him the cold shoulder by saying nothing to him. Jack watched from the motorcoach hoping T would be okay, but he knew it would be a long weary race.

T looked at his men and stood still in silence while thinking hard about what to do. He smiled and urged them to huddle up. They hesitated, but finally did. He looked them in the eye. "Okay, I know this was a shock to you, but I wanted to be honest with you. I respect you guys, and you having nothing to fear because I don't want to date any of you—I want to win you a championship, starting with this race today. I know with your help I can win, and I can't wait to see that championship ring on your fingers. Can I count on you to help me do that?"

He bravely stuck his hand into the center of the circle. There was a long moment of hesitation before the youngest guy on the team put his hand on top, followed by a tire changer, the jack man, and soon the rest of the team. They gave out a big old yell, and for the first time that morning, Charley felt a bit of optimism return to his team. T climbed into the car. He was too pumped up to even feel his sore ribs. The crew started getting him ready.

Drew steered his motorized wheelchair from the media room to the various pits of his other teams assuring the sponsors that everything would be fine. Many were upset, but Drew knew that in his heart, T was right. His company and his sponsors, along with his drivers and teams, could help the world a bit more, but he was still ready to jerk a knot into Thad for not telling him in advance. He would deal with that later.

He guided his chair to T's pit and over to the chair lift, and rode up to the pit box. He put on his headset and clicked the microphone button on the side of his left earmuff. "T, you copy?" The crew fell silent recognizing the voice.

"Yes sir," replied T quickly, while afraid he was about to be fired.

"I just wanted you to know it took a lot of guts to do what you did this morning. Not many folks would stand up to the press, the sponsors, and especially me like you did. I respect the truth, and I expect to win today. Can you do that for me?"

T grinned, "Yes sir I can, and I will—if the boys will help me!"

The crew let out a cheer that made the other teams turn to see what was going on. Before long, the Star-Spangled Banner had been sung by one of the latest American Idol winners, and four fighter jets flew over. On command from a guest celebrity, the drivers started their engines. T looked back at his crew one more time and gave them a left hand salute. He pulled out behind the pace car and drove slow, allowing the rest of the field to catch up. He had an early goal of leading a lap, and leading the most laps to pick up some more championship points. He knew it would be hard today, but he had to stay focused. As the pace car pulled off, he prepared to lead the group to the green flag.

Suddenly with the flag still at the starter's side, car number 50 bumped him hard from the rear. T had been rocking the tires back and forth to clear the rubber from any debris, and failed to notice the car behind him moving up quickly. The hit sent him bouncing in to the car alongside him. That driver cursed him. T mouthed he was sorry but knew no one would hear him. The green flag dropped so he put the pedal down and the race was off.

Twice on the first lap, the number 50 car hit him again. In spite of Charley's protest of rough driving, the race officials didn't seem to care. T knew his only chance was to out run him. He flew around the track and obtained goal one of leading a lap. After about sixty laps the race settled down, and the 50 car was farther back in the pack, but that was the least of his troubles. T pitted, got four fresh tires and two buckets of gas, and just as they dropped the jack for him to speed away, car number 67 pulled alongside and shut his engine down blocking T from getting out. The driver acted like his car cut off, and they could hear the starter turning, but what they couldn't see was the driver switched the on switch to off. He let T sit there for about fifteen seconds, and long enough to put him in the back of the field.

"What kind of horse shit is that!" screamed Drew. Janet flinched as Drew slammed his hands down on the railing. One of their crewmembers started running down to the number 67 pit and yelling at that team. They yelled back, and soon they were swinging fists. T's team ran to their teammate's rescue, and the officials came to break it up.

Jack saw it all on television, but the announcers never said what started the fight. Charley broke in on the radio, "Ok, crew. I want you to settle down right now. We have a race to win, and we'll take care of those boys later. T, you ready to roll son?"

From the back of the field, T prepared for the restart of the rest, and replied, "Yep, I can get back to the front."

"I know you can, but be careful coming up through the field. There might be another asshole waiting to put you in the wall."

"Roger, no problem," replied T as he gulped.

Charley looked up at the spotter on the roof and then called him on radio, "Gary, you got eyes on T?"

"Yep, no problem."

"Anybody saying anything up there?"

"Not a word. Everybody has been avoiding me like I didn't take a bath last night."

T and the crew could hear the conversation. Charley chuckled, "Hell, Gary, you probably didn't take a bath last night!" They all laughed and then seriously, "Gary, make sure he gets through the field clean. You tend to watch what is in front and beside of him, which is why I hired you, but today I want

197

you to watch what is behind him. If you get a hint of trouble, speak up quick! Roger?"

"Roger that," promised Gary.

Twenty laps later, T was bumped in the rear just as Gary was telling him to watch out. T just put the throttle down and said to hell with them. He passed five cars in one lap and was soon near the front, but then his right front tire went flat. He limped around the track and reached the pit line just as the caution went out. Now he was going to be two laps down. Charley cursed. Drew spit tobacco into a cup, and Janet safely moved to the far end of the pit box.

His team changed the tire quickly, and he began racing through the cars that were a lap down, so he could get to the position in the field to take advantage of the lucky dog rule, and get a lap back which happen with a caution on lap 103. On the pit box, Charley called for two tires instead of four, and he told them he wanted it done in six seconds. T slammed his brake pedal and skidded to a stop. "Get ready son. Just two and go. Go, go, go!" he yelled.

T was first out of the pits and mission accomplished, but they were still one lap down. At lap 156, he came in under green flag, and got four tires and gas. "Now get in the lucky dog spot again," demanded Charley.

It took Jack a while to catch on to the strategy, but sure enough on lap 167 a caution was flown, and T got his second lap back. He pitted with the field, but since he only had a few laps on his tires, he just took gas and came out ahead of the field. The announcers went wild over the move, and the crew jumped for joy. Drew nearly swallowed a plug of tobacco he felt so happy.

T said on the radio, "Way to go Charley. That was a great call!"

After the restart, he was bumped no less than three times by a car coming down on him. He tried to stay in front, but they were sure making it tough on him. At lap 212, he obtained the most laps of the day, and objective number two was accomplished. Seconds later a lap car ahead of him slid up the track to allow him to go pass. T waved thanks failing to realized it was the 90 car, and on the same team as the 50 car. Suddenly, the 90 car quickly slid back down, hit T right in the door panel knocking him off the track, and wildly into the heavily painted and decorated infield grass. T's car spun sideway, throwing grass and dirt into the air. The crowd stood expecting the sidewall to dig into the grass throwing T's car in a multi-somersault spin. T quickly turned the steering wheel in the direction he was already going, like he use to do when driving dirt cars in the mud, or his father's truck in the snow. The car straightened up, and to everyone's amazement T never let off the throttle. He cut across the front of the pits just missing a wall, and bounced right back up on the track and in fifth place.

"Way to go T," yelled Charley. I doubt you hurt the tires in the grass, and in a lap or two you'll shake all that dirt and sod off. You can breathe now," laughed Charley, "while I restart my heart." The crew laughed. "Thad, I know you'd like to scoot up there and knock the number 90 car over the fence and into parking lot D, but as a favor to me, would you mind if we won the race first?"

T grinned, "No sweat. How many laps to go?"

"Oh, let's see," fended Charley, "Just eight—nothing to it, right?"

The crew fell silent waiting for T's response, "You just count the laps off and the cars left, and I'll take care of the rest." The crew cheered, and in the motorcoach, Jack turned down the television sound and turned up T's radio channel. He smiled and excitedly shook his fist in the air.

Thad reached the fourth place car by the second turn and passed him clean. It took two laps to get to the third car. He went a car length high around him to be sure he missed him, then cut down sharp in front of him, and took third place away—two cars to go, and five laps to get it done.

Charley felt afraid to say anything on the radio except the lap read out and two cars to go. T caught the second place car, number 53 and tried to go low, but the driver blocked him. T tried high and was blocked again. The driver never really thought T could pass him, so with four laps to go, T faked high, then came back a little, and when the driver went low, T was already even with him on the high side. He had about a quarter inch of pedal left and he put it down. By the second turn, he was around the second place car and in sight of the leader or the 46 car.

"Three laps and one car. Go get 'em!" yelled Charley. The crew stood on the wall. Jack was busy biting his fingernails, Janet kept crossing her arms never finding the right position, and Drew spit out his tobacco. He clinched his fists, and said to no one, "Come on T. You can do this!"

T knew the driver of the 46 car. He was an experienced multi-year veteran and a winner. There would be no faking high or low. He would try very high first, and if that didn't work, he would have to bump and run to win. He hated to do it, but he had to win. He dug low when he reached his bumper, and gave him a love tap on the straightaway to rattle his cage a little, but not hurt him. T went very low, but received an instant block with just two and half laps to go.

T quickly went high, but 46 came up as well. T came back in line behind him. He had two laps to go. 46 expected another fake low, but T went high, and 46 came up. T didn't stop and went up another lane and sailed even with him, and almost out of 46's mirror, but a quick turn of his head, and a scream from his spotter let him know where T was.

T slowly brought his car back down and once again put the pedal down as far as it would go. There were just one and half laps to go, and they were now just inches from each other. 46 slid up and gave him a love tap in return, but it almost sent T in the wall. He anticipated it and let the car absorb it, and then he cut down hard and looking to crash the 46's front right bumper.

The 46 driver made a simple mistake—he tried to protect his car, and gave the wheel a quick pull left to move him over just a foot, but slightly let up his foot on the pedal. It took a half second for him to slam his foot down to the floor. T took the lead and slid down in front of him with only one turn to go.

The pit box stood. Jack stood in the coach. Janet stood. Drew wished he could from his wheelchair. All the charity kids stood. The sponsors rose from their box seats. T's enemies stood. More than half of the forty-two televisions cameras zoomed in on him. The finish line crew double-checked their cameras. The starter unfurled the checker flag in his hand. The race officials rose up. The hundred and sixty thousand in attendance stood, and for ten seconds, it was as if time stood still.

As they came out of the fourth turn the 46 six car made a desperate attempt to win by bumping T's car once again. Thad assumed the worst, held on tight, and zoomed across the finish line one foot in front of the 46.

The crew and Janet cheered. Charley sat down exhausted. Gary, the spotter, wiped the sweat from his face. Drew grinned as big as he possibly could. Jack leaped around the coach, and then quickly sat down, and put his shoes on. He locked the coach, jumped into the golf cart, and headed for Victory Lane.

Charley came on the radio as T let down his window net. "Way to go, son. That was a hell of a race. I am so proud of you." He then talked to Gary on his radio. "Great job Gary. Let him do his burn out, and then talk him through to Victory Lane, and don't let him hit anything." Finally, he spoke proudly to his crew, "Way to go boys. You just proved how much of a champion you really are. Out!" He took off his headset and climbed down off the box, he helped Janet down, and waited for Drew's chairlift to lower him down to the ground. "What do you say, Drew? Are you in the mood for a little champagne?"

"Hell yes! What a day. That boy is something, isn't he," replied Drew.

"From what I hear, he's a hell of a brave man, too."

Drew nodded knowing what Charley was talking about. Janet loaded up Charley, and they both chased T and Drew to Victory Lane. She parked just as Jack got there. He ran over and gave her a hug. She smiled, "I had a feeling you were his lucky charm today. He always seems to win when you're around."

"He's the winner, I just make a good breakfast," replied Jack.

Janet laughed and hugged him again.

On the track, T reversed his car, picked up the checkered flag, and began a Victory Lap. To his surprise, many folks in the stands started throwing empty cans and plastic bottles at his car. He had been booed a lot, but never trashed. When he reached pit row, he slowed down and started watching for the officials. Gary told him forty more yards, so he slowed down some more until he saw them waving him in and telling him to slow down. He turned the key off, and spotted the TV reporter and cameraman making their

200

way over to his door to interview him. He saw his team on the other side of the car laughing and yelling, so he gave them a thumb up sign. He pulled off his gloves, undid the steering wheel, and threw it up on the dash. He managed to pull his helmet off, though it hurt his ribs, unplugged his ears, unbuckled his seat belts and safety straps, and then Charley leaned in the window and handed his street hat and sunglasses to him.

"That was an incredible save across the grass. Not many drivers on this track can do that."

T smiled, "I guess I was just lucky."

Charley patted his arm, "Yeah right. You need help getting out of there? Are the ribs killing you?"

"Thanks, I can do it, and I'll cry later."

Charley stood back as T came out of the car. His team cheered and started spewing champagne and Pepsi everywhere. T stood on the door thrusting his arms up as high as he dared, while feeling thankful for the chest vest. He turned and jumped down, and began the interview.

The reporter said, "Congratulations, Thad. This puts you in fifth place for the championship with just four races to go. Can you win the big championship?"

T responded, "Fifth place? I only have to beat one a week. It will be a piece of cake."

"You started the day with your big charity press conference and your other announcement; did this pump you up for the win?"

Jack frowned at the failure of the reporter to tell the truth, but T smiled, "It sure did. The kids always make me feel great, and I love helping them. I hope our fans will get behind these charities now. In addition, as to the announcement, well, I just feel great. It is like a huge burden has been lifted off my shoulders, and now I feel I can drive twice as fast."

The reporter came back one more time, "I doubt your competitors will be glad to hear that."

"Oh, don't get me wrong. They are fantastic drivers. I am just more determined than ever to win the championship this year, and give Drew his second big win from me, and Jack's first! Thank you very much."

The reporter turned to the camera to conclude while T started talking with the dozen or more other reporters all begging for answers to questions. Jack walked around the outside of the circle after hearing T say his name, but wasn't quite sure what that was all about. He found an empty bleacher spot and climbed up on it. Now he could see T and began waiting patiently.

After answering a few questions, T turned to answer a sportswriter for the USA Today, but immediately caught sight of Jack on the stands behind him. He smiled and winked at him, and made the reporter repeat his question having lost his train of thought. "Oh yeah, that move across the grass is not something you practice. I learned how to drive on dirt and snow when I was a kid, and just turned the car in the direction it was going until I could steer back on the track. He didn't hurt me—he just made the mistake of making me mad enough that I was going to win no matter what!"

The interviews continued for an hour, then a live TV spot on the Victory Lane show, finally he said goodbye, got in the cart with Jack, and they drove back to the motorcoach. Once inside they kissed long and deep.

"I'm so glad you're okay," began Jack as he unzipped the uniform. "How are the ribs?"

"They are still there and yep, sore." T stepped out of his boots so Jack could pull his socks off, and slid down the uniform.

"Boy, this suit sinks."

"Just put it in that big plastic bag and tie it off. Duke will take care of it tomorrow. The dry cleaners do a great job of getting that smell out. This week will be harder for them as I have gas, burning rubber, dirt, and grass for them to handle."

Jack pulled the fire underwear down and off, and then T's soaked boxers. "Come on buster, it's time for you to go to the car wash."

T laughed as Jack led him into the shower and scrubbed him from head to toe. They ate a good dinner of leftovers, and lots of pie before turning the lights out.

"You really did a great job today," stated Jack as he cuddled in close.

T kissed him, "You mean when I gave away the million dollars."

"No."

"When I challenged the sponsors and Drew to support the charities?"

"No."

"When I came out to the world?"

"No."

"No? Then when I won the race?"

Jack laughed, "You did a great job when you did all of that, and yet remained your sweet loving self. I could just eat you up"

T laughed, "Well, that's a start!"

EIGHTEEN

Thad and Jack slept in, but at the home office, Janet fielded call after call from newspapers, magazines, and television networks all wanting an interview with the new out and proud Thad. She anticipated more calls due to his winning the race, and called her staff from Drew's plane on the way home from the race to report in early the next morning. She quickly wrote press releases for both the race and T's announcements, doing all she could to maximize the donations to the charities and minimizing T's coming out. The press wanted just the opposite.

The photography department working quickly to produce high quality photos of every presentation of the big checks, and the hug from Sammy with T. She loved the pictures. Her graphics team rapidly updated T's personal website and the team's website with the stories about the charities, and his win. At the end of the releases, she put a quote or two from T's speech about his coming out and telling the world he was gay.

Her media team prepared electronic press kits of all the photos, stories, and digital copies of his speech. By ten o'clock, every media person on her list had received her emailed package. She then went to work on updating the media press section of the team's website that required a password from her for approved journalists to download.

Once accomplished, she met briefly with her staff to discuss what T would accept and what he would not, as to live and arranged interviews. She told Mary that T would do three phone interviews for various syndicated satellite radio racing shows. Her computer guru set up a spreadsheet that would appear on the staff computers so they could all see what, where, and when they booked Thad, but in harmony with Jack's plans.

Four ladies fielded calls and began returning Janet's numerous voicemails. Much like a stockbroker in the middle of a hot deal, Janet accepted or declined one call or request after another. Drew stuck his head in the door to speak to her, but took one look at the situation and backed off. He, too, had numerous calls to return from the sponsors, and he knew what they wanted to discuss. He had his secretary arrange conference calls for each one beginning at two.

His motorized wheelchair took him to the corner of his office where the big windows went all the way to the floor so he could look out to the horizon, as well as down to giant hauler parking lot. He saw the haulers for his teams arriving, and let a sigh of relief as he always did when the gigantic eighteen wheel units arrived safely. Behind them were motorcoaches for all the drivers except T, and at the end of the line, he saw his own special built coach with a built in lift for his wheelchair.

He picked up the phone and called Clint Barnard his operations manager, "Clint, where's T's bus?"

Clint smiled and looked up at Drew's window at how fast and quick he was when things in the shop weren't quite normal, "T told Duke he would be staying overnight. He said something about going to Omaha this morning."

Drew frowned, "Okay, let's get 'em ready for the weekend."

"Roger," replied Clint, knowing the boss was talking about the cars and haulers as well as the crews.

He hated to interrupt Janet, but he wanted to know what T was up to this time. Her secretary slipped her a note while she was talking to NBC, and so she put their coordinator on hold, and took Drew's call. "Hey, Drew. Congratulations on the big win yesterday. How are you this morning?"

"I have a knot in my stomach, and I'm sorry to interrupt you, as it looks like this thing with T has mushroomed."

Janet sighed, "No kidding. My marketing team has handled over two hundred calls, and we have T booked on live interviews with television and radio shows, and press interviews for the next two days. The sponsors are going to love all the free publicity they will receive."

"That's great. I'll tell them. Listen, a quick question, do you know where T is? His motorcoach didn't come in with the others, and he told Duke he was staying over and going to Omaha today?"

"Shit! I thought he came in last night on his plane." She recalled him going AWOL earlier in the season. "I've got him booked all over the place. I will find him, and get back to you. I'm sorry I didn't know."

Drew smiled, "I think we are learning that Thad and Jack are smarter than most of our driver teams. I think they have a marketing plan, and we'd better get on the same page. Call me when you know something. Thanks."

Janet hung up and yelled for everyone to stop what they were doing and listen, "T did not come home last night, and apparently going to Omaha, so now we have to stall all interviews until I can get him on the phone and get the plan. Thank you."

She quickly got off the phone with NBC, and dialed T's private cell phone number.

They enjoyed making love before falling asleep last night and again this morning. Jack made breakfast while T finished dressing, and came to help set the table, fix juice glasses, and sat down. Jack brought the food to the table and smiled.

"Morning gay boy," he said.

T laughed, "That I am. This looks great "

"Your phone has been buzzing on vibrate, and there are some faxes in the machine."

T frowned, "I had hoped this would be a quiet day, but I sort of knew it wouldn't. I better check in with Janet. He began listening to all the voicemails, and except from one from his mom, they were all from Janet. He smiled. "She must be in a tizzy. I got eight calls from her."

He set the phone down, and quickly finished his breakfast, and then sat back and dialed her. Janet's secretary stood up and ran to tell Janet, who was talking with a reporter for Sports Illustrated magazine. "Janet, T's on line seven!"

Janet quickly got off the phone, "Well, about time you called me!" She smiled, "You act like you won a race yesterday or something."

T laughed, "Come to think of it I did. I gave away a million dollars, and now we're fifth in points for the championship race."

"You also came out of the closet, and we've had zillions of calls today. I have booked you all day long for TV and radio interviews, as well newspapers and magazines. Drew just told me you're playing hooky again, and didn't come home last night."

"Home is where the heart is, and you're right—we're still in Indianapolis."

Janet took that to mean that Jack was with him. "Well, I'm glad you two boys are safe. What's this about Omaha today?"

"Dang, I forgot to tell you in all the excitement. I'm sorry. I'll put Jack on to explain, but first I need to make a couple of changes. I want you to continue to handle everything to do with the media when it comes to racing and sponsors, and I want Jack to handle my personal schedule and charity work. He'll be the final say on whether we can or cannot book something for your team, but don't worry, I'm not going to hide from you. We'll do them all, but I just want Jack with me to get everything done."

"He'll also write my speeches, and I need for you to work out a way in future sponsor commercials to plug my charities. I'm going to call my personal manager Herb Ellis and have him set up a charity foundation for me, so that folks can go to my website and donate money. I think we'll call it the TNT Foundation. I know all this is a big change, but it is all for good reasons. Is this all right with you?"

"Of course," Janet smiled, "but what do I tell the folks we've already booked?"

"Call one of the Omaha television affiliates, and set up a satellite feed. What time is it?"

Janet grinned, "Well, you must have experienced good sex last night if you can't remember what time it is. It's about 10:30 here."

T blushed. "Okay, set up one after the other starting about noon. Call me back with which station we are working with. We're flying there shortly. Thanks again for all your help. We'll manage—don't worry. Here's Jack."

Jack explained the purpose of their trip, the donations, etc. and Janet made some notes including the presentation at two central time. She hung up and got her media team to find the list of Omaha stations. She picked one out, and got on the phone. In twenty minutes, she had the details worked out, and then her team began rearranging the live interview appointments, and giving them the satellite feed information. It was going to be an open feed so each station could just record audio and video feed as they switched from each source.

She then called Drew to explain. He laughed, "Thad and Jack are very smart. This is a good plan. It will be hard to hate him with all the good he is doing. I hope I can hang on to the sponsors.

Janet smiled, "One more thing, "T wants to meet with each sponsor at their corporate headquarters on Tuesday, and Jack gave me the schedule. He wants full media coverage, and he intends to win them over. Should I fly up?"

"Hell yes. Tell him I appreciate this. I will start calling the sponsors, and we'll all see them tomorrow. He wants to start with RESTAR. You and I will fly up on the jet. Make sure we have tons of media coverage. It will be far harder for them to back down with the publicity T is going to give them. Yes!" he exclaimed again as he slapped his open palm on his desk.

T and Jack got Duke to drive them to the airport where they found Al warming up the jet. By 11:30, they touched down in Omaha, and the limo Jack arranged picked them up. They stopped at Burger King, and surprised everyone as they picked up hamburgers and fries, knowing it would be a long afternoon with no time for food. They ate on the way to the television station.

The staff at the local station became very excited, and every office emptied as T arrived into the studio. He took a moment to shake everyone's hand. A stage manager brought Jack a list of the interviews. Jack, new to all the mass media hysteria, kept his cool, and together, he and Thad talked while a nice lady did his makeup. They discussed a few comments, and Jack gave him a few lines of copy he wrote on the plane and printed out. Minutes later, they were in the studio while the lighting crew adjusted the big lights and his chair. T suggested to the director they super impose a picture of his car behind Thad, and told them how to download it from the team's website. Five minutes later, the car appeared in the monitor.

T asked, "How many?" He sat down while an audio technician put a wireless microphone under his shirt and flesh colored earpiece in his left ear. He hid the cables and returned to his booth for a sound check.

"Thirty, I think," replied Jack as flipped through the pages of the schedule.

The director carefully checked with each of the technicians and satellite controllers until they were all ready to go. He also had tape rolling in case of a failure on the satellite, or on the reception around the country. The last time he had done something as big as this was when a Presidential candidate in the last election stopped in. He was enjoying T's visit a whole lot more.

206

Jack stepped around to the back of the camera, but stayed just slightly in view so T could see him. He smiled and said, "Bob Matthews at ESPN is up first."

T smiled as the cameraman began giving him a five second countdown. The stage manager gave Jack a headset, so he could hear audio from the director, as well as from the interviewer, and T. He heard Bob introduce T and then ask, "Thad, congratulations on the big win yesterday. It didn't come easy with lots of problems, but how does it feel to come back after all the adversity and win?"

"It made the victory all the sweeter, and it put me in fifth place and chasing another championship."

"When you were knocked into the grass at hundred and eighty miles an hour, I thought you were done for."

"So did I," laughed T.

"Must folks would have put on the brakes, but you must have kept the throttle down. Is that right?"

"Yes, I drove it like you would drive if you were in snow. I turned the wheels in the direction I was already going, and gradually brought it back on the track."

"We have just a minute left, so let's go through your day. You start by giving a million dollars of your own money to charities, then announce you're gay, and somehow win the race. Did you plan this amazing complicated day like it turned out?"

"Yes, my partner and I did. It was time to get the secret behind me, and more importantly, it was time I grew up and started spending more of my time helping others instead of just myself. I am counting on my sponsors and fans to help support all the charities in our new TNT Foundation. At the meeting yesterday, I told everyone I would win the race and I did. I had also promised my little friend Sammy I would win it for him. You can't let that remarkable boy down."

"Have there been any repercussions since you announced you were gay?"

This question made Jack frown, because he felt the question encouraged the public to create problems for them as if they were expected.

T answered, "The world today is more accepting than ever before, but we still have a long way to go. There are thousands of gay kids all over America, and millions around the world who need our help."

Bob thanked T and closed out the interview.

"Next." T grinned as Jack gave him the next name.

The routine continued until 1:30 central time. After the last one, T and Jack thanked everybody, and rushed out the door with T wiping the makeup off with a handful of paper towels the stage manager handed him. The limo took them straight to the Boys and Girls home and over to the administration office. Henry Wilkins, the director, led them to the library and continually thanked T for helping them with their air conditioning repair at the library. T and Jack smiled as they were going to do more than that at the press conference in front of the library. He also met the President of Office Depot, and shook hands with the driver of the 99 car, Tim Jones. They all walked down the hall and out to the front of the library to the top of the steps. T grinned when he saw over thirty-two hundred children, and another thousand teachers, administrators and workers waiting for them. Upon arriving, the boys learned Father Flanagan started Boys Town in 1917, and how it became Girls & Boys Town in 2000. He also learned there were many other campuses all around the country. Jack made a note to get the list.

The children clapped and cheered when they saw T and Tim Jones in their uniforms. After a while, Henry walked to the podium and began his remarks by thanking the drivers and sponsors for their visit. He then introduced Thad. He told the kids how glad he was to be here, and he heard the heat and air system for the library had died.

He teased them by saying, "It doesn't get hot here in the summer does it? Or cold in the winter?" The kids laughed and replied it did. "I heard you had a need for a new air system, and so I called my good friend Bob Miller." Bob gave the kids a wave. Thad continued, "Bob, let's don't keep them in suspense. Please come tell them what we're going to do."

Bob gleefully walked to podium and thanked T and Henry Wilkins for the opportunity. "Kids, my company, Rheem Manufacturing, have some bad news, and thankfully, some good news. The bad news is your old system is history, and we're going to haul it out of there. The good news is, and with Thad's help, we're going to install a brand new heat and air system for the entire library!"

The kids yelled and cheered as well as the faculty. Henry came up to the podium along with Thad and the media took numerous pictures. Henry thanked him many times before Thad took back over the microphone.

"Now that you have a new system in the works, Henry told me the kids were running low on school supplies. I called my good friend Howard Huntley who is head of Office Depot. He has a solution for you. I want to call Howard and fellow driver Tim Jones to the podium."

T shook their hands and then T stepped aside so they could make their presentation. Howard said he was pleased to get a call from Thad asking for his help. He turned to the kids, "Office Depot is proud to be here today. Our driver Tim Jones is going to wave the checker flag for a surprise for you."

Tim stepped to the side of the podium and waved the flag high over his head. From around the corner of the building came a long huge Office Depot truck. The driver held the horn down to get the kids' attention.

Howard spoke up again. "Henry, on behalf of Office Depot, I am pleased to present the Girls and Boys Home an entire truckload of school supplies!"

The kids cheered and again the men posed for more pictures. Henry made some final pictures, and then T and Tim began signing autographs for the kids. It took a little over an hour for them to sign something for every kid. Then Howard took Thad, Tim, and Jack on a tour of the facility. Calling Tim a quiet guy would be an understatement, but whenever they came upon a group of kids, Thad would stop and get off the golf cart, and tease and play with the kids. Before long, Tim was doing the same. By 5:30, they said their goodbyes and left in the limo.

"Good job," stated Jack as he gave T a kiss.

"Thanks to your hard work, an amazing idea, and very good planning. Tomorrow we take on the sponsors. Do you want to go home, stay here, or what?"

Jack opened his laptop and brought up the sponsor tour. "We start at nine in the morning in Boston. Why don't we fly there tonight, have a nice dinner, and we won't have to worry about an early flight in the morning."

"You got it." T dialed Al at the airport, so he could file his flight plan. He then called Janet, gave her the update, and said he would meet her there. He did not tell her where they staying. After he hung up, he asked Jack, "Can you book a hotel on that thing?"

"Of course," replied Jack. By the time, they reached the airport he booked them into the Marriott Custom House Hotel overlooking the harbor, and they had the penthouse suite on the twenty-fourth floor. They exited the limo, and went aboard while Al was warming up the engines.

"Hey Al, are you ready to go to Boston?"

"Yes sir, and may I say that was awesome what you did in Omaha. I saw it on the television in the cabin quarters. That's a great place and they do such good work. Well, have a seat, and I'll take care of the rest."

Jack came forward and handed Al the next day's itinerary. "Al, I'm still new at this, so I hope I didn't book us on too tight a schedule. T said you could handle it, but if you see a problem, please let me know, and I'll adjust it."

Al scanned the list. "I've been to all these stops before so nothing new there. I'll make it work."

"Do you want me to book you a room in our hotel?"

"No, I already booked myself near the airport. I like to get to the plane at least an hour before flight to check everything out, but thanks anyhow. Let me get the door, and we'll get out of here."

Thad and Jack were starving, so they ate some fruit and cookies in the galley, and a split a quart of ice cream. Afterwards they curled up together and took a nap. The limo met them at the private hanger, and soon they were taking in the sights of the harbor by night from their room. They changed clothes, and went out of the hotel to eat. The concierge suggested an upscale restaurant on the harbor, and they enjoyed walking to it. Their table was waiting for them in a corner providing a little privacy. Jack protested how much money they were spending, but Thad said they needed a good meal, and reminded Jack they could avoid admirers and fans. The meal totaled a hundred and fifty a piece, but they worked hard to get their monies worth by eating several lobster tails, shrimp, and some kind of a veggie dish that neither heard of, but they loved it. They even ate dessert, left the restaurant ninety minutes later fat and happy, and began walking to the hotel. A large truck pulled up at the corner and gave T the finger, but they just assumed he was rooting for another driver. At the next block a cab driver called T a fag, but T smiled and said, "Yes I am!"

Jack laughed, but pushed T along afraid something more serious might happen. Just as they reached their hotel block, the cab driver returned, and threw a beer bottle at them. The driver also yelled again and sped off.

"Does this sort of thing happen often?" asked Thad.

"All over America, replied Jack sadly. " This kind of thing is one of the things we have to work on, and it will be a long battle. "Come on—I'm sleepy," urged Jack anxious to get T off the street.

T smiled, knowing Jack was protecting him, "You're just horny and can't wait to get to my body."

Jack laughed as he pulled him forward, "Well, now that you mention it—I am!"

Drew and Janet met Thad and Jack at the lobby door to the giant RESTAR corporation headquarters and the home of Thad's major sponsor. They paid thirty million dollars a year to sponsor the team, and in return they got twelve different commercials, numerous print shots, car and hauler exposure, and most importantly they were on the top of T's uniform in numerous places.

They spotted Drew and Janet in the lobby. "Hey, Drew," said T as he leaned over and gave his boss a hug, and then turned to Janet. "My goodness, Janet, this engagement stuff is making you even prettier than before." He gave Janet a kiss. Jack shook Drew's hand, and gave Janet a hug, too.

They both laughed. Drew said quickly, "We don't have much time. I appreciate you doing this sponsor blitz as the companies have just about chewed off any ass I had left. They are wondering why this coming out stuff happened during the race season. They are worried about their customers, and mostly they are just worried. What in the hell are you going to say?"

Thad smiled and winked at Janet, "I'll show you. Did anyone ever tell you that you worry too much?"

"I've made it a career of worrying. That's my job."

"Just trust me. It'll be fine." T began leading them down the hall.

They took the elevator to the top floor and immediately welcomed by Greg Bell, the president of RESTAR. "Gentlemen, so nice of you to come—we're looking forward to discussing the situation with you."

They all shook hands and were ushered into a conference room where their board of directors assembled. Around the table sat the heads of various departments, including their marketing division, and the head of their advertising agency. Thad and gang took seats near the front of the table, as Greg Bell walked to the podium. "Let's get this meeting under way. Drew, Thad, and guests, we welcome you to our board meeting. Drew, we were uninformed of Thad's announcement on Sunday, and left no opportunity to prepare a response to our customers, stockholders, and staff. I think the value of our investment in your company and team has gone down as a result. We pay millions of dollars for quality representation by the top driver in racing, and we want only the best representing us. I expect you're here to try to save your ass, but I'm hoping you're here to introduce Thad's replacement driver—the other young man sitting with you. Drew, what in the hell are you running down there in Charlotte?"

Janet saw the veins in Drew's neck tighten, a sight she didn't see often, and she knew the result could be a huge temper outburst colored with a litany of four-letter words. Thad looked over at Drew and winked, "I've got this one." He then leaned into Jack and whispered, "Are you planning on driving my racecar?"

Jack shrugged his shoulders and whispered back, "Hell no. I'd look awful in that uniform. I don't have the ass you do."

Thad nearly busted out laughing as he walked to the podium. "Ladies and gentlemen, I am so happy to be here today. I asked Drew to allow me to answer your questions and comments. First of all, Drew and his entire company didn't know about my announcement on Sunday. I was born gay—all gays are born gay. It is not a choice, only a choice as to when to come out and tell your family and friends. I kept it a secret all my life. I performed exactly as you would want me to. I did great commercials for your promotions, and mentioned your company at every single opportunity for three years now. I have visited your plants and tried to boost morale by shaking the hand of every person there. I have spoken at your hospitality tent meetings prior to a race, and signed countless thousands of autographs for you. Your name is on my car and my uniforms and prominently displayed everywhere I go. I have spoken at your banquets and any other requests you have—even some that were not in my contract.

"Gay people are forced to keep their life a secret, and in many cases—it is the only way they can flourish in their career. However, I learned a man I never met discovered I was gay. He tried to blackmail me in Daytona. When I refused, he handed out memos to the media. Most of the reporters took it as a joke, but a few began to look into my personal life a little deeper than most. I have since learned a reporter went to see my mother and my schoolteachers. The blackmailer also made a huge scene at a charity event at the Cincinnati hospital.

"So as you can see, before long the reporters would have eluded to my sexuality preference via innuendos and more. My team would have noticed it, as well as other drivers and teams, and it would just have snow balled into a disaster.

"I chose a more honest and direct approach. I told the truth on my own terms, and I'm determined to make this a good thing for your company and customers, as well as dozens of charities all around the country. To start the ball rolling, I gave away a million dollars of my money to twenty charities. I spoke about my sponsors at the press conference, and mentioned your name to millions watching television before and after the race—which I won.

"Yesterday, I appeared in Omaha and gave the Girls and Boys Town a new air system for their library and a truck load of school supplies. Two companies that are not my sponsors were more than happy to do this for me, for the kids, and for free. They spent about a half million dollars in Omaha."

"You said you were paying for the top driver in the series, and implying that because I was gay, perhaps I was not the top driver. My being gay has nothing to do with my driving ability. Did you forget after the announcement I went out, won the race, and moved up to fifth in points? I am also going to win this championship. How much publicity do you think you'll get as I move up in points these final races and win the championship? I will tell you, far more than the thirty million dollars you've invested. I'd say the value in your investment just went way up.

"If I had waited, the rumors could have hurt all of us. By being bold and telling the truth about something so very private, then what I say about your company must be true, too. Don't you see—this announcement is going to get you more publicity than any other team?"

T turned to Drew, "I think we should charge our sponsors more because I'm going to get them more media coverage than we promised last year!"

Thad smiled, "Don't worry Greg. I'm just teasing, but I am going to give you more. I'm going to do a number of public service commercials and I'll be wearing my uniform with your name on it. I'm going to give thousands of interviews in this same uniform, and I'm going to drive my car with your name on it all the way to the championship. In addition, when they hand me those trophies, I'm going to remember to thank RESTAR! How much is that worth?

"I asked you on Sunday to support these charities. I've formed a foundation called TNT Foundation with the slogan—Racing For A Better World. I'm hoping you will take the high road, and support my foundation, so that you will always look and feel great about how you're helping the world with your products.

"But I will tell you Greg, if you really want to drop your sponsorship, we have just four races left, and one month left so the refund would be about

212

three million. Drew will write you a check for that amount right now, but remember, you'd have to drop me from all your commercials, print ads, and billboards. Your company name would come off the car and my uniforms, and in one hour, I'll have another company lined up to take your place for fifty million dollars just as we did with just one phone call for the Omaha deal yesterday.

"Okay, that's all I've got to say. I'll do all I can to help your company, or you can quit now. You choose." T turned to sit down, but stopped and went back to the microphone. "For the record, that young man sitting over there by Janet is not another driver. He's my partner."

Greg stood to take the podium, but a woman on the other side of the table stood up and spoke first. "Greg, Thad's right. My department has received about a thousand angry calls. Not one said anything about his driving talents, nor did they have anything to say bad about RESTAR. Millions of people saw the race, read the stories about his coming out, and yet we only had a thousand complaints. What is that—about .001 percent? This is best publicity campaign I have ever heard of."

Greg interjected, "But it brings…"

The head of marketing stood up, "Greg, Thad has done everything we have asked him to do. Four times this year I called to ask if he could help with a project that quite frankly was not in the list of appearances his contract calls for, and each time he showed up on time and cheerfully did a great job for us. As I see it, his private sex life is none of our business. There are thousands of gay people in our company. We advertise we hire without prejudice to sexual preference, and we threaten to fire anyone for abusing someone for his or her sexual orientation. Why choose to treat our extended employee Thad any differently? He has brought pride to the minority gays in our company and our customers." He paused and added, "And he is a brave man on and off the track."

Greg tried again, "But…"

The advertising agency head stood up. He was taking a chance as he could lose a hundred million dollar account if he went against Greg. "Greg, I'm technically an outsider at RESTAR, but I have been handling your advertising campaigns for ten years. I have hundred and eighty people whose sole job is to promote RESTAR. My wife and I have a gay son. My graphics head is gay, and probably twenty percent of my company is gay. We shouldn't fire him for being gay, we should go on the offensive and say we support him, and deplore anyone that offends another by words or violence. To fire him would create a firestorm. You would have to pull all our commercials with Thad, and instantly spend millions creating new ads without him. That's a huge waste of talent and money. He's offering to make you millions more, and we should take him up on it."

213

The members of the board applauded, as did many of the guests around the room. The knot in Drew's stomach reduced a bit, and the veins in his neck went back to normal. Greg stood there while the applause continued with the realization taking hold that he had been wrong.

He finally spoke, "I see your points. Thad, on behalf of the company, we accept your offer to help, if you can accept my sincere apology."

Thad smiled and stood, "I'm looking forward to working with you."

Drew rolled his chair up to the microphone, "Greg, if you don't mind I'd like to say a word." As usual when Drew asked if you mind, it meant get the hell out of my way. "I want to thank you for your support, and I understand how you feel. When this thing hit me, I had the same reaction, but I soon realized I was madder for not knowing and being surprised, than I was that he was gay. I fought in Vietnam and I wrestled in college, and I built this team from scratch. I have a Purple Heart and Silver Star in a case at home for my wounds and bravery beyond the call of duty. I thought I was a brave man, but let me tell you, standing up to the whole world as a super star, and telling them you're gay, is by far the bravest thing I've ever seen. My sport began with redneck drivers and mechanics and we're slow to change. Thad will be called every name in the book, probably spit at, and if you saw the race, they're going to bump our car around a little bit. He didn't yell back at them—he went out, whipped them, and won the race. Thad Nigel Thompson and his partner Jack are the bravest men I have ever known. Thank you for the visit. I'll let your staff and ours work out how we can help your company help the world through T's foundation. The goodwill and publicity you're going to get from Thad's effort is going to be worth ten times what you've paid for."

The audience stood and applauded Drew. Janet had tears in her eyes while Thad and Jack were beaming. They followed Drew as he rolled out of the room to the elevator. As the four of them started down in the elevator, Drew spoke up first, "Jack, you wrote Thad's speech—didn't you?"

Jack looked over at Thad and smiled, "Yes sir, they were my words, but Thad's heart, and as usual he changed a few phrases on the fly."

Drew smiled, "I don't know what we're paying you, but you deserve a raise."

Thad laughed, "Sir, we aren't paying him anything at the moment."

The group laughed as Drew added, "I'll fix that as soon as we land. You should have your own money as a reward for your talented artistic abilities, and because you have to put up with Thad." He laughed heartily along with everyone else. "I could use your help with the other drivers and all of our publicity materials."

"I am happy to help in any way I can," replied Jack humbly.

Drew winked at him, and then his smile fell somber.

Drew looked up to Thad. "Son, when we get home. I'm going to give you my Silver Star."

214

Thad smiled and shot back, "Well, that's the least you can do since I'm going to give you a big old championship trophy!" The foursome laughed all the way down to the lobby.

The rest of the day, they went from one board meeting to the next, and one by one, they all stayed onboard. Drew, exhausted from the stress, was greatly relieved. Thad and Jack waved goodbye, as they flew out of the last city for the day and headed home.

"Where to?" asked Jack.

"We've got two days off. Let's go to my house. I'm tired." Thad took Jack's hand as they walked to his jet and let Al take them home. Emotionally and physically exhausted they slept leaning in to each other shoulder to shoulder and head to head, comfortable and confident in just slightly touching the person they love the most, and feeling safe and secure, and sleeping safely.

NINETEEN

They took the two days off by sleeping in the sun, swimming in the pool, and taking long drives in his boat on Lake Norman. They wore hats and sunglasses everywhere they went in an attempt to hide from fans, as well as new enemies. For decades, the press in Charlotte considered the homes of a racecar driver 'hands off', but every morning since Thad's coming out there were satellite trucks parked along his street with about fifty reporters and camera operators. When Thad bought the property, Drew sent Duke over to help Thad design his security. His suggestions included installing a ten-foot fence on the perimeter of his property along with a motorized wrought iron gate at the front entrance. Thad didn't like the fortress look of the fence, so at great expense he had landscapers install grown trees and bushes in front of the fence, and from the outside, the fence remained hidden.

Duke also cut a road out the side of the property that traversed near the lake, and came out at the highway in the midst of a thick forest with another electric gate. He installed cameras for monitoring the gates and the fence. They camouflaged the escape route with plants, and rarely used it, so even a news crew in a helicopter would not recognize or discover the road.

Twenty yards from shore, the fence cut across his acreage securing the property. Thad could go through a locked gate, so he could walk down to his boathouse and dock. There he had an upper deck to lie in the sun that also served as shelter for his boat and two Yamaha personal watercraft vehicles. Duke placed cameras in the trees to help secure this open area as well.

The house featured the latest security system including twenty-four hour monitoring by an alarm company. Once completed, Thad thought the system was overkill, but about once or twice a year, someone tried to invade his property. Most offenders were women determined to sleep with him, others were just slightly crazy, and Duke said those were the most dangerous because you could not predict what they might attempt or do.

They woke late on Thursday morning and found themselves looking for something to eat in the kitchen when Jack happened to look up at the camera monitors displaying the front gate. "Thad, look at that crowd."

Thad returned from the refrigerator with a half-gallon of orange juice, set it on the table, and walked over to Jack. He studied the array of small monitors. "What do they want?"

Jack thought for a second, "I guess they want to talk to you, or they hope to catch a picture of you having sex with your good looking boyfriend."

Thad smiled, "Let me know if you see this 'good-looking' boyfriend. I'd like to meet him!" He turned and gave Jack a kiss. "Should I go talk to them?"

"I don't think so. That would encourage them to stay here because they'll know they are aggravating you. Why don't we set up a press

216

conference upon your arrival in Atlanta this weekend? I'll create a press release and distribute them to the media, so they'll understand they are wasting their time here."

"Hold on Jack. Look at that." Thad pointed at a line of white buses.

"They look like an army. Who are they?"

Neither boy spoke as they stared at the approaching convoy of over twenty white buses. The first bus came to a halt across the street from the front gate. Together they read the sign on the side of the bus, "God Hates Fags.com" and in smaller print, "Support Family Focus". The men and women began unloading from the buses and each carried a sign. As the first bus emptied, it pulled forward, and the next bus stopped and began unloading its passengers. They were very efficient and well organized.

"At thirty people a bus—that's about twelve hundred protestors," stated Jack.

"I guess we have stirred up a hornet's nest. I'm going to call Duke. We need some help."

Thad picked up the phone as Jack added, "I think we'd better call the county cops, too. This could get out of hand."

Duke called Drew after talking to Thad, and immediately made a plan to protect their number one driver. Drew made a few calls and hired the biggest security company in the area, while Duke called in their own security guards including his off duty staff. They loaded up in two vans and drove over to Thad's. Duke's men gradually ordered the protestors across the street and off Thad's land. The crowd began chanting, "Adam and Eve, not Adam and Steve!" They held up signs with ugly abusive epithets about gay people and Thad in particular.

Duke encouraged his men to stand strong, though he began to feel like Custer at Little Big Horn. His eye caught sight of the blue spinning lights before he could hear the sirens. A second convoy of a dozen county patrol cars raced to the scene. They pulled their cars in line on Thad's side of the street. Duke went over and introduced himself to a captain. "Thank you for coming. I wasn't sure what the legal situation is, but this side of the road is Thad Thompson's property, and he has asked us to protect it."

"Okay, give me a second." He turned and spoke in his radio and ordered his men into a crowd control position. He then took out a bullhorn and reminded the protestors they could not step on private property, and would have to remain across the street. He then turned back to Duke. "I need to speak to Mr. Thompson."

"Can we take your car?" asked Duke.

"Sure, get in."

Together they drove pass the long line of parked white buses. "Where did these people come from?" asked Duke.

"We've had a run in with them before after they showed up at a military funeral. I think folks call them the religious right. I know they have a right to protest, but you would think Christian folk could do it with less vulgar signs and animosity. Where are we going?"

"There is a secluded private side entrance to his property. It'll be much easier to get in. Duke dialed Thad on his cell phone. "T? This is Duke. I'm in the captain's patrol car. He needs to speak to you. Can you open the side gate?"

"Roger, will do. Come ahead," replied T as he hit the gate button, and then to Jack. "We'd better get dressed. A cop is coming up the back road."

Thankful, they had taken a shower together before breakfast. They quickly dressed, and were sitting at the bar at the edge of the kitchen when they arrived. Jack was busy working on his laptop and reading up on the Focus Family Web Site. Their home page was urging people to show up to protest.

Duke introduced the captain while Thad and Jack shook his hand. T tried to detect if the captain was a bigot or not, but so far he remained very professional. Thad quickly said, "I am sorry this has happen."

The captain smiled, "I guess your announcement on Sunday has snowballed into an opportunity for this religious group to stir up the masses and increase their fundraising efforts. How long are you in town this week?"

"We leave early Friday morning. I do not plan to go out and speak to them as I suspect it would get ugly," stated Thad.

"That's right. If you have to leave, I'd go out the back way, but only with some of your security team waiting for you. If you need help, call this number," said the captain as he handed Thad and Duke business cards. "Tell me about your security?"

Duke took over and explained the fence and gates as well as the cameras. The captain appeared impressed. He said to all, "If anyone breeches that fence, which I doubt they can, please call me immediately. Keep the house locked, and we'll catch them and haul their butts to jail. If the protests and media stay more than a few days then I'll talk to my boss to find out where we stand legally with moving them along. Do you know who owns the property across the street?"

"Mr. and Mrs. Thomas Jenkins. I tried to buy it from him, but he said he planned to build a home there when he retired. He is a banker and lives downtown," added T.

"I will contact him, and see what his thoughts are about the protestors and media setting up camp on his land. I hope he tells me to stop them from trespassing on his private property. Okay, I'm done here. Nice to meet you and sorry this happen, but remember, the right to protest is part of our list of freedoms. Try not to take it too personal. It is hot out there and not much shade, so hopefully the heat will discourage them from sticking around.

After all, they will already have their picture on the front page of the paper, and the on network news shows, and usually publicity for their cause, and the financial support it brings, is what they're really after."

Duke returned with the captain to the front gate. They each spoke to their men before the captain returned to his car to call into his office.

He had been correct about the pictures. Photographers snapped away at the throngs of bouncing signs and protestors, as they marched in a long circle on and off the road in front of the gate. To their dismay, Duke and the officers saw a line of cars approaching and they, too, joined the protestors. He assumed they were church folk as well.

Thad felt like a captive in his own home. The chanting made him tense, so Jack turned on the satellite television and found a good loud action movie for them to watch. Jack sat beside Thad on the coach with his laptop and clicked online. "According to their website, they view homosexuals as Satan amongst them. They say God hates fags, and they should all die— sounds like a friendly bunch to me," added Jack sarcastically. "Since we're sort of stuck here for a while, why don't I go ahead and get things rolling for the weekend. Are you up to more charity work?"

"Hell yes!" replied T. "They are not going to stop me from helping the kids and less fortunate.

"I knew you would say that. I'm so proud of you. You're just so sweet." Thad and Jack looked each at each other and busted out laughing at how silly Jack sounded.

He gave Thad a kiss and returned to the kitchen to go to work leaving Thad to his movie. He started by calling Janet and updating her on the situation. He asked if their legal staff could look into Thad's property rights, and the rights of the protestors. He also told her he was going to spend the day working on T's charity work. He then told her Thad wanted a press conference upon his arrival in Texas, so he could answer their questions about his coming out, but after that, he would not say another word about it until after the race. "Race only interviews for the rest of the weekend."

Janet said she would prepare a press release stating time, location, and the ground rules, and she asked, "How are you boys holding up?"

Jack smiled as he looked back at Thad in the great room, "I think T is about ready to kick some butt, but we'll stay in control."

"Let me know what I can do to help. Will you inform me when you have your promotion and charity schedule figured out?"

"You got it and thanks."

Jack pulled up the checklist he had made last week, and went online to start his research. Jack was about as far from being a racing fan as anyone could be until he met T, so he started his research at the Texas Motor Speedway web site to find the location of the track. It was just north of Fort

219

Worth, and a tad east making it ideally situated for thousands of fans from both cities to attend. He began his list of charities to call, and two hours later, his plans came together. The next few hours he organized and arranged support through gifts to these institutions.

He emailed the plan to Janet and created an itinerary for Al. He sent the travel plan over to Al by fax knowing he hated email. Thad came over and gave him a hug while looking at the travel schedule on the screen. "Are you done?"

Jack leaned into him and kissed him on the cheek, "Yep, but pooped. Let's go for a ride on the lake, and then I'll work on your speeches tonight."

"Boat or personal watercrafts—choose your relaxation weapon!"

Jack laughed, "Let's try the personal watercraft, but how long until the sun goes down?"

"With fall here, it seems to be setting earlier. We didn't get up until after lunch. I'd say about three hours. The water should be flat and smooth unless there is some wind."

They headed down the hall pushing the other before stripping out of their clothes, putting on bathing suits, and choosing hats and sunglasses. T put a loose rubber strap over Jack's head and down to his neck. He then put clips on their sunglass strap and their hats to the rubber strap. Jack realized this was to keep the hat and glasses from blowing away. They grabbed a towel and went out the back door after Thad set the alarm system. They used T's golf cart—a gift from Drew and the team after his first win in the top series. The crew modified the cart with chrome wheels, a roll bar, and a powerful stereo. They drove down to the dock, and soon they couldn't hear the chants at the front gate.

T unlocked the rear gate, and they stepped through leaving the cart behind. He locked the gate before strolling down the hill to the dock. They checked the oil on each craft, and then filled the gas tanks. Jack thought they looked like a Sea-Doo, but had Yamaha emblazon in bright red on a purple metallic background. T showed him how to start it, slipped the safety key coiled strap over this left wrist, and pulled it tight.

Jack asked, "What's that for?"

Thad grinned as he pushed the first boat in the water and walked over to push his. "That's so the boat will instantly stop when I knock you off with a huge spray of water!"

Jack laughed, "You wish. I hope you can swim."

T started his motor and led them out of the cove at idle speed, "Once we break out of the cove we can go as fast as we want, but be careful, and don't get too close to me or too close to the shore. Allow some room in case you do fall. Oh, and one more thing. Watch out for wakes from some of the big boats on the lake. They're fun to jump, but if they catch you wrong you'll flip over. Ready? Let's go!"

T turned the throttle handle and his boat took off. Jack was a bit more timid, but gradually picked up his speed so he could catch up to T, as they invaded quiet coves and leaped over small boat wakes. They zipped through pretend slalom courses, and cruised along some of the bigger homes on the lake. They saw a beautiful sailboat and cruised alongside to study the fine craftsmanship. No one caught on that T was on the watercraft. After about fifty minutes of cruising at high speeds, they slowed down and entered a small cove with a long S curve entrance providing some privacy from the big lake.

They shut off their engines, removed their safety engine straps, and leaped off their crafts into the cool water. They splashed each other and dove under the other while reaching up to pull the partner under by the back of his swim shorts. One thing led to another and soon their suits were on the boat, and they began enjoying a good swim in the nude. Once tired, they swam between their boats with Jack putting his arms over the rails, and T kissing and playing with him. With only a few more weeks of racing, and winter rapidly approaching, they knew this would be the last time the water would be warm enough to swim in.

They arrived back at the dock just before dark and stowed the boats. They dried off, walked the path to the gate, and road the golf cart back to the house. They both made their way to the kitchen, and felt sad that the protestors were still in the monitors of the security system.

T grilled some steaks while Jack went to work on a short speech for the press conference, a list of questions he thought the media might ask, and other speeches for the charity groups. He then asked T a question, "What do you want to say when they ask you if you have a boyfriend?"

T flipped the steaks on the inside grill at the far end of the kitchen and smiled, "I'll tell them yes."

"And if they want to know who?"

"I'd be proud to say you, but what do you want to me say?"

Jack thought a second, "I guess if you finger me, pardon the pun..." began Jack as T rolled his eyes at the pun, "that would make it harder for me to get out of the public eye. But if you don't tell them it is me, it feeds the bigoted flames that gay people have no morals, we sleep around at the drop of a hat, and we want sex with as many people as possible."

"That sounds like fun. Gays can do that?" T laughed.

"I think we should show that we are in love only with only the other, just as they probably are with their wives."

"I bet most of them are divorced, but I agree. Should we hold hands or kiss, or do the nasty to prove it?" T laughed again as he swiveled his hips in a doggie style pump.

"You're incorrigible and irredeemable," he teased. "No I don't think we should push it too far yet. Their mindsets are the result of centuries of

221

hate—I don't think we can change that in just six days. Let's play it cool, but if you need to touch me or hold my hand, just do what you feel."

"I'd like to feel a lot more than your hand!" laughed T. "Dinner's ready." He lifted the steaks off the grill, and brought them to the table, and then leaned into Jack and kissed him passionately.

They arrived at the track the next morning by helicopter from the airport. Janet picked them up in the golf cart, and drove immediately to the back of the media building. She gave them both a hug and warned, "There's a lot more people here than I anticipated. Are you doing this alone, or with Jack?"

"Alone," replied T. "We think we should try to avoid questions about our sexual activity or other personal intimacy questions. I have short speech, and I'll take questions for about thirty minutes. Then you signal me, and I will close at the next opportunity and come straight back here. We'll go to the motorcoach and get ready for practice."

Janet nodded her approval. Jack pulled open the door, and T stepped inside. Forty electronic flash bulbs from the still cameras immediately blinded him. He was thankful he knew the way to the stage. He walked up the steps as the press turned to follow him, while Janet and Jack slipped inside, and pulled the door shut. With every chair taken, the media packed the room, as well as the center aisle filled with video cameras.

Thad raised his hand asking for quiet and smiling, "Good morning, and welcome to Texas. I'm going to make a few comments, and then you can ask questions one at a time. If this gets out of hand then I'll stop and walk out that door, so stay civil and I'll give answers to your questions. First of all, I assume you're here to ask about my personal life and not about my win last week, or the fact that I'm going to win the championship. That is a shame, but I understand how the media works. So be it, but at some point in the future, I'm going to ask you to help me on a charity project, and I hope you'll return the favor. I'm proud to be part of DMI, proud to have Drew McClain as my boss, and RESTAR as my major sponsor, as I am of all my sponsors. I believe they are proud of me even though I'm gay. There are millions of gay people all around the world that deserve fair treatment, with dignity, and with the ability to grow in the relationship of their choice and feel loved. Okay, end of speech. Questions?" He had hope there would be none, but he knew better, and picked a reporter from Speed Channel.

"Do you think coming out is going to affect your driving style, or the chase for the championship?"

T smiled, "Thank you—a sneaky question about me hidden in the middle of a racing question." The press group laughed. "I think my coming out took a huge burden off my back, and I'm not just talking about being gay, but trying to keep it a secret. I've always been gay—it was the secrecy that was killing me. Now that I'm free, I think I will race even better, but don't tell my competitors, okay?"

A lady reporter from Speed News quickly asked the next question. "Do you have an active sex life, and if so, is the lack of sleeping going to hurt your stamina in the race?"

T rolled his eyes, "Another clever question. Goodness you guys must have gotten up early this morning." The press laughed again. Jack knew T was making these light comments to allow his brain time to reel in a response. So far, he had been able to use various parts of the guess questions they had gone over, along with Jack's answers. "It would only be fair for me to answer such a private question about do I have an active sex life by first asking you the same thing. Do YOU have an active sex life?" Before she could respond, T continued, "And you?" he pointed at another reporter. "And you? You? You?" He smiled as he kept pointing at various members of the press and watching them blush. "Ah, that would be rude, wouldn't it, but I'm a nice guy, so I'll tell you this. He lowered his voice to a whisper and paused while the room fell silent, "Yes." They laughed again.

Returning to his normal voice, T said, "The person I love increases my stamina for the race because the love between us makes me even stronger!"

The Dallas Times reporter got the next chance, "I was in Daytona when I got the memo from some unknown figure stating you were gay. Did this note have anything to do with you coming out now?"

"To be blunt, that person attempted to blackmail me. He did not know me, but he knew my partner and managed to put two and two together. He was right about us being gay—he was very wrong to try and extort money from me. To prevent this from ever happening again, we decided it was time I came out. I waited my whole life for the chance to come out, and in the end, I'm grateful, because his note, and attempts at extortion, gave me the extra push I needed to tell everyone."

The reporter from Race Magazine began his question, "How do you think the other drivers and crews will treat you? After all, you're the first gay man to come out at the track."

T smiled, "I'm not the first gay man in racing—just the first one to come out. There are others. Statistically gays make up about ten percent of the population."

Jack knew what was going to happen next and he lightly elbowed Janet and whispered, "Watch this.'

T grinned and raised his hand to start pointing and counting, "So let's see, there's about hundred in here so that means probably at least ten of the press group is gay. Let's see, is it you? You? You?" he continued until he reached ten. "You see, your colleagues or even your best friend could be gay, but afraid like I was to come out. Don't make it so hard on them, and stop telling all those dirty jokes.

"I hope the teams will treat me with the same respect they expect me to give them. I hope on the track they will race me hard but clean, and I'll do the same."

Jack smiled and glanced at his watch. Fifteen more minutes and it'll be over. Janet marveled at how strong and confident Thad was. When she gave the signal to wrap it up, Thad could not have been more gracious, and then quickly left the stage. Jack and Janet were waiting in the golf cart as T climbed aboard. She quickly whisked them away and over to their coach. T changed clothes while Jack fixed bowls of fresh fruit for them to eat, and for the fun of it, they both ate a huge large orange muffin with the real bits of orange inside. They were licking their fingers after that.

Jack drove Thad over to the garage. T said hello to several drivers and competitor team members as they rode along. He thought he heard someone behind him called him a name. He turned and saw no one. Jack dropped him off at his garage and drove back to the motorcoach, and began going down his checklist for the engagements later that afternoon and Saturday.

T climbed aboard his racecar and for the first time he did it without his rib vest. He was just a little sore, but relieved he could breathe easier with the thing off and without pain. He backed out of the garage and drove over to his pit where his team waited for him. Charley followed in a golf cart. Once Charley had his headset on and reached the top of the pit box, he radioed Gary to see if their spotter was ready. Gary came back quickly on the headset with an all-go verdict. Charley looked down at T and his car. "Okay, T, let's go. Take it easy at first so you can break in this new car and motor."

"Yes, mother dear," replied T as the crew laughed. He started the engine and made his way out to the track. T went through the first turn with ease and began pushing the throttle down. By the time he whizzed by the pit he was already doing a hundred and forty miles an hour.

"So much for taking it easy," muttered Charley.

There were about twenty cars practicing by going low, to see what the bottom of the track felt like, and if it had a good groove. Then they would move up a lane hoping for a second groove and even higher. They took turns drafting off the lead car and passing others. T was now doing a hundred and eighty miles an hour. He had just finished the backstretch and was the number two car in a line of cars drafting. He pulled hard to the outside and began accelerating for a pass.

Gary suddenly came over the radio, "Crash turn four!"

T heard him just as he was coming out of turn three. He was side by side a car on his inside that blocked his view of turn four. Ahead of them, they saw an oil slick as the 22 car had blown an engine and hit the wall hard. The remains of the wrecked car had stopped directly in his lane. The lower car went to the grass, but T's only choice was to go high. To avoid slamming into the car, he turned his wheel hard to the right. The left front and rear tires hit the oil, and in a flash, he slammed hard into the wall.

"Shit!" exclaimed Charley. "Gary! Is he all right? T can you hear me?"

Gary came back on the radio, "I don't see movement. The car is torn up, and we'd better get the backup car ready."

"Thad? Can you hear me?" asked Charley over the radio again, as he wiped nervous sweat from his lip.

Jack looked up at the television where he had turned the audio down. He grabbed the remote and hung up the phone. The announcers were explaining the oil slick. Suddenly, a replay came on the screen, and Jack's heart skipped a beat when he saw T's car hit the safe wall barriers. A long moment later, he saw the net come down and T climbed out. Jack and Charley both sighed with relief.

Charley began climbing down from the pit box. "Okay boys back to the garage, and get the backup ready. I'm heading to the Med Center."

Jack heard Charley over the team radio on the table. He locked the coach, and began driving to where he thought the Med Center was. T was required to go there even if he felt fine, but he didn't feel fine. He was a bit dizzy, and now the soreness in his ribs returned. Janet saw him walk in and winked at him. He smiled, "I'll be back in a minute. Better watch for Jack." He went in and the big double doors closed.

Jack parked as close as he could, and then jumped out and ran to the Med Center. Janet saw him coming, "Calm down, Jack. I just saw him and he is fine."

He put his arms on her shoulders and stared into her eyes. "Are you sure?"

She smiled at him, "He told me to watch for you, and I think he was right. It is not easy watching someone you care about slam into the wall at a hundred and eighty miles an hour, is it?" She gave him a hug.

Jack's face went white, "A hundred, and what?" He started getting dizzy. "I've got to sit down."

She laughed and led him to her golf cart. He quickly sat down on the front seat. Janet repeated, "A hundred and eighty. He'll be fine. The car and the safe wall barrier protected him."

It was a long twenty minutes later before T appeared from behind the double doors of the entrance of the medical center. Jack saw him, wanted to run to him, but held fast. T came over and gave him a hug, "I'm all right, so don't you worry. It was just some oil on the track. I'll be fine. In the moment he hugged Jack, a photographer snapped their picture and turned away unseen. The Speed Channel cameras also caught the hug, as their reporter and cameraman walked up to ask if he was okay. T told them he was fine, and they watched Jack drive him back to the garage. To Jack's amazement, T got out, climbed in the backup car as if nothing happen, and drove back out on the track. Jack drove over to the pit to watch for a while.

Two men in the pit of car 50 saw Jack and one whispered to the other, "I think the oil slick worked just fine. We'll save the rest for Sunday." Jack never saw or heard them. No one did.

After a shower, lunch, and a rubdown by Jack on Thad, they settled down for a nap. Later, Al flew the boys on a short hop to Houston where T made an appearance at a housing development set up for victims of the recent Hurricane in the Gulf of Mexico. Soon they were heading to Dallas to visit the headquarters for Rainbow Days, a non-profit group that provides the children living in high risk areas the skills they need to come out of it crime and drug free. Jack had the head of a computer company there and lots of press, as he and T gave the group two hundred computers and a donation of three hundred thousand dollars.

The next stop was to Treasured Friends, a group with the purpose of finding homes for rescued pets. T and Jack played with the dogs and cats, and thanks to a popular dog food company, they presented the organization with another big check. They left with the thankful group cheering Thad's name.

The last charity stop was to the office of Wipe Out Kids' Cancer, whose mission it was to raise money for research to cure, and eradicate cancer. They arranged for about twenty kids to be there who were in the midst of cancer treatment. T hugged every one of them, and thanks to Janet, he had hats and t-shirts for all. Jack had called Greg at RESTAR, and they gladly donated a half million dollars to the group. Greg flew in for the presentation. He arrived with smiles and hugs, and delighted to see Thad and Jack carrying out their promises.

By five, they arrived at the first of six television stations with Jack prompting T with the names of the Sports Directors. They invited Greg to join them, so he could see T in his uniform promoting RESTAR at every single opportunity. They were back at the track by dark, changed clothes, and drove in the Hummer to Fort Worth. T told Jack he was taking him somewhere special for dinner. When they turned down streets lined with corrals and stockyards, he thought they were going to a gay bar in a seedy part of town. T made two quick turns and pulled up to a place with a huge neon sign called Billy Bob's. After parking, he climbed into the back seat, stripped out of his uniform, and put on street clothes.

They walked in wearing tennis shoes and jeans, and immediately felt out of place as everyone else was wearing cowboy hats, western shirts, and boots. T laughed as Jack took in the enormity of the place. There were six thousand people dancing in front of three stages, and the sign said thirty-six bars. Off to the side he saw numerous restaurants and even a giant buffet line. T grabbed two beers, and told Jack to follow him through the crowd. T walked fast so folks wouldn't stop him for an autograph, and before they knew it, they were on the far side and in the bleachers watching a live rodeo show followed by a horse show with trick riders.

"Come on, you've got to try something!" said T as he led Jack back through the crowd where they found a big mechanical bull surrounded by about fifty stacked tumbling mats.

"I ain't getting on that thing," protested Jack.

T leaned in close and whispered, "You will if you want any of my ass later tonight."

Jack laughed, "It ain't all that good!" He quickly turned, faked leaving, and then spun around, "Gotcha!"

T laughed and pushed him to the line waiting to ride. They finished their beers and T went first. The crowd soon recognized him and cheered him on. He made it about seven seconds before hitting the mat. He bowed to the applause and laughter. Jack climbed aboard and thought he was holding on tight, but three spins, a few butt leaps by the bull, and he tumbled off to the mat. T picked him up, and they both waved at the laughing crowd.

"Come on before the fans swamp us!" yelled T as they made their way through the crowd, and off to a restaurant in the far corner. Jack was puffing by the time they got there.

"Dang, you walk as fast you drive."

T held the door for him. "Sorry, I have to, or I'd be signing autographs the rest of the night."

They sat down at a table in the darken corner. T sat with his back to rest of the restaurant. Jack had the feeling T had sat there before. A waitress came up and recognized him. "Hey T, what-a-it-be?" Jack laughed as she rolled her words together.

T laughed, "Get us two beers, salads, loaded bake potatoes, and two thunder steaks, and could you ask Ralph for a little help?"

"You got it darling. You want them medium or still walking when they get here."

"Medium please. I left my spurs at home, and thanks."

"Walking?" quizzed Jack.

"The steaks," chuckled T. "Wait until you see them. They are as big as tire on my car."

A tall man wearing a red vest and black cowboy hat approached the table, "Good evening, Thad. We're glad you're back. What can I do for you?"

T pumped the man's hand, "Good to see you Ralph. This is my friend Jack. Can you keep the fans off for a while, so we can try to eat our thunder steaks?"

"No problem. I hope you enjoy your meal."

They had celebrities just about every night, and he knew exactly what to do. Ralph spoke into his radio, and in a few minutes, a man blocked off their table with red velvet ropes, and two men stood guard. The salads appeared in a flash, and fifteen minutes later the waitress returned with a huge banquet serving platter, and put twenty-four inch plates for each boy on the table with a potato and the largest T-bone steak Jack had ever seen sizzling in the middle. It literally hung off the edge of the huge plate. Jack forgot the salad, and went to work on the steak. "Oh my gosh, this meat is so tender and the taste is divine."

"Sadly, that steak was walking around this morning. We're in the middle of the famous Fort Worth stockyards where they load the cattle up and ship them all over the country." Then he quickly changed the subject, "You sure went down hard on your ass after flying off that bull you were riding. Are you okay?"

"Yep, the adrenalin was pumping so fast I didn't feel a thing—other than embarrassment!" laughed Jack.

They ate laughing and teasing each other and enjoying the music. Near the end of their meal, the lights went down in the back of the building and a popular country singer took the stage. T wanted to dance so bad with Jack, and at first he thought they might could get away with it as the dance floor was packed, but he knew he would be inundated with fans. They enjoyed the music and dinner, and then T paid the bill, tipped Ralph and his boys, and gave the waitress a big tip, too. He signed a few autographs as they were leaving, and then they ran to the Hummer and drove off.

T didn't win the pole, but was in the second row in the third position for the start of the race on Sunday. He gave no interviews prior to the race other than the short ones by the network crews covering the race. He plugged his sponsors at every opportunity. He saw Greg Bell, shook his hand, and thanked him for his support and help before Jack whisked him off to his pit. Driver introductions drew about the same reaction with a lot of fans booing him and some loving him.

Together, they sat in the shade of the golf cart waiting for time to climb aboard the car. "Why do they boo you?"

T smiled at Jack. "It is sort of like wrestling. Everybody pulls for their favorite and loudly boos anybody else. Because I have been lucky to win quite a few races, and did it while so new to the sport, well, I guess I pissed them off. At the worst, their booing means they are noticing my victories. Don't take it personally," added T.

"Well, they need to grow…" before Jack could finish his sentence a guy came up behind them with a huge cup of ice and Coke, reached around, and threw it violently into T's face, drenching him.

Jack leaped out of the cart, but the guy had taken off through the crowd. A few people saw it, but kept moving. The ice stung Thad's face and bruised one eye. Jack looked around and spotted Charley. He ran to him. "T's been hurt!"

228

Charley leaped off the pit box and ran to the golf cart with Jack. "What's wrong?"

"Some fan slung a big cup of ice and Coke in his face. I think it must have damaged his right eye," said Jack.

Charley got on his radio and called the team doctor over. He was there in seconds. He carefully looked at Thad's eye while Jack grabbed some towels from the pit box and tried to clean him up.

"I'm okay," said Thad, as the doctor let go of his eyelids. It just stung a bit. I wish I had put my helmet on." He got up and walked around the cart.

"Are you sure?" asked the doctor.

T smiled, "It was Diet Coke. I hate Diet Coke."

Charley and the doctor sort of laughed. T gave Jack a high five, and said he would see him after the race. T climbed over the wall and into his car, and began hooking up his safety gear. Janet arrived and gave his hand a squeeze. "You better push hard today, and by the way I hear gay boys can run real fast, is that right?" she teased.

"You got it. Do me a favor and check on Jack for me. He'll tell you why."

She gave him a puzzled look as she climbed over the pit wall and walked over to Jack who sat in the golf cart seemingly deep in thought with a somber look on his face. She saw the wet seat beside him and the ice on the floor. She put her arm on his back, just as a country star was singing the Star - Spangled Banner. She waited for it to finish, and then the Air Force jets flew over before asking, "What happen?"

"A guy slung a large cup of ice and Coke in T's face. We thought it damaged an eye, but the doc says he is okay. T says he is okay, too."

"I take it you're not okay," she added.

"I'll be fine. It was just a shock. We were just talking and having a good time, and then bam! We didn't see the guy sneak up on us."

"Are you going to watch the race from here, or head back to the motorcoach?"

"I am going back to the coach as I have to work on next week's events. Did I tell you I got him booked on the Today Show?"

"He is going to be on the Today Show? When?"

"I got the call this morning. We're doing it Tuesday in New York City. T is very excited about it. Mary will do the interview, and she has been known as friendly to gays, so we hope this will help. We do the Brad Allen show afterwards."

Jack stopped talking for a moment, and then asked, "Do you think we need more security for him at the track?"

"Yes, I do. I'm going to go talk with Drew about it, and I'll see you after the race. T will be fine. He's tough, so now you need to be tough for him."

"Yes ma'am," said Jack as he smiled, and pulled away in the cart.

The start of the race went well, while Drew put a call into Duke who arranged to have a group of four cops ready to meet Thad, and give him protection at the end of the race. He then turned back to watch his drivers go to work. T had moved up to second just before the first caution, and with a quick pit time, he came out of the pits in first. Drew, Charley, and Janet were elated on the pit box.

After all the cars pulled back on the track and waited for the restart after that caution stop, a crew member in the pit next door to T's team, began sweeping his pit area with a broom. He went over the line into T's box, but no one really cared, as it was not unusual to do so. As the race started T's crew stood on the wall to watch, failing to see the sweeper drop several roofing nails to the asphalt just behind his broom and hidden from the crewmembers. He finished his sweeping and stepped over the wall.

T continued his lead, but remained challenged constantly by the driver of the 90 car. This continued until time for a green flag pit stop. T pulled off the track to the apron and began slowing down. The 90 car was in the pit group ahead of him coming around the back stretch, but at the last second he pulled a hard right, didn't take to the pits, but continued on to pick up five points as the new race leader.

"Charley yelled into the radio, "Okay boys, four tires, gas, and a slight spring correction on the right rear. Let's do it!"

T came into his pit and screeched to a halt. He put the shift in neutral, and let out the clutch, keeping his other foot on the brake. He took a big swing from his Gator Aid plastic drinking tube as his right side of the car went down and up came the left. He looked in the rearview mirror and saw the second tank of gas go in. He pushed in the clutch, dropped the shift to first just as the left side went down. He popped the clutch, roared out to the apron, and back on the track.

He had just reached top speed when he felt the right front tire go down. "Flat tire!" he yelled in the radio.

"Dang, bring in it. Which tire?"

"Right front..." before he finished the right rear went down. "Shit! The right rear is down, too. I'm coming in."

He let off the gas, went back down on the apron, and returned to his pit. He slammed on the brakes, up the right side went, two tires on, and he was back out in just six seconds. T spun out to the track and down at the tail end of the field. The crew lifted the flat tires over the wall, and began studying them to see what had gone wrong. The front had three nails and the rear two. They showed it to Charley and Drew. They even showed it to the nearest race official.

Charley complained, "What the hell?" Then up to his spotter, "Gary, did you see anything weird going on out there?"

Gary came on the radio, "What do you mean by weird?"

"T had three nails in the front and two in the rear. That is too much of a coincidence. If someone threw them on the track he might have hit one or two, and someone else would have hit the rest, but he got five, and no one else hit any." Charley slowly caught on that it had happen right in front of him in the pit. He came back on the radio, "Crew, I want you to watch the pit the entire race. Someone put nails in our pit stall. Sweep down our pit."

"Two flats at hundred and ninety miles an hour could have killed him," stated Drew.

Charley replied, "We were lucky he noticed while accelerating."

"Damn. The person that planted those nails should be tarred and feathered."

"That's too nice. I was thinking skinned alive," replied Charley while looking at his laptop with a display of T's gauges electronically reproduced in front of him. He clicked on his microphone for T. "Well, there were nails in your tires. How they got there, I don't know, but we'll watch the pit area from now on. You piss anybody off this week?"

T clicked his microphone button as he came out of the fourth turn, "Just the religious right, and fifty million homophobic folks in America."

Charley said with a straight face, "Is that all? And I was worried. Come on son; let's beat these bastards. Take your time, but let's get back to the front. I bet it smells back there."

T grinned, "Roger, will do!"

Late in the race, following a three car wreck, the crew hastily got T out of the pit picking up five more spots, and put him in third with forty-eight laps to go. He was behind the number 90 car and the number 50 was in the lead—teammates. T began working the number 90 car trying to pass high or low, but met with a block with time running out. He weaved in and out a couple of times, frustrated he couldn't pass.

The driver of the 90 car guarded and blocked him at every opportunity. He yelled at Thad, even though T couldn't possibly hear him over the engine noise, "Come on, you faggot. Give me a little bump. If you don't you're going to lose, you fudge-packer!"

With twenty-five laps to go, and as they excited turn two leading into the long back stretch, T pulled up close and gave him just enough bump to force him to let off the gas. He prepared to pull left and go low hard, as he knew the 90 car would have to go up the track to gain control.

The 90 driver yanked hard on a string that fed behind his seat and to the right of his two car batteries. The big mouth cap instantly came off the bag of a clear lubricant hanging like the IV bags in the hospital. The oil spewed down to the pavement. Because the cars were so close, no camera spotted it. He laughed as he saw T lose control in the mirror and begin spinning. He, too, spun like the bump started the mess, and put his car into wall sideways so it wouldn't hurt much. He turned the wheel hard, drove down the track, as if out of control, and deliberately crashed it into the interior wall messing the front engine compartment up badly. This put his car out of the race, and out of any chance of an after race random inspection of his car. He knew the remains of his car would be loaded and on the way home within the hour, and under no suspicion.

Meanwhile, Thad's car spun out of control several times before catching the front bumper of a passing car knocking a wheel off his car, and sending him out of control and into the grass and out of the race.

Jack stood up in the coach and watched the accident happen over and over again. Not one camera caught sight of the clear oil.

Charley clicked his microphone button, "T you there?"

"Yep, I'm here, but this car ain't going anywhere. The wheel broke off."

"We'll get 'em next time." Then up to Gary, "Gary, did you see anything happen to his car?"

"No, he just gave the 90 car a small bump so he could pass, and the next thing I know he is spinning all around."

By the time the wrecker trucks removed the two cars and cleaned up the mechanical mess, the hot Texas sun evaporated liquid, leaving no evidence. T dropped to a thirty-second spot in the race finals since a lot of other cars had gone out ahead of him. He had led a lap, and led the most laps, which saved him a little in points, so he was still in fourth place in the championship.

Charley and Drew looked over the car, and couldn't figure out what happen. They watched the video replays finding no evidence of foul play. T came out of the Med Center, and immediately the new security detail met him. They put him in a car and drove him to the coach.

"Jack? You here?" T ran up the steps into the coach after closing the door.

Jack was at the table where he had been working. "I hope you're okay. That looked like a hell of a spin."

T gave him a kiss. "It was. Come on, they want us to get out of here as soon as we can. They're afraid someone else might throw something. Please pack as quick as you can, and let's get going. We're done with Texas!"

T changed out of his uniform while Jack packed their clothes along with his laptop, and together, they were out the door in ten minutes. The guards drove him to the heliport. T thanked the cops and shook all their hands. They lifted off just as the race was finishing. The number 50 car won. Al was ready for them when the helicopter landed, and soon they were in the air and safely heading home to Charlotte.

TWENTIETH

The flight on Tuesday to New York City was the first activity of the week for the boys, as Monday was a recovery day from the large amount of physical and mental stress heaped on their shoulders. Jack felt guilty for all Thad was going through because of their relationship, but every time T smiled at him, the gesture managed to suppress the guilt for a while. As they began to descend, the skyline of New York City Jack reminded T of his last visit to the city with a friend in the summer prior to the terrorist attack on the World Trade Towers. It was his third visit to the top, but his friend's first. The rapid ride to the roof made their ears pop with the change of air pressure, but the moment the elevator doors open they could see through the giant windows, and the shock of just how high they were almost took their breath away.

Jack and his friend had walked around the observation tower noting they were taller than most aircraft circling the city while the people on the streets looked like ants. They watched a short film on the building of the towers in a small theater in the center of the floor, and took pictures of each other standing in front of the windows with the skyline in the background. Jack felt sad T never experienced the Trade Towers before their demise on September 11, 2001. He still could not believe they were gone, and the number of people who died.

There were four other race drivers arriving on Wednesday, but the boys came a day early so they could take a holiday in the city. T had his sunglasses on, and his hat pulled down tightly. Jack used his new Master Card to check in, a card Thad arranged for him so the bills would go to his accountant, and the hotel would not know T was there. He hoped the media would not find out either. Jack also had a debit card so he could withdraw cash for tips and small expenditures.

They tipped the bellman, and as the door to their room shut, T tackled Jack and they crashed onto the bed, made out for a bit, but reluctantly, they broke the embrace and left the room with Jack's camera over his neck. To speed their tour up, they took numerous cab rides from one attraction to the next. They went to the top of the Empire State building, visited Times Square, decided to buy tickets to a Broadway show that evening, and Jack dragged T around the Natural History Museum. After Thad stood under the skeleton of a giant dinosaur, he was hooked on seeing the rest of the exhibits. T acted as if he was going to say something profound, but instead asked Jack if he knew how large a dinosaur's penis was? Jack laughed at him as he they made their way through the vast hallways. By afternoon, they were strolling through Central Park.

The entire day no one noticed them or called Thad by name. It was as if they were invisible, and T loved the feeling of freedom. They were afraid to hold hands in the park, but playfully bumped into each other from time to time while laughing and smiling.

They devoured their dinner at Elaine's including dessert before walking to the theater. T had never been to a Broadway show, so Jack picked a revival of the Odd Couple with Nathan Lane and Matthew Broderick. It was a hilarious comedy, and they sat in fourth row seats in the middle. They laughed the entire show, and T confessed afterwards how amazingly talented this company was.

They walked to Times Square and watched the startling cast of city characters walking the streets. This included two men who had spray painted their body in silver and glitter, and did a dance routine. Next, they heard an amazing solo saxophonist who played for tips, while balancing on a ball, but the winner of the weirdest was a naked cowboy wearing only small briefs and white hat playing and singing songs with his guitar.

They ate Hagen Das ice cream while watching the crowds stroll by before finally heading back to their room. They had a message on their phone stating the limo would be there at six in the morning.

"That's too early," complained T.

"It's a morning TV show—they can't come in the afternoon," laughed Jack, as he began undressing after arranging a wake-up call on the phone.

T laughed and replied, "I can. I can come anytime you're around!"

T brushed his teeth and began undressing, while Jack brushed his teeth, and moments later the lights were off, and they were making love once again.

T did not really wake up until they walked into Rockefeller Center to the studio for the Today Show on NBC. The producer's assistant walked them to their dressing room. A make-up artist came to the door and knocked. Thad and Jack's gaydar alarm went off the moment they saw Jimmy. He was a short, skinny man with big white teeth, and bright red hair housing a ton of gel, causing the hair to remain straight up as if he had stuck his tongue in a power receptacle.

Jimmy smiled, "Mr. Thompson it is so nice to meet you."

"Just call me T," replied Thad as he shook hands with Jimmy. "This is Jack." They shook hands as well.

Jimmy rolled his cart over to the dressing table with the numerous bulbs of lights trailing the edge of the mirror. "Just sit over here, and I'll do the rest. Is this what you're wearing?"

"Yes, nothing too fancy for me—just this shirt and a navy blue blazer," replied T as he sat down.

Jimmy carefully removed his race hat and frowned, "You must have been in Central Park as there is a squirrel nest on your head."

The boys laughed. T asked, "What are you trying to say?"

Jimmy replied, "I'm saying we're going to evict the squirrels!"

They all laughed again as Jimmy threw a cape over T's clothes and went to work on washing T's hair, and making a few snips before firing up his blow dryer. He then went to work on his face by first shaving him, and then applying the makeup for the television interview.

"Honey, on the streets you don't need any makeup, as you're beautiful, but the lights and cameras can make your natural face look like craters on the moon, and remember, folks are eating breakfast while watching our show, so we don't want to scare them!"

Jack laughed, "I think you better get another makeup cart, as it will take a lot to make his face look good."

T flung a brush at him. "Yeah, I'll catch up with you later."

Jimmy smiled, "So how long have you two boys been a couple?"

T grinned, as they couldn't fool Jimmy, "A few months. How'd you know?"

"Well, that was easy: you winked at him twice, he smiled back, and your story is all over the news. I just didn't know who the lucky guy was until now. I didn't see his picture in any of the stories."

T smiled, "Well, I hope we can keep it that way, but we do love each other very much."

"That's good. I wish you well," replied Jimmy as he took the cape off, and put tissue paper in the collar of T's shirt to avoid any makeup powder getting on his jacket. "I had a boyfriend once. We were together for eighteen years before he finally succumbed to cancer. He's been gone seven years, and I still can't imagine starting over again." He paused before adding, "Of course if I could find someone as cute as the two of you I might!"

"Thanks for your help," replied T, as Jimmy pushed the cart to the door.

"Good luck today and remember, you're talking about your gay life, but you're also giving gay people all over the planet encouragement, and if we're lucky, another step up the ladder of acceptance. I'll be watching."

Thirty minutes later, they were ushered to the studio. The stage manager assumed Jack was T's manager, and took him to a couch in the corner where he could see a monitor. T sat on the interview couch while the news anchor finished their previous story. "Coming up in our next half hour, we're doing a story on a new model of Segway, the motorized units that allow you to stand on a platform as it whisks you about town. And now we go over to Mary and her special guest."

Mary was sitting in the chair opposite from T. The camera operator gave her a cue as his red light lit up on the top of his camera, "Thank you, Jane. I'm excited about our next guest. He is a racing champion, and currently in fourth place in the race for the championship right here on NBC, and preparing for this weeks' race in Atlanta. I am happy to welcome Thad Thompson, or as his friends call him TNT. Welcome Thad."

Thad smiled, "Mary, you can just call me T—that's what my real friends call me, and I'm glad to be here." Jack marveled at how easily T handled the interviews. Not long after Drew signed T to a five-year contract, Janet hired a media coach, and for six weeks, they drilled T for all types of interviews including television, radio, and newsprint. He nervously stuttered and stammered a bit at first, but with their help, he soon became a favorite of the reporters. He was clear, to the point, and most importantly quick with his whit, and short and concise with his timing. She then arranged for several directors to work with him until he could produce amazing, very professional, top quality commercials. He learned to easily edit on the fly making various versions of the same commercial in precise lengths of ten, twenty, thirty, and sixty-second versions. He was even more skilled at making local station promos on the fly, to the delight of the entire television station staff.

Mary replied, "Are you okay after the big spin you took on Sunday?"

"Yes, I'm fine. The car has tremendous safety features, but I did feel like I was caught up in a giant salad spinner."

She laughed, and Jack smiled, as that was a line he wrote for T.

"You have just three races to go, and you're fourth in points. What will it take to win the championship?"

"Oh, I'm going to win, but I need to win a pole or two, lead the most laps for bonus points, and place in the top three. And if I'm lucky, I'll also win at least one of these last three races."

"I want to run a clip from a press conference you held a few weeks ago. Let's take a look."

Jack's stomach tightened as if twisted in a knot. He watched excerpts from T's coming out speech on the monitor across from the couch. The boys knew this would happen, and they were prepared. T pretended to watch while his brain rewound some of the phrases they practiced.

Mary continued as they video went away, "So you came out to the entire world as the first gay driver. Were you afraid to do so?"

"I've been afraid to do so all my life. Afraid my family would turn against me, my teams would throw me out, my fans would desert me, and my friends hate me. However, once I made the decision to come out, I couldn't wait to get it done. Now I'm free to be who I am and no longer a robot going through what is expected of me. That press conference took only a few minutes for me to come out, but the rest of it was about doing good things in this world. I gave away a million dollars to charities and urged my sponsors, my team, and my fans to support charities all over our country. Since then we have flown to many cities and given away more money in a few weeks than I did all of last year."

"But aren't you afraid someone might hurt you on the streets, or in the garage, or even on the track?"

236

"I want to help as many people as possible, and I want to be a beacon of hope for the all the gay people on the planet, urging each to come out when they are ready, and to not be afraid. So you see, if I want to lift them up, I can't be afraid."

"I can't imagine driving a car two hundred miles an hour, but to come out in the middle of a stunning career, for that I think you are indeed a hero. T—thank you for coming, and good luck on Sunday."

"Thank you Mary. It was a pleasure to be here."

They sat still for five seconds until the stage manager said clear. Mary shook his hand as Jack walked over, "Is this the lucky boy."

T smiled, "This is Jack, and I'm the lucky boy." She shook hands, and smiled, "You boys take good care of each other. Thank you for coming." They were ushered back to the dressing room. Jimmy quickly got the makeup off his face. T stood up, and gave him a hug as did Jack. They made their way to the stage door where the limo took them to the Brad Allen talk show, featuring the final top five racers who had flown up the night before.

Back into another makeup room he went as the show came on the air. He joined the rest of the racers in the green room. He and Jack sat on a couch together. At first, no one said anything, so T decided to break the silence, "After makeup, we all look like we just came from the morgue."

Some of them laughed as Robbie replied. "Don't lick your lips. I made that mistake last year. This powder makeup is nasty tasting stuff."

"Are you guys sightseeing today? It's a beautiful city."

Sam, a big redneck driver, said, "Not me. I hate this town—too many weirdos for me."

The door opened and an assistant walked them to the stage. They were in commercial break so they were seated with T in the middle. The host of the show, Brad Allen, walked over, shook their hands, and sat down. He looked up from his notes as the cameraman gave him a cue.

"We're here today with the top five drivers in the country—all vying for this year's championship. Welcome fellows. Let me start by asking, "Which one of you is going to win?"

The audience laughed as they all raised their hands. Jack held his breath as Brad asked a question of each one leaving T for last.

When he finally got to T, he said, "Thad, I watched you win last year in Richmond when I got to do the start your engine command. You're a heck of a driver. Do you think your coming out is going to hurt or help you win?"

Jack winced as he tried to smile at Thad, "It is going to help. I no longer have to worry about the big secret. That's done, and I have devoted myself to helping as many charities as I can, and seeing those kids with their eyes full of hope, gives me hope that I can win this championship for all the kids."

Brad laughed, "Well being gay in New York is no big deal. Half my staff is gay, but you're in the heart of Georgia this weekend—isn't that redneck country?"

T smiled, "Well, actually Atlanta is pretty liberal with Elton John heading up the list of most popular gay men in town, but I'm a proud gay man, and all I can do is to take one day at a time—and win the championship."

"Thank you fellows—good luck this weekend."

As they were leaving the makeup room, Jack heard one of the drivers call him a faggot, but Jack forced a smile, and said with a smirk, "Have a nice day."

They ate an early lunch, and visited the city's first gay academy, the Harvey Milk High School. T presented them with a check for fifty thousand dollars, and got one of his sponsors to donate a truckload of computer equipment. The media took many pictures of the presentation, but once that was done, T was ushered into the auditorium without a single reporter or camera present. The staff wanted the kids to feel free to ask him anything without showing their faces to the media. Once introduced, T didn't walk up and onto the stage with the principal, but reached up from the floor and shook her hand, and then sat on the edge of the stage to be as close to the kids as possible. Someone handed him a microphone so the two hundred students and faculty could hear him.

"Before I take questions, I would like to introduce my partner, Jack Langston. The students clapped for him. "Jack, get your butt over here and help me." The kids laughed as a reluctant Jack sat beside T while planting a playful elbow to his shoulder. "Okay," began T, "ask away."

A tall skinny girl on the front row stood up. T and Jack smiled at her. "When I came out, my family kicked me out of the house. I was homeless for a year before a gay couple took me in. It was hard losing my family, but now my fellow students are my friends as well as my family. What was it like for you to come out?" She sat down.

T spoke up, "For me and many others, it was a major decision. I'm in the public eye all the time, and once I met Jack I had to decide whether to lose Jack by staying in the closet, or keep him and come out."

Jack said, "Well, it wasn't that simple. I knew he loved me and I loved him, but we experienced someone trying to blackmail us. The man could only take advantage of us if we wanted to keep our love a secret. I could tell T was not yet ready to come out so…"

"So he left me!" exclaimed T as he took over with a grin. He began pouring on the sob story with sly smile. "Yep, the man I love just left me cold without even saying goodbye," teased T. "It was so sad. I could probably write a country song about my despair," he added as the kids chuckled, and he pretended to dab at a tear.

"Yeah, well, the note I left said it was because I didn't want to hurt you, and I didn't want to force you out of the closet," said Jack. "But what it didn't say was that I just couldn't stand your bad breath any longer!" The kids laughed.

T blushed, "I can't help it if I smell like burnt fuel and smoking tires."

"I know, but I'm having a hard time making out with you with my gas mask on!" The kids laughed again.

"Uh, next question," urged T feigning embarrassment.

An overweight boy stood up, "I'm teased for both being gay and fat. I am trying to lose the weight because no one is attracted to me like this, but do you think a person can change from being gay? My family sent me books to read and tapes to listen to, and they all promise to convert me."

T slipped off the stage, "Okay, first things first. Come down here." As the boy started to the front, T reached back, took Jack's hand, and urged him off the stage as well. "Okay, group hug." Jack and T enveloped the boy in a big hug. They held that for a minute as the boy sobbed. After breaking the embrace, T looked over to the principal as he pulled his microphone up to speak, "Ma'am, is it legal to kiss in this school?"

The students snickered as she replied, "Yes, but not during class."

T quickly kissed the boy on the lips as did Jack. The boy blushed as T turned him around to face the students while keeping an arm around him. "Now students, look at this boy's face. How could you not like this gorgeous smiling face? I didn't have a single boyfriend until I met Jack in my twenties. You're still in school, and have plenty of time to find mister right. There are many amazing people in this world that also fight the weight problem. Goodness, most of America is trying to lose weight. I urge you to do all you can to lose weight so you'll be healthy, and live a long, long time.

"I want your journey through this world to be a fun one. I've learned that you feel better when you stop worrying about yourself, and stop helping others. I have a little friend in Cincinnati that taught me this. His name is Sammy. He got so upset at the cancer treatments he just stopped eating, but we became friends, and he is eating and now healthier. The more he grows the more I get excited. You have to work harder on helping others so the magic of how others see you will just happen.

"As to can you be converted—I don't think so. God made you as you are, and He doesn't make mistakes. You are not a mistake, but I think it would be a mistake to pretend to be straight when you know He made you gay. Be proud of how you were made, and that you now have a chance to enjoy life and all the gifts we have been given. What is your name?"

"Jonathan," replied the boy.

"Soon I will have to leave to continue my career, but I am going to check up on you from time to time to see how you're doing, but I need some help from the whole school," he added as he pointed to the audience in assembly. Is there anyone here that will help me by being friends with Jonathan?"

T's held his breath, until finally a student stood up and said aloud, "I will!"

Rapidly one by one the entire student body stood and yelled "I will, too!"

They had stayed at the school for two hours trying to provide all the support and inspiration they could. Jack told the students he was a writer and learned to enjoy writing while in high school. He urged the students to take advantage of their education. He told them to start writing in a journal, so they could see their problems in their own handwriting, and it would be like releasing the problems or letting go. He closed by saying, "By the time you're twenty-five, you'll start losing brain cells, so if you want to get ahead in this world, now is the time to study and learn all you can."

They received a standing ovation as they left the auditorium. The boys gave the principal a hug while other kids hung out the windows to wave goodbye to Thad and Jack.

They spent the afternoon doing various interviews for the media before finally leaving New York for Atlanta. Their trip there had been a welcome oasis, and the opportunity to help others was indeed helping them, too.

Duke met their helicopter as they landed at Atlanta Motor Speedway. It had been raining all day, but in the last hour, the skies cleared, and the track crews and trucks were rapidly drying the track. Jack saw a sea of motorhomes and campers already parked around the track's perimeter, and ready for race weekend. T noted there were two other golf carts waiting for him with some big guys aboard, "Who are those guys?"

Duke smiled, "Our new security team. Everywhere you go this weekend they are going to be there, so we don't have any more problems with ice or rednecks."

"I hope we don't need them. Hey, Duke," smiled T, "did I tell you I'm going to win this race this weekend?"

Duke laughed as they went through the gate at the heliport and turned towards the track. The drivers were always met by groups of fans hoping to get an autograph as they drove towards the tunnel leading to the infield. Jack saw it first, and tapped T on the shoulder.

"Do you see those protestor signs? I think the church groups beat us here. Look at the way that one is spelled. Obviously he skipped a few years of school." The sign read 'fagits go to hell' instead of faggots.

Duke spoke, "Boys, don't you worry about them. My men can squash them like a bug if they get in our way, but you know I fought in a war so folks in this country could enjoy their freedom of speech."

240

T replied, "Yeah, I agree they should have a right to do so—as long as they don't hurt anyone physically."

Once they arrived at the coach Duke went inside with the boys and shut the door. The security detail remained outside. "When it comes to security you're my responsibility. I bought something for you to help me take care of you. He gave each boy a very small device with a button on one side attached to a key chain. If you're in an awkward spot, or if you sense trouble, just hit the button and it'll alert me. I've already tested them all over the track, and they work even in the bathrooms. Okay, I'll wait outside while you get ready for practice."

Once he shut the door, T and Jack kissed, as it had been too long since they kissed after their jet landed. "Those guys look like the secret service detail for the President," stated T as he began undressing.

Jack retrieved his uniform and fire suit from the closet. "Well, if that what it takes to keep ice out of your face, I'm all for it. I worry about you all the time—both on and off the track. Do me a favor and just win the pole, lead the race the entire time, and win the darn thing."

"If only it were that easy," laughed T. "Of course, that is exactly what I need to do to get closer to winning the championship."

They drove over to the garage with their security detail. There were fans roaming around everywhere with their expensive pit passes around their necks on a yellow lanyard. This was the only sport in the world that allowed the fans to get so close to the stars. They arrived safely and as T walked up to Charley who had his head under the hood, a crewmember of another team yelled from across the garage, "Well, it looks like the superstar faggot has arrived. Boy, aren't we lucky." The rest of his team laughed, as did other crewmembers from various teams in the garage.

T wanted to yell back, but Jack had done his yelling therapy before they left the coach by once again calling T every queer name in the book. T just gave them a slight wave and turned back to Charley. "How's the car?"

"Great," replied Charlie, and then to the crew, "button it up boys. Let's go racing." He turned back to Thad, "Don't encourage the local rednecks. Just ignore them. You ready to practice?"

"Does a fish like to swim?"

Charley laughed, "So do the ones I tried to catch on the lake this week. I did catch an old boot."

T laughed, "What kind of marinate do you use on a boot?"

Charley chuckled, "I guess the same one you use when you put your foot in your mouth! Now get your ass in that car and let's go racing!"

Jack and two of the security detail drove over to the pit along with Duke. Duke called the team to a huddle, and went over why his men were there. After studying the tapes of last week's pit work, and failing to discover how the nails got there, he urged them to keep an eye on the pit this week.

T drove by in his car followed by the rest of the detail. He made about eight laps before speeding up, and so far, all was going well. Jack left to head back to the coach and get some work done. He always worked while T drove in practice, qualifying, and the race as it helped him manage his worrisome nature. Previously, he arranged several charity visits for the afternoon along with the usual visits to a few of the local television stations. Atlanta was also home to CNN so he agreed for T to do the Larry King Show that evening. It was going to be a long day, so they planned to rest most of Saturday except for practice and qualifying.

They would be in Phoenix next week, so he went to work researching the charities and stations in the Arizona area. T came in the door about one o'clock, hot and hungry. He changed clothes while Jack heated up some barbecue Duke obtained, and fixed plates of potato salad, coleslaw, cantaloupe, and fresh corn on the cob. Once showered, T joined him and together they ate discussing the afternoon. Jack showed him two pages of answers to questions he guessed Larry might ask him. He knew Larry would go for more depth, as they had the full one-hour show to fill. There would also be call-in questions.

They took a nap, and then drove the Hummer and followed by a second car filled with Duke's men to the first charity. After the television station visits, they drove downtown and picked a restaurant near CNN headquarters that Jack found on the Internet. They parked the Hummer and went inside. Jack reserved a table for just the two of them, and a bigger one for the men. They were half way through their steaks when a short man wearing dark sunglasses and a pink starched oxford shirt began approaching the table. Duke was the first one to see him and grabbed him by the shoulders just as T and Jack looked up.

"Hey, fellow," began Duke, "you'd better go back to your table!"

T and Jack looked up, and it was Jack who realized who the man was first, "That's Elton John!"

T smiled, "Duke, I think Elton John is okay. Thanks."

Duke let him go, and immediately apologized. Elton laughed, "Thank you. It's been a while since such a strong butch man grabbed me like that. The pleasure was all mine!" Duke blushed.

"Please sit down," urged T.

Elton did and removed his sunglasses. "Let me apologize for intruding. I had intended to write you a note of support for all you're doing for charities since coming out. I have a big AIDS charity event at the Oscars each year, so I hope you'll come. This is verbal invitation, and we'll send you an official printed version."

"Why of course. We'd love to," replied T.

Elton looked over at Jack and smiled, "Is this your boyfriend? My, my—he is cute."

Jack blushed and T smiled. "Yes, he is and yes, he is cute."

Elton reached over and patted Jack's arm, "Is Thad as wild in bed as he is on the track?"

"Yes, but he smells much better in bed."

T blushed this time. "I smell good all the time."

"What are you boys doing while waiting for the race?"

T related about practice, the charity visits, and the television stations, and then said he would be on Larry King in two hours. Elton looked pensive for a moment while thinking a little.

"Why don't you come for a visit tomorrow after..." he couldn't think of the right word.

T helped him, "qualifying. It is a time trial, and you start the race based on who has the fastest time."

"Qualifying," said Elton slowly, "I wish I had qualifying before I found some of my earlier boyfriends. If only I had qualified the boys that turned out to be jerks, well, life would have been so much easier."

They all smiled as Elton continued, "So why don't you boys come over after qualifying to my place, and we'll have dinner together. My boyfriend is an excellent cook, and you won't have to worry about fans finding you there. I have excellent security."

The boys responded affirmatively. Elton gave each a hug, put his glasses back on, and returned to his table. T and Jack did not say a word for about a minute, as they were still star struck, but then laughed at the opportunity.

They got quite a shock at the enormous building housing CNN. A member of the crew walked them back to T's dressing room. He changed clothes and waited for makeup. They shook hands with Larry just minutes before airtime. Larry touched on a few headlines before introducing T. They spent the first half of the show talking about racing, how T got his start, and what his goals were including winning this weekend. After the mid break Larry touched on the charity work, he was doing, and then he asked T about his coming out so publicly. T had Jack's phrases in his brain, but as usual he spoke mostly from his heart. Jack thought he did very well.

After a commercial break, they began taking live calls. The first four went well with fans asking him how old he was, what kind of car he drove on the streets, but the fifth caller asked him if he was prepared to go to hell for being a homosexual.

"Well, sir, I'm sure God made you just as He wanted, but like most folks it is up to us to learn how to be the best person we can. I understand you believe God hates gay people, but I believe in God, too. You and I both believe God made us in His own image, so he made you straight and he made me gay. Are you saying you think I should argue with God's wisdom?" T didn't wait for a reply, but kept going, "I certainly don't plan to argue with

Him when I get to heaven. He also said we should love one another, so even if a Christian doesn't like the fact that He made me gay, aren't you suppose to love me anyhow?"

The man replied, "You can twist the Scriptures any way you want, but you're still going to hell."

T replied again, "But didn't He also say you are not supposed to judge. Aren't you judging me now?" The caller hung up.

Larry said, "Is there a particular group that gives you the most trouble for being gay?"

T hesitated while Jack nervously popped his knuckles before T said, "You're not going to believe this, Larry, but the protestors are mostly Christians who say vile, ugly things to me, and right in front of their children. They make signs and scream out at me everywhere I go. I've done nothing to them or anyone else. I just want to be what God made. Jesus preached mostly about love...love for your neighbors, strangers, and for the world. I love my partner and together we're simply trying to help as many people as possible. We don't hand out flyers encouraging folks to be gay or even to come out. We don't have a club or a gay church for them to join. We don't ask for money as most preachers do. Our goal is to just help—what's the harm in that?"

Larry went to a commercial and soon the show was winding down. Larry could not have been nicer to them, and said he would watch the race on Sunday to see how T did. T told him he was going to win the race. Once in the car Jack asked, "Why do you always tell people you are going to win the race or the championship? How do you know that?"

"Because it gives me that extra edge or reason I need to push myself to win. I don't like for someone to say you lied—you didn't win, but I am going to win. You'll see."

As they drove back to the race Jack said, "I'm hungry."

T laughed, "I'm horny."

They both laughed, "Okay, we'll eat ice cream in bed."

T shot back, "Good, I love it when you lick..."

"Your elbow, right?"

They laughed hard and long as they drove into the gate to the track with their security detail right behind them.

Practice went well the next day, and T drew the last qualifying number so his run would be the last attempt of the day to win the pole. The times were good by all the drivers, but so far, the 93 car was on the pole with the fastest time of the day.

"You can whip it," stated Charley in the headset.

"I know," replied T solemnly, as he was already going through the turns in his mind. Jack watched qualifying on the television in the motorcoach as T pulled out onto the track. The announcers talked about his appearance on Larry King the night before. T made his warm up lap while steadily speeding up. He did well through the first two turns, but bobbled a little in turn three, which would put him in the eighteenth starting position, but he shook it off, and took the white flag for his second and final lap time.

He zoned out everything and sped through turns one and two while being careful to hit his marks this time. He sped to turn three and flew through turn four. Everyone watched the clock and five seconds later the team realized T had just won the pole. They cheered, as did Jack in the motorcoach.

Jack hustled to the media room in the golf cart while T posed with the pole award beside his car, and then Duke and the security detail drove him to the media center. As T made his way through the crowd, someone called him a faggot, but he paid no attention. When he reached the podium, he spotted Jack in the back. He instantly felt better and more confident as Jack winked at him and T smiled.

The questions went well before a reporter asked, "T, are gay people faster than straight people?"

T laughed, "What? Are gay people faster than straight people? Well, you have me there. I never thought about it." The audience chuckled. T said, "Well, yes I guess we are because we spend our whole life outrunning those big old rednecks." The audience laughed. T added, "Seriously, when you're in the closet, you're lying to everyone, so we learn to think fast to outsmart families, friends, and sometimes total strangers. I guess if you think fast long enough—you learn to drive fast." T felt relieved when media director called an end to the questions.

There were a few protesters outside the media center when T came out, but his men kept them at bay, and before long, he and Jack were safe in the motorcoach. They ate lunch, took a nap, and then called the telephone number Elton gave them. Jack wrote down the driving instructions so they quickly kissed, showered together, and walked to the Hummer. "T stopped the men as they walked behind him. "Boys, thank you, but you can chill tonight. We're off to a private home for dinner so we won't need security tonight. Take the night off and relax a while. I'll see you in the morning."

Duke started to protest but said nothing other than the men had the night off, and to be there at nine the next morning for race day festivities. T drove as Jack read out the instructions. They made it downtown after about a forty-minute drive from the track, found the right street and quickly passed the high rise, and had to turn around. Elton had told them to pull into the parking garage. A large bald black man met them at the gate.

"May I help you?" he asked as he walked up to the driver's window.

T hit the button to down the window. I'm Thad Thompson and this is Jack Langston. We're here to see..."

The man interrupted as he looked at his clipboard, "You're on the list to see Elton. Park on the D row, and then walk back here to catch the elevator. He's on the twenty-eighth floor."

David, Elton's boyfriend, met them at the door and began showing them around. Elton came in, gave the boys big hugs, and together they continued the tour of the house. The boys marveled at the fantastic framed prints and paintings on display as well as a large room with glass cases for all his awards.

"Elton," began T, "if you keep on winning stuff, you're going to need a museum."

"From what I hear, you're wining just about as fast as I am, and you already have a museum."

T laughed, "Well, not a museum, I guess that will come later. My trophies are on display at our headquarters. When the fans come to see our vast car garages, they walk through a hall with all the awards. Have you ever been to a race?"

"No, I have been asked to sing at a few but no, I prefer sports where the men don't wear helmets or suits, but rather skimpy shorts like track and field, or even better Olympic swimmers. I just love Speedos!"

They all laughed as they made their way to the dining room where dinner was ready for them. The roast duck just melted in their mouths, and the key lime pie could not have been better. Their talk turned to Elton and David. Elton explained David had helped him sober up and after that, he really fell in love, and has been sober ever since.

David asked, "Can you boys go dancing at a gay bar?"

Jack said, "No, we haven't tried to. I'm afraid they would mob T."

Elton replied, "I know the feeling. I have an arrangement at the biggest club in town. Hang on a second. I have an idea. I'll be right back." Elton left while the boys chatted with David, and after about twenty minutes Elton returned, "Okay, it's all set. The club will be ready for us, and I took the liberty of inviting a few friends I can trust to join us. I have to change clothes. I'm ready to go dancing."

Elton thought it would be fun to ride in the Hummer so the foursome pulled out of the garage with David becoming the navigator. As they pulled into the parking lot, it was already about ten o'clock, and there was a long line waiting to get in. David showed T how to pull around to the back where a guard met them. Elton hit the button for the back window, "Barney, it's just me and a few friends."

"Yes sir, Mr. John," replied the smiling man, as he opened the gate for them to enter.

They came in the back way through a narrow hallway, up the steps, and into a room with numerous tables, and a dance floor in the center with the lights low and making patterns in rhythm to the music blaring from the speakers.

"Come over here boys," urged Elton as he took T's arm. "Look down through these windows, and you can see the bar's big dance floor just filled to the brim with dancing gay boys. I wish we could join them, but we'd be mobbed." He turned to see a group of friends coming in the door. He gave them hugs, and introduced T and Jack. Groups of four to six kept coming inside the room for the next half hour until the fifty or so men began dancing to the music. T and Jack had only danced a little in the motorcoach, but they felt such freedom and joy to be in the company of these gay men. It was a special gift Elton presented them, and they would not forget the kind gesture.

The party lasted a few hours until T knew he had better get back to the track to sleep. He and Jack bade Elton and David goodbye after friends promised to take them home while T and Jack made their way home to the racetrack. Jack was soon sore as T felt a bit horny once they got there, but they slept soundly in each other's arms, with T resting his head on Jack's shoulder, and his hair just lightly touching Jack's face. Jack kissed his hair lightly, smiled, and closed his eyes to drift off to sleep.

TWENTY-ONE

Jack woke up first, checked the clock on the dresser, and sighed. He reached for the remote and clicked on the television. He had left the television on Speed Channel, and when the screen lit up, he could see the replaying of last night's Race Live Show. The chatter concerned the championship, and their analysis of the anticipated outcome of the Atlanta race. Thad stirred and rolled into Jack's arms, managed to open one sluggish eyelid, smiled and kissed Jack.

T yawned, "Let me guess—it is time for the wonder boy to get out of bed."

Jack smiled, "I don't think they'll let you play hooky, and remain in the running for the trophy."

They kissed again, and began making their way out of the bed and into the shower. "How busy is the schedule this morning?"

Jack turned around while T poured shampoo on Jack's head and began massaging his hair.

"Oh that feels good. I am beginning to think we should try the hooky approach after all." T reached down and pinched his butt. Jack laughed, "Oh, let's see, you have three sponsor tents to visit, a Speed Channel interview, and a live network interview. Not too bad. Then you race, you win, more interviews, and then we fly home later tonight, and make love after we get out of the Jacuzzi."

"That's sounds doable," replied T as he rinsed Jack's hair, and then turned around for his turn. "Let's hurry up. I'm starved, but I had such a good time last night," as he turned and kissed Jack once more.

As they finished the last of the huge omelet Jack made, T read a note Duke left taped on the door. "Now hear this," began T. "Duke says for us to call him when I'm ready to come out of the coach so he can assemble his troops. Gees, he sounds like General Patton or something."

"I guess you better call him, because you're due at the first tent in fifteen minutes, and you still have to put on your uniform." Jack cleared away the table by putting the dishes in the dishwasher, while T called Duke on his cell.

T was dressed in ten minutes while Jack gathered his notes and comments for T to read just before his interviews to keep his brain cells on fresh ideas. They assumed Duke was there, opened the door, and stepped out. NARC parked all the driver coaches in low rows about twenty feet apart. They did not see Duke, so they moved out of view into the shade, and a bit farther back along the side of the coach.

T looked up in time to see the color instantly fall from Jack's face. "What is it?" he asked as he adjusted his sunglasses and hat tightly on his head.

"I'm sorry, but turn around," stated Jack as he reached out to T's shoulders and turned him around.

T read 'Die Faggots!' in bright pink paint on the side of his 1.6 million dollar motorcoach, and his heart skipped a beat. He turned back to Jack and tried to cheer him up. "Boy, Duke is going to be pissed!"

"I thought only drivers and teams could get in this parking lot."

"Unfortunately, you're right, so I guess someone with the teams doesn't like us. Well, too bad. They just made me mad, and I'm going to win this race today!"

Jack smiled, "That a boy. Show the bastards queers can drive very fast!"

They both laughed as Duke drove up in a double row golf cart followed by two carts of the security detail.

"Morning, Duke. How are you?" asked T with a smile.

"I'm fine."

"That's good. Now don't get mad, but Jack and I have something to show you." The boys slowly stepped aside as Duke got out of the cart and followed them to the side of the motorcoach.

Duke face immediately turned bright red. "What the hell? When did this happen?" yelled Duke.

Thad thought he saw steam rising from Duke's ears, as he focused on the graffiti. "We just found it. I didn't hear anything last night. Thankfully, I slept through it," said T as he led the way to the golf cart.

Duke shook his head in disbelief that someone in the private coach lot would do such a thing. "I will have that cleaned off during the race. I'm so sorry. From now on I'll post a guard at all times." Duke climbed aboard the golf cart as Jack took the seat behind him. He stepped on the pedal.

"It's just paint, and they didn't harm us," stated T.

"You don't understand. If they were brave enough to paint your coach, then next time that might decide to set the coach on fire."

Jack gulped. T looked back at him and tried to smile. Minutes later they arrived at the first hospitality tent where Jack beamed with pride as the three thousand fans clapped and cheered throughout T's speech. Meanwhile, Duke called Charley who ordered two crewmembers to clean the wet paint off the bus. Forty minutes later, T gave a similar speech in another tent with even more enthusiasm than the first, and more determined to put the attack on his motorcoach behind him.

An hour later, he did the Speed interview and managed to plug a few local charities. The network interviewer dared to jump in, and ask how his life had been since coming out. Jack and Thad anticipated the question and as usual, T first began speaking Jack's answers before moving along with his own words. Jack smiled and winked at him.

Thad replied, "I wish I could say all had been well, but there have been a few problems. Sometimes a race fan yells a bigoted narrow-minded slur, throws a soft drink or beer bottle at me, or maybe spits at me, but I anticipated this would happen. It is just ignorance and generations of hate that spew out like a long overdue volcano. People always fear what they don't understand, but what they should know is that I believe God made me just the way I am with my blue eyes and dark hair. I also believe he gave me the talent to drive fast and helped me develop a lead foot on the accelerator. Thankfully, my partner helped me realize that I can handle all the world might throw at us, as long as I stay focused on helping as many charities as I possibly can, and hope others will join me. We're off to a great start by giving away two hundred million dollars in just a few weeks."

They concluded the interview, and Duke drove them over to the stage for driver introductions. "I've got to pee," said T as he left the group in a hurry, and walked over to a line of portable toilets. He moved away so fast that Duke's men could not get through the crowd. Jack stood on the golf cart trying to keep T in view. He saw the top of his hat as he stepped in and closed the door. Jack's heart skipped a beat when he saw three members of a competitor's team walking briskly in the same direction. He felt they would probably turn over the toilet, and perhaps hurt T.

Jack quickly turned around to search for Duke but didn't see him anywhere. He hit the button on the panic device. He yelled at the closest security detail member to get to the line of johns. They all began pushing through the crowd trying to make their way to Thad. Jack looked back at the portable toilet and suddenly, he saw Duke stand up in front of the opposing team members. Duke snarled at them, and they cursed him before turning to walk away. Thad came out and quickly made his way to the stage just in time for his introduction. Jack sighed heavily, but remained tense. The graffiti paint attack apparently affected his attitude and confidence more than Thad's.

Duke felt helpless to protect him as T climbed into the back of a bright red pickup truck, and followed the driver ahead of him around the track, so he could wave to his fans. He reluctantly took his men to the Thad's pit where the pickup truck would drop him off after his lap. Thad felt the folks yelling boos were louder than ever, but he did see many people standing and clapping for him. He decided to find such a person every fifty yards to concentrate on, smile and wave to, and give them a great photo opportunity.

After the start of the race, Jack returned to the coach with two men guarding his door. He now knew how the wives of the drivers must feel when their loved ones are driving alongside forty cars at hundred and eighty miles an hour. He tried to work on his laptop, but kept nervously looking up at the screen as the laps ticked off.

T maintained his lead of the race until a green flag pit stop put him in twenty-third place. Forty laps later, he had moved up to the top ten when suddenly, the car ahead of him blew a tire. Jack leaped to his feet as T whizzed by the spinning car, briefly scrapped the wall, and somehow managed to get clear of the out of control spinning car. Jack sighed heavily and fell onto the couch.

Near the end of the race, Thad was trying to pass the car ahead of him by going high and low. He and his spotter forgot about watching his rear until it was almost too late. T looked up just as the 50 car tapped his bumper from behind. T swerved, but held on while fighting to keep control of his car. The 50 car managed to pass Thad, as T had to slow a bit to straighten the car.

T cursed at the 50 car as he fell back to fourth, and fell in line behind the 50 car. "Keep your cool," urged Charley over his radio.

T smiled, "Don't worry. I'm still going to win this race. How many laps to go?"

"Thirty-two laps."

"Do I have enough fuel?" asked T.

"Yep, with a pint or two to spare," replied Charley, somewhat sarcastically.

T laughed, "Well, then, no need to waste it. Out."

T heard Charley tell his spotter to keep an eye out for him. T caught the 50 car with twenty-six laps to go. It took four laps of trying to get around him before he finally returned the favor, and gave the bumper of 50 car enough of a tap to cause him to lose his line, allowing T to slip by.

The final two cars were on the same team, and both did their best to keep him from passing. The second place car dropped back from the lead to concentrate on blocking T. He was successful down to the ten laps to go. T knew if he didn't pass him soon, he would not have time to catch the race leader. He pushed the nose of his car under the left bumper of the blocking car.

The driver tried to come down the track, their fenders bumped, but T held his ground. The rival car slammed into him, and T slammed back, pushed the throttle down, and passed him. The lead car was fifty yards ahead of him.

"Charley?" asked T.

The call surprised him, "Yes, I'm here."

"How many laps to go?"

"Eight and a half," replied Charley calmly.

"Oh, and I was worried. Out," replied T.

In the motorcoach, Jack smiled, as he heard his lover's voice over the radio. On the pit box, Charley grinned as Drew winked at him. Janet laughed, "He's going to win—isn't he?"

Drew laughed, "Yes he is!"

He gained about eight yards a lap and caught the 67 car with just three laps to go. He swerved high and low trying to get around him clean, as the final laps ticked off. He finally got a fender to the inside, and shoved his way alongside the 67 car as it came down hard into the side of T's car. The blow sent him off the track just enough for his left tires to fling up dirt. T yanked the wheel hard to the right to get his car back on the track. He looked up in time to see the white flag fly indicating they were now on the last lap.

He realized he was in a dead heat with the 67, and with his pedal all the way to the floor, there was nothing else he could do, but fight for position. Since he was on the inside, he technically had less pavement to the finish line, but he felt attached to the 67 car like a Siamese twin. He tried to shake him loose, but the driver wisely kept slamming downward with his car, hoping to cut one of T's tires.

T slammed him back as they made it around turn two. The entire hundred and sixty thousand fans stood anticipating a tight finish. The battle between the two cars continued all the way down the backstretch with thousands of sparks flying into the air.

T gasped when he felt his right front tire go down. For a brief moment, he thought he saw a smile on the face of the driver of the 67 car as he glanced quickly at him. Abruptly, T saw the man's left front fender drop and he knew, he too, had a flat tire.

They made the third turn as their tires came apart shredding the fenders sending cascades of sheet metal high into the air behind them. As the following cars hit the flying metal particles, a huge gigantic crash began, as car after car slammed into the other, blocking the entire track except for the leaders. They came out of turn four, and began fighting their way to the finish line on three tires instead of four.

T saw the flagman raise the checkered flag. T faked a slight left, as if ready to hit the 67 car again. After pausing for a second, he dropped a bit more, and then yanked his wheel hard to the right, slamming into the side of the car. The impact locked onto the other car's front bumper with just a foot of T's bumper in the lead as they careened across the finish line, and then crashed into the wall in turn one.

The fans cheered at the wild finish, and Charley stood in disbelief as the entire field of cars came to one final screeching stop. The carnage left the spotters as well as the reporters with few words to describe the event. Everything happened in less than three seconds. Belatedly, the caution lights lit up, but there wasn't a single car capable of moving. Smoke, steam, and burning rubber filled the air, but as the cloud lifted, the fans could see the entire disaster that began in turn four, and all the way down the front stretch, ending in turn one. They stood there in shocked awe, not quiet believing what they had just seen.

The cameras zoomed in as T helped himself out of the car and ran over to the 67 car. He yanked down the net and helped the driver out, relieved to see that he was okay. They shook hands and began walking back to the pits.

With no car for a victory lap, T's team ran to him, lifted him on their shoulders, and marched to Victory Lane. The reporters began the usual television interviews for the conclusion of a most unusual race.

Drew looked over at Charley and Janet, "Well, I have never seen a race end like this one, but the boy kept his word—he won the race!"

"That he did," said Janet.

"Let's get out of here. I feel like champagne!" Drew hit the button lowering his wheelchair down to the ground. They joined the team as they celebrated the win. When T saw Drew, he came over and gave him a hug, as well as Janet and even Charley.

Two men arrived with Jack on the golf cart. Jack held back from the crowd surrounding Thad, but when T saw him, he ran to him, hugged him tightly, and then he kissed him on network television for the entire world to see. A hush fell over the celebrating crowd as T broke the embrace, turned and threw his hat into the air, lifted both his fists over his head, and yelled as loud as he could.

The crowd cheered once more as Jack's face flushed red with shocked embarrassment, but with a face portraying a huge smile.

T's kiss was on every sports report and made the national newscasts later that day. It was also on the front page of almost every newspaper in the country bumping the President to page two, and by Tuesday on the cover of many magazines. This brought a larger crowd protesting his homosexuality in front of his house. The county requested more help from the state after the protestors tripled in numbers. Eventually, the officer in charge decided to close off his street, preventing any more protestors from joining the marchers. After they left for the day, they were not allowed to return. They officers also began requiring the protestors to remain quiet after nine o'clock, providing some peace to the rest of the neighborhood. This sent more protestors home for the evening. A few broke the rules, and the police made a big show of arresting the lawbreakers. There were handcuffed and family members were told the transgressors were going to county jail for the week.

Outside his gate and fence was twenty-four hour bedlam, but inside his home, T and Jack were happy. They slept late on Monday, took the boat out on the lake that afternoon, but left early Tuesday morning for Frisco, Colorado to just get away from it all. Thankfully, the cabin was available, and by late morning, they were hiking the trail along the lake. Many of the leaves had lost their green color, and fallen to the ground in huge piles of bright colors. They wore warm jackets, as the breeze off the water was cold in early

November, making their nose and cheeks red. The weather forecast predicted the first snowfall of the year for later that night.

They laughed, talked, and held hands as they walked down the trail. The serenity of the isolated place gave each boy a peaceful heart. Jack knew that in a few months, the lodges and cabins would start filling with ski tourists, and they would have to find a new place to get away from everyone.

Wisely, Jack did not talk about racing, or the pressure on T since coming out. He also did not debate the wisdom of Thad kissing him on live television, because he knew T only did what any other racer did when he won—he kissed the person he loved most in the world. Instead, Jack and Thad talked about what they would like to do after the last race. Jack thought they could leave right after the final race in Homestead since they were already at the bottom of Florida.

T explained they would have two weeks off, but they would have to return to New York City for all the marketing promotion and commotion leading up to the annual awards banquet. Jack sighed, but went to work on researching two vacation ideas—a short trip and a much needed longer one.

He found there was an annual Gay Cruise on one of the largest passenger ships in the world, and scheduled to leave on Sunday morning out of Vancouver Canada a few days before Thanksgiving. He knew all too well that many gays have a tough time during holidays, especially Thanksgiving and Christmas, because those holidays were heavily family oriented. Many gays find themselves left out of family plans, or felt uncomfortable attending. Often gay couples see their families separately if the family members haven't accepted the partner, or they stay home and do nothing. A few lucky ones find their partner invited as well, and thus, the family celebrations continue through the years. Jack and Jessie often helped serve Thanksgiving dinner to thousands of homeless folks. It was their way of helping themselves by helping others. He hoped he and Thad could do the same next year, but this year they needed time to celebrate alone.

The cruise helped gay couples and single gays have something cool to do during Thanksgiving, and together, they would enjoy the huge feast put together by the talented world class chefs employed by the cruise line. T agreed to the trip, and so Jack signed them up. He also approved the press release the gay organizers put together announcing T would be onboard. He emailed press photos to help them. He insisted on paying for their trip, so they wouldn't feel obligated to do anything but chill out and have a great time. While the cruise line agreed, they sent four complimentary tickets for their friends. They gave two tickets to Jesse, and the other pair to Jonathan, the boy they met at the gay school in New York. Jack arranged plane tickets for all four, and bought clothes for Jonathan, luggage, and sent him some traveling money.

They discussed the longer second vacation trip that would begin after the awards banquet, and both agreed they would be ready for a trip filled with sun, sand, and adventure. Jack found several gay cruises on large sailboats, but after some discussion, they agreed to do something privately.

It took Jack a few days until he found several charter sailboat companies in the Caribbean, but the price per day blew him away, as he still was not use to the expenses Thad encountered everywhere he went. He showed T the websites, which T liked, but suggested they save that idea for an off week during race season.

"I would still be recognized in the Caribbean," protested Thad. "Let's go farther, to the other side of the globe."

Jack laughed, "It could be expensive."

"I wish you would quit worrying about the money. They pay me a lot for what I do, so let's enjoy it. I tell you what—I'll give you a budget of say a half million. Can we have a great time for that?"

Jack gulped, "We could buy an island for that."

T kissed him, "So get to work on the web and plan something cool for us to do. I don't care where it is, as long as long as I get to spend every day alone with you."

Jack spent part of every day for a week doing his research and planning until he had it all mapped out. When he showed T the vacation plan, and the schedule, Thad laughed and gave it a big two thumbs up.

Jack explained they would fly from New York to Fiji where they would board an eighty foot chartered sailboat with a crew of three: a captain, first mate, and chef. They were all gay with the captain and the first mate in a long time relationship, and the chef a long time friend. They would spend four weeks visiting many secluded islands while scuba diving below the water, and just about anything and everything on the water. The large sailboat also had two personal watercrafts onboard.

At end of their sail, they would fly to Kenya and into the heart of Africa, and stay at one of the few gay resorts on the continent. They would experience numerous camera safaris, and live in a giant tree house cabana. They would take a rope swing down to the main house for their meals and adventures, but the rest of the time, they could enjoy complete privacy in their tree hideaway. The boys both liked the plans, and that gave them reasons to survive the final two races, as well as the onslaught of the throngs of protestors.

The night before flying to Phoenix, they planned a romantic dinner in Keystone before returning to the cabin to enjoy the Jacuzzi, and finally to bed to begin a few hours of much needed lovemaking.

TWENTY-TWO

Their flight from Fresno Colorado to Phoenix Arizona only took ninety minutes, but the serenity in the mountains ended the moment the jet wheels touched the tarmac. T stepped out of the plane and immediately found himself surrounded by his security detail, an army of reporters, camera and sound operators, and producers. With two races to go, the championship race tight, last week's amazing win in Atlanta, and the front page kiss between Thad and Jack, the press corps's hunger for responses from the star driver quadrupled.

"Thad? Thad?" yelled a reporter from ultra conservative Fox News. "Are you sorry you kissed your boyfriend after winning the race in Atlanta?"

"Sorry? Why would I be sorry? Were you sorry when you kissed your wife or girlfriend goodbye this morning? I hope not. I have absolutely no regrets, except for not doing it sooner. I did what all the drivers do—celebrate the joy of winning with the person they love most."

A lady reporter asked, "Thad? Are you guys planning to be married?"

"Well, we've only been dating a few months, but so far we're very happy. However, we're not happy that America has not yet accepted that gay people can laugh and love, and have cherished families just like our straight friends. Many states are legislating against love. Shouldn't they create laws that encourage love and peace instead of anger and hate? I believed the Pledge of Allegiance—especially the last few words…with liberty and justice for all. We are all supposed to be free, and I hope one day soon gay people will receive the same justice that many of you often take for granted." He paused briefly, "We'll see you at the track and the press conference. Thank you."

T grabbed Jack's hand as they made their way to his waiting Hummer. Along with Duke and his men, they sped off to the track. Thad and Jack ate lunch in the motorcoach before T changed into his uniform. He gave Jack a kiss before hustling off with Duke to get ready for practice. They drove over to garage where his crew was making the final changes to his car.

"Hey, Charley, are we ready to go?"

Charley smiled at him, "This car is more than ready. You're going to love it. I walked the track early this morning. The repairs they made to the asphalt are fantastic. It is smooth and unless we get a downpour, you should have plenty of tire grip. We might even have three grooves. Are you ready?"

"Yes sir. Let's do it."

T put his helmet on and climbed in. It took him a minute or two to buckle in with Charley's help. He fired up the engine, backed out, and roared over to the track. The official waved him onward, and he began going through his gearshifts building speed rapidly.

Jack looked up at the television and watched T work his way around the track while moving high and low testing the surface, as well as how tight or loose the car was set up."

"How's the car?" asked Charley over the radio.

"It was a little loose at first, but now it is just fine."

"After each change of tires I suspect you'll feel the same—loose until the air pressure heats up in the tires, and then you'll be flying. We'll have to be careful near the end of a fuel run in case it gets too tight. Let's work on your qualifying."

"Roger, I will, but please give me one more lap, and I'll be ready for lap times."

T flew down to the lower groove just above the yellow line, and did his best to hold the line with the throttle down the floor. The car held, but he felt like he was about to lose control at any point. Going into the fourth turn, he soared up the track and crossed the finish line as fast he could go. Charley clicked his stopwatch, and began watching him take the first turn. He clicked the split button to see how fast he was so far. He smiled.

"You're looking good. Keep it smooth and hit your marks," added Charley.

T heard him but did not respond. Charley knew he was in his quiet zone where he said nothing while concentrating solely on his line.

"Twenty-nine thirty-two!" said Charley as flew across the finish line.

"It'll do better. One more," replied T as he made his way around the track to prepare for another lap time. After an even faster lap, he decided to stay out for additional practice.

There were other cars practicing so T made his way in and around them to get a feel of any draft possibilities. Suddenly the 50 car swerved upward cutting him off. T reacted quickly, avoiding the potential collision as well as the wall. T could have sworn he saw the driver smile.

Charley asked, "What the hell was that?"

T smiled, "I don't think that 50 car likes me."

"No kidding," laughed Charley.

"He'll like me even less after I win on Sunday."

Charley smiled, "Oh, you think you can win?"

T laughed, "You know I can! Let's go for another lap time. I want to go into the fourth turn just a little higher before zipping back down to cross the finish line."

"Roger!" yelled Charley with a grin.

Qualifying went very well with T winning yet another pole position to start the race. Afterwards they went to the media room for the press conference. There were questions about the race, but eventually, they asked more about his private life. He had just answered the second one when he saw

Janet step into the back of the room and move alongside Jack. Jack gave her a sheet of paper with updates as to T's charity personal appearances, and the list of television stations scheduled for Thad to visit.

She winked at him and smiled, and he smiled back. As Jack turned his face from looking at Janet with the intention of looking back to the stage, a familiar face caught his eye in the crowd standing near the back of the room on the far side. He turned his head left and right searching every face.

"What is it?" whispered Janet.

"I thought I saw Tim in the crowd."

"Gees, are you sure?"

"No, I'm not. I just caught a quick glimpse, but now I don't see him."

"I'll tell Duke to watch out for him." Janet went down the outside aisle, and found Duke standing at the corner of the stage. She whispered to him that Tim might be in the audience.

Jack turned back to Thad as he finished the interviews and made his way to him to exit the building and drive back to the motorcoach.

"How was that?" Thad climbed aboard the golf cart as Duke stepped on the gas pedal.

Jack leaned into him. "Very good."

T noted Jack was not smiling. He gave him a second look, and realized the color had gone from Jack's face. "What's wrong?"

Jack sighed and looked into T's eyes, "I think I saw Tim at the press conference. I think he was in the back of the room on your far right."

"So, he can't blackmail us now. The whole world knows we're gay. Even the Pope and President know."

"I'm probably being apprehensive—he just gives me the creeps."

"Let's go get some lunch, I'm starved. What time are we going to the children's home?"

Duke parked outside the coach as Thad and Jack went inside. Jack turned from pulling the door closed while answering. "We have to be there at…"

Thad planted a deep wet kiss to Jack's smooth lips effectively cutting off his speaking ability while pulling him to his chest. Thad came up for air, "I'm as horny as a frog."

"3 o'clock," continued Jack with a laugh. "Well, take me to your Lilly pad, Mister Ribbit!"

"Roger, cowboy." T bent down bending Jack over his shoulder like a fireman, and hauled him to the bedroom where he unceremoniously dumped him. Jack laughed as T began pulling Jack's shoes off, pants, and underwear while Jack managed to get his shirt off. Suddenly, he stopped after Jack was naked.

Jack gave him a puzzled look, "What's wrong? Did the frog swallow a distasteful bug?"

258

T grinned, "No, I was just marveling at how beautiful you are. Your body is just perfect."

"Yeah right, I'm skinny with no muscles except for the ones in my fingers because I type too much. My left arm is longer than my right because I'm always lugging my laptop around with it."

"Yeah right. Your right hand is strong from all that masturbating you do," quipped T.

"I haven't done it once since you found me in Fresno. I have no need to. Would you hurry up and dive on me? I'm getting a chill lying naked on this big, soft bed."

T pulled the Velcro apart on his uniform and began stripping out of it, followed by his inner fireproof long johns, his underwear, and his socks. He knelt down and kissed the top of Jack's feet.

"That tickles," protested Jack.

T paid no heed, but slowly kissed the calves of his legs, rolled a tongue up his thighs, and grinned when he looked up at Jack's arousing penis. He reached for a condom, put it on Jack, straddled his hips, sat down on his jimmy, and began to rock. They took turns for top and bottom roles, but the lovemaking was always spectacular and satisfying, and after a while, they drifted off into naptime forgetting about lunch for now.

The last stop of the day was at a children's hospital Jack picked from a list on the Internet. The boys felt sad to see so many children with cancer, but they never let on as they laughed and teased with every single child. Toy R Us came through again for Thad, and so he delighted in giving each child something new.

The television interviews went well including the usual questions about his coming out, and what it was like in the garage or at the track since he came out. T began to feel like a robot, but tried to answer with a difference twist each time.

"Its time for some dinner," protested Thad as they climbed into the Hummer.

"Do you have a suggestion as to where to go, or do you want to eat back at the track?"

Duke broke in, "It would be easier to maintain security at the track."

T responded, "I think the track is where anyone would expect me to be. Let's go to Pedro's Bonanza!" he said with a wicked grin.

Jack laughed, "What the hell is Pedro's Bonanza?"

"It's an incredible Mexican restaurant. While you're feasting on their great food, mariachi bands will entertain you. They're awesome. Duke, are you up to it?"

"Yes sir. Best food I have ever had. I'll tell the others to follow us and where to go if we get separated in traffic." He used his radio as Duke spun the tires as he went out of the parking lot.

T and Jack bounced in the back seat. T laughed, "I think Duke's mouth is already salivating for one of Pedro's giant chimichangas!"

Twenty minutes later, they entered the restaurant. A cute hostess ushered the party to a private dining area just off the main floor so they could overlook the other patrons. The wait staff quickly served Mexican beer, tequilas, bowls of warm fried chips, and hot salsa. Duke and his crew sat at one table while Jack and Thad sat at the other.

A guy wearing a large beaded Sombrero and a flashy uniform, stepped from behind the curtain, and proceeded to play a slow catchy song on his silver trumpet. As he finished the chorus, he doubled time the tempo and played the same song twice as fast. Upon completion of that verse and chorus, he jumped an octave higher, and picked up the tempo again. This time the curtain went up, and about twenty mariachi band members began playing as well. The group all belonged to one family with the oldest about thirty and youngest about six. Some played guitars, others violin, two drummers, and the rest played various brass instruments. They walked among the audience as they did their show. After each number, they received lots of applause from the enthusiastic audience.

T ordered platters of food for Duke and his crew, as well as for him and Jack. Starving, they started with freshly baked chips and hot salsa, followed by beans and rice, with hot chimichangas, covered in a delicious cheese sauce, a few burritos, a couple of sizzling fajitas, and finished the meal with a few beers, and hot Mexican ice cream—deep fried. Jack and Thad were stuffed, but the mariachi members knew how to settle their tummies. The young boy took Thad's hand and pulled him to his feet. He did the same to Jack, and put one of each hand together forming a line. As the music played, they danced around the room picking up more diners until almost fifty patrons were snaking their way around the tables. By the time they sat down, they were all laughing and applauding. T covered the bill and gave the waiters large tips, and a five hundred dollar tip to the band. He shook all their hands before leaving.

By ten o'clock, Thad and Jack were safe asleep in each other's arms with legs somehow intertwined, and T's ear listening to Jack's heart as he slept.

Race morning came all too early. T made three appearances in large hospitality tents receiving a few boos and hand gestures while in route. Jack forgot all about Tim until the last tent, but in the back, he spotted him, and this time made a positive identification. He retrieved his cell phone and called Duke. While talking to Duke, he helped him get a visual on Tim. Once Duke spotted him, he picked up another man and began working his way through the huge crowd towards Tim. Meanwhile, Tim deliberately turned so he was facing Jack, smiled, and then turned and disappeared. The smile sent cautionary chills across Jack's spine. By the time Duke arrived, the mystery man vanished.

Jack listened to Thad speak while wondering if he should worry Thad with the discovery of Tim, but finally decided he did not want Thad to hold back anything from him, and so as soon as he left the stage, Jack told him he had spotted him.

"Do you know what he wants?" asked T as they drove away.

"No I don't. It is like he stalking us. What a psycho. You keep your eye out for him until you get in that car, and then go out there and win the race."

T laughed, "Now you're beginning to sound like me. I will win the race. Let's go get some lunch. It'll be race time in ninety minutes."

The first two thirds of the race were uneventful with T already securing the most led laps, and of course leading a lap to get additional bonus points. The computers finally scored him in the championship lead, but there were seventy-six laps to go. They had one more planned pit stop when T came out of the fourth turn, and knew instantly he had a right front tire going down.

"I've got a flat!" he yelled over the radio. "Right front. Get ready!"

"Roger that," replied Charley as he watched the crew get ready knowing they were monitoring the radio chatter.

T made his way down to the bottom of the track, and slowed down, hoping the tire would not come apart and shred his sheet metal off his car frame all the way down the right side. The other cars began passing him, but there was nothing he could do but hang on. He finished turned three and peeled off to the inside and onto pit row.

"Watch your speed," warned Charley. "We're going to gamble and put four tires and fuel on."

"Roger. I hope you're feeling lucky, as we're going to come out a lap down."

"I'm feeling very lucky!" exclaimed Charley.

The jack man dropped the handle for the second time, and T sped out to the rear of the field and one lap down. He began making his way up through the slower cars. It took forty laps to catch the rear of the lead lap car. He thought he was in the lucky dog position, but the 42 car passed him just as the caution went out.

"Dang I missed it!" he yelled over the radio.

He struggled for a few laps trying to put his car in the lucky dog position, and five laps later the 17 car blew an engine just as T passed the 42 car, and the caution flag flew putting T on the lead lap.

"Now we're ready to race for the win!" exclaimed T.

Twenty-four laps later, caution went out again for debris on the track. The leaders began slowing down preparing to enter the pit for the last time of the race.

"Plenty of time and only twenty-two cars ahead of you," responded Charley as he glanced down at Drew. "Stay out T. Let the leaders go to pit."

T grinned, "Boy, you are in a gambling mood."

He fell in line with all the cars lining up to head to pit road ,but at the last minute he hung a hard right, and just missed the orange cone at the entrance to the pit. The announcers went wild as the crowd began to murmur. T was now leading the race under caution.

"Do I have the tires to make it to the end?"

"You'll be close."

"Do I have the gas?"

"Nope," the radio barked with the solemn reply.

T sighed heavily, "So we're hoping for another caution before the race ends or divine intervention. Is it going to rain?"

"Nope."

"Are you sure you know what you're doing?"

"Nope."

T laughed. "What's a matter Charley? Cat got your tongue?"

Charley laughed, "You said you were going to win this race, I'm just wondering how in the hell you're going to do that with tires that are wearing down and not enough fuel!"

T grinned, "Okay, get a gas can ready for a splash and dash. How many laps left?"

"Twenty-eight."

"Okay, let's do half of them as the leader, and if we don't get a caution, then I'll zip in for a touch of gas, and back out, and hope we don't lose too many positions. At the worst I might be able to get near the front, but we'd lose."

"Right."

"If they call a caution before then…"

Charley broke in, "If we get lucky and the caution does come out, come in for a splash of gas and right side tires. That should give you enough to get to the front."

"Okay. Boy this is going to be fun."

Charley looked over at Drew who was shaking his head nervously. Jack listened on the radio trying to understand the strategy while two of Duke's men patrolled around the outside of the coach. The men failed to see Tim, who remained hidden just fifty feet away. Tim studied the situation for a few minutes, noted the two big men watching the coach, and decided to back off.

"Here we go son. Don't jump the start and let's go racing!" yelled Charley.

262

T put the pedal down as they rounded the first turn. He drove like a mad man figuring he needed as much lead as possible should he have to take the first option and just get a splash of gas.

"That is smart. Keep it up," said Charley as T pulled away from the rest of the pack. "Eighteen to go."

Jack became very nervous when they got down to fifteen to go. Suddenly, he saw T peel off the track, slow down rapidly and then ease down pit row holding his speed just a click under the speed limit and the infamous radar gun. The pit crew quickly changed the right side ties, and got some gas in as T sped back out again.

Charley spoke into his radio microphone, "Leader is in turn three, and we got an excellent job by the pit crew. Way to go boys." He turned back to see T enter turn one. "Son, this is when you need to turn it up a notch. There are just thirteen laps to go."

T's radio remained silent and Charley instantly knew he had gone into his zone. He broke radio silence only to tell him the lap to go, and his position as he crossed the finish line. T caught back up to the fifteenth car on the lead lap in short order with his fresh right side tires. He moved on pass fourteen and thirteen with ease.

"He's on a roll!" yelled Drew as he watched the monitor from the pit box. "Go boy, go!

With eight laps to go, he passed three more cars and was in tenth place. Two laps later, he was in eighth, but then it got tougher as drivers began blocking him. When he saw the white flag, he was in sixth place and by the finish line, he made it to fifth, and the race was over. Thad was not happy with the result, feeling great disappointment in his finish.

Everybody along the pit wall on his team sighed heavily. They had hoped he could do the impossible, but he ran out of time and laps. Frustrated with the outcome, he rapidly drove his car to the garage, and climbed out. Most of the media ran to the winner's circle paying T little attention. The pit crew and the security detail were working their way through the crowd. Jack left the coach in the final laps and drove the golf cart to the garage to pick him up. Behind him in the crowd was his security detail, but they were cut off as the number 45 car stalled on the way to his garage after running out of gas.

T took his helmet off and tossed it in the car, and bent over to remove his heel guards, out of the corner of his eye he saw Jack driving up. He smiled, but suddenly he focused behind Jack, and spotted Tim rapidly running towards him.

T dropped the heel guards into the car, and began jumping up and down, and waving at Jack to warn him. Jack gave him a puzzled look, but couldn't fight his way through the crowd in the golf cart, so he slammed on brakes, and jumped out thinking T wanted him to hurry to him for something.

Another racecar sped behind him as T yelled something, but Jack couldn't hear him over the noise of the car. T yelled again and pointed. Jack slowly turned as if in a slow motion video, and caught sight of Tim. Jack turned back to T who took a step or two towards him. T reached into his pocket and pressed the panic button. He glanced left and right looking for Duke. Jack didn't see Tim pull the pistol from a Ziploc bag hidden in the bottom of his beer cooler under the ice, but T saw it, and yelled again at Jack.

Jack turned and saw Tim, and frantically looked for the security detail, or Thad's team while pressing his panic button in his pocket. He realized the pit crew was forty yards away and too far to help. The security detail abandoned their golf carts due to the after race crowd stampede to the parking lots, and though rushing towards the garage on foot, they would not make it in time to stop Tim. Jack turned and saw the gun. Instinctively, he ran towards T to protect him, but it was T who was trying to yell and warn Jack. At twenty yards, Tim began firing wild repeated shots from a 9mm Glock at Thad. He had only fired the pistol once after he bought it a few months ago, but he got lucky. The crowd immediately scattered in all directions.

Jack heard a bullet whiz by his ear just missing him, and saw the punch, as it hit T in his right side, knocking him against the entry wall of the garage, where he fell to the ground. The second shot went high, hitting the wall right behind Thad's rapidly slumping body, and just missing his head.

Tim realized he could not aim well while running, so he stopped a few steps to his left, and took dead aim around Jack while concentrating his shot on T's head. As he pulled the trigger Jack impulsively leaped towards T, and the bullet caught him in the air in the left rear shoulder, sending him hurtling into the back of T's racecar where he hit the trunk, and slowly slid down the back of the car leaving a blood trail in the process.

One of the security detail almost reached Tim, but Tim quickly turned, fired a shot at the man and missed, but sent the crowd into panic driven frenzy. Tim turned slowly to shoot at Thad once more, hoping for a kill shot.

Duke never slowed his run towards the garage. He counted the shots—six so far, and he knew at least three more could follow. He wasted no time as he pushed his way through the crowd, knocking men and women out of his way. Once he got within forty yards of Tim, he drew his pistol, rapidly brought back the breech, took aim, and fired three rapid burst shots without hesitation.

The first hit Tim in the right shoulder causing him to drop his gun. The second hit him just above the heart, and the third slammed into his head. His skull exploded onto a pile of tires, but he was dead as his bloody body hit the black asphalt face first. A bright red pool of blood cascaded outward across the pavement like melting ice cream.

Duke ran to T while holstering his gun, saw the blood at his waist, and felt for a pulse. The rest of his men finally caught up to him including

264

Jack's detail. "He's alive! Get an ambulance here quick. Don, put pressure on Thad's wound. Stretch him out carefully. Watch his head."

He then turned to Jack, "Steve, help me with Jack." He felt Jack's neck for a pulse. "He's alive, too."

Together, they turned Jack's limp body over and laid him down. Duke saw the wound in the left shoulder, and hoped it was high enough, but he knew it was dangerously close to his heart. If the bullet hit the heart, he would bleed out in seconds. If it had hit a major artery, he would bleed out internally before they could do anything.

He heard sirens behind him as the ambulance team began making their way through the growing crowd of onlookers. He pulled away Jack's shirt and saw the hole. He quickly took off his own shirt, rolled it up, and pressed it to the wound. Steve did the same putting his shirt in a roll on Jack's back where the bullet exited.

Janet arrived next with Drew and Charley behind her. She nearly fainted at the sight of the bloody boys, but tried to keep her wits about her, but with so much blood, she began sobbing as she turned to Charley. The crew chief put his big arms around her, as he scanned the horrific scene. "Hang on honey. They're tough. They'll be okay."

The EMT technicians paired off with two men surrounding each boy and examining them carefully. One of the men looked up at Duke and smiled, "Good job. This one has lost a lot of blood, but you were treating him correctly. We have to get him to the infield medical center fast. Keep the pressure on the wound while we get him on the gurney." Duke and Steve kept the pressure as they helped lift Jack's limp body onto the gurney, and walked alongside to the ambulance.

Janet watched as they rolled Jack away. Blood, bits of asphalt, and dirt covered his beautiful face. Duke climbed into the ambulance with him as the doors closed, and they began making their way out of sight around the corner of garage to the med center.

The two men working on Thad cut away his uniform so they could get to his wound just above his hip. The powerful bullet went in and out of him, too. T's face was pale, and he remained unconscious due to either the shock of being shot, or it appeared he had hit his head on something on the way to the pavement.

They carefully put Thad on a gurney, loaded him in the second ambulance, and drove off. Janet looked like she was going to throw up and cry at the same time. Drew decided to take charge.

"Janet, get me to the Infield Care Center. Make this crowd get out of your way, and I'll follow you. Charley, get your boys together and clean up this mess."

A deputy walked up, "Now hold a second. This is a crime scene. My boss will be here in just a minute."

Drew shot back with anger and frustration, "The crime is over. That piece of shit..." he pointed to disheveled body belonging to Tim, "shot my driver and his friend."

"I gathered that, but who shot this man and killed him?"

"I don't know."

"Then my men and I have a lot of work to do. If you didn't see anything you may leave." Then he turned to the crowd, "If there is anyone here that saw this shooting then please line up behind me. If there are any cameramen who have footage of the shooting please come to me now."

Drew turned his wheelchair away from the crowd as they began following the deputy's instructions. "He called to Charley again. Stay here, look after our equipment, and help the deputy any way you can. I'll be at the Infield Care Center." He turned to Janet. "Come on, honey. Let's get out of here."

TWENTY-THREE

Drew and Janet had to fight through a swarming gang of reporters and news crews waiting outside the track's emergency medical center for news on the shooting, and Thad in particular. A race official spotted Drew and came over.

"Drew, you'll have to wait here. The doctors are stabilizing Thad. They plan to fly him by helicopter in a few minutes. I can tell you the bullet went through his right side just above his hip and barely missed the hip bone and exited it out his back. They don't know if there is internal bleeding, hence the need to get him to the hospital, x-rays, and if need be, surgery as soon as they get him ready. He'll be going to City Hospital. I will let you know if there are any changes. Just wait here." He turned to walk back down the hall.

Janet suddenly came out of her shellshock, "What about Jack? How is he?"

The official frowned as turned back towards her. "He's lost a lot of blood. He'll be flying out first, as he is in very critical condition. I'll be back shortly."

Tears slowly dripped from Janet's eyes as Drew reached over and took her hand. "Let's find a place for you to sit down."

They found a chair in the corner for her, and together they waited in silence finding nothing useful to say in such a stressful mess of a situation.

Twenty minutes later, the medical staff rushed from a room down the hall, and pushed a gurney covered in hanging bags and tubes. They moved quickly, but Janet caught a quick glimpse of Jack's face. They turned the corner and rolled him out the side doors to the helicopter. The news crews shot footage not knowing if the patient was Thad or someone else.

"Oh, Drew. He looked awful."

"He'll be fine," began Drew trying to comfort her when he really had no idea what to say.

They heard the helicopter take off and moments later, a second chopper set down. They looked down the hall as the medical staff began rolling a second gurney down the hall. Janet stood up, and caught a brief view of Thad's face, as he remained unconscious and pale.

As they pushed out the side door Drew took charge again, "Nothing we can do here. Let's get to the hospital."

Numb from the experience, Janet obediently followed her boss, as he made his way out another door to avoid the reporters. He knew the race officials would update and handle the media, and he wanted to make sure Thad got the best medical care possible.

As they reached the exit doors, Drew heard Duke call to him. "Drew?"

They turned, and saw Duke with blood all over him. He had tried to wash up in the restroom, but it just made the stains worse.

"Duke, are you okay?"

"Yes, just messy. Jack was bleeding profusely, so I had to stuff my shirt on to his wound, and hold it there."

"You probably saved his life," stated Charley. "How is he?"

"I don't know, but the doctors seemed very concerned."

Drew asked, "What about Thad?"

"I think he'll be fine, but they are worried about internal bleeding. Are you on the way to the hospital?"

"Yes, we're going to fly out. Why don't you get a quick shower, put together a team of your security men, and meet us there when you can."

"Yes, sir." He paused searching for the right words, and finally said, "I'm sorry this happen. Thad drove straight to the garage and quite honestly, we thought he was going to win, and didn't anticipate him coming here. The crowd stopped us from catching up with him. Jack stopped the third bullet aimed carefully at Thad. I don't think Tim saw Jack, or he was just hell bent and determined to kill Thad."

Wisely, Drew reached up and shook his hand, "Don't you worry. No one can prevent a single-minded killer. Now go on, and get cleaned up, and we'll see you in a while."

Janet, Drew, and Charley boarded his helicopter that flew them to the airport where they took a car into town to the hospital. Although this took an extra thirty minutes, he surmised it would have taken hours to get away from the track by car with all the spectators heading home.

When they entered the hospital Drew turned to Janet, "Go find the hospital administrator, and tell him I want to talk to him now."

Janet immediately began reading the hall directional signs as she made her way to the main office.

"Got to keep that girl busy," said Drew to Charley, as they watched her go down the hall. "She's really shook up."

Charley asked, "Aren't you? I can't believe that man shot Thad. Why?"

Drew responded, "I'm not sure why, but I always seem to be able to take charge without emotions in the heat of a situation. It is afterwards, when alone, that I suffer. Duke and his men will be here soon. I want to make sure that Tim was the only shooter. We'll need to protect Thad's room."

Charley didn't know what to say, so he found a sofa to sit on, as Drew followed him in his wheelchair. Janet returned with a tall man with a full head of styled gray hair and no tan. He contrasted greatly with anyone in the racing business. They always had great tans from all their work in the sun, and most had already pulled their hair out while their teams battled for a win.

268

"Drew, this Albert Watson, he is the hospital's administrator." She turned to Albert, "This is my boss, Drew McClain." She then politely stepped out of the way, as Albert shook Drew's hand.

"Thank you for coming to see me. As you probably know, you have my best driver and his friend in surgery right now. I just want to assure you that I'll personally take care of the bills. I want you make sure you have your best team on hand, and that they get the best possible care. I also insist you instruct your staff not to talk to the media. Janet here is our public relations expert, and she'll handle the media personally."

"Why of course, sir. We always have our top staff on call during a race weekend, but we never imagined there would be a shooting. I can assure you our best surgeons are working on them now. I'll be happy to have you handle the media, as I am sure you have more experience than we do. I'll have my media person bring you up to date first. We can have the media placed in our press conference room where they can wait for the any news."

"Thank you," replied Drew. He gave Albert his business card, "Invoice everything to the address on the card. I'm counting on you to make sure the boys survive."

"We'll do our very best." Albert shook his hand again, nodded at Janet and Charley, and turned to leave.

The hours ticked by ever so slowly while they waited in the modest waiting room. Thad's surgery went well. The bullet missed key organs, while leaving only a few fragments that the surgeons found and removed. After they stitched both sides of his abdomen, the surgery finished. X-rays pronounced his head okay with no fractures, but a goose egg of a bruise that would hurt for a while. Thad was now in the recovery room.

Janet received the news Thad would be all right, though they were still monitoring him carefully for any sign of internal bleeding. She decided it was time to face the media. Drew and Charley followed her to the stage, though they remained off to the side, as Janet bravely walked to the podium.

"Ladies and gentlemen, I'm pleased to report that Thad is out of surgery. The bullet apparently went through his body just above his waist. It did not hit any organs and so far, there is no sign of internal bleeding. He must have hit his head pretty hard when he fell back, but he does not have a skull fracture. They will watch him carefully over the next twelve hours, and we hope we will know more then. Are there any questions?"

A reporter asked, "Who shot him?"

"I'm sure the sheriff's office will release the details, but I recognized the shooter as Tim English."

"Isn't that the man that threatened to blackmail Thad?"

Another reporter added, "Wasn't he the guy that caused the scene in the hospital in Cincinnati?"

Janet sighed, "Yes. He was the same man."

"Had he made threats on Thad's life?"

"None that I know of," replied Janet. "I'm sorry, I'll let you know more when I know. Thank you." She turned to leave.

A lady reporter on the front said loudly, "What about the other boy? Rumors have it that it was Jack Langston—Thad's boyfriend. Is that right? How is he doing?"

Slowly, Janet walked backed to podium, "The second victim was indeed Jack Langston. He leaped in front of the killer's final shot aimed directly at the fallen and wounded Thad. He is still in surgery and his wound is more severe. The bullet hit him in the upper left side of his chest. He lost at lot of blood. I'll let you know more of his condition when I can."

She left with a quicker pace to avoid any further questions. Once they were back in the waiting room Charley asked them, "Is that true? Jack stopped the second shot?"

Drew nodded, "Duke said the killer fired while running towards Thad, and got lucky with the first shot that hit Thad, but he slowed his run, made another wild shot, and then stopped running, and took careful aim at Thad and fired. Jack threw his body in front of Thad, and most likely saved Thad's life—perhaps at the expense of his own."

Charley shook his head, "Dow, that's like the secret service detail saving the President."

Janet smiled, "He didn't do it because it was his job—he loves Thad more than anyone or anything on the planet."

Charley smiled, "Amazing. I don't think my wife would do that for me."

Drew grinned, "No, you big lug, but I bet you would do it for her."

They moved Thad to a private room several hours later, and Janet was allowed in to wait for him to wake up. Jack was still in surgery. Drew and Charley continued to wait in the waiting room. Finally, about midnight, a single surgeon entered the room and walked over to him.

"Are you the family for Jack Langston?"

"Family? Uh, no," began Drew, "he works for me, and is my driver's best friend. How is he doing?"

"He lost a lot of blood, and we gave him two transfusions. Fortunately, the entry wound was just above his heart. The bullet just missed his lung, too. As far as the bullet wound goes, I'd say he was lucky, but it is still early. I've stitched him internally and externally, and I hope I have the bleeding under control. We'll know more tomorrow. He is in the recovery room now, and will remain in the intensive care unit for the night."

Drew asked, "Is there anything else we can do?"

"No, but you might pray for him. I've done all I can."

"Thank you. Of course we will."

About three in the morning, Janet heard a slight moan, and slowly stood up from the poor fitting recliner she had been trying to nap in. She walked slowly over to Thad's bed so she could see his face. His eyes were open, but he appeared to be staring into space.

"Thad? How are you feeling?" she asked in a whisper.

He moved his eyes to her face, paused as they slowly focused, and then he made a slight attempt to smile upon recognizing her. Without hesitation he replied, "I hurt like hell."

"Are you alright?"

"I think so."

"The surgeon said the bullet went in your side and out the back, and didn't hit anything vital. You should recover with time. They are monitoring you in case there is some internal bleeding. Your face looks normal again. You were very pale when they took you to the hospital."

"My head hurts," he protested.

"You hit your head when you fell back after being shot."

"Did they get Tim? That fool shot me."

"Yes, he's dead. Duke killed him."

"Oh," he replied with a pause before asking, "Where's Jack?"

Janet's face went white.

"What's wrong? Where is he?"

Janet said softly, "You didn't know. After Tim shot you the first time, he tried to shoot you again. His next shot went high, but he stopped running, and took careful aim for his third shot. Jack saw his aim, and leaped in front of you. He was shot in the left shoulder."

"Oh my gosh! Where is he? Is he okay?"

"You both came to the same hospital, and were in surgery at the same time. His surgery took a lot longer. He has loss a ton of blood. He is in the intensive care unit."

"Take me to him," demanded Thad, as he tried to get up.

"You can't move. You'll tear your stitches, and they have you drugged for pain. They'll know more in the morning. You should try and sleep."

Reluctantly he stopped trying to move. He sighed heavily. "Wake me the moment you hear anything about Jack."

"I will."

"Promise me," he said with more determination though still weak.

"I promise. Now you just sleep. I'll be right here next to your bed."

At eight the next morning, the surgeon entered T's room and found him awake, "Mr. Thompson. I'm David Bell, your surgeon. How are you today?"

271

"I'm sore and my head still hurts."

"Let me see your head," he said as he gently lifted Thad's head. "Well, the swelling has actually gone down a bit since last night. That's a good sign. Let's see your wound." He pulled the covers back, and then said to the nurse waiting at the corner of the bed. "Please get a tray. I want to remove his bandages, and check the wound for bleeding."

The nurse left the room, returned with a blue tray, and brought it to the table over Thad's bed. The surgeon carefully removed the tape and gauze, helped Thad turn a little, as he studied the rear exit wound, and once satisfied, he and the nurse put new bandages back in place.

"Your wounds are in good shape. I need to feel the area around it and probe a little for internal bleeding. It might hurt a little."

"Go ahead, doc. It can't be as bad as my head."

The surgeon smiled, and began feeling his abdomen carefully. Once satisfied, he returned the bed covers. I don't think there is any internal bleeding, but we'll keep monitoring you for the rest of today. We're giving you an antibiotic to prevent infection via two capsules in the morning and at night. I'll check on you again this afternoon."

After he left, Thad looked up at Janet, "That hurt a lot."

Janet smiled, "You stubborn drivers are so brave."

"What do you know about Jack?"

"I've heard nothing."

"I'll be fine. Why don't you go find out for me? Please."

"Okay, but don't you get out of that bed," she warned.

"Yes mother dear," replied Thad sarcastically.

She winked at him before turning to leave the room. In the hall, she found Duke sitting in a chair, and across the hall two more of his men. Duke looked up at her, "How's he doing?"

"He'll be fine. He's gone back to sleep. I'll be back. I'm going to see Drew. I hear you were quite the hero—killing Tim and stopping him from hurting anyone else."

"That's not exactly true. He wasn't shooting at me. Jack is the one that took a bullet for Thad. He's the hero. I'm just sorry we couldn't stop Tim before he fired a shot."

"You did the best you could. It was chaos after the race. Don't worry. They'll be fine. I will see you in a while."

She walked down the hallway to the waiting room, and found Drew asleep in his chair, and poor Charley trying to sleep on a couch way too small for his large frame.

"Drew? Are you awake?" she asked.

Startled, he quickly looked up to her, "Oh, yes, I was just resting my eyes. Of course, although I have to pee like a racehorse, but I'm fine. How's Thad?"

"Good. He awoke several times, and the surgeon doesn't think he has internal bleeding. He has an awful headache from the bump on his head."

"That sounds better."

"How's Jack?"

"He's still in the intensive care unit. His surgeon came to see us last night, but no news since then."

Janet smiled at him. "I'll go find out. Get Charley to get you to a bathroom."

"I will. Thanks."

Janet walked down the hall until she found the Intensive Care Unit. She went up to the nurse at the counter, explained who she was, and asked about Jack.

"He's still asleep. His surgeon just checked on him. We're monitoring him carefully."

"Shouldn't he be awake by now? Thad is awake."

The nurse smiled, "He had a horrible wound with much more extensive blood loss, and perhaps his body is just letting him rest a little longer."

"I'll be in Thad's room if you need me. Will you let me know how he's doing in a while?"

"Yes, of course. I see your name on his file with orders from Mr. Watson our administrator. I will let you know."

Janet went back to tell Drew and together, they knew they needed to update the media. Reluctantly she entered the media room, and walked to the podium.

"Ladies and gentlemen, I want to give you an update. Thad has awoken from his surgery. His surgeon has examined him, and doesn't think at this point there is any internal bleeding. He has a headache from his backward fall after being shot, but he is talking and that is a good sign.

"As for Jack Langston, his surgery went well, but he is in the Intensive Care Unit. The blood loss was large, he was given two transfusions, and so far he is not yet awake."

A reporter asked, "The sheriff announced a while ago that Duke Pendleton shot the killer. Doesn't he work for DMI?"

"Yes, he is head of our security detail for Thad."

She sighed, and took a breath before continuing. "If Duke hadn't stopped the assailant, he would have shot Thad again, and most likely killed him, Jack Langston, or others. I will let you know more as soon as I hear from the doctors. I don't expect any updates until later today. Thank you."

She left the room before any more questions could be asked. She waited outside, and watched in secret as the reporters began packing up their gear and leaving. She felt great relief preferring to send out press releases electronically, as opposed to live briefings.

The day passed slowly. Drew and Charley flew back to Charlotte. Duke placed two men outside Thad's door, and two more in the Intensive Care Area, but it was more of a ward and harder for them to guard, but they stayed available none the less, while watching everyone as they entered and left.

Duke returned from the Sheriff's office where he gave a full report, surrendered his weapon for ballistic testing, allowed the deputy to make a copy of his gun permit, driver's license, and then they let him go. There would be a formal hearing, but the deputy said there would be no charges, and eventually, his pistol would be returned to him.

He checked on his men on duty at the Intensive Care Unit protecting Jack, and then took the elevator to Thad's floor. He spoke to the men on guard sitting outside, and then knocked as he entered the room. He found Janet feeding Thad some grits.

Thad saw him and began complaining, "Oh, good Duke is here. Duke, please find me a hamburger or pizza. She is trying to kill me with these unsalted grits and no butter."

Duke smiled, "You're sounding better."

"I'm better until the pain medicine wears off, and then my side and head hurt. They'll give me two pills, and I sleep some more."

"That's good."

Thad and Janet noticed Duke looked more somber than usual, and they both feared he had bad news. Janet stopped trying to feed Thad, and put down the bowl.

"What is it?" she asked of Duke.

"Thad, I'm so sorry my men and I could not stop this from happening. It is my fault. I didn't have the garage covered. I thought you were going to win, so we were heading to the winner's circle."

Thad smiled, "You have nothing to be sorry for. I lost the race, felt upset, drove straight to the garage, and probably drove there too fast. With the crowd, I'm sure you had trouble catching up to me. It was my fault. However, in the end, you saved Jack and me by stopping Tim from shooting either of us one more time. I am so grateful for you. Any news on Jack?"

"No, I just came from there. He's still asleep."

"Janet, are you sure I can't go down there and see him?"

She smiled at Thad, "The doctor said you were to stay in bed."

"Ye ma'am. Well, since Duke is back, why don't you take a break, go to the hotel and get a shower, and clean up. You're beginning to smell."

She laughed at him, "Thank you very much. You sure know how to talk to a lady."

"I didn't mean it that way. You've been here all night. Go get some rest, eat a meal that doesn't have grits involved, and I'll see you tomorrow."

"Are you sure?"

"Yeah, Duke will tell me some bedtime time stories, won't you? Tell me the one that begins once upon a time there was a crazy racecar driver that no one could beat!"

Duke gave him a sheepish look, but caught Thad's winking eye, "Uh, don't worry, Janet. I'll take good care of him. You go rest now."

She leaned over and kissed Thad's forehead. "You'd better behave, and get well. I'll see you tomorrow."

"Thank you for your help."

"You're welcome."

After she left, Thad said, "Check the hall and make sure she is gone."

Duke gave him a puzzled look, but returned quickly, "No sign of her."

"Good, now help me get out of this bed." Thad began pulling the covers back.

"But the doc said you're to stay in the bed."

Thad grimaced, as a shot of pain raced to his brain, "Have you ever known me to do exactly what I'm told?"

Duke smiled, "No I haven't. Slow down. I'll get you out of there." He pulled Thad to a sitting position. "That's good, now just rest there, and I'll go find a wheelchair. I can't take a chance on you fainting, and putting another knot on your head."

"Okay, you win. I'll wait." Thad didn't really put up much of an argument, as he felt a little dizzy.

They made their way slowly down the long hallway before Duke pushed him up to the counter in the Intensive Care Unit. An older gray haired nurse came to see what he wanted.

"Ma'am I need to check on Jack Langston."

"Are you family?"

"Yes ma'am, I am."

"Hold on." She walked to the end of the counter, pulled a chart, read it, and then returned. "The chart says he is doing fine, but still unconscious. There has been no sign of internal bleeding."

"Very good. May I see him?"

Her brow wrinkled, and took a breath to say no, but T didn't wait for her to answer, "I must see him. He saved my life. He took the second bullet for me, you see. I must see him."

She bit her lip, and the grandmother in her sighed, "Well, only for a minute. We don't usually have visitors in here."

"Thank you." Thad reached and patted her arm.

She looked up at Duke. "You wait here. I'll take him back."

Slowly she wheeled Thad down the hallway behind the counter as T searched the patients of each bed until at last he saw Jack. His heart sank, as he looked so awful with bandages on his head from the scrapes when he fell, and they he stared at the big bandage over his shoulder. She rolled him alongside, and then left the room to give him some privacy.

Gently as if afraid he might hurt Jack, he gripped his hand softly, and gave it a cautious squeeze. He carefully caressed his forearm before speaking. "Jack? Jack? It's me, Thad. Do you hear me?" He waited, but Jack remained still. "Jack, thank you for saving me, but you shouldn't have done that. You might not have been shot. I know you saved me, but I can't stand the thought of you being wounded on my account. Jack? Jack? I need for you to wake up. I need to see your eyes, and feel the warmth of their glow on my face. I need to see your smile. Jack? Jack? I love you. We have so much more to do together. Please wake up. Jack? Jack?"

Thad stopped and stared at Jack's face hoping to see some kind of sign that he was awake, but seeing none he allowed the tears to flow from his eyes, and slowly slide down his face like icicles melting in the early spring sun. "Jack, don't you die on me. I need you. I love you. Jack?"

Jack's arm twitched. Thad nearly jumped out of the wheelchair. He looked up, and saw one of Jack's eyes slightly ajar. He saw the blue of his pupil and smiled. "Can you hear me?"

Jack blinked his eye twice.

"Very good. Okay, you just rest, and I'll be back in a few hours. I bet they have you drugged so you'll sleep well while your body is healing. You're going to make it. You'll be fine. We've got a cruise to go on, and a trip to Africa. Therefore, you just rest, and tomorrow we'll get some grits in you. The hospital makes wonderful grits," he lied. "They'll stick to your ribs for sure."

Jack blinked twice and closed his eye.

The nurse returned Thad to the counter in his wheelchair. Duke was going to roll him to his room, but Thad stopped him. "Ma'am?" he asked the nurse. "Do you have a cafeteria around here?"

"Why yes, just down that hallway, and turn left across the breezeway." She pointed towards the turn in the hallway.

"Thank you. Duke, let's get something to eat."

"But I should get you back in bed."

"And you will, but not before I eat something besides grits!"

Duke laughed and pushed him down the hallway.

276

TWENTY-FOUR

Although Thad selected a large plate of food, once he got started, he began to slow down, as he began thinking about Jack.

"Do you think he'll pull through?" Thad asked Duke.

Duke stuffed the last part of a buttermilk biscuit with butter and honey dripping off the side into his mouth. Swallowed, and drank some milk to wash it down. He wiped his face and hands with the napkin, "Dang, this is pretty good for a hospital. Thad, I've seen many injuries in my time, both on the track and off. Jack is young, strong, determined, and most of all he has a reason to live—you. I have to be honest. I have never known a person that was gay. I mean I knew of gay people, and I have seen gay people, but I never knew one, and now I know two. Like most folks, I was probably afraid it might rub off on me, so when you're afraid, you act like you absolutely hate them.

"I have known you for a couple of years now, and though it was a shock when you came out, I don't think I could hate you. In fact, I really admire your bravery, both behind the wheel and especially off the track. Now that I have gotten used to it, I don't see what the big deal is.

"I'm nothing pretty to look at it, so I know how important love is between two people. My Betsy and I have been together twenty-two years. She was the prettiest thing I had ever seen. I was a big old college football player that just enlisted in the military. I told her I didn't understand why she loved a big old dope like me.

"She'd always smile and say that it was not just the outside shell that she loved, but rather the inside. She said I had the most beautiful heart in the world. Can you imagine that? Me beautiful? Ha, I am not stupid. I asked that girl to marry me right then. She had to wait until I got out of the service, and she did wait, because I didn't want to take a chance on making her a widow while in the war.

"So Thad, I've seen the way you and Jack are when you're together. I would never have figured it out, but you're like bookends. You excel at racing, and he excels at writing and planning. He's smart, and the things the two of you have done to help charities all over the country is absolutely amazing.

"If that was me up there in that hospital bed, there would be nothing that could stop me from getting back to my Betsy. I think in that regards, Jack and I are alike. He won't let a little old bullet stop him from coming back to you. He'll be fine. Don't worry. He's tougher than you think, and he has a big heart like old Duke. He'll be fine."

Thad smiled, "Thanks, Duke. I can see why Betsy loves you. Come on, let's get out of here."

Thad's doctor saw him early the next morning, and reported he could check out today, but he would need to change the dressing on his wound twice a day for about a week. He gave him prescriptions for a strong antibacterial ointment, pills for infection, and some for his headaches. Thad still hurt some, but felt far better than yesterday. He thanked the doctor for taking such good care of him.

Everyone left the room so he could dress. He walked over to the closet by the window to retrieve some clothes Duke had brought by earlier that morning. He heard what he thought sounded like chanting, so he turned to the window and looked down. There were thousands of people standing outside, and for a brief moment he thought they were there praying for his recovery, but as his eyes began to read the signs they were holding, the reality of this mob took hold.

The signs read 'All Homos Should Die', 'Faggots Go To Hell', 'God Punishes the Wicked with Death', 'Thad Should Die Now'. He saw the long line of white church buses, and wondered how such followers of Christ learned to hate with such zeal. He shook his head in disbelief that they could actually be praying for him and Jack to die.

Disgusted, he began to dress although pulling up his pants was painful. He left his shirt hanging out to help cover his bandage. He found Duke in the hallway waiting for him. "Let's go upstairs to check on Jack."

Duke anticipated he would say that, and so he followed him to the elevator. "The boss called to see how you were doing."

Thad smiled, "I'll call him back in a while. Did you see that mob out there?"

Duke turned his head left and right to see who else was listening on the elevator, and then whispered, "The sons of bitches ought to be horsewhipped if you ask me. The gall of them to pray for another person's death—what the hell are they thinking?"

"Apparently they are not thinking at all. Do you have a plan for getting us out of here?"

"There's a heliport on the roof, and I have a chopper standing by at the airport. We'll figure that out after we see Jack."

Thad smiled at the nurse at the Intensive Care Station. "I'm Thad. May I see Jack?"

She looked up and smiled. "His doctor is back there. Stay here a second, and I'll see if the doctor thinks it is okay." She left before he could reply, but returned quickly. "Come on back."

Thad followed while Duke took a seat on the couch across the hall where two of his men were also sitting.

"Good morning Doctor…" began Thad.

"Herschel, thank you, and good morning to you." The doctor was in his mid fifties with little hair left, but his smile and warm eyes put Thad at ease quickly.

278

"How's he doing?"

"Well, his vital signs are good, but he hasn't awakened yet."

"Yes he has," replied Thad.

"What?"

"I came to see him last night, and he opened his eyes and looked at me."

"That could have been a muscle twitch."

"No, I asked him to blink twice if he could hear me and he did. Later he did it again. Shall I show you?"

Slowly, the doctor stepped aside. "Please," he said with some skepticism.

Thad took Jack's hand in his and began speaking to him. "Hey, buddy—time to wake up. Your grits are getting cold. The doc is here to see you. Come on, wake up sleepyhead."

Jack opened first one eye and then the other. Thad smiled.

"Good morning. How are you feeling? Do you feel like the bus ran over you? I'm sore, too but luckier than you. The bullet went in and out of my flesh, and didn't hit anything serious. See, I have my street clothes back on. Can you speak?"

The doctor moved around to the other side of the bed feeling astonished that Jack opened his eyes on command. "This is a really good sign that he is awake." He pointed a light into Jack's right eye. Satisfied, he moved to the other. "Can you speak?"

Jack whispered, "Yes, but my throat is dry."

Thad quickly found a cup of water and a straw, and let him take a sip. Jack sucked it loosely letting some water drip down his chin. T wiped it up and smiled at him. "How's that?"

"Better. What happened?"

The doctor looked over at Thad, so T took over, "Let's see, our old buddy Tim decided he was mad at us for not paying the blackmail money and thus he shot me. He just lightly wounded me, but falling backwards, I hit my head knocking me unconscious. Duke says he was running trying to get to Tim when he saw Tim take a more careful aim at me. Then this cute superman type of guy named Jack," he paused and pointed at Jack and smiled, "well, he bravely jumped in front of the gun, and stopped the bullet with his skinny ass. Duke then shot and killed Tim. Stay tuned—film at eleven."

The doctor didn't know the whole story, and looked over at Thad and then back to Jack with great astonishment.

"So you see Jack—you're a hero, a real live hero. All I ever do is drive a racecar real fast."

Jack smiled, "This hero doesn't feel so good. I am sore."

"After you were shot, you hit the pavement pretty hard. I've got a big knot on the back of my head, too. I guess we're a sorry lot."

"Can I get out of bed? Can we go home?" Jack asked.

T looked up at the doctor. The doctor smiled and replied, "Not yet. Your wound was more serious than Thad's. The bullet just missed your heart and left lung. You were very lucky. The bullet went through you, and they found it in the dash of Thad's racecar. It was fragmented, but we don't know if that happen upon impact with the steel in your car, or was a small piece left behind in our body. I didn't find anything during surgery, so I am hopeful we got it all. You also loss a lot of blood, and it will take a few days to get your full strength back. We're also monitoring your urine to see if there is any internal bleeding. I think we can move you to a room now. You just rest, and we'll get you moved, and see if you can eat something."

"Oh boy, Jack—you aren't going to believe how good the grits are in this place. You're going to love 'em," he lied with a sly grin. "I'll wait outside. Now you do what they tell you to, and I'll see you in a few minutes."

"It's for you," said Duke as he handed T his cell phone.

Without asking who it was he said, "Morning boss. How was your flight back?"

"Miserable," replied Drew. "I was so worried for you and Jack, I just couldn't sleep. How are you? How's Jack?"

"I'm fine, dressed and just have to be careful with bandages, and try not to tear any stitches loose. Jack finally awoken, and they are moving him out of Intensive Care and into a room."

"That's good news. Are you flying back today?"

"I don't think they are going to let Jack out of here yet. His wound was much worse than mine."

"Should I get a substitute driver ready for this weekend?"

Thad thought for a second and replied, "We have six days. I'll be fine. I'll meet you in Homestead. I've got a deal I want to talk with you about."

"A deal?"

Thad smiled, "You'll like it. I will call you later."

He turned around, and saw Janet step off the elevator. "Oh my gosh! You're up and around." She gave him a hug.

"Don't squeeze too hard," he warned as he kissed her on the cheek.

She immediately stopped and stepped back, "Oh, I'm sorry. How are you?"

"Good, sore and I have a headache. The wound will heal. They're getting ready to move Jack upstairs."

"How's he doing?" she asked timidly, half afraid of bad news.

"He just woke up. They're going to monitor him for a few days. I'll fly from here to Homestead on the weekend."

"You're going to race?"

"I've got a championship to win."

She laughed, "You're incorrigible. You don't think someone will take Tim's place, and try to shoot you again."

Thad sighed, "Tim wanted money and was willing to kill when he didn't get what he wanted. The religious nuts haven't been violent, just annoying."

"What about your wound?"

"They put a Band-Aid on it. I'll be fine," he replied with a sly grin.

"Yeah, right. I hope you know what you're doing."

"I know I'm going to win a championship."

By late afternoon T cranked up the hospital bed so that Jack was almost sitting up. Thad spooned him some soup. Duke kept a man outside, while he and another guy obtained rooms in a nearby hotel. Duke realized they were going to be there longer, and each man would need to work at least an eight-hour shift. They ate and went to sleep. Janet spoke to Drew several times confirming that Thad intended to drive in the final race.

She pushed into Jack's room, and found it full of flowers. "I didn't know Jack was so popular," she said as she admired the flowers.

"They're not for me. They were for Thad. He already checked out, so they sent them up to my room. Did I ever tell you I was allergic to flowers?" Jack winked at T who gave him a puzzled look in return.

"Oh my gosh. Do you want me to move them out of here?" she set her stuff down on a chair to start the move.

"I'm just kidding. They're fine."

She whirled around and smiled, "I see you are doing much better. Your wit has returned, but I wish you wouldn't take after Thad. One of him is enough for this planet."

"Hey, I didn't do anything," protested T.

"How do you feel?" Janet sat down on the edge of his bed.

"I'm full of the worst tasting chicken soup I've ever had. I wish I had a hamburger."

T smiled, "I was thinking of sneaking out of here, and getting us both something good to eat. Would you like something, too?"

Janet laughed, "So you're going to sneak in some good food, huh? I think I can help with that. T you'd better not go outdoors—the big mob of religious nuts is still out front. What would you like? I'll go get it."

Jack spoke first, "A big burger, fries and a milkshake."

"Make that two," laughed Thad.

"Okay boys. You're on, but don't blame me if the nurse fusses at you."

Jack added, "Janet, when you get back I need to go over the charity plans for the weekend in Homestead. I don't think I'm going to be much help."

281

"I'll be glad to assist. I'll be back shortly."

After she left Jack looked up at Thad, "Are you sure you can race this weekend? What if you wreck and tear the wound open?"

"I'm going to wear my favorite chest protector again. They will strap me in very tight so that the only things moving will be my feet, hands, and head. No problem. It'll hurt getting in the car, but I won't feel a thing getting out after I win the championship."

"I am worried a little about the race, but troubled that someone will try to copycat Tim, and take another shot at you," added Jack.

"I'm a little worried about that because I don't think anyone else would jump in front of a bullet and stop it for me like you did. What were you thinking?"

"I wasn't thinking. I just leaped. I was desperate. There was no time to get to Tim, or push you out of the way. I just did it."

"Well, don't do that again. I can handle it."

"Yeah, right. You were already shot and unconscious. He had a dead aim on you. You'd be dead, and who would I love then?"

Thad teased, "I'm sure with your formidable looks, and fast typing skills, you could find some old bloke to love you."

They both laughed before Jack added with a serious tone, "Well, you go to Homestead, and if at any time you don't think you can drive then promise me you'll get out of the car."

"Yes, mother dear. I promise." T leaned over and kissed Jack.

Jack was asleep when Janet returned with a large shopping bag. He immediately smelled the food and woke up. "Oh my gosh! That smells so good," he said.

"I got a lot of weird looks from the hospital staff, but I made it. We'd better eat quickly before they catch us." Janet brought a takeout box to Jack's table as he pushed the button to bring his head up to an eating position. T grabbed a towel from the bathroom and laid it across Jack's chest and up to his neck. Seconds later they were all eating and chatting about this weekend's race.

It took Jack about twenty minutes, but he ate everything in the Styrofoam box. He then laid it aside, put a big straw in the milkshake, and gave it a hard suck.

"Oh, my! It's strawberry—one of my favorites. Thank you very much."

"My pleasure," replied Jane. "Did the doctor say when you could get out of here?"

Thad spoke up, "As you can see they still have an IV drip in him because of the blood loss, so I think near the end of the week."

282

"That burger should help me make a bunch more blood," added Jack between sucks on the straw. "My next meal should be a rare steak!"

They all laughed. Thad added, "Let's just hope he keeps mending as fast as his wit."

Janet cleaned up the evidence of their meal, and took it down the hall to the trash bin. When she returned, Jack said, "Janet, Duke brought my laptop. It's over there with T's jacket. Turn it on, and I will show you the plan for this weekend. I've got some calls I hope you can help me with."

She brought it to Jack after it booted up, and he loaded an Excel spreadsheet with his checklist in one workbook tab, and the itinerary in another. He showed her the lists. "Thad is doing four television stations on Friday late afternoon, visiting a children's hospital in Miami, and going over to the Homestead Air Force Base to visit the soldiers in the hospital there. On Friday night, he has a press conference scheduled to announce that TNT charities will partner up with Macy's to help orphanages all across the country with gifts for the kids for Christmas. We need to raise ten million dollars to make this happen. T is going to auction off one of his cars on EBay, and auction off a dinner for two with the high bid couple to have a dinner with Thad and Jack. It'll be in New York during the awards week, and finally, we will auction off T's helmet, the one he'll wear in Homestead. When he wins, we expect that auction to go through the roof."

Janet set there stunned, "Okay, I'm impressed. When did you have time to do all this?"

"I usually work on my ideas during his races to help me control how nervous I get. I watch the race on the LCD in the front of the coach while doing my research on the Internet. All of the people involved in this project will need to be called to let them know that T will be there in spite of being shot. We need to write some press releases and work on his speeches."

She scanned down the list, "Okay, no problem. I will make the calls, and perhaps tomorrow we can work on his speeches."

"I am hoping they will let me out of here before the race so I can join T there. He says he is leaving here Friday morning. Please let Al know so he can prepare for the flight."

"Al is staying at the Sheraton next to the airport in case you need him. He wants to come see you. He is very worried for you."

Thad smiled, "Tell him we would love to see him."

"Thad you're getting a ton of mail. I hired some temp workers, and they are sorting through it, putting the bad mail in the trash, and saving the good mail for you to scan through."

They all jumped when the phone by Jack's bed suddenly rang. Janet decided she should answer it in case one of the religious nuts got through. "Hello?"

The caller rapidly spoke for a moment and then Janet replied, "Just a moment." She put her hand over the mouthpiece, "Jack, there's a woman downstairs by the name of Jesse. She wants to come up to see you."

Jack smiled, "Jesse is here? Yes, please tell her to come up."

Janet relayed the message and hung up. I'll go back to the hotel to work on this list. May I borrow your laptop for a while?"

"Yes, of course."

She gave T a card, "This is my room number and telephone should you need me, and I'll have my cell phone."

Just as she stood to leave, the door pushed opened. In came a woman wearing dark sunglasses, holding a cane as if blind, and holding on to a dog in a harness, which to Janet looked like a lead dog for this blind lady.

Janet turned around as Jack and Thad started laughing loudly. She gave the boys a puzzled look, thinking they were being rude.

Jack spoke up first, "Jesse! Please come in."

Janet looked back at Jesse as she removed the sunglasses, and smiled. She set the glasses on the tray table, laid the cane down on a chair, and let go of the dog.

"Bailey! Come here boy," urged Jack.

Bailey took quick steps and put his big front paws on the edge of Jack's bed. Jack began scratching his ears while Thad came around the bed and gave Jesse a big hug. "We're so glad to see you. What's with the blind lady getup?"

"It's the only way I could get the dog in the hospital. They have such silly rules," she said as she gave Thad a kiss.

"Wait until you try their grits," laughed T.

"Or their pitiful chicken soup," added Jack with a grin as Jesse came over to hug and kiss Jack, too.

Janet remained standing with her mouth agape. Thad rescued her, "Jesse, this is Janet. She handles all my public relations kind of stuff, and is our dear friend. Janet, this is Jesse, one of Jack's oldest friends and a big help to me when old Jack went on the lamb."

Jack added, "And this is Bailey, the best Labrador in the whole world. He and I have hiked many a mile together."

"I thought he might cheer you up a bit." Jesse turned, and held out her hand to Janet. "I see you have been spoiling these boys. I smell hamburgers. I doubt that is hospital food."

Janet blushed, "Guilty, and I am so glad to meet you. I was on the way to the hotel to do some work. Would you mind making them behave for a while? They are such rascals. Both of them were shot, yet Thad intends to race this weekend, and Jack insists on getting work done. I'm out of here. I'll see you later. It was so nice to meet you, and I hope to learn more about Jack from you soon."

"Nice to meet you, honey. I'll keep these boys straight," she laughed, "well, sort of straight!" They all laughed.

"How did you get here? Did you drive?"

"No, it would have taken too long. I called about flying with a dog, and they said only blind people could take a large dog onboard, so that gave me the idea of pretending to be blind. I borrowed the glasses, cane, and harness from my aunt. They were her husband's before he died. We boarded the plane with no problem."

"Well, thank you for coming. I'm so glad to see you."

"I've been keeping up with the two of you since Thad came out. By the way, dude. I am so proud of you for being brave and stepping forward. I still can't believe you kissed Jack on live television. I nearly had a cow, and fell off the couch. Wow, what a moment!"

Thad laughed, "I didn't think about it ahead of time. It just seemed natural to do. I had just won a big race."

"And you're going to drive the final race this weekend?"

"I was the lucky one with just a flesh wound. I'll be fine. It's my head that's killing me. I got a bad bump on the back when I fell backwards after Tim shot me."

"Your face is killing me," joked Jack.

"And how are you?" she asked of Jack.

"I am a little weak due to the blood lost, and my shoulder is very sore. Now that I had my first decent meal, I'm feeling better."

Suddenly, Bailey was tired of standing on his hind legs, so he leaped up on the bed, turned around at the foot and carefully laid down beside Jack with his head close enough so Jack could rub his ears. He closed his eyes and went to sleep.

Jack sighed, "I think Bailey has a good idea. I think I need to take a nap for a while. Leave Bailey here, and you guys can go take a walk or something."

Thad leaned up and kissed him. "We'll just walk around the hospital floor a while to build up my stamina, and work out some of the soreness. I'll see you in a while."

T stepped out of the room and closed the door. He saw Jack's name taped on the door and got an idea. "He snatched a pen from a cart and piece of paper, and wrote in bold letters, "Do not enter, enema in process!" and taped it to the door as well.

Jesse laughed at him as they walked down to the elevator, but finding the waiting area, they decided to sit a spell. "How you doing?" she asked.

"I'm fine. I just need to make as many laps around this wing as I can, so I can loosen up a bit."

"How is Jack really doing?"

Thad noted the worry lines on her brow and smiled, "I am amazed. When I first saw him, I thought I was going to lose him. His face was pale and ashen in color, and nothing moved, not an eyelid, nostril, or the veins in his neck. I don't even think I saw his chest move, but when he opened that one eyelid, and blinked twice at me, I knew he would be okay."

"What did the doctor say?"

"Well they are afraid a bullet fragment might be left behind in the surgery, but nothing shows on the scans, and of course, they are afraid of infection."

"How long will he be here?"

"I guess until he feels like leaving. He has been great this afternoon. Janet brought some decent food, and he ate every bite of it. Now that you and Bailey are here, I think he feels not only safe, but also confident. I guess we'll know more in a few days."

Jesse smiled at him, "I'm here for the duration. You just tell me what you boys need and I'll do it."

Thad gave her a hug. "Thank you. Thank you very much. We both love you, and are thrilled that you came to see us. Come on, let's walk, and talk some more. Other than Jack, you're probably the only person I can talk to about Jack, and how much I love him."

"You're right—you can talk to me about anything, but especially Jack. He and I have been friends, close friends, for a long time. I wouldn't have made it without him—now I feel you sort of feel the same way. However, if we asked Jack, he would say he is the one that can't do without us. He would say love as friends or lovers is a circle which is why the wedding ring is a circle of never ending love from one to the other and back again." She suddenly laughed, "Whoops, I'm sorry. I'm getting mushy way too fast. Come on, let's take a stroll." They left the waiting area, and began walking laps along hospital corridor so T could build up his strength.

The nurse was taken aback when she saw Bailey on the bed, but she was a dog lover and gave him a quick pat, as he looked up at her with just one eye open while she checked on Jack and then left the room. The surgeon came after her and he, too, gave Bailey a pat, checked Jack's medical chart and left the room.

Jack slept longer than intended, so T put Jesse on the recliner, and he took the empty bed on the other side of Jack. It was a double room, but Janet arranged for it to be a private room for security purposes. Duke's men came and went with one man on guard outside his door at all times. Church groups still marched outside the hospital praying Thad and Jack would die from their wounds. However, inside things were peaceful as the three adults and a big dog slept soundly through the night in spite of the occasional checks by the nurses to see how Jack was doing.

On Thursday morning, T awoke with the sound of Jack heaving. Jesse was over at the hotel with Janet to get a shower, and Bailey smartly scampered off the bed and leaped onto the recliner. T quickly got a towel and hit the nurse button. Jack threw up everything he ate the night before. She helped to clean him up, picked up his chart, and looked at the monitors. All looked normal, but when she took his temperature, it was 102 degrees. She sighed, and said she was going to call the doctor.

The surgeon arrived in an hour, and after checking Jack thoroughly, he felt like he had an infection of some kind. He prescribed an antibiotic that the nurse injected in his IV port, plus Tylenol, and sleep medicine. At times Jack's skin became very hot, and then later he was freezing with chills. T felt helpless. Jack was barely awake most of the day. Jesse said he had caught the flu one time while staying with her, and acted the same way.

They took turns looking after him, but T wouldn't leave the room to go to the hotel. He showered in the bathroom, and Duke brought him more clothes he'd gathered from the motorcoach before a substitute driver took it to Homestead Florida. T knew he would have to leave Friday morning on the jet to the track, but he didn't want to leave Jack behind. He ran through his mind what would happen if he didn't race, and without hesitation, he didn't like that outcome. The entire season lost in the last race, and with his coming out, he could not let that happen. He had to race, and he had to win.

As the only out of the closet racecar driver, he felt like it was important he win the championship to show everyone he was as much of a man as they were. He knew the race would be hard as the stakes were as tough as they get. Anything could happen big or small, like a chance of a lost with just the drop of a lug nut on a pit stop. Or a busted radiator, a blown engine, a cut tire, or perhaps pushed hard into a wall on purpose, but he felt in his heart he could win and win he vowed to do.

Jack's fever went a little higher that night, worrying the surgeon and his nurse a little, and Thad a lot. The surgeon contemplated more x-rays and scans, but decided to wait another twenty-four hours before signing off on the procedures. He also knew he might have to take Jack back to surgery, but he hoped the boy's fever would break.

About five the following morning, with Thad asleep in the recliner by his Jack's hospital bed, Jack suddenly awoke, "Thad? Thad?" he called in a hoarse whispery voice. T stirred. Jack called again. "Thad?"

T leaped to his feet, and then flinched at the pain in his side. "Jack. How are you?"

"Thirsty. How about you?"

T held a cup full of water so Jack could suck the straw. Jack drank every bit of the water before replying, "More water. I'm fine. Gee whiz, that was an awful fever. What day is it?"

"Friday early morning."

"You've got to leave soon, huh?"

Feeling guilty, Thad didn't reply, but slowly nodded his head.

"It's okay. I'll be fine now. You go on and win the race, and I'll watch it on television as usual."

"I don't want to leave you behind."

"I'll be fine. Take Janet with you to help with the appearance schedule. Jesse will take care of me here. Once they'll let me out of this place, I'll catch up with you."

"Are you sure?"

"I'm fine—just sore. You didn't sit on my head last night did you?"

Thad smiled, "I think you're delirious from the fever." He felt Jack's face, "I don't think the fever is there." He pressed the nurse call button on the side of the bed. When she came in he asked, "Would you mind checking him for fever? I think the fever broke."

They waited in silence until she said, "You're right, he's back to normal."

"Thank God," stated T, "at least we hope he is back to normal."

Jack laughed and replied quickly, "If I was normal," he stopped to see if the nurse was listening and she was, "I wouldn't be hanging out with a racecar driver that has drivers and cars trying to do him in at two hundred miles an hour, and an idiot shooting at him!"

Thad started laughing and couldn't stop. It was a laugh of relief and joy because he felt Jack was going to be fine.

T said goodbye to Jack as Jesse fed him some of those pitiful grits. "I hope you bring me back a hamburger after you win," said Jack.

"I hope you get well enough to eat a steak with me to celebrate," replied Thad with a grin.

They kissed several times, then T played with Bailey, gave Jesse a hug, one more kiss for Jack, and they left. Duke took Thad up to the roof to board a helicopter. He left two of his men guarding Jack while Janet, Thad, and Duke flew to the airport. Al was waiting for him. A few hours later, he was at the Homestead track. The motorcoach had arrived the night before—stocked with food and ready for him. Clean race uniforms hung in his closet.

T put on his favorite rib brace or lifejacket, as they called it, to protect his chest and new wound, suited up and went through qualifying and ended up starting in the top ten. Not as good as he wished, but in the top ten would do. Janet led him through the day schedule and by nightfall, he did a masterful job at the press conference announcing the auctions, and the purpose behind them. By nine o'clock, he was on the phone with Jack for a while, and then fell asleep quickly though alone in the bed.

Jack improved quicker than he thought he would, and managed to get out of bed Friday night, take a much overdue pee, and walked to the bathroom on his own. Saturday morning they removed the IV, and he began the first of his laps around the ward with Bailey as his guide dog. By that afternoon, he took Bailey up to the children's ward and together, they went from bed to bed letting the children rub his ears. Bailey was excellent with every child. They met one boy with a silent sullen look on his face. The nurse said he had cancer and had started chemo. When he didn't immediately rub Bailey's ears, Bailey just up and licked the boy's face with a long hot tongue. The boy giggled so Bailey did it again. Soon the boy was smiling, and Bailey got his ears rubbed.

At the track T made it through the day of practicing, speeches, appearances, and ate dinner in the coach with Janet, talked with Jack on the phone, and went to bed early. He was exhausted, but he told everyone he was just fine.

Jack sensed Thad was down, so after hanging up, he used his cell phone to call Al, and make a personal request. He called Jesse at the hotel and after his second call, it took him a while to fall asleep, but he finally did, with Bailey resting against his leg. It had been a long week since the last race, a lot had happened to them, but they were still breathing, and still in love with each other. It brought a smile to his face as he drifted off.

TWENTY-FIVE

Thad woke up after dreaming of meeting Jack, and the sex they later had that night on the motorcoach. His groin ached for him. He pulled the pillow tight to his chest, and wished it still smelled like Jack. He opened his eyes and sighed. He rolled out of bed, took a leak, and got in the shower. He picked at his breakfast as Janet knocked on the door. He got up, let her in, and gave her a hug.

"How's the wounded racecar driver?"

He grimaced as he sat back down in the booth. "It only hurts when I move, or when I sit still for a while." He winked at her.

She laughed, "I guess that doesn't leave much peace, huh? Are you ready for the press conference?"

"I will be. Let me brush my teeth, comb my hair and change clothes." He got up slowly, and she watched him as he moved gingerly down the hall.

Janet fired up the laptop and checked the schedule. She was worried about the press conference because she knew the subject T was going to talk about. Jack arranged for twenty kids from a gay youth home to visit the track as T's guests.

Janet drove the cart with four security men tailing them, and tried not to hit any bumps as T held on tightly to keep from getting sloshed around, but when she parked the cart at the back entrance of Media Building, T spotted the teenagers waiting for him. Suddenly, he came to life. She grabbed the plastic bag on the back seat and quickly stepped out to keep up with him.

T shook the children's hands, while Janet gave them a TNT shirt and hat from her big bag. They were all smiling and excited about meeting Thad. After he finished meeting the last one he turned to them, "Kids, huddle up with me a moment. I want to ask you something." He waited for them to pull in close. "Inside this building is about a hundred reporters and cameramen from all over the world. I asked them to come so I could introduce you to them, and ask the world to consider helping gay kids just like you. Would you be kind enough to join me inside and let me show you off to this group?"

The kids immediately said yes as he knew they would, but he wanted to be sure they didn't mind being on television, or maybe having their picture in the paper. Janet led them inside and looked up to see Drew and Duke at the back of the room wondering what T was up to this time.

"Ladies and gentlemen," began T as he took the stage but before he could continue, the press corps assembled stood giving him a standing ovation. The applause continued for several minutes. It really touched Thad. He motioned for them to please sit down and finally they did. He sighed hard, and took a good breath. "I want to thank you for coming on this early Sunday morning. You can ask me questions after I make a statement if you like. First of all, I am doing much better, and I'm ready to race. As a matter of fact, I'm going to win the race and the championship today."

The kids clapped and cheered, and reporters were wondering who they were. After they quieted down, T continued, "These fine kids behind me are my guests today. They are from a gay youth home. Their facility was created because all of their parents kicked them out of their house when they found out their children were gay. Many were forced to roam the streets and beg for money. They weren't old enough to get a real job, and no money to go to school. Some ate from dumpsters behind a restaurant in the middle of the night. Others were beaten by street punks and spit on by church groups. Schools refused to accept them even if they did find a place to live. No one wants a gay child, they said.

"Thankfully, the Albertson Home was financed by two gay men who own a clothing store. Each year they have a charity auction to help with expenses, but there is never enough money to accept every gay child, so there are many gay kids still roaming the streets waiting on their chance to stay at the Albertson Home.

"Last week my best friend used his body to stop a second bullet from finishing me off. He had a rough week, but he is going to make it just fine. In honor of his love and devotion, today I'm going to donate one million dollars to the Albertson Home. I challenge my sponsors, my team, and my fans, and all Americans everywhere to support other worthy groups like this one."

He turned to the kids and then back to the reporters, "Friends, these are the kids of the Albertson Home." The audience politely clapped. T once again went down the row, but this time he gave each child a big hug.

When he returned to the podium he rolled his eyes, smiled at the reporters, and said, "I don't suppose any of you have a question."

They laughed, and one reporter up front asked, "How are you really feeling? Are you going to be able to drive four hundred laps?"

"Is it that far?" teased T. "Well, I think I have come up with a system to get me through the day. To conserve energy I am just going to step on the gas, and only make left turns all day."

The group laughed again. Another asked, "Do you think you were shot because you are gay?"

Jack had warned him they would ask. "Yes, I am afraid I was. You know people have been marching outside my home for weeks begging God to kill me, and then after I was shot, they marched outside the hospital hoping me and Jack would die. Well, I am here to disappoint them. The man that tried to blackmail me because I was a gay man in the closet shot both of us. Now that I'm out—he could no longer attempt blackmail. I guess that pissed him off, and so he came after me. I was lucky, but many gay folks are the targets of hate crimes every day. Some are killed with baseball bats. Many are injured severely, so I was lucky indeed."

The press conference broke up after a few more questions. Drew found T sitting in the golf cart waiting on Janet as she passed out press releases about the Albertson Home.

"How you feeling?" Drew drove his wheelchair beside him and squeezed the brake handle.

"I'm good. I'll be fine. Listen, I want to have a team meeting before the race. Is that okay with you?"

Drew looked at him out the corner of his eye. "What for?"

"I think we can win if everyone on the team gives a hundred percent today. Don't you?"

"Okay. What time?"

"How about now, and then I'll go to the coach, and rest until driver introductions."

Drew left with Duke trailing him in the other cart while Janet drove T to the garage. The security men were right behind them and followed T everywhere he went. Drew gathered the race team members in a circle. T stepped in the circle and leaned back against his car. His side was throbbing. Slowly, he turned looking each man and woman in the eye and smiling.

"I asked Drew if I could speak to you before the race. I know when you signed on this year you didn't expect to be crewing for a gay driver. I bet you didn't think we would be this close to winning either. I can promise you this today—if you'll give me a hundred percent one last time, we can win this race, but that's not good enough for me.

"I want to ask you to sign up right now for next year. I know crew negotiations don't usually start for another week, but if Drew doesn't mind, I'm inviting every one of you back for another great year of winning races. If you'll stick with me, then I want you on my team. If you'll agree to sign up right now, I promise you we will win the race today and the championship. I can't do it without you. I know you all were probably brought up to hate gay people. I understand that. However, you're human and humans can change, and the world can change, but it changes one person at a time.

"Okay, it is time for you to decide if you're a winner or not. I want everyone to back up to the wall over there." They all moved as directed. T waited for the murmuring and whispers to quiet down. T backed away from the group and then said. "Okay, if you're willing to sign up for next year right now, ready to win today's race, and this crazy championship, then you only have to join me over here."

Drew's palms began sweating. If no one moved forward, he would lose the championship before the drop of the green flag. He wished he could have stopped T, but he knew stopping Thad was something no one could do. Drew gave each one of his men a long look, but no one was looking at him. They were all staring at Thad as if in shock. Charley suddenly pushed his way from the back of the group, shook T's hand, and stood beside him. A tire changer was next, then the jack man, and so on until the entire team made it across the garage. T shook each hand firmly. Drew sighed heavily.

Thad laughed and smiled broadly. "Thank you. Thank you very much. Do you feel like going out there and winning a championship?"

They cheered loudly before Charley put them back to work. T walked over to Drew and smiled.

Drew grinned, "You are one risky racecar driver. I thought you wanted to discuss something with me."

Thad smiled, "That's what I was going to discuss, but you know me, I just got on a roll and kept on going. I could only win if everyone is on the same page, and they get over the gay thing. I will leave their new raises up to you."

Drew frowned quickly. "Raises?"

T gave him a playful bump to his shoulder, and then climbed in the cart with Janet. "Home please. I'm pooped."

"Yes sir," she replied with a grin.

As they crossed from the garage area, they passed by the long line of the team haulers where many of team members were hanging out before the race. Off to her left Janet heard an unknown voice call Thad a faggot, but T was so exhausted he just kept his eyes straight ahead, and paid no attention to anyone. Janet pulled the golf cart to the door of his motorcoach and slowed to a stop. She gave a smile to the guards sitting in the shade of the awning.

"You go on in and get something to eat, and drink plenty of liquids, and I'll be back in a while," said Janet.

"Thanks," replied T as he opened the coach door and immediately ran into the lapping tongue of Bailey, who seemed to actually be smiling at the sight of Thad, while rapidly thumping his tail gleefully back and forth.

"Bailey? Hey, boy. How did you get here?"

Jesse reached down and pulled Bailey back, so T could come into his coach. "Al flew us in. We thought you might need a few extra cheerleaders today. I hope you don't mind. How are you?"

Thad gave her a big hug and kissed her on the cheek, "It's fans. Football has cheerleaders, but you're right, I do need you today. I need all the cheerleaders and fans I can get, and of course, I don't mind. I'm thrilled to see you."

T broke the embrace in time to see Jack slowly walking down the hall. "Oh my gosh—you're here! How are you?" T took a few quick steps, and gingerly hugged Jack, pulled back and looked into his face, smiled, and began kissing his face. "You're supposed to be in the hospital."

"I'm fine. I think getting out of the hospital did me some good. I was just taking a nap when I heard your voice. It is so good to see you."

"I'm overjoyed at the sight of you, Jesse, and old Bailey."
Emotionally spent, T led Jack to the couch, and they all sat down. Bailey went
over to Jack. He climbed on the four thousand dollar leather sofa, stretched
down beside him, put his soft head in Jack's lap, and closed his eyes. Jack
rubbed his ears, "Good boy."

T protested, "Hey, I could use some of that attention. Do I have to
wag my tail to get it?"

Jack laughed, leaned over, and kissed him. "There's a joke there, but
I'll let pass for now, as you need to rest before the race."

Thad laughed, "I need to eat something, and then rest. Let's see what
kind of food we have on board. Jesse, are you hungry?"

She replied, "You stay on the couch with Jack, and I'll make lunch. I
found tons of food in the refrigerator."

"Thank you. Thank you very much for coming, and bringing Jack
and Bailey with you."

Thad slept for more than ninety minutes, a long nap for him, and did
something he had never done—he missed several appearances at the
hospitality tents, but Drew covered for him, explaining he was recovering
from his hospital stay, and he would welcome them next time.

Jack sat on the bed while T dressed. He grimaced, as he pulled on his
fire suit, and once again slipped on the chest brace to hold his ribs and his new
bandage in place. Jack checked his bandage, and pronounced it clean. Jack's
left arm was still in the sling, but he managed. T pulled on his uniform, his
boots, and then zipped up the front.

"This is going to be a long day. I'll be glad when it is over," stated T.

"Me, too. I have never been to a championship. I can't wait to see
you with your trophy," added Jack optimistically.

T smiled, "Oh yeah, I promised everyone I would win the race and
the championship, didn't I. Piece of cake, right?"

"Just take one lap at a time, and if the pain is too great then fake a
small crash and end the thing."

T looked over at him on the bed, and frowned. "No, can't do that.
There are too many folks counting on me. You just relax here in the coach,
and I'll be back in a few hours." He came over, and kissed Jack several times.
"I love you. I love you very much."

Jack grinned, as he kissed him back and said, "If you win, I think I
can have sex tonight."

T laughed, "Boy, what a sight that would be. I am wounded on the
right, and you're wounded on the left. It would be pitiful."

Jack faked an astonished grin, "Yeah, but the vital parts are still
working!"

They laughed together. T heard the coach door open. "That'll be
Duke. It's time for me to go."

Jack got up and together they came down the aisle holding hands as if saying goodbye before a long trip. T saw Janet. "Hey girl, are you ready for a win?"

She smiled, "Of course I am. If you don't mind, I brought a visitor to cheer you on."

She stepped aside, and behind her was little Sammy with a TNT hat on his small head, his eyes were shinning, and he had a huge smile on his face.

"Sammy! Oh I'm so glad to see you." T sat down on the couch, and beckoned Sammy to him. He gave the boy a big hug, and tickled him gently. "How are you?"

"I'm fine, but I heard you were sick, so how are you?"

"I'm doing well, and I'm even better now that you are here." T quickly introduced Sammy to Jesse, and instantly Sammy loved Bailey and his big swinging blond tail.

"How did you get here?"

"Your boss called me. His name is Drew. He flew to Cincinnati, and gave me a ride in his electric wheelchair. He asked me I had ever flown on a plane, and would I like to see you race. Of course, I said yes, but we had to wait for my mom to get there, but after a little pleading, and a final okay from my doctor, Drew took me to the airport, and we got on his private jet. Man was it cool!"

Sammy's audience laughed at his child-like explanation of the experience. Sammy continued, "I brought you something." He had an envelope in his hand, and gave it to T.

"Why thank you," began T as he opened the envelope and removed a picture of T and Sammy at the hospital. "Oh my, this is a great picture. Thank you, I love it. I think I'll put it on the dash of my car, so I can see it during the race. Would that be okay?"

"Sure, do I get to see your car?" he asked gleefully.

"Of course—let's go."

T stood up, gave Jesse another hug, Bailey a rub of the ears, and then a long hug with Jack before a final kiss. He then surprised Janet with a hug and kiss, too. They left the coach with Janet driving the golf cart, and Sammy sitting in T's lap on his good side. Duke and his security boys followed closely. Duke began feeling like he was guarding the President, as he couldn't help but scan everyone they came in contact with, constantly on the lookout for weapons.

Janet drove them to the back of the stage to get Thad ready for driver introductions. Janet said, "Sammy and I will wait for you at the truck exit to get you to the pits."

"I think I'll take Sammy with me, if that is okay with you."

She laughed, "Of course it is."

Many of the drivers were waiting in line for their turn on the stage. T introduces Sammy to the drivers that were friendly to him, and then deliberately introduced him to some of the drivers he knew hated him. These guys never smiled at Thad, but they warmed up immediately to Sammy.

T was the second to last to be introduced, since he was second in points. Because this was the final race of the year, and the race winner could easily win the championship as well, a television reporter waited on stage to interview him live after the stage announcer introduced him. The fans in the stands could see and hear this last minute interview as well.

T led Sammy by the hand as they went through the curtain onto the stage. Jack moved to the recliner in the coach, and turned on the large LCD screen in time to see the interview. T noted the fans against him were not quite a vocal as usual. He hoped that was a good sign.

The television reporter walked across the stage to him with a microphone in his hand. "Thad, welcome to Homestead, and how are feeling?"

"I got out of the hospital earlier in the week, and I'm still pretty sore, but I'm ready to go."

"Do you think you can win today?"

"I hope so. How many laps is it?"

The reporter laughed, "Oh just a few hundred. Who is your little friend?"

The camera zoomed back as T knelt down beside Sammy. "This is Sammy. He has cancer, and this is the boy that started me on my journey to help as many kids in the world as I can. He escaped his hospital room with the help of my boss, so he could come down here and watch me win."

The fans fell silent as Sammy's face was beamed to the large projection screens around the track.

The reporter asked, "So you're going to win?"

"I have to. I promised my crew, my boss, and the kids from the Albertson Home, my partner Jack, and Sammy. I can't let them down. I'll win the race and the championship."

"Well, good luck to you today."

With the interview over, T and Sammy climbed into the back of a red pickup truck to begin the slow drive around the track, so they could wave to the fans. T waved left handed to protect his right side. After the ride, Janet picked them up in the golf cart and drove them to the pits.

T introduced Sammy to his crew. They each gave him a big high five with the open palm of their hands. T showed Sammy his car. Sammy wanted to get inside, so T lifted him and set him inside.

Drew rolled up behind them in his wheelchair, "Which one of you is driving today?"

T turned and smiled, "I am, and thank you for bringing Sammy to the track."

296

"You're welcome. It is the least I could do for the driver that is going to bring me the championship trophy today."

T laughed, "You're right about that. Look at this." He handed Drew the picture of Sammy and him in the hospital. "I'm going to put this on my dashboard. I will win for everyone, but especially for Sammy."

"Time to climb aboard," said Drew. To Sammy he beckoned, "Come Sammy. How would like you to watch the race alongside the crew chief and the boss?"

Sammy smiled. He gave T a big hug, and then climbed into Drew's lap. They both waved as they turned, and rolled over to the pit box. Janet was waiting for him, helped put on his headset, and even sunglasses to protect his eyes from the pit dust.

With great anticipation and some expectation, the race finally began with T in tenth place. Almost every lap he caught a glimpse of Sammy's picture and smiled, but usually he was too occupied with moving through the field to think at all. The television video showed him on the move. He had taken over ninth, then eighth, and finally seventh after just twelve laps.

Jack laughed as Jesse came off the couch and yelled, "Go T! Go!" Bailey barked.

"I didn't know you were such a rapid race fan," stated Jack.

Jesse smiled, "How can you not be when someone you care about is in the race?"

"I tend to keep it all inside and nervously watch him make every lap, and thankful when he safely crosses the finish line. When they throw a caution, I quickly hold my breath until I see T's car and find it safe. Let's face it, when it comes to racing, I'm a race track bitch!"

Jesse laughed as T moved into sixth. "Go Thad!"

Twenty minutes later, Thad was in fourth and trying to get in front of the car in third. He came around the second turn with a fake to the outside and a dive to low inside putting his right fender alongside the driver. He knew he now had him, and would take the position by the fourth turn.

Suddenly, T felt a tire give way. "Blown right front!" he yelled into his radio. "I'm coming in get ready!"

Charley replied, "Okay, slow down. We don't want it to rip the sheet metal off."

"Roger," replied T solemnly, as he put on the brakes on the back stretch, and moved down low on the track towards the yellow pit entrance line. He heard it almost as quick as he felt it. The tire abruptly blew, he had to fight to hold on the steering wheel, and immediately felt the pain in his right side, as he struggled to hold the car on the track.

"Oh no," stated Jack quietly, as the camera zoomed in on the blown tire.

T turned towards pit row, and the turn caused the entire airless tire to slip off the rim making steering even more difficult as sparks flew into the air from the hot rim scraping along on the asphalt. The car became unwieldy. T almost veered out on the track, but he managed to pull it to the left just missing the outer wall. Sparks flew along the right side of the car for twenty yards.

T heard Charley call for four tires and gas from the pit crew. He complained, "Four tires?"

"Yes, we're going to come out almost last in the field for a green pit stop, so we're going to use some pit strategy. Don't worry, with fresh tries you should fly through the field. We will get this lap back."

Charley yelled into his microphone to the pit crew, "Grab the lift bar!" Just as Thad skidded to a halt in front of the pit box, one of the over the wall crew placed the bar under the car body on the rim side. With the help of several of the crew members, they managed to lift the car just enough for the jack man to slide the jack under, and lift up the car high enough to get the right rear tire off the asphalt, and new tires on front and back.

It only took his crew thirteen and half seconds to get his tires changed and two buckets of gas. When the jack man dropped the car, T sped out while being careful not to speed and receive a penalty. He was now in forty-third place or last. He once again began to move up through the field. It took a hundred laps, two pit stops, until he could finally see the front of the field, though he was currently in twelfth place.

"What lap is it?"

Charley pushed his red microphone button on the side of his headset, "Two hundred twenty-three."

"I should have asked how many more," replied T.

Charley replied, "A hundred and seventy-seven. Are you all right?"

"Yep, I'm fine, just tired. Out"

Charley's brow wrinkled with worry, as he glanced over at Drew who gave him the 'I heard it too' nod. They were afraid his injury and stay in the hospital had diminished his stamina.

At lap two hundred seventy-two, a caution went out, and all the leaders were pitting. T fell in line automatically, but his mind put him in a daze, as he crossed the pit lane entrance.

Boom! He felt the bump from behind by the 50 car. Before he could put his foot on the brake, he tapped the car in front of him. "What the hell?"

His radio crackled, "Penalty on Thad's car, the number 69 for speeding."

Charley cursed. "Damn, he was bumped from behind for crying out loud!"

The crew changed the tires, and filled the gas tank before T sped out. Charley got down from the pit box, found a racing official, and began protesting the speeding call, but it didn't do him any good. After the pit cleared out and the cars were in line to restart the race, T was summoned to his pit.

He cursed as he pulled down pit row while carefully watching his tachometer to keep from speeding again. The official stood in front of his car as the race began. They held him for one lap that now made T two laps down.

"Dang!" exclaimed Charley. "Okay, T, we'll have to take advantage of the lucky dog rule. Get to..." he paused while looking at his computer printouts, "twenty-fifth place, or the number 39 car. Once you are in the right spot, just stay there until we get a caution. That will get us a lap back."

"Roger, will do."

T worked quickly up through the lapped cars with his newer tires. Twenty-eight laps later, he was in the lucky dog spot, and then waited for thirty more laps before the 73 car blew an engine resulting in a caution.

"Good job, we're now just one lap down. Thad, I think we saved some fuel by keeping you in the same spot for thirty laps. If the leaders pit, I want you to stay out putting you back on the lead lap."

T asked, "Do we have enough fuel?"

"I think we have enough for twenty laps or so. If we reach that point, we may have to pit for splash and dash of gas so we can stay on the lead lap. It's a gamble, but we have hundred and eighteen laps to go, so time to start working on winning this race. Save as much fuel as you can."

A few other desperate souls stayed out as well, and the race restarted with T in fourth place. Lap by lap ticked by as Charley began chewing harshly on the head of his pencil. Drew knew it was a good call, but he worried if it would pay off. At ninety-eight laps to go, and T still in fourth place, the fuel would soon run out.

In the coach, Jack and Jesse watched and listened as the announcers showed video of the previous leaders working their way through the field. The 53 car had been the leader, and was pushing his car back to the front as fast he could. Thad was stuck behind the 42 car that continued to block every move he tried. Two laps later, his patience ran out. He dove low on the 42 car, giving the 42 car 's left rear bumper just a slight tap, but he had done it at the wrong time, as they had just begun entering turn three. The 42 car got loose as the 53 car drove by him. The 42 went up the track and bumped into the 75 car sending them both in to spins before slamming into the wall.

"Caution is out!" yelled a gleeful Charley.

"Yahoo! I thought I was going to have to pedal this car in," said T.

A large part of the field pitted this time. "Can we go the rest of the race, or do we need one more stop."

"No we can't. We'll need either a full pit stop or splash of gas. We'll be prepared for either. You're in fourth, and on the lead lap. Take your time and let's get to the front."

"What's the point standing?"

"You're in third if the race stopped right now."

"Okay," replied T somberly.

Drew broke in on the radio something he rarely did as the owner, "You can do it T!"

T smiled, as he glanced down at Sammy's picture, "Thanks, I know I can, too."

After a few caution laps with the big guns still behind him, T hit the gas pedal as the green flag dropped. He had eighty-nine laps to go. He used twenty of them to get to first place. Jack and Jesse cheered him while Bailey barked once again. On the pit box Janet, Sammy, and Drew cheered him on as well.

The 43 car was three cars back, but immediately followed by both 50 and 90 cars, teams Thad experienced trouble with before, including the 50 car t-boning him in an earlier race cracking several of his ribs.

"Gary? Keep me posted on the 43, 50, and 90 cars. That's where the trouble will come from," stated T on the radio.

"Roger will do. The 43 car will take third on the next lap."

"Stretch it out," urged Charley. "Get as far ahead as you can while they are still slowed down in traffic."

T agreed and slowly gained a half car length with each lap. It took ten laps for the 43 to get to second and start working on cutting T's lead. The 50 and 90 car took third and fourth with thirty-four laps to go when a caution went out for a blown engine on the 66 car.

"What do you want to do?" asked Charley.

T thought for a second, "Well, we don't have a lot of choices. The caution tore away my lead. We know we have to get some gas so I can't stay out. There may be a few that do stay out, but that would make moving up through the entire field pretty tough if we took four tires. Let's take two right side tires, and splash of gas. How far back will that put us?"

"Probably tenth," replied Charley. "Can you make it up in thirty laps?"

"Yep," replied the unwavering and strong-minded Thad.

Charley looked over at Drew for sympathy, approval, or both. Drew smiled. "Go for it!"

"Okay, pit boys. I want the fastest time of the year. Give T two right side tires and one bucket of gas. Let's do it. We can win this thing right now!"

His men ran to the right side of his car, old tires off, new tires on, gas in and down. T sped off but being careful not to speed on pit row. He moved up and onto the track.

"What spot?"

Charley sighed, "Eleventh, but seven of the cars in front of you didn't pit because they are out of pit sequence, but they have fifty or more laps on their tires. The 43, 50, and 90 are in first, second and third, but Gary reports they didn't take tires just gas."

"So with a bit of patience, I should be able to get by the seven cars on old tires, and then do battle with the final three cars that took only gas, but have fresher tires. This is a piece of cake. How many laps to go?"

"Thirty."

"Got it," he replied and paused. "Out." Just as Charley started to sit back down T came back on the radio. "Jack? I know you're listening. I'm going to win this race!"

The pit crew cheered. Charley stood back up laughing and cheering. Janet laughed, and Drew just shook his head with admiration.

"How'd he know you can hear him?" asked Jesse from the couch in the motorcoach.

"I always have his radio on low, so I can understand what the heck is going on when the television announcers have the cameras and attention on other cars. He's going to win!"

On top the pit box Sammy stood up in his chair as he heard all the talk on the radio. He let out a big yell for such a little guy that Charley, Janet and Drew heard him even though they had their headsets on. "Go Thad!" he yelled again.

The green flag dropped. They had thirty laps to go. T wasted no time by passing the tenth place car on the backstretch. At twenty-seven to go, he faked high, went hard low, and took ninth place. Eighth place was harder, but he got pass with twenty-three laps to go.

T got a bit lucky when the car ahead of him ran out of fuel and dropped low off the track avoiding a caution. At lap twenty, he passed the sixth place car. Two more laps, and he went very high and around the next car to fifth place. Three laps later, he took fourth with seventeen to go when suddenly a yellow caution flag went out for a blown tire putting a car near the rear of the field into the wall. This event created a tighter field for the restart. If there had been ten laps to go they would have restarted in single file with T in fourth, but with seventeen to go the cars lined up in double file, putting him on the outside of the second row and closer to the front.

It took the track crews a long fifteen minutes to clean up the crash scene while the field continued circling the track behind the pace car. With thirteen laps to go, and the fans standing with great anticipation for a tight finish, the green flag finally flew. Gary began calling everything he saw the leaders do over the radio, but T had no time to respond. He knew he had at least two enemies up front with him—one on the outside, and one on the left. He didn't want to wait until the cars stretched into a single file. He moved low pushing the 90 car lower than he wanted to go. The 90 driver called to the 50 driver to watch out as T soared up the track faking to the high outside. T jerked the wheel back to the left, as if preparing to go back down the track, and then abruptly, he pulled to the right and got his right front bumper beneath the 50 car.

T thought he had him beat when the 90 car recovered enough, and slid up the track bumping T's left rear. Thad's front right bumped the 50 car accidentally, but the 50 car didn't see it that way. He jerked the wheel down squeezing on T, as the 90 car squeezed up the track, making Thad feel like he was the baloney in a baloney sandwich.

The crowd leaped to their feet assuming a huge wreck was about to ensue. There were ten laps to go. T was afraid he was going to cut a tire if he stayed between 90 and 50 cars, He had no choice but to hang on. The three cars continued banging and bumping for a full lap. T knew he had to get out of there quickly if he was going to catch the 43 car.

He did the opposite of what they expected by tapping the brakes while briefly coming off the gas pedal. The 90 and 50 instantly began flying by him wrongly assuming he had a flat tire. T hit the gas and jerked the wheel just slightly to the right, bumping the 50 car causing him to get very loose. The driver of the car was good, and saved his car from the wall, but he lost two positions. T fell in line behind the 90 car, and then took two laps to catch his bumper, and wasted no time.

The 90 went high and low while continually blocking T's moves.

The spotter barked on the radio, "The 43 is pulling away."

T knew he could no longer do battle with the 90. He came down hard in the fourth turn, bumped the 90, who also became loose, and fell in line behind T, as Thad took over second place.

The entire pit crew let out a huge sigh of relief, and watched with great anticipation as T went after the 43 car that was two full car lengths ahead, and only six laps to go. He pushed his car hard, and finally reached his bumper with three to go, when he heard Gary on the radio.

"Look out. The 90 and the 50 car are about to catch you."

"Damn!" yelled Charley. "It's time to go boy. You can do it!"

T glanced up at his rearview mirror and saw the 90 car coming up fast. He pushed hard on the pedal, went high, and then low on the 43. With newer tires on the right side, he managed to cut low quickly, and get below him. It took two laps for him to get the nose of his car pass the 43 car, and a lap later, he broke into the lead and in the clear, but a glance to his dash gauges almost stopped his heart, as he noted his water temperature needle pegged hard to the right. He knew his engine could blow a rod and fail at any moment. He had no choice but to ride it out, and hope for the best.

The white flag came out as T drove over the finish line as fast as he could. They had just one lap to go. The 90 car suddenly pulled low and got pass the 43 car with ease and only a car length behind T.

Gary broke in on the radio from the spotter's roost, "His lap time is a half second faster than yours. You're going to have to block him."

T had no time to respond, but he heard Gary's report. He glanced up to see the 90 car coming as he came into the next turn.

By the second turn, he was on T's bumper. The fans were cheering. Everyone in T's pit was yelling. The announcers were going crazy. The statisticians reported if T wins the race, he wins the championship. They had a half a lap to go when the 90 car made his move to the inside. T couldn't block him. They entered turn three with the 90 car alongside him. He slid up the track and gave T a slight bump.

T's heart nearly leaped out of his chest, but he held the steering wheel as tight as possible, and reacted by returning the bump, and pulling down hard into the 90 car. It was the 90 car's turn to hang on. He moved back up and bumped T again, as they came into turn four. T fought back with a downward move, and then surprisingly he faked high as if out of control. The 90 car driver grinned feeling the victory was his, but Thad, counting on his new right side tires to grip, suddenly yanked the wheel down hard as they straightened up on the front stretch heading for the finish line at hundred and eighty miles an hour. He hit the 90 car with fifty yards to go pushing the 90 car harshly down below the yellow line, and at angle to the finish line allowing T's car to be slightly ahead. T never let up on the 90 car staying tightly in the 90's car right front side so he couldn't get loose.

The driver of the 90 car yanked his steering wheel hard back to the right, but the downward momentum was to T's advantage. T held on as tight as he could, and crossed the finished line at a forty-five degree angle with his front right corner beating the 90 car by inches. T had no time to celebrate as he began spinning, and Charley feared he would crash hard into the wall. The 90 car spun low into the grass and hit the lower wall.

The crowd watched as T's car went around in eight rapid continuous circles, with tires squealing and smoke bellowing until you could no longer see his car. The crowd fell silent, anticipating a huge impending crash, but suddenly, from out of the far side of the cloud of smoke, T's car broke into the clear. He quickly straightened the car, and slowed down, as he coasted through turn one and took in his first winner's breath.

The crowd cheered, the announcers sighed in relief, and T's team began jumping for joy. Sammy looked over at Drew, "Did we win?"

Drew laughed, "Yes, son. We won!"

In the motorcoach Jesse leaped to her feet, "He did it!"

Jack laughed, "He said he would. Oh my goodness—he's the champion!"

The cameras followed Thad as he went around the track doing a few burnouts, and then stopped at the finished line, took off his helmet, removed the Hans device, his safety straps, dropped his window netting, climbed out of the car, and stood on the window sill to wave his arms in the air triumphantly. The flagman tossed him the checkered flag. T caught it and waved it high over his head feeling no pain, as his adrenalin pumped hard through his veins. He dropped back down into his car, and drove to victory lane where his team waited anxiously for him.

The television announcer was waiting for him as well. Thad put on a TNT hat, took a deep breath, climbed out of the car, stood up on the window sill, and threw his hands high over his head while producing the biggest grin of his life. Janet held Sammy up so he could see as the champagne spewed in every direction like fire extinguishers. Overhead fireworks exploded in the air and millions of tiny pieces of confetti showered down like a paper blizzard. Sammy squealed with glee. Drew sat off to the side in his wheelchair waiting for the celebratory melee to subside.

Finally, the drenched announcer was able to talk to T. "That was some finish. Congratulations. You won the race and the championship. How does it feel?"

T laughed, as he wiped his face with a towel, "I don't think I feel anything. That was so exciting. I can't believe it is over. I had promised many folks I would win, and finally we did it. I couldn't have done it without my team, Charley, and Drew. I am so lucky. I want to thank my sponsors..." he began rattling off the list of sponsors while Drew moved his wheelchair forward stopping a few feet away from Thad. His face beamed with such pride and a great feeling of accomplishment. He couldn't believe they had won, when just a week ago his favorite driver had been shot. His eyes watered, as he waited patiently for the interview to conclude, but T stopped talking when he saw him, and immediately embraced him. He pulled off Drew's hat and kissed his baldhead. Drew blushed, and together they laughed and hugged again.

T laughed, "I told you I would win you another championship, and we did."

Drew grinned, "I never doubted you for a minute. Way to go, Thad. Way to go!"

T turned back to the announcer as he said, "Take us through that final lap as we watch it on the monitor."

T looked down at the small monitor. "I knew he was coming. He drove hard, and he is a good driver. The 90 car fought me, and I just made a slight fake up, and then down hard and hung on. Not much to it. I just had to hang on until I crossed the finish line."

Over the back of the monitor T suddenly looked up and his eyes locked on to the person standing ten feet behind it. He sighed hard with a lump forming in his throat. He could no longer speak. Tears filled his eyes, but they were tears of joy. He winked at Jack and smiled. Sammy stood in front of Jack smiling from ear to ear. T waved at him, and yelled for Sammy to come to him. T picked Sammy up and set him on his shoulders. T then waved at Jack to come over, too. He spread his arms, and Jack walked to him. Not wanting to hurt Jack's shoulder, T carefully gave him a hug with Sammy laughing while still sitting on Thad's shoulders. The camera swung around to catch the embrace. Out of one eye, T saw the camera, pulled back from the embrace, and planted a huge kiss on Jack's lips. The whole world saw the two men kiss live on television once again. Then the team sprayed them with more champagne. Sammy got wet, but he loved it. Together, they marched over to the stage for the presentation.

The General Manager of the track, along with the race sponsor, presented him his race-winning trophy. The crowd cheered. The President of NARC, along with the series big corporate sponsor, made the presentation of the gigantic championship trophy. T made sure that Jack was at his side, and Sammy still riding his shoulders as the cameras flashed. There would be two pictures on the front of newspapers all around the country in the morning, featuring the infamous and iniquitous kiss, and the team with the race and championships trophies along with T, Jack, and Sammy on one side, and Drew, Charley and Janet on the other.

Once the official pictures were completed, the sponsor shots began with his crew around him, as they put on a brand hat for each sponsor and smiled for the camera. It took about forty minutes to do all of them. Once done, they left the stage, and Janet drove them to the media center. He did interviews with media representatives from all the around the world for the next two hours. Jack and Sammy went back to the motorcoach to rest.

It was late by the time T arrived exhausted. He saw Sammy asleep on the couch, sleeping soundly under the blanket Jack gently put over him. Thad smiled at the sleeping boy, feeling happy he could experience the race and the win. They left Sammy warm and comfortable, while they moved to the bedroom. Jack helped him out of racing suit with his one good hand, watched after him as he showeredwhile noting the new scar from the bullet wound, and then kissed him as he toweled off. T dressed and came up front to say goodbye to Sammy. He hated to wake him, but Janet said they had to catch their flight.

T knelt down beside the sofa. "Hey, Sammy. Are you awake? Did you have a good time?"

Sammy yawned and smiled, "I had the best time of my life. Thank you."

"Oh, I have to thank you. With your picture on my dash, I knew I would win. You gave me the confidence to push the car to victory."

Sammy gave him a big hug, and T felt sad to see him go, but laughed as Sammy became excited to be flying home with Drew in his jet. T promised to call him. Janet said her goodbyes as well, as she had much work to do on preparing press releases for the new champion. She took Sammy with her to the helicopter to shuffle over to the airport to fly out with Drew.

After they left, T said, "I'm hungry. Do we have anything left to eat?"

Jesse said, "Sit at the table, and I'll heat everything up for you. You must be starved."

T sat at the table holding Jack's hand as they waited. Jack spoke first, "Did you ever doubt you would win?"

"Yes, of course, but only during the first 399 laps."

"I felt you could win, too, but I was more afraid as to what the other forty-two drivers might do."

"I know, but you can't think of what someone might deliberately do, you only have time to figure out how to get around the next car."

Jack smiled, "Champion—that's impressive."

"Two time champion," grinned T. "Have you started thinking about how we can use it to do some good in the world?"

Jack laughed, "I'm still in shock, but yeah, the appearances will be bigger, and the money will pour in."

"I'm ready for that, but not for a while. We have a cruise to go on, then awards in New York, and a big vacation in Pacific and then on to Africa."

"Thank goodness. I have had enough stress for a while. Let's eat."

Jesse brought the food to the table, and the three of them ate while chattering away. T would toss a bit of food to Bailey from time to time, and when he forgot, old Bailey would bark to get his attention.

"You're spoiling him," protested a grinning Jesse.

"Yeah, I know, but he's worth it!"

After they finished their dinner, Jack punched away at the keyboard on his laptop, and pulled up the pictures of the race on the NARC racing league website. He stared at the posed picture of Thad with Sammy on his shoulder, Jack at his side, both the race and championship trophies in the front, along with Charley, Drew, Janet, and the rest of the team, and an idea popped into his head.

To the group Jack said, "I think I know of a way we can continue to help all the charities while we're on vacation."

T smiled at him. "Don't you ever rest?"

"Yes, but hear me out." He spun his laptop around so T and Jesse could see the picture. "This is an awesome picture. I'm sure Janet's photographer got the same shot. We could have the photographer print two thousand large full color copies, you'll sign each print, and we'll get them framed with a brass tag."

"Ugh, I'm so tired of my name," protested Thad.

"Hang on. We'll send each charity two signed pictures—one for their wall to encourage others to give, and the other they will auction off in their local area. There will be a thousand auctions all happening at the same time. I bet we raise a ton of money, and it will help a lot of kids."

Thad laughed, "Okay, I'm in." Bailey got up from the floor and pushed his nose into Thad's left leg. "What is it boy? You want some more rubbing?" Bailey suddenly barked loudly, and they all jumped. T laughed, "I think he's mad he's not in the picture." Bailey barked again, as T began playing with the big lovable dog.

TWENTY-SIX

It was long after midnight before the hot sticky air finally cooled down. Thad began rolling his head back and forth on the pillow where he slept with sweat drops rolling off his brow like water from a windshield. He saw smoke rise from the barrel tip of the gun. He strained to focus until he recognized the face of the man running towards him. He shuddered as he hoped to never see that menacing diabolical face ever again. He saw the pivotal puff of smoke, and felt the deep thud of the spinning bullet as it entered his side knocking him viciously off his feet.

He saw the shooter's face and recognized it. He continued falling backwards as the 9mm bullet plowed its way through his flesh when suddenly, he saw Jack's face as he ran towards him. He glanced beyond Jack and saw Tim take a sturdy aim. He thought he was about to kill his innocent lover by cowardly shooting him in the back. He tried to yell out an alarm, but abruptly the memory cells went blank as he hit the wall with his head and fell to the ground bleeding and unconscious. The dream's abrupt end yanked him awake like a sudden break in the film in a darken theater, filling his brain with extremely bright white light.

He woke with a jolt as he rose to a sitting position in the bed. Across the floor he could see the dancing shadow glow of a small flame against the canvas walls. He realized a net covered the bed as if trapping him. It puzzled him, as he wiped the wetness from his face. Where was he? What happen?

"Have you got to pee?" asked Jack unexpectedly.

T swung around, and saw Jack's sleepy face in the shadows of stray light as they produced dark circles through the netting. Suddenly, reality returned, and the realization as to where he was, and with whom, became vividly apparent. So feeling foolish, but greatly relieved, he smiled, while shaking his head in disbelief, "No, I'm fine, it was just a very bad dream."

Jack opened his arms, "Come here, and I'll kiss that old dream away."

T sighed, and fell back onto Jack's well-healed shoulder. "My hero," he said as he kissed him.

"What were you dreaming about?"

T lied, "Oh nothing that made any sense."

From beyond the canvas, they suddenly heard a loud, oddly sounding, grunt. Jack asked, "Did you just fart?"

In a whisper, T replied, "No, it came from outside the tent."

Jack whispered back, "How high is our tree house?"

"I think it is about eighteen feet off the ground."

"So it's not a small animal but a large ..."

They heard the grunt again mixed with a crunching noise like a big dinosaur eating the metal off a trapped car. They both sat up in the bed. Something began poking at the canvas pushing it inward until the ties became tight.

"Do we have a gun?"

T replied, "No, they aren't allowed. It's a camera safari."

"What do we do?"

"Shh! Hold still, maybe it will go away."

They heard the groveling grunt sound once more, but no longer at their thin canvas door.

T got out of bed. "I'm going to see what it is."

"You'll be killed."

"The Will is in the safe."

"Oh great, I'd rather have you than a piece of paper."

T turned and smiled, "Me, too. So you're the oldest you go see what it is. You've already lived a long healthy life while my young life is just beginning."

Jack laughed, "I'm only three months older than you. What long life?"

T laughed. "Okay, I'll do it. Now be quiet."

He walked cautiously and carefully across the damp bamboo floor, and over to the entry door of the tent. He parted the tent seam and carefully looked out.

"Come here," he whispered to Jack.

Naked and no longer aroused, Jack crept out of the bed, made his way through the netting like trying to work his way through a giant sticky spider web, and came alongside Thad. T put his index finger to his lips indicating for Jack to please be quiet. He held open the seam, and in the light of the fire in the center of their camp down below, they both watched the largest giraffe they had ever seen slowly pick, push, and poke at the leaves on the limbs of the tree they were sleeping in.

"Night eaters, huh?" grinned Jack.

"I wish we had something to feed him."

"I've got some M & Ms in my pack."

"I don't think we should feed him chocolate. Come on, let's go back to bed. He can eat all the leaves he wants. Let's just hope giraffe's aren't meat eaters."

Jack laughed and took T's hand and led him back to bed. They cuddled tightly, kissed several times, which led to making love once more in the middle of Africa, on a big limb of a giant tree, in a spectacular tree house with their new pet just outside crunching and chewing away on the little green leaves. The giraffe never stopped chewing, but it puzzled him a little at the slight steady movement from the tree house on the limb above his head. Life is good, the boys thought, as they rested peacefully once again in each other's arms—very good.

TJ Johnson
October 2008

EPILOGUE

I am a big race fan and enjoy all the hoopla and expectations leading up to a race weekend. I pull for a heavily booed, but successful driver. However, I wondered why no one in this amazing sport has come out as a gay person. This is where the idea for **The Raceboys** began. The rough draft happened over the course of 2005 and into the following year. I began the final editing process in 2007 after writing the rough draft for another book.

I combined my love for racing, with the beauty of one of my favorite places to visit, the Western North Carolina Mountains, to create a story about this highly talented driver who happens to be gay. It should not be an unusual story, but for now, it is.

TJ Johnson
October 7th, 2008

Acknowledgements

I must give high praise to my editing team and their amazing patience to put up with my typos and mistakes, and want to thank them for helping me.

I must also give thanks for my sister who makes me laugh so often. You can't buy a better sister than her. Her charm, wit, and generous loving attitude help me over and over again.

TJ Johnson

Author TJ Johnson

TJ spent most of his early years hating to read, and thinking even less of his senior English class. Fortunately, a special teacher insisted he write a fictional short story, a two page tale about something he found interesting. Instantly, TJ became hooked on the fun of writing fiction. Thankfully, he now reads constantly, going from one book to the next, with several in queue waiting their turn. His favorite part of writing is the crafting of a rough draft. A period in the process when the words fly from the storage center deep in his brain like a movie stuck on fast-forward. The agonizing part begins with the painstaking restructuring, as TJ edits one sentence at a time until he is either happy, or exhausted into believing he is happy with his conclusion.

His new release is **The Raceboys** about a national champion forced to come out a gay driver.

Coming Soon: TJ is currently polishing "**A Writer's Fantasy**" about his favorite college sport basketball, as well as his favorite player. In the story he plays himself as he writes about the fictional Taylor University's historic basketball program, and the circumstances that led up to meeting their star player. The story tells how they fell in love, and TJ begins writing a book called "A Backstage Pass to Taylor University's Basketball Championship." It is meant to a be a funny, improbable, love story, but as TJ states in the beginning, "It's MY fantasy, and I'll write it anyway I please," which means in the story TJ is thinner, has more hair, and far better looking!

Currently TJ is editing **The Blackfeet Boys** set in the northwest in a time when two young warriors must abandon their home with the most feared and blood thirsty tribe in North America, and search for a safe and isolated world together. Followed by **Gay Grifters:** Chris Connors learns his new friends not only steal your wallet and gold, but also your heart and soul! With little honor among thieves, these young gay men take pleasure in robbing their tricks, while aiming for bigger scores. Will the biggest thief in America give up a life of crime for a lifetime of love? Only the tale will tell.

Fans of the War Series (**The War Apart - Part 1**, **The War Ahead - Part 2**) will be pleased to know that the research is finished, and the writing has begun on **The War Beyond - Part 3**.

Future works include several new stories: Followed by: **Forever Alone...Again** a funny sentimental tale about a man's countless attempts to find real love, only to watch his new perfect relationship self-destruct before he can move their love from third base to a home.

Requests for additional information and Inquiries can be obtain from
Hard Title Publishing, at **Info@ItsFiction.com**

WWW.ItsFiction.Com

Contact TJ Johnson at:

Info@ItsFiction.com

1. I try to answer all my email myself; however please read "Bio & Info" before writing as your question – saving time for all! Many readers ask the same questions repeatedly.

2. Please do not add my email address to any group for jokes, thoughts, prayers, or riddles, etc. I always delete these without reading.

3. I do not open any emails with attachments as these may contain viruses or other nonsense!

4. Please do NOT write suggesting plot lines as I delete these quickly, too. I like to write my own stories. If your plot is good, write it yourself! Do not send your manuscript to me – I am a writer, not a publisher, and I do not have the time.

5. All characters and names are part of my imagination and indicate no one particular. If I like a person's name, I may use the first or the last name but never both at the same time. It is true some of the events in my books are historical in nature but many are not. Choosing which to believe is your job, but this is why fiction is fun.

6. If you do not receive a reply, perhaps "Bio & Info" contain the answer already, or your email address is not functioning correctly.

7. If you have read all the above, I cannot wait to hear from you!